BEYOND the VELVET ROPE

TIFFANY ASHLEY

D0110612

HARLEQUIN® KIMANI PRESS™

Recycling programs
for this product may
not exist in your area.

BEYOND THE VELVET ROPE

ISBN-13: 978-0-373-09134-8

Copyright © 2013 by Tiffany Ashley

Printed in U.S.A.

To my readers.

Thank you for your love and support. Without you, there would be no me.

Chapter One

She had made a mistake.

Thandie realized it the instant she woke up. Before she'd even had a chance to open her eyes or take a sip of coffee, she knew the truth. She'd made a big mistake, and she would pay dearly for it.

She buried her face into the pillow, and breathed in a familiar scent. His scent. She groaned. This only confirmed last night had really happened. Images came back to her in flashes of vivid clarity. She wished she could blame it on the champagne, but she'd barely finished one glass before everything fell apart. How could things go horribly wrong so fast? And on the most sacred of holidays?

It was the first day of Fashion Week. The streets of New York were abuzz with excitement. Celebrities flooded the city for a chance to preview this year's winter collection. For every self-proclaimed fashionista, Fashion Week was like Christmas extended for seven wonderful days.

It was too bad Thandie would miss it. And all because she'd

had a moment of weakness. Now that she thought about it, this had been building for weeks. But never, in her wildest nightmares, did she think things would have played out like this. And she certainly hadn't imagined it would be so public.

Thandie buried her face deeper into the pillow, refusing to open her eyes; refusing to face the mess she'd created. She wished she had something to focus on other than what had happened hours before. She muffled a groan as her mind unwillingly recalled the sequence of events preceding her waking in a bed that was not her own....

Several hours earlier...

Thandie had been in Bryant Park, seated in the front row, watching the new Beverly Horton Collection being revealed. The tent where the show was taking place was filled with famous faces. Thandie had only to look across the aisle from her to see actress Nia Reynolds and fashion icon Victoria Beckham whispering to each other.

On Thandie's left sat her former boss and good friend, Gage Ali. Gage was a heavyweight in the public relations field. Her contacts were everywhere, and her influence was boundless.

On Thandie's right sat Bailey Woods, a celebrity publicist from Los Angeles. Like many present, she was in town for the shows. Bailey was another dear friend, but Thandie had seen little of her since Bailey relocated to California a few years ago. Having recently survived a hard breakup from her actor boyfriend, Bailey was going through a rough time in her life. Thandie and Gage were having a hard time trying not to mention he-who-must-not-be-named, or beg for all the gorry details. At least, not until after the shows.

And then Cam had shown up. The timing could not have

been worse. Thandie had been praying she would not run into him tonight. But fate has a bizarre sense of humor.

Cameron Stewart was tall and boyishly handsome, with a lopsided grin and thick shaggy dark hair. The instant Thandie laid eyes on him, her earlier reluctance melted away. She hadn't seen him in weeks, and she missed Cam. There was a certain comfort his nearness offered that few people outside her family supplied. She would always have a special place in her heart for him.

Cam was Thandie's ex-boyfriend. They'd been together for nearly three years. Many believed the two of them would eventually get married. Until recently, Thandie had thought the same thing. Their breakup had been a gradual conclusion; an end to an era that had long outlived its usefulness. She had seen it coming, but had been unwilling to acknowledge it. She'd hung in there, hoping the tide would turn and they would regain the special relationship they'd lost.

But had it never happened.

Their split had ended on agreeable terms. Although Cam hadn't been in favor of the decision, he'd accepted the decison because Thandie had wanted it. But he'd made it clear if she ever changed her mind, he would be waiting for her.

Cam had approached her group and partly out of instinct, but mostly out of habit, he leaned forward and kissed Thandie breifly on the lips. The mishap was further compounded by Thandie leaning into his touch. Quickly realizing their error, the two awkwardly pulled away from each other. To mask the discomfort that had settled over them, Cam began to tease Bailey, a mutual friend of theirs. As usual, Cam's easygoing nature brought smiles to the faces of those around him. Thandie could literally feel Gage and Bailey's spirits lift in his presence. Thankfully, his visit had been short. Cam, a fashion photographer, was working the Horton event, and had to get back to his seat before showtime.

Thandie watched as Cam crossed the tent and took his place among the other photographers. She wasn't sure if her eyes were deceiving her, but there seemed to be something different about him. Something she couldn't see, but sensed.

Thankfully, the house lights suddenly darkened, and the show got underway.

She pushed all thoughts about Cam from her mind, hoping that would be the last she saw of him tonight. But fate had other plans.

Hours later, at the after-party, Cam showed up with his new girlfriend. Thandie spotted him the moment they'd entered the club. She'd always known he would find someone else sooner or later, but actually seeing him with another woman made something tighten deep inside Thandie. It wasn't jealousy exactly. It was something more basic, something more carnal.

Suddenly, in a room crowded with strangers, Cam's eyes found hers. As if seeking her out, his dark gaze locked with Thandie's and refused to let her go. In that instant, Thandie was able to define what she'd felt earlier. Desire. She desired Cam. It was as if seeing him with someone else stimulated her sexually in a way it never had before.

As if reading her thoughts, Cam's gaze grew darker, and then he did something shocking. Cam disengaged himself from the statuesque beauty at his side, and purposefully crossed the room. When he was standing less than a foot away from Thandie, he wordlessly took the flute of champagne out of her hand and deftly pushed the glass toward a shocked Bailey.

Not caring who was watching, Cam pulled Thandie into his arms and kissed her with a passion that left them both shaken.

Details became blurred after that point. Thandie vaguely remembered Cam guiding her onto the patio. There, the two of them began frantically kissing and pulling at each other's clothes. Cam lay her down on a chaise longue, and the two of them became wildly intimate.

They were so enraptured in each other, they paid little mind to the crowd of partygoers surrounding them. Thandie vaguely recalled Gage pushing her way through the throng of voyeurs, hurrying her and Cam out a back exit, and shoving them into the backseat of her waiting town car.

The short ride to Cam's apartment was filled with more hot kisses and a great deal of fondling. Things only escalated when they arrived at their destination. Their lovemaking was quick and fervent; their climaxes hard and satisfying. Afterward, they tumbled back onto the damp sheets; too exhausted to move. They fell asleep to the sound of Cameron's cell phone ringing incessantly; no doubt from his girlfriend.

5:45AM

Now, in the light of day, Thandie regretted everything. She should have never given in to such madness. It had been satisfying for her, but the big problem was that Cam would assume more from their encounter. Thandie cringed at the thought of hurting him further.

Ashamed, Thandie buried her face deeper into the pillow. Perhaps she could escape before he woke? Maybe she could sneak out without being noticed. She wouldn't be able to entirely evade their showdown, but she could at least put it off for a day or two. She would run and hide until she was ready to deal with Cam on her own terms. And preferably with clothes on.

Opening her eyes slowly, Thandie surveyed the room. Although dimly lit, she could make out Cam's shadowy bedroom. In their haste to get to the bed, they'd made a mess of the room. She could see a trail of discarded clothes starting from the hallway and ending in a heap at the bedside. She groaned inwardly. It would be impossible to find all her clothes among the debris without making noise.

Turning her head slightly, Thandie noted where Cam lay. He was sound asleep in his favorite position, on his back with one arm tossed over his eyes. This might be her saving grace.

Clenching her teeth together, Thandie slowly and soundlessly attempted to ease herself out of bed. Inch by precious inch, she slipped free of the sheets. With one hand pressed firmly on the floor, and one foot extended to brace her weight, she was almost there. Thandie knew she looked ridiculous, but if she could just slide the rest of her body out of bed, there was a chance she could collect her clothes and sneak out of Cam's apartment undetected. Holding her breath, she inched farther off the mattress.

She might have made it had it not been for the sound of a cell phone chiming at that very moment. It shattered the silence of the room like a bullhorn. Thandie froze. She watched in horror as Cam jerked awake and then rolled out of bed. The movement pulled the bedsheets with him, making them spill off the foot of the bed. As if in a sleep-induced trance, Cam shuffled to the dresser and snatched up his cell phone. Rubbing his eyes, he looked at the display. And then he swore. He seemed to be debating whether he should answer. Deciding not to, he tossed the phone aside, and then looked up.

"Oh, shit," Thandie grumbled.

Cam blinked, taking in her bizarre position. Half of her was hanging off the bed, while the other half was outstretched toward the floor. Her intentions could not have been more obvious. Cam leaned his hip against the dresser and simply stared at her. His expression was solemn. "What are you doing?"

Awkwardly, Thandie came to her feet. Self-conscious because of her nakedness, she grabbed a pillow and held it in front of her. It offered little coverage, but since her clothes were not easily accessible, it was her best option.

"I have to go," she said, her voice husky from sleep.

Cam looked up at the ceiling, hurt settling onto his features. "Why are you leaving?"

She sighed. "You know why I'm leaving."

Cam threw his hands up helplessly. "I thought after last night…" His voice trailed off.

Thandie looked away, too ashamed to meet his pleading eyes. She regretted her actions last night, regretted the way she'd fallen into his arms without a care to the world. Regretted the way she'd blindly disregarded the consequences. There would be plenty of time to feel humiliation over the public episode. Everyone would be talking. It might even be reported in a local gossip column.

But Thandie couldn't be bothered with that right now. She was too guilt-ridden to consider anything except that she was hurting Cam again.

"I made a mistake," she said.

"You made a mistake? That's all?" he said with a humorless laugh. "I had a girlfriend, Thandie."

"I—I can fix that," she stammered. "I can try to explain to her—"

"Explain what?" he snapped. "Explain that in the blink of an eye, I chose you over her? Explain that I'll always choose you over her?"

"I'm sorry," she whispered.

"Yeah, well I'm sorry, too," he snapped.

"I'm sorry, Cam. I truly am."

"And your mother?" he asked quietly. "Does she know about us?"

"Don't," Thandie said sharply. "Don't you dare bring her into this." The mention of her mother caused Thandie's eyes sting with sudden tears.

Cameron swore, all the fight gone out of him. "I'm sorry, I shouldn't have said that. I'm just so…" he dragged a hand through his tousled hair, searching for the right word. Then he froze, a thought having occurred to him. He looked at Thandie with tired eyes. "You don't love me anymore, do you?"

She'd been expecting this question, but was still unprepared with where the answer would leave them. "Of course, I love you," she confessed. "Just not like that anymore."

"But last night—"

"I'm sorry," she said in a small voice. "Nothing has changed. Last night should have never happened."

"Thandie, please don't do this," he groaned.

"Cam, we've been broken up for weeks. What did you expect? Did you think things would magically go back to the way they were?"

"Yes," he said defiantly. "Yes, I did."

"Oh, Cam," she choked out. "I thought you understood—"

"Get out."

Thandie's head popped up. "What?"

"I said get out," he repeated in a voice void of any emotion.

"Cam." She took a step toward him, but he turned his back on her and abruptly walked out of the room. Thandie jumped when she heard the bathroom door slam shut.

She stared at the spot where Cam had stood. She hated hurting him. Cam deserved better. He deserved to be with someone who would mirror his bright, happy personality. It hadn't been that way between them for a long time.

She called out to him again. When he did not respond, she debated going after him or simply leaving.

Her indecision caused agitation to bubble up inside her. She couldn't stand for Cam to be upset with her, but she also did not want him to entertain any notions of them rekindling their relationship.

And then it happened. Thandie felt her breathing catch and then quicken to a pace she could barely control. Soon she was doing more gasping than breathing. Her hands began to shake frantically, and beads of sweats dampened her forehead. She was suddenly hot, so hot she was burning with it.

Oh, God, no, she thought. *Not now.* She reached out, steadying herself on the edge of the bed. Clenching her fingers tightly in the sheets, she struggled to slow her breathing before the panic completely overwhelmed her. Forcing herself to focus on an imaginary spot on the wall, she repeated her breathing exercises. Inhaling deeply through her nose and exhaling through her mouth. It was difficult to concentrate. She had to try three times before she found her rhythm. Once found, she concentrated on it with desperate determination. It took several painstaking minutes before her breathing returned to normal. When she felt the crippling hold of fear loosen slightly, she reacted with cat-like instincts.

Her still hands shaking, she quickly dressed and got the hell out of there. Twice she had to lean against the hallway wall to brace herself and catch her breath. She needed to sit down, but the urgency of putting distance between herself and Cam pushed her forward. No one knew she suffered from panic attacks. And she had no intention of broadcasting this fact; not even to Cam. Aside from being embarrassed by it, she knew it was a scary thing to witness.

Thandie had been plagued by panic attacks ever since she was a little girl. She had learned to control them as she got older. Her experienced episodes had become less frequent, and often occurred while she was alone. But every once in while, she was caught off guard by the sudden grip of anxiety. They were brought on by stress. It was an oddity that she would choose a high-pressure career. Strangely enough, Thandie never had an episode while at work. Her attacks were remarkably selective. They chose only to present themselves when she was dealing with personal issues.

It was just after dawn, and the sky was just beginning to brighten with flecks of sunlight. Taking a cab to her loft uptown would be ideal, but the streets were empty. Apparently, it was too early for taxi drivers to earn a living. Taking the bus was out of the question. She was dressed for a fashion show. She'd rather walk before facing the curious stares. But it was cold outside. Too cold for pride. And certainly too cold for a woman to walk around in six inch suede boots and a sequined miniskirt. Stares or no, she was not walking home.

The closest bus stop was around the corner from Cam's building. Thandie hobbled in that direction, trying as much as possible not to attract any attention. It was a challenge, but she managed to do it without grimacing once.

As luck would have it, as soon as she reached the end of the block, she saw a lone taxi puttering down the dark street. Relief flooded through her as it drew nearer to the curb. Once tucked inside the backside of the taxi, she released a heavy sigh. The temperature in the cab was only marginally warmer than outside, but it was an improvement nonetheless.

Thandie clenched her hands together tightly, until the shaking subsided a little. It took a while before she realized her hands were not the only thing trembling. Reaching into her purse, Thandie pulled out her phone. It was Gage calling.

Suppressing a groan, she answered, "Hi Gage."

Laughter greeted her. "How's my favorite little porn star this morning?"

"That's not funny," Thandie said unamused.

"You know what else isn't funny?" Gage asked in her crisp British accent. "Threatening every snitch at that party not to release your name to the press. I assure you the task lacks hilarity. I've had a full morning already and it isn't even six o'clock yet."

Thandie checked the time. "My goodness, Gage. Have you slept at all?"

"I'll sleep when I'm dead," she said with a dry laugh.

"Thanks, Gage. I owe you—"

"Trust me. You'll never be able to repay my generosity on this one."

Thandie cringed. "Was it that bad?"

"Are you fucking kidding me?" Gage scoffed. "You and Cam were seen doing the deed in public. Couldn't you have had the decency to screw each other in Central Park, like a normal New Yorker? No, you aimed for the big leagues. You had to put your sexcapades on display at a Marc Jacobs's party of all places. And on the first day of *Fashion Week*."

Gage added the last part as if the untimeliness of the stunt was her biggest offense. With a sigh, Thandie had to admit Gage was right.

"I wasn't thinking," she admitted.

"No. You were too busy screwing. Not very smart."

"What should I do?"

"Not a damn thing. I've taken care of it. There may be some whispers, but rest assured no one will print either of your names."

"Thank you, Gage"

"Stay out of sight for a few days, to give this time to blow over."

"I can't," Thandie said helplessly. "I'm hosting a party tomorrow night."

Gage gave the sigh of a martyr. "Fine. But do me a favor and try to stay out of trouble for a while. I think I've used up all my favors."

"I'll keep that in mind."

"Make sure you do."

Miami, Florida
12:57PM

Elliot stretched lazily before rolling onto his back. Opening his eyes slowly, he stared up at the mirror mounted above the bed. Fuzzy memories of last night came back to him. He was in his playroom. The one room in his home where his bed partners were welcome. It was conveniently stationed just off the foyer, the first room closest to the front door.

For Elliot Richards, privacy was his most treasured possession. His home was next in line. He hated the idea of bringing women home; this was his haven, his utopia away from the loud and busy life he led on the mainland. It annoyed him that he was reduced to bringing his conquests here. But there were few choices available to him.

Miami was a small city, gossip ran rampant, and he was easily recognizable. Hotels were simply not an option. Elliot was not a vain person who relished the attention of others. He was quite the opposite. He shied away from publicity, often refusing to be interviewed by the press. However, as the owner of a string of successful South Beach businesses, he was often photographed sharing a drink with celebrities. The paparazzi had unknowingly made him into the one thing he worked hard to avoid: famous.

The redhead sleeping to his right rolled into his side, nuzzling his chest with her nose. The movement caused the blonde lying on his left to toss her arm across his naked hips. Bored, and somewhat uncomfortable, Elliot nudged her limp body away from him and slid out of bed. He looked around for his pants, but after a few quick glances, he gave up the endeavor.

The redhead awoke. "Where are you going?" she asked.

He answered her with a question of his own. "Did you drive here?"

She shook her head; her auburn locks curtained her eyes. "You drove us. Where are you going?"

By this time, the blonde had come to life, yawning deeply before giving him a sexy grin. "Come back to bed, baby."

Spying his phone on the floor, Elliot scooped it up and punched a number stored in his auto dial.

"Security," a gruff voice answered.

"This is Elliot Richards. Call a cab, please." He hung up the phone and winked at the women. "Ladies, I have a busy day. You should go." Stepping over miscellaneous sex toys used the previous night, he pulled open the door. Before leaving, he turned back. "Please don't be here when I get back."

He closed the door closed behind him.

When he stepped into the hall, he ran into Romero Latez, his personal assistant. The twenty-something Pennsylvania State University graduate had been employed by Elliot for over a year, and he was the best assistant Elliot had ever had. He was discreet and well-groomed. Romero held himself with the arrogant air of someone who was a decade older and had seen everything. He showed no obvious surprise over Elliot's nakedness. It wasn't the first time, and it definitely wouldn't be the last.

He handed Elliot a chilled bottle of water. "Are you ready for your messages?"

Elliot took a modest sip before shaking his head. "Not just yet." Nodding his head toward the door that led to the playroom, he said, "Get them out of here before Lucinda sees them."

Romero nodded and Elliot turned away. He crossed the living areas, passed the kitchen, and headed toward the west wing, where the master suite was located. He pushed open the door, closing it immediately behind him.

This was the one room in the house where no one other than himself was allowed. It was the single place where he could truly be left to his private thoughts. Oftentimes, the scant half hour he used getting dressed for the day was the only time when he was by himself. He relished these moments. And he guarded them passionately.

Elliot rarely had time to be alone. He was often surrounded by people. There was always someone waiting for him, needing an answer to a series of questions, or just plain wanting his insight. This was partly his fault. He'd purposely mapped his life so that every moment of the day was strategically planned. He liked to make the most of every minute. He had to. There were simply too many people who worked for him to keep track of it all without relying on a rhythm to the madness. Yes, it was often madness. And yes, there was a definite rhythm to it.

Tossing his phone on the bed, he headed into the bathroom. Once showered and clean-shaven, he entered his expansive closet. After surveying the array of neatly hung expensive suits, he selected a pair of black slacks, matching jacket and a dark dress shirt. He triggered his phone to play his messages on speaker, so he could listen while he dressed. There were only a handful of people who knew his mobile number. And Elliot was particular about returning calls in a timely manner.

Message 1: "Elliot, it's Nick Sinclair. I'll be in Miami soon. I thought you ought to know. I'll call you later with details. Tell Lucinda I said hello."

Message 2: "This is Nico. Three words: Matrix. Party. Tonight."

Message 3: "Hi Elliot. This is Daria. I'll be in Miami on the twenty first for a photo shoot. I'll be there for the entire weekend. [giggle] I'd love to see you again. Call me."

Message 4: "Hey, Elliot. It's Eddie. Don't forget we have the financial meeting at three this afternoon. I think you'll find the marketing budget interesting."

Elliot considered the messages, making note of the order in which he would return each call. He'd grinned when he'd listened to Nico's cryptic message. Nico could always be counted on for a good laugh. The mention of Matrix throwing another one of his parties was good reason to call Nico back first.

Afterward, Elliot planned to call Nick Sinclair, another longtime friend. The two spoke often on the phone, but due to the fact they lived on opposite coasts, they rarely saw each other. He wondered what would bring Nick to Miami this time of the year. Regardless, it would be nice to see his old friend again. Elliot made a mental note to call his comrade as soon as possible. As for Eddie, there was no need to return his call. Elliot would see Eddie within the hour.

Daria was another issue. Her trips to Miami seemed to be coming more frequently. He would have to talk to her about this. If she was forming expectations about their arrangement, he would have to set the record straight.

Now dressed, Elliot shot a fleeting glance toward his bed as he left the room. Equipped with the news Nico had delivered, it was doubtful he'd be sleeping in his own bed tonight.

Romero was waiting for him in the foyer. Elliot was pleased to hear the house was silent; hence, the women were gone. Romero tossed him his car keys. Wordlessly, Elliot stepped onto the sprawling patio which wrapped around the front of his home. Elliot hit the key fob dangling from his keychain, and the headlights of a shiny black Porsche lit up. Sliding into the driver's seat, he turned the ignition, pausing only long enough for Romero to sling into the passenger seat. Throwing the car into first gear, pebbles kicked up as Elliot sped off Star Island.

A short time later, they pulled in front of a four-story building. On its broad side, a large sign read Club Babylon in sleek silver letters. On a typical night, the street would be lined with cars, and the sidewalks crowded with eager partygoers. But it was daylight, many hours before the club opened for business. Parking steps from he front entrance, Elliot tossed his car keys to Romero and strolled into the inside like he owned the place; which he did.

With Romero close on his heels, Elliot crossed the now empty dance floors, and jogged up the steps which led to his office. It was a large airy room, with stylish low-slung furniture and many shiny surfaces. It was positioned in a corner of the building. The architecture enabled it to jut out at an angle so that it was suspended over the main dance floor. With three of the walls made of glass, it allowed Elliot an unfiltered view of the club. Presently, the room glowed a dreamy orange hue, a reflection from the stage mood lights; and a clear indication the technicians were testing the lights before showtime.

There was a cluster of men waiting for Elliot when he arrived. He nodded to each before taking a seat behind his desk. He punched a series of numbers on his speaker phone, and instantly two investors were conferenced into the meeting.

"Hello, everyone," Elliot began. "Let's not waste time. We have a lot to cover in a few short hours." He looked down at his watch. "It's 3:00 p.m. now. We can break for lunch around six." He turned to a thin, freckle-faced man seated on a sofa across from him. "Eddie, where do we stand with the financials? I want cost analysis for the added security, transportation and entertainment. Let's hold off on the marketing for now. We need to make sure we can handle the traffic we currently bring in." Inclining his head toward Eddie, he said, "Please begin."

Chapter Two

Thandie stepped out of the limo to see the line outside the club was so long it wrapped around the corner. The rowdy group traveling with her filed out behind her. Two of her assistants, Len Harris and Amanda Karl, were working the front door, checking in VIP and special guests. They both waved at Thandie frantically.

"Wow, I'm glad to see you!" Amanda shouted over the crowd. "Working the door is crazy business. It's not ever midnight yet, and we're already close to capacity. Craig keeps threatening to shut the door, but I have thirty people on the list who haven't shown yet."

There was a time when Thandie would have had a meltdown over such news, but after five years in the business and many clients later she had dealt with bigger problems. Amanda had only worked for her for a year, and though she was very attentive and detail-oriented she often panicked during showtime.

"Let me see the list." Thandie scanned the sheet. Amanda

was right. If these people showed up, they had to be let in. She checked her watch. "Keep a sharp eye out. I want them escorted in immediately. Leave Craig to me."

"Good," Len said, "because he told me he wants you to come see him as soon as you arrive."

Fighting back the urge to groan, Thandie nodded her head.

Recognizing her, the bouncer waved her towards the entrance, causing the long line of people to watch her curiously. When it came to New York's nightlife, Thandie Shaw held the master key to almost every VIP room in the city. And that made her a hot commodity. She was currently marketing several clubs at once, and she was doing it with great flair. Celebrities loved her and the cameras adored her. But she couldn't do it alone. Between sending press releases, creating VIP lists, and making sure the right people were at the right place, having assistants was a must.

Turning her attention to her guests, Thandie ushered her group inside the club.

A woman in line recognized the man standing beside Thandie and started screaming. This created a wave of screams as word soon spread that actor Ruark Randall from the hit cop show, *LA Homicide,* was there.

Thandie ushered Ruark and the rest of his party through the door. As soon as they cleared the threshold, Thandie spied another one of her employees, Raja Travis, across the room. Tall and exquitsite, Raja was doing an excellent job of working the room, making sure everyone was having a good time. This was a must in their line of business. Getting people to the club was only a fraction of her job; the next step was keeping them there.

Thandie guided her group toward the back of the building. The VIP hostess welcomed her with air kisses before unhooking the velvet rope that gave entry to a secluded room where only the most exclusive of guests were welcomed. Thandie had purposely arrived just before one o'clock. This was when the crowd was usually in full swing. Tonight was no exception. Neon lights lit the darkened room, and everyone except for herself seemed to be quite drunk.

Ruark Randall and his group of rowdy friends were among the most obnoxious clients she had ever escorted. Ruark wasn't necessarily cute, but he had a certain charisma about him that made people watch him. Perceived by the press to be relatively reserved, Thandie was surprised to discover that Ruark was very affectionate when he had been drinking. Right now, he was making a scene by practically humping her. She tolerated him as long as she could before disappearing to look for Craig, the manager.

As she made her way through the dancing crowd, she told herself that although she was getting paid very well, it simply was not enough to be pawed at by a drunk idiot. It didn't matter how famous they were, a drunk idiot was still a drunk idiot. She swore if Ruark asked her go home with him again she would punch his perfecty capped teeth out of his mouth

"Thandie, baby, you did good." She turned just as Craig Sanders strepped out of the crowd. "The Pussy Cats were spectacular," he grinned.

Thandie smiled tightly at the compliment. Craig was referring to the troupe of exotic dancers she'd hired for tonight. She'd arrived just in time to catch the tail end of their performance. She was annoyed to discover they were performing a recycled routine.

Thandie nodded her head toward the DJ booth. "Who's spinning tonight?"

"The Freshman."

"Excuse me?"

"That's what he calls himself."

"That name is pretty lame. Why on earth would he insist on it?"

Craif shrugged. "At least it's accurate." He smirked. "He's a freshman in school."

Thandie looked up at the DJ booth. The boy in question held headphones to his ear, while his hands moved busily, spinning and exchanging records. "He doesn't look old enough to be in college," she said under her breath.

"That's because he isn't," Craig said, amused. "That kid is in high school."

The news caught Thandie by surprise, making her blink several times. "He's a freshman in high school?" She lowered her voice. "What is he doing in here, Craig?"

"Hey, that kid has been working in clubs since he was in middle school. He's one of the top underground DJs. He's a pretty big deal. I actually had to get on a waiting list to hire him. Never mind the fee I'm paying. Don't get me wrong. I've paid more, but those jerks were twice his age."

Thandie nodded her head. He might be a kid, but one thing was certain: The Freshman definitely knew his music. His transition from one song to the next was flawless. Club guests showed their appreciation by rushing to the dance floor.

Pulling her attention away from the excited crowd, Craig pointed toward the VIP room where Ruark Randall and his boisterous cronies were tossing girls over their shoulders and spinning around in circles. "Do you think he'd take a picture with me for the website?"

Thandie rolled her eyes. "Please don't tell me you're a fan."

Craig looked sheepish. "I watch the show from time to time. I can't be at work all the time."

"The show comes on in the evening while you're at the club."

"I record it."

Thandie shook her head in disbelief.

"Len tells me you're trying to close the door."

He nodded. "Our capacity is borderline. I can't have the fire marshal on my ass."

"Just let Len pass through twenty more people."

"Twenty people? Are you kidding me? Thanks to that group you just brought in, I'm likely over capacity now."

"Allow my guests entrance when they arrive. Trust me, Craig, their presence will ensure the club gets a mention in *The Post*."

"Okay, okay," he said with a groan. "Len can let them in, and then the door closes."

"You're wonderful, Craig."

"Yeah, yeah." His eyes suddenly brightened with interest. "Hey didn't you go to the Marc Jacobs party last night?"

Thandie stiffened. "Yes, why?"

"I heard it got pretty wild. Did you see anything?"

"No," she said immediately. "Nothing out of the norm."

Craig shrugged. "Figures. I finally score an invite, and I can't go because I'm working." His beady eyes scanned her body. "You know, Thandie, you should really consider being my woman."

She folded her arms across her chest, and gave him her best no-nonsense expression.

"I was just kidding," he weakly.

Thandie placed a hand on her hip and said, "If you want a picture with Ruark, let's get it over with. I want to wash my hands of him as soon as possible."

"That doesn't sound like a team player to me."

"Get the camera, Craig."

They made their way back to the VIP area, where Ruarke was making a scene popping the cork off a bottle of champagne. After easing their way through a throng of curious on-lookers, Thandie quickly made introductions. Ruarke smiled pleasantly, but when Craig asked for a picture, the actor tossed his head back and laughed.

"Dude, I'm not taking pictures with another guy. I'm not gay." He pulled Thandie to his side. "I'll take a picture with Tammie here instead."

Craig's disappointment was evident, but he eagerly agreed to take the photo. Just as Thandie had expected, Ruark used the photo opportunity to hold her unnecessarily close, even going as far as to kiss her on the mouth on one of the takes.

It was going to be a very long night.

By the time Thandie got home, she felt as though she had been mauled. It was four o'clock in the morning when she unlocked the door to her loft apartment door. The lower level of her home doubled as her office, and the upper served as her personal living quarters.

She had come a long way in her career. Before starting her own firm, she'd worked five years with Gage Ali. Gage was the director of public relations for one of New York's top fashion houses.

The years assisting Gage had been the most informative of her life. She'd met more celebrities than she ever dreamed possible and established many business contacts. Although demanding at times, Gage had been a thorough instructor. She had a strategy for every situation. Promoting Manhattan nightclubs was a far cry from managing press releases for a fashion company, but many of the same rules applied. One, keep your cool. Two, take control. And three, keep your cool. Due to her discipline, Thandie had rose quickly in her field. There was not a VIP lounge in the City she could not gain access to, and earn a generous commission while doing it.

Thandie was thankful to Gage for guidance and found herself calling her mentor for advice when she faced an emergency. Gage always had the right answer. Gage had introduced her to just about everyone worth knowing, including her ex-boyfriend, Cam Stewart.

Cam. It hurt every time she thought of him.

They hadn't spoken since she'd woken in his bed the previous morning. Thandie did not like to idea of him being upset with her, but it was probably best this way. Better they go their separate ways once and for all, instead of prolonging the inevitable.

She climbed the steps leading to her bedroom. One of the girls had left a note on her pillow, a reminder of her massage appointment at ten. Thandie looked at her watch and groaned. Her appointment allowed her only five hours of sleep. She would love to reschedule, but her masseur was hard to book.

Thandie eased into bed, fully clothed. She could smell cigarette smoke in her hair. She yearned to take a shower but was too tired. When she'd dropped Ruark Randall and his friends off at their hotel, Ruark had invited her up to his room to do ecstasy. She had to refuse five times before he got the point. She swore if she never saw the man again, it would be too soon. If she had the energy, she would vent her frustrations aloud, but in the grand scheme of things it didn't really matter. In spite of for her frustration and weariness, Thandie loved her job. The satisfaction of hosting a successful event far outweighed the aggravation of babysitting spoiled A-listers. Besides, tomorrow night would involve another celebrity with a different story.

Miami, Florida

Elliot Richards slid his hands into the pockets of his slacks. He looked out over the crowded dance floor below. There, beautiful people swayed to loud techno music. Club Babylon was very much alive tonight. Babylon was his jewel, his mistress, his one true love. And his greatest accomplishment. What had begun as a thought was now reality. He'd spent years cultivating the idea, observing the industry, and building his knowledge. He was the man behind Club Babylon, the chic, multilevel dance club whose fame was growing by the minute.

Elliot owned a string of businesses throughout Miami, but Babylon was his obesssion. He was heavily involved in all interactions. He managed a team of fifty workers, comprised mostly of dancers, bartenders and cleaning crews. It was a large undertaking. Mercifully, he did not do it alone. His management staff was the best in the business. He was fortunate to have them, however, very little was done without his approval. Elliot was known for his innovative marketing strategies and extensive knowledge of the industry. That being the case, his staff rarely moved on anything without his say-so. Between the operation of Babylon and his other enterprises, Elliot barely had enough time to sleep. But this was the life he had chosen. Even on the worst of days, he couldn't think of anything else he'd rather be doing.

Elliot checked his watch. In another hour, he would be expected to make his rounds, offering complementary drinks to VIP members and hugging beautiful, tanned women. It was his job. As the owner, he was obligated to work the crowd. If there was one thing that made Miami different from other party cities, it was its well-connected night scene. Everyone on the strip wanted to say they knew someone important. It seemed to work out that a majority of the people who walked into Club Babylon claimed they were close friends with Elliot, and thus demanded star treatment. His staff had their hands full, catering to the wave of celebutantes who flooded his VIP lounges. Managing a thriving business required long nights and countless favors.

However, there were advantages to being Elliot Richards. He'd been blessed with physical attributes most men could only dream of possessing. Elliot was tall, lean and handsome. His chiseled features were softened by an unusual combination of thick black hair and clear silver eyes.

And Elliot had one more thing working in his favor—he was wealthy. A series of smart business investments made early in his career had paid off, and he now had a vast fortune. Because of his good looks and money, Elliot never had trouble attracting attention from members of the opposite sex.

"Elliot, are you listening?"

Elliot turned to his management team: Adam Parr, Markie Duran, Rex Barrington, Eddie Bloom and Tom Comber. They were all looking at him expectantly.

"Yes, I heard you, Rex," Elliot said in his low, untroubled voice. He moved to face his director of marketing. "I agree. We need to push the marketing campaign for the grand opening."

"Everyone loves the changes," Rex offered, "but if we want to hit the numbers that the renovation was geared for, we need to decide how we want to do it."

Elliot nodded. He knew Rex was right. Rex was his director of marketing. The club needed a serious marketing push, and he had his hands tied with other projects.

Elliot inclined his head to his general manager. "Markie, your thoughts?"

Markie's ears perked up. "I know we've all been busy trying to make sure we had all the supplies needed to open our doors on the scheduled date, but now that day is passed. We should focus on how we're going to keep the club full. As it stands, we're hitting good numbers because people are curious about the remodel. But that won't last long."

Eddie Bloom, the efficiency expert, spoke up. "Elliot, you bankrolled a lot of money into renovating the club. If you plan to recoup your funds, we need to do some serious marketing. Otherwise, the investment goes unnoticed."

Elliot nodded. "Our campaign needs help." He turned to look down at the crowd again. A lovely blonde woman hovered near the bar. She'd come with a date. A boyfriend? A husband, perhaps? It didn't matter. Neither would be much of an obstacle. "We need to hire a PR firm," Elliot mused aloud. "A well-known professional."

Rex clapped his hands together. "Good idea. Perhaps someone who has connections up north? This would be the perfect opportunity to expand Babylon's reach beyond SoBe."

Elliot turned to address his team. "Is everyone in agreement?"

They all nodded.

"So, it's settled," Elliot said with finality. "Rex, call Warren and tell him I'm leaving the promoter assignment up to him. That way, if the investors aren't happy with the results, they can point the finger at each other." The men laughed collectively.

Elliot pulled himself upright, smoothing his palm over his suit lapel as he did so. "Gentlemen, if that's all, please excuse me. I have something to attend to."

He waited until the last man filed out of his office before descending the staircase which led to the arena floor. It was time to make his rounds.

Chapter Three

Staten Island, New York

Thandie carefully placed the bouquet of flowers on the counter and waited for someone to acknowledge her. As usual, she felt nervous. These visits were always filled with mixed emotions. She looked forward to them with the same intensity that she dreaded them.

As if alerted to her growing sense of unease, a nurse materialized from a corridor. She was a heavy woman with wide hips, rosy cheeks and smooth pale skin. Her name was Nurse Joanne.

As soon as she saw Thandie, her face split into a brilliant smile. "Ah, Thandie! I'm so glad you came. She'll be so excited to see you."

Thandie's face lit up with elation. "Has she been asking for me?"

Nurse Joanne paused and then made a slight shake of her head. "No, dear, but I know deep down she'll be thrilled you're here."

Thandie's initial joy vanished, quickly replaced with embarrassment. She felt foolish for having asked. It was silly to think her presence would be desired, least of all remembered. It had been this way for years. It was silly to expect anything anymore.

"There there," Nurse Joanne chided. "There's no need in upsetting yourself. You'll ruin your visit before it even begins."

Thandie gave a half-hearted smile.

"That's a good girl," Nurse Joanne said reassuringly. "Now let's get you upstairs. Did you sign in yet?"

Thandie pulled the visitor log book in front of her and began filling in her information. Next to the date, she wrote the patient's name: Josephine Shaw.

After waving to the nurse, she made her way to the elevators, where she rode the lift to the second floor. The corridors on the upper level were abuzz with whispered conversations and occasional laughter. The environment was warm and inviting. This reassured Thandie she'd made the right decision years ago.

Following the hall, Thandie arrived at room 216. The door was open, and inside the sunlit room sat a lone figure. Turning at the sound of someone entering the room, the woman lifted her head and gazed at Thandie.

The sight of her face made Thandie catch her breath. Not yet fifty-five, Josephine could easily be mistaken for someone ten years younger. She was a small African American woman, with a heart shaped face and slender nose. Her dark hair was swept into an elegant bun at the nap of her neck and her soft brown eyes were bright with curiosity. Her lip quivered slightly when she smiled, making her smile all the more endearing. She was beautiful. Thandie had always believed she was the most beautiful woman in the world.

Thandie approached her slowly, careful not to make any sudden movements. She placed the flowers on a table and knelt before the woman. Taking her hand in her own, she kissed it before pressing it against her cheek. "Hello," she cooed softly. "How do you feel today?"

Josephine Shaw's smile faltered just a little, but she managed to keep the grin in place. "I feel well," she said pleasantly. "Thank you for asking."

Thandie could tell by the tone in her voice she was confused. "Do you know who I am?"

Josephine peered at her closely. "You're very pretty," she whispered. Her eyes slid to the side, as if she were sifting through a multitude of emotions and memories. "What... what is your name?"

It was a blow Thandie should be familiar with, but it hurt just as much now as it had the first time. Thandie blinked back tears and said evenly, "My name is Thandie Shaw. I'm your daughter. Do you remember me?"

Her mother looked uncomfortable, and gripped her hand tightly. "I'm sorry," she said with a helpless shake of her head. "I don't remember your face." She fidgeted, seeming to become agitated.

Thandie patted her knee reassuringly. "Perhaps next time you'll remember," she promised. These were empty words, but they always seemed to have a calming affect on both of them.

Every once in a while, her mother had a moment of clarity. She never remembered everything, but she remembered enough to know Thandie was her daughter. During those rare occasions, she stroked Thandie's face and wept openly, apologizing for leaving her at such a young age. Thandie clung to those memories. They always ended with heartbreak, but for those brief moments, she had her mother back. However, they always ended too quickly, and she was left anxiously awaiting the next time her mother would return to her. But it had been over a year now, and she was beginning to lose hope.

Thandie marveled at how much she favored her mother.

They had the same shade of pale brown skin and long ink-black hair. Like her mother, her facial features were small and delicate, making her look younger than her twenty-eight years.

But there where distinct differences. Chiefly amongst them was Thandie's height. Measuring just a few inches shy of six feet, she was taller than most women. In contrast to her mother's petite stature, Thandie had a long lean figure, with subtle curves.

Abruptly, Josephine broke off mid-sentence and said, "When will Cam come to visit me?"

Thandie lurched at the words and stared at her mother. The mention of Cam had always been a strange happening. He'd accompanied Thandie on these visits only a handful of times, but her mother had always remembered him. Even at her most cloudy moments, she would ask about Cam out of the blue. But this time there was a lift in her mother's voice that startled her. She searched her mother's face. There was a faint glimmer in her eyes. A glimmer of recollection?

"Mom," she said, suddenly desperate. "Cam won't be visiting you anymore. We broke up. Do you recall me telling you that a few months ago?" She leaned forward, watching her mother's every move.

As if not hearing a word, Josephine gave a gentle laugh. "He's such a dear. He brought me this shawl last week. Isn't it lovely?"

Thandie looked down at the worn piece of fabric wrapped around her mother's shoulders. It was gray, made of soft cashmere. It was indeed a gift from Cam. A Christmas gift to be exact. He'd given it her two years earlier.

Thandie began to deflate. Disorientation of time was another symptom of dementia. Thandie knew at that moment her mother had yet again retreated. She'd lost her. Like so many times before, Josephine Shaw had slipped away from her daughter when she needed her most.

"Yes, Mom," Thandie agreed. "It's very lovely."

Hours later, Thandie was back in her apartment. The visit with her mother had taken a lot out of her. Before leaving, she'd kissed her mother on the cheek and promised to return in the next few days. It was a pledge she always made, and always kept.

There was a lot to be done, following last night's event at Phenomenon. After taking a calming bath, Thandie set to work calling her contacts at local newspapers to find out how much coverage the party secured. Within half an hour, Thandie's three assistants arrived: Amanda, Raja and Len. Without preamble, they quickly went about sending emails and making calls.

Shortly after noon, the office phone rang and Amanda scooped it up. "Shaw Public Relations," she said cheerily. "This is Amanda speaking."

"Thandie, please."

"Who's calling?"

"Tell her it's Warren Radcliffe."

A moment later, Thandie was on the line. "Hello, stranger. I haven't heard from you since you moved. Where are you?"

"Miami," he said, with a smile in his voice.

"Miami? Why on earth would you ever leave New York?"

"I ask myself that question every day." He laughed. "But I have family down here. I moved to be closer to them in my old age."

"I don't think you'll ever be considered old, Warren. But Miami over NYC—it doesn't sound logical."

"If you could see the sights I see every day, you would think differently."

She smiled. "That means there are a lot of half-naked women running around. Careful, Warren, you'll have a heart attack."

Thandie had known the retired corporate CEO for years. They had met on the club scene. She met a lot of interesting people in her line of business, and Warren was by far one of the more memorable characters she's ever come across. In his late sixties, the man had a weakness for the nightlife and young women. It was a flaw that had caused him to endure four divorces over the span of seven years. Shaky matrimonies never seemed to bother Warren. They only gave him a reason to party hardier, which eventually led to him marrying another young trophy wife.

"How are you, Warren?"

"I'm wonderful. I finally put my money where my heart lies."

She laughed. Where Warren was concerned, there was no telling what that statement meant. "I'm listening."

"I'm an investor in a club down here."

"Where, exactly?"

"South Beach, of course. It's awesome, Thandie."

"I can hear the excitement in your voice. What's the name of the club?"

"Club Babylon."

This got her attention. "I'm familiar. Word has it that place is a growing hot spot on the strip."

"Yeah, business has been really good."

"Sounds as though you've got your hands full, but I hope you're calling me because you're visiting Manhattan soon."

"Actually, I was calling to see if you would consider coming to South Beach. I think I might have a business proposition for you."

"Me in Miami? You've got to be kidding."

"On the contrary, I'm very serious. Moving down here was a major change for me. I was used to the hustle of the City, but it's a complete different world down here. There are beautiful people everywhere, white sandy beaches and crystal-blue water. It's unbelievable."

"Sounds like paradise."

"It is. I spent the first months just soaking up the place. Of course, you learn about the movers and shakers very quickly. But there is one in particular I would like you to meet."

"Who is that?"

"His name is Elliot Richards."

"I think I've heard of him."

"He's a young guy. Probably a year older than yourself, I'd guess. He's a serious tycoon down here, a real sharp thinker. He owns several local health gyms, smoothie shops, nightclubs, and a restaurant. And get this—he personally manages them all at the same time."

"Impressive," she said, mildly intrigued.

"Everything he touches turns into gold," Warren went on. "So when I heard he was opening his newest club, Babylon, I jumped at the chance. Two other guys invested with me. None of us had ever invested in a nightclub, so there was a lot we had to learn. There were a few nervous moments, but Elliot talked us through it like a pro. In the end, Club Babylon was a success. The revenue that place brings in one night is unbelievable."

"Sounds too good to be true."

"That's what I thought. We all make a healthy cut, so you can image how shocked I was when Elliot proposed to shut down the club five months to renovate the building."

"Five months? That's a death sentence."

"That's exactly what I said, but somehow Elliot talked us into it. Looking back on it, he didn't have to because he owns seventy percent of the shares. We invested two-point-eight million into the renovation. We just reopened a few weeks ago. So far, everyone loves the changes, especially the VIP lounges. The turnout has been decent, but we know we can do better, much better. So that leads me to why I'm calling you."

"I'm listening."

"I'd like you to come down and promote the club. Of course, Elliot would have to give the green light, but I'm sure after he talks to you, he'll be sold on the idea."

"I can't move to Miami, Warren."

"It would only be temporary."

She flinched at the word. "How temporary?"

"Three months."

"Three months? That's an eternity."

"It could be done in two months if you really work hard. If you think you can recoup our venture in less time, go for it."

"Warren, I'd love to help you, but I haven't been able to survive outside New York for longer than a week. Besides," she hesitated, "I have responsibilities here. I can't leave town for that long a time."

"Then visit the City on the weekends. This isn't a regular nine-to-five job, kiddo. If you have to fly back to take care of a few things then do it."

"I can't."

"Thandie, I need you. Babylon will reach its mark eventually, but you could give us the boost that gets us over the top. I've seen you work, Thandie. You're the best."

"You have the wrong person. I barely know Miami. I wouldn't even know where to stay."

"You'll stay with me. I have a house near the beach. You'd love it."

"Warren, this is a huge undertaking. I would have to bring my staff."

"That's fine. There's plenty of room at my place. I'll even offer you my home office. It'll be perfect for you. My home is your home. You should know that."

"Warren, I can't put you out like that. Aren't you married again?"

"Separated. Wife Number Five and I have been split up for months. In all honesty, I see her credit card bills more than I see her. Anyway, it's a big house—plenty of room. You'll have all the privacy you need. No one will bother you. So stop stalling. Accept my offer."

She laughed. He was making it sound too easy. "There are plenty of firms who could do just as good a job."

"But I want you. The pay is top-notch. Thandie, this is a once-in-a-lifetime opportunity for all of us. What are you holding on to in New York?"

Immediately an image of her mother popped into her head. She did not like the idea of putting distance between them. What if there was an emergency and they needed her to come to the care center? Or worse, what if her mother remembered something and Thandie wasn't there to share it with her? She wasn't willing to risk that possibility, small as it might be.

However, hadn't Warren mentioned she could return to the City when she needed to? Would she be able to somehow cover the costs of her travel expenses? If so, Warren had asked a good question. What was holding her back? The answer certainly wasn't Cam anymore. Lately, it only reminded her of her failed relationship. Why shouldn't she get away for a bit? It would only be for a few months. What would it hurt? She could hand her big assignments over to Amanda. Of her three assistants, Amanda was the most reliable and showed the most promise. Besides, the assignment would give Len and Raja great work experience.

"Okay, Warren." She gave a dramatic sigh. "I'll consider your offer, but only because I miss you so much."

"Excellent. I'll have Elliot give you a call later this week. Trust me, everything's going to be perfect."

Later that week…

While Thandie was wrapping up her phone call with an editor from *Daily News America,* her assistant Len waved frantically signaling her that she had another call.

"Who is it?" Thandie asked.

"He says his name is Elliot Richards."

She picked up the line. "This is Thandie speaking."

"Hello, Ms. Shaw, this is Elliot Richards. I understand you've been expecting my call." His voice had a deep seductive timbre, instantly sending a shiver of arousal down her spine.

"Yes, Mr. Richards. Warren spoke with me briefly, regarding the nature of your business. I understand you may be in the market for promotional assistance."

"That would be correct." There was a soft chuckle from his side of the line. "Warren was gracious enough to give me your résumé, and I must say it's very impressive."

"Thank you."

"It appears you're the perfect person for the job," he added smoothly.

"Again, thank you." Thandie could feel her excitement rising.

"However," he said, "I'm not going to hire you."

"Excuse me?" She was certain she hadn't heard him correctly.

"I'm not going to hire you, Ms. Shaw," he repeated.

Biting down her disappointment, she asked, "May I ask why not?"

"Read between the lines."

"No, I'd much rather hear the words from you."

"You're a woman," he said quite simply. "And I don't hire women."

Thandie was momentarily stunned speechless.

"To be frank, Ms. Shaw, females can make things complicated, particularly in a club environment. Do you understand what I'm saying?"

She was still too shocked to speak.

"But I do appreciate your taking the time to speak with me," he continued smoothly. "I wish you the best. Have a nice day, Ms. Shaw."

The line went dead.

Thandie stared at the phone. She wasn't certain if she should be upset or think the whole thing comical. In this day, it was hard to believe such blatant sexism still existed. She was tempted to call him back and give him a piece of her mind, but before she could, her cell phone rang.

"Hello?"

"Thandie, it's Warren."

"Warren—"

"I heard what happened. I'm so sorry."

"How did you hear so quickly?"

"Elliot had you on speaker phone."

"He what?"

"He talks to everyone on speaker, but nevermind that. I'll talk to him."

"Was he serious?"

"Unfortunately, yes. He has good reason, but that doesn't excuse his behavior."

"Seriously, he won't hire me because I'm a woman?"

"Not to worry, kiddo, I'll talk to him."

"I'm not sure I want you to talk to him."

"Don't be silly. He's just being difficult, and you're offended."

"'Offended' is hardly the word, Warren. I'm pissed."

"Let me talk to him."

"He's an asshole."

"That's a bit harsh," he said defensively.

"I thought I was being kind. He hung up on me, Warren."

"I'm sorry about that. Elliot is always pressed for time. You'll see that soon enough. He called you during one of the staff meetings. He's already on another conference call."

"He interviewed me for a job during a staff meeting?"

"I'm making things worse, aren't I?"

She didn't answer his obvious question.

"Not to worry. I'll talk to him. Everything's going to be okay. Are you still interested?"

She was silent for a long while. She'd done her research on Elliot Richards. Having the club magnate as a client would add major weight to her portfolio. But having him hang up on her not only wounded her pride, it made her mad as hell. Just who did he think he was? She was now determined to make him eat his words. "Yes, I'm interested."

"That's my girl. I'll talk to him. Just sit tight, and I'll call you back.

The call disconnected.

Again, she looked down at the phone, still reeling from Elliot's quick brush-off. Her initial shock melted away, leaving only angry determination in its wake. Her resolve to capture his account now lit her on fire, and she made a silent vow that she would be on his payroll. She'd been in the business for years, and she had worked with the worst of the worst. Whatever Elliot Richards had to dish out, she was confident she could handle.

★ ★ ★

Thandie was still fuming over her conversation with Elliot Richards days later. True to her word, she'd placed daily phone calls to his office and was informed he was either in a meeting or on a conference call. She was impressed to learn that he was never out of the office. His assistant insisted that, "Mr. Richards is always working." But knowing this did not help her get him on the phone. He was becoming as unattainable as Bigfoot. To make matters bleaker, she hadn't heard from Warren in days. She'd taken his silence to mean he hadn't been as persuasive as he'd hoped. This didn't deter Thandie. If anything, it made her more persistent.

It was 10:00 a.m., and Thandie was beginning her morning meeting with her assistants. As always, the women were avid listeners, and took detailed notes. Amanda, her lead assistant, shouldered the more important responsibilities. It wasn't that her other assistants weren't good at their jobs; they just tended to be easily excited when in the presence of a celebrity or really cute guys, which unfortunately for Thandie was a common occurrence.

"Raja, call Chantel and see if we can get some gift certificates. Chantel's little spa is the newest hot spot for models. And while we're on the subject of models, Amanda call Sookie and confirm Jarvis will be at the Simmons party. I know his people have already confirmed, but he's notorious for double-booking and then blowing off both commitments. If we can guarantee he'll be there, then we can be certain the other music honchos will be there." Thandie snatched up her phone and began entering a cryptic message. "And just to be certain, I'm texting his girlfriend, Tamika. I can't stand the woman, but she's media-hungry and can't turn down a chance to be seen. If she comes, he'll be there."

"Thandie."

She turned when Len called her name. "Yes?"

"You have Warren on the line."

Sending off her text message, she plucked the cordless phone out of Len's hand and cradled it on her shoulder. "Warren, I'm in a meeting. This'll have to be quick."

"You're in."

"Excuse me?"

"You're in. Elliot has agreed to hire you. You'll need to come down here ASAP. I guess all those messages you've been leaving him worked." He laughed good-naturedly. "Elliot's agreed to meet with you on the eighth at 5:00 p.m.. This is the only time I could get him to confirm, so make sure you're here and on time. Call Romero, Elliot's personal assistant, tomorrow morning and tell him when you can come, and he'll set up the plane tickets. Whatever you say to him *will* be repeated to Elliot, so try to keep the 'he's-an-asshole' comments to yourself, please."

"Do I have you to thank for this?"

Warren laughed. "Elliot's a complicated guy, but once he had some time to think about it, he saw this was the right thing to do."

"That sounds a little far-fetched."

"Well, I do have my ways."

She could hear the humor in his voice, and it made her smile. "I'll call you later."

"Excellent, kiddo. I'll take care of everything else. Oh, and Thandie?"

"Yes?"

"It'll be nice to see you again."

"Same here."

Chapter Four

Miami, Florida

As soon as Thandie entered the baggage claim area, she saw a sign reading T. Shaw. The man who held it up was handsome, with bright brown eyes, spiky brown hair and a perfectly trimmed goatee.

She made her way toward him, catching his gaze when she was only feet away from him. He smiled brightly.

"Hi," he said.

"Hi." She smiled and pointed at his sign. "I'm Thandie Shaw."

His eyes widened. "You're T. Shaw? Shit, nobody told me you're a..." He cleared his throat and collected himself. "Forgive me. It's just that...you're not at all what I expected."

"So I see," she murmured coolly. It's just that we've never worked with a woman."

"So I hear," she murmured coolly.

He blushed rather innocently. "Sorry to stare. I've worked for Babylon for two years, and this is the first time I've known a woman to be hired before. You must really be good at what you do." He folded the sign up and tossed it into a nearby trash bin. His hands now free, he offered to shake her hand. "I'm Adam Parr. Elliot thought it would be good for me to collect you, since we're going to be working so closely together. I'm the VIP host."

She nodded her head appreciatively. Adam helped her with her bags, and the two headed outside.

Adam smiled. "So how do you know the big boss?"

"Big boss?"

"Elliot Richards. How do you know him?"

"I don't," she said simply.

"Oh," he paused. "I thought you two knew each other and that was how you landed the job."

"No." She pulled her sunglasses down over her eyes. "We've never met. I'm actually a friend of Warren Radcliffe."

"Oh, the other boss." He lifted her bags into the trunk of his car. "Warren's cool. He's very…active for a guy his age."

Thandie smiled. "I bet they were saying that when he was twenty."

"Knowing Warren, you're probably right." Adam slammed the trunk closed and opened the passenger door for her. "I was told you would be traveling with a group."

"Raja and Len had to tie up a few things for me at the office. They're flying in later this week."

"Sounds like a plan. Have you ever been to Miami?"

"Not as often as I would have liked."

He laughed. "Well, you're in for a treat. There is no place on earth like South Beach."

Adam drove Thandie around the city, taking her through Coral Gables, Coconut Grove, and passing by Star Island. Adam turned out to be a great tour guide. He pointed out all the best spots. By the time they turned onto Washington Avenue, Thandie was relaxed and ready to meet the rest of the staff. Finally, Adam pulled in front of huge four-level building, and killed the engine.

"We're home," he announced.

"Home?" she asked.

"Club Babylon." Adam waved his hand, indicating she follow him toward the building's entrance. When Adam pushed through the front doors, Thandie was surprised by the activity. It was the middle of the day, and people were rushing about in every direction. Men were carrying bags of ice, crews were cleaning the floors, and the lights changed from gold to blue, then purple. Movement caught Thandie's eye, causing her attention to be pulled toward the stage.

She tapped Adam. "I thought you said you didn't work with women?"

Adam followed her stare and then grinned. "Oh, that's the entertainment. We have plenty where that came from."

Adam must have caught her reaction. He jutted his chin toward the women who were gathered on the elevated catwalks. "We have plenty of girls."

That was an understatement. Thandie was astounded by the parade of pretty women strutting about. Everywhere she looked there were beautiful, tanned bodies. Some were on stage, practicing a dance routine that easily resembled a striptease, while others lounged near the bar.

"This place wouldn't operate as well without eye candy," Adam explained. "And Club Babylon has the best in the city." He pointed to the stage. "Every club needs dancers, and Miami is a haven for professional dancers. Working at clubs is a great gig for them. It pays the bills and allows them to go on auditions during the day. That means we get to pick from the cream of the crop."

"Adam," a pretty brunette from the stage called out. "Tell Elliot to come down here."

Adam's brows perked. "Why, Marina?"

"Because I want to tell him I love him," she said with a wicked grin.

Adam laughed. "You and every other female here." He turned to Thandie. "Get used to that. The women love Elliot. He has a certain effect on them."

She nodded. "I've been warned."

Adam laughed. "You think I'm joking, but I'm offering you sound advice."

"That's sweet, Adam, but I can take care of myself."

"Suit yourself," he said with a shrug. He turned to look up a wide stairway that ended at a closed door. There was a huge beast of a man guarding the entrance. "That's Elliot's office through there," Adam confirmed. "It looks like he's busy right now. How about I give you a tour of the VIP area?"

She nodded.

"Please follow me." Adam pointed the way as he led her toward another staircase. "VIP is up this way. I would recommend you lead your guests along the south wall. Crossing the dance floor to get to the stairs is a nightmare, and going by the bar is a deathtrap. I'll need to introduce you to Bruno. He checks VIP guests in. He's very thorough. If you aren't VIP, you don't get past him. Security will give you bands for all your guests when you come in. That way, your party can come and go through the different areas as they please."

He went up the stairs, pointing out certain areas of the club that could only be seen from his vantage point. She was amazed by the beautiful details of the building. The higher they climbed, the more she was able to discover. Without question the most awe-inspiring part were the hanging gardens that appeared to float above the dance floor. She imagined the view was more spectacular when the theater lights illuminated their perfection.

Adam paused to let her admire the view. "It's spectacular, isn't it?"

"Breathtaking," she agreed.

"It was Elliot's idea. He had this vision to make the club resemble the Hanging Gardens of Babylon. He flew in a historian and a landscape architect to recreate it. We were all skeptical at first, but the results speak for themselves." He leaned forward and wiggled his eyebrows mischievously. "And they retract. See those cords?" He pointed to one of the gardens. Thandie could just make out thin black cords attached to the planter's metal railing. "The cords go all the way up to the ceiling," he explained. "That's how the gardens are housed and maintained. We have a gardener who comes in daily. Because they're delicate, we don't display the gardens often. But when we do, this place is magical."

Keeping them on task, Adam nudged her to continue moving. At the top of the steps was yet another door. Adam pushed the large door that opened into the VIP room. It was a three-level, glass-enclosed "club within a club." The wall facing the main arena was made entirely of glass, giving everyone below a great "envy" view.

Adam stood alongside Thandie. "I've managed VIP rooms in Miami and LA," he confessed. "This is by far the coolest lounge I've ever been in. It's six-thousand-square-feet. Seats up to two hundred, holds up to five hundred standing. There are three full bars, one on each level. Five bartenders and eight servers. Private bathrooms are on the left of the bar on all levels. A DJ is always stationed on the main floor; however, if we have a guest DJ performing we pipe in the music. Pretty cool, huh?"

Thandie was speechless. As Adam walked her through the rooms, she was impressed by the display of sheer luxury.

"If you think this is nice, wait until you see the Tower," he said.

"The what?"

"Just a minute." He walked over to a hidden elevator and waved his hand over the panel. "Only the staff is allowed to use the elevator. During working hours, we ask everyone to refrain from using it. However, you and your guests are welcome to use it during off hours. It leads up to the Tower. You can take the stairs if you like. It's more scenic, but if you prefer a straight shot, the elevator is always here. The code to go to the Tower is one-two-two-one."

He punched in the code, and they rode up to the Tower. When the doors opened, she couldn't suppress her gasp. It was a beautiful oasis of hanging gardens, private balconies, open fountains and satin pillows. Adam seemed happy she was impressed with the room.

"I knew you would love it," he boasted. "We call it the Tower of Babel. This room is reserved for the ultimate VIP guests. There is a private entrance that leads up from the parking garage. This is the pinnacle in intimacy and privacy. It seats up to thirty, standing room for up to fifty. There are six servers and a private restroom. As you can imagine, this room is in high demand. This is Elliot's best idea yet. It's been a huge hit since we reopened from the renovation. We've had several parties up here already. It's a great revenue-turner. Even on slow nights, the Tower brings in serious cash. We've already got a waiting list."

She felt his gaze on her as she walked about the room running her fingers along the smooth furnishings.

"It's ten times more impressive at night, lit primarily by candlelight. Sexy stuff."

She nodded her agreement. "This is amazing, Adam."

"It is." He clapped his hands. "Bruno should be here by

now. Let's go downstairs and get you two acquainted. If we're lucky, Elliot will be free to speak with you soon."

The office door belonging to the mysterious Elliot Richards was still closed when they returned to the main floor; however, Bruno was available. He didn't have much to say, only grunts and occasional nods. Adam helped by briefly explaining Bruno's role and indexing a long list of responsibilities that fell under his authority.

Almost as soon as Adam and Bruno finished their overview, Thandie was introduced to Markie Duran, the club's general manager. He was pleasant enough and eager to bring her up to speed on Babylon's network of rules and securities. There was so much to take in, Thandie doubted she absorbed half of it. She was coming to realize Club Babylon was not simply a nightclub—it was a money-making machine. It was unlike anything she'd ever seen before.

"I should have brought a notepad to take notes," Thandie commented once Markie finished his presentation.

"Don't worry," Markie said with a laugh. "In a few short nights, you'll know this place like the back of your hand."

Thandie hoped he was right about that. The sheer size of the club was intimidating.

"It's too bad you weren't in town a week earlier," Adam added. "You missed the birthday bash." He winked at Markie, and both men gave a wicked laugh.

"Whose birthday?" Thandie's question faded when the door leading to Elliot's office suddenly opened. The reaction was immediate. The muscular man guarding the door stepped aside to allow several men to exit the office and descend the staircase. Thandie craned her neck, trying to get a good look at each man. "Which one is Elliot?"

"None," Adam confirmed with a quick glance. "It looks like Elliot's free. We better grab him while we can."

Taking hold of Thandie's elbow, he guided her up the stairs, pausing only long enough to quickly introduce her to the burly black man who stood guard outside the office door. She learned his name was Vincent Michelle, but preferred to be called Michelle.

Thandie crossed the threshold and stepped into a spacious, sleekly decorated office. The walls facing the arena were made entirely of one-way glass, providing an uninhibited view of the club without being seen. Oddly shaped lamps lit the room, which softened the modern furniture and created an intimate atmosphere.

Thandie's gaze continued to sweep over the room, and then she faltered. There he was. The man she'd flown over a thousand miles to meet—Elliot Richards. He was leaning casually against the edge of a large glass desk, staring at her. It was as if he'd been patiently waiting her for the entire time, and not the other way around.

The instant her eyes met his, Thandie froze in place. She watched, spellbound, as the sinfully handsome man pulled himself up to his full height and approached them. He was tall, tanned and mouth-watering. A one-of-a-kind Ferrari. He was perfection in motion. With every step he took, Thandie became more convinced of one thing: Elliot Richards had been well worth the wait.

He had satin black hair, captivating silver eyes, a strong chin and kissable lips. He was dressed in a crisp white button-up shirt and black slacks that could only be tailor-made to fit. His shirt pulled tightly across a muscular chest, his golden skin a stark contrast against the crisp fabric. He had a cool air that drew her to him, with very little effort on his part. Now, she understood why Adam had warned her.

"Hello." He gave her a slight grin, one that was all business and too damned sexy to be permissible. "I'm Elliot Richards.

You must be Thandie Shaw." He held out his hand. "Finally, we meet."

Thandie struggled not to gawk at him as she shook his hand. "It's a pleasure to meet you, Mr. Richards."

He blessed her with a dazzling smile. "Believe me, Ms. Shaw, the pleasure is all mine. You must forgive my tardiness. My meeting ran long; however, my delay doesn't in any way reflect your importance. I'm eager to see what you can do for us." He waved his hand toward the couches. "Please, have a seat."

Thandie walked toward a long leather couch, feeling Elliot's gaze on her the entire time. He waited for to take her seat, before sitting down himself. Adam took the opportunity to excuse himself, mumbling he had some things to see to.

Elliot waited until Adam left before turning to her. "I trust the tour you received was sufficient."

"Yes, very much so." She said with a guarded, yet nervous smile. "You have an amazing place."

"Thank you. It was quite an investment, but I'm happy with it."

Thandie had to force herself to concentrate on the conversation. Elliot Richards was gorgeous, alarmingly so. It was hard to believe this charming and very handsome man was the same person who'd hung up on her weeks before. When his lips began to move, Thandie became transfixed.

"I'm sure Warren has already spoken to you, but please allow me to reiterate." He checked his watch before continuing. "I currently own three night clubs. Lush, Red Door and Club Babylon. Lush is a fetish club, with very select membership. Red Door is a nightclub marketed toward the lesbian persuasion. It's the smallest of my businesses, but it holds a consistent clientele. Then, there is Club Babylon. It's my largest undertaking. The club has done very well on the strip, but we recently decided to update the look to grow our service capabilities. We reopened our doors last month. The changes have been received quite well, particularly the amenities marketed toward our members. However, we want to see major returns in a relatively short time. I expect to see a return on my investment in three months' time."

"Three months sets a vigorous schedule," Thandie warned.

Elliot nodded. "Yes, it does, but I'm confident we'll hit our mark on time. With your help, of course." He smiled. "Warren sang praises of your abilities. He was quite vocal that you are the person we need."

She blushed slightly. "Warren is very kind."

"If that were all it was, you wouldn't be here." He looked at her seriously. "Please allow me to be frank."

"I wouldn't have it any other way."

"I don't normally employ women, and for good reason."

"May I inquire why?"

His gaze was level. "In my experience, women become… unfocused."

She immediately understood. He was the reason for his previous female employees losing their focus. How could they not? He was a walking, talking, breathing distraction.

"In all honesty, Ms. Shaw, I'm not entirely sold on the idea of you being here. Club Babylon is quite the exception to the typical club expirence. This is not a place for emotional beings and and from past experiences, women often get attached to the wrong thing. Which is why working with an all-male staff is not only beneficial but necessary in my line of business."

She stared at Elliot. His sharp profile and flawless skin made it very clear what those "wrong attachments" might be. Fixing him with a hard stare, she said, "May I ask you a question?"

"Please."

"What the hell am I doing here?" She could tell her frankness momentarily shocked him. "As you can see, I'm not a man."

Elliot's silver gaze roved over her body slowly and intentionally. "That is a fact I have been unable to ignore." His stare was heated when he added, "And neither will the rest of my staff."

"I assure you I'm a professional. As long as your staff operates on the same level, then we should have no problems." She smiled thinly. "You've reviewed my portfolio; you know what I'm capable of. So if there is an issue with my gender, again I ask, what the hell am I doing here?"

"You're here because Warren insisted on it," he said simply.

He flashed her a devilish grin that made her mind conjure up every dirty thought imaginable. He really was too handsome for his own good. Her gaze unwillingly floated over his body, and there was no doubt in her mind the man was created for mind-numbing, can't-walk-in-the-morning sex.

"Although I appreciate Warren's confidence in me," she began, licking her lips in a struggle to tear her eyes away from his body, "I assure you I come highly recommended. Feel free to check my references."

"I have."

"And?" she prodded when he did not elaborate.

His eyes sparkled. "As you said, you come highly recommended. You wouldn't be here otherwise." He crossed his legs in one fluid motion. Somehow, he managed to make the action appear very masculine. "I thought it only fair for you to know where I stand."

She felt as if he were studying her unemotionally, as if he were shopping for a new car, mentally accessing value versus usage and lastly, appeal.

"I appreciate your candor," she said, somewhat irritated.

"I promise you I have an abundance to give." He disarmed

her by giving a boyish grin. "Babylon is my woman. I love her to obsession. Her success is my own."

"I understand."

"So I haven't frightened you off yet?"

"Not even close."

He grinned at her. "I like that you're not afraid of me."

This time, she laughed. "I'm from New York. Nothing frightens me."

"We shall see about that."

His words were delivered so softly, Thandie did not immediately catch their meaning. Did he intend to frighten her out of the job? She considered asking him this very question, but at the last minute stopped herself. Instead she asked, "Whom will I be working with?"

"Myself," he said. "Very closely." His eyes openly assessed her again, but this time was a little different from the first. This review was sexual. Whether he was impressed or not, she could not tell. "As well as my managing staff," he added. "You'll meet them tonight before we open. We get together for an action-meeting during the first hour of business. You should make yourself available. We go over the themes for the next night, as well as address any issues. Use tonight to acquaint yourself with the ins and outs of the club during showtime. It's easy to get confused when the lights are down."

"I'll be there."

"I know you will be."

"Can you give me an idea of what you expect from me?"

Elliot inclined his dark head gracefully. "I want you to host a series of events here at the club, leading up to our grand re-opening."

"Aren't you open now?"

"This is a 'soft' opening. It allows us to work out the kinks and formulate our operations. A dress rehearsal, if you will. We're showing only half our potential."

"Oh," was all she could think to say. She felt a little embarrassed, because she should have known the answer to her question. She'd seen a soft opening before, but certainly not to this extent. "When will I learn specifics regarding the project? Goals, budget, etcetera?"

"Over dinner."

Thandie frowned. "I'm sorry?"

"Do you have plans tomorrow evening?"

She heard herself answering before thinking. "No."

"Good. I'd like you to have dinner with me at Peppers at eight o'clock. The attire is formal. I suggest you wear a dress. My assistant Romero can give you directions."

"Why?" she blurted out, immediately suspicious of his intentions. "Why are we meeting there and not here, in your office?"

Elliot folded his hands in his lap. Thandie could tell he was not use to being questioned. Although his face remained a mask of cool indifference, his silver eyes flashed with what looked like annoyance. In spite of this, his voice was even-tempered when he spoke. "We are meeting at Peppers because I enjoy the food and I have a reserved table there. The timing of our meeting is because of my schedule. My day is filled with meetings. The only block I have available for you is while I'm dining." He arched a dark brow. "Is this going to be a problem?"

Feeling embarrassed for having jumped to the wrong conclusion, Thandie immediately shook her head. Mercifully, there was a heavy tap on the office door seconds before it opened. The large, beefy head of Michelle appeared.

"Elliot, Warren is here to see you."

"Thanks. Let him in." He stood, brushing his hands across his perfectly pressed pants. "Any last questions, Ms. Shaw?"

"No," she said quickly, avoiding eye contact.

"Before you leave, I should mention the Tower of Babel is off-limits during business hours. Take my word for it and just don't venture up there."

The office door opened wider, and Warren Radcliffe entered the room. In his sixties, he was a man who'd aged well. His pure white hair was worn long enough to brush the collar of his shirt. It was stylishly cut, and professionally highlighted. His mustache and beard were trimmed low, and well groomed. Adorned in a colorful Hawaiian shirt and khaki shorts, he looked as if he didn't have a care in the world. If Elliot were an exotic car, Warren was more like a lovable childhood toy, worn in presentation but holding all the jubilance of its younger days. In spite of his features, weathered from years of hard partying, his boyish nature could not be ignored. He was a great reminder that life never got boring because one grew older.

When Warren smiled at her, Thandie resisted the urge to run and curl herself up in his natural sunshine. As if reading her mind, he pulled her to her feet to give her a tight hug. "You're finally here. It's great to see you, Thandie. You look great."

She kissed his cheek. "So do you."

He shot a curious glance at Elliot. "I see you two have met. I hope he hasn't seduced you yet."

Elliot gave a dry laugh. "I'll leave the seducing to you, Romeo."

Ignoring Elliot, Warren looked down at Thandie. "We need to get you settled in. Adam loaded your bags into my car. Where are the girls? I'm here to help, but you'll need them. Damn, listen to me rambling like a woman. Wow, it's good to see you, Thandie. I feel as if I'm five years old again on Christmas morning."

"That was a long time ago," Elliot remarked.

Warren slanted his eyes in his direction, before returning his attention to Thandie. "Fun times, kiddo. This is going to be the adventure of a lifetime."

There was a knock at the door and Michelle popped his head in again. "Elliot, your next meeting is here."

Elliot checked his watch, then waved his hand. "Let him in." He turned to Thandie. "Until tonight, Ms. Shaw."

The door swung open, and a tall, dark-haired man entered the office.

Before Thandie could figure out who this new visitor was, Warren ushered her out of the office. Michelle quickly closed the door behind them.

Warren huffed. "No need for us to get caught up in that stuff."

"Who was that?" she asked.

"Your guess is as good as mine. Elliot has his hand in so many ventures, it's difficult to say." Warren was about to add more, but before the words could escape his lips, a beautiful Asian woman with long dark hair wrapped her arms around his neck.

Surprised and obviously grateful, Warren grinned from ear to ear. "Susan, how are you, honey?"

"I've been looking everywhere for you," she said.

"Well, I'm all yours now."

"Did you forget your promise to me?"

Warren paused for a moment and then snapped his fingers. "Of course not. How could I forget you?" His eyes ran over her long legs. "You're always on my mind."

"I better be," she laughed lightly. "Tonight, right?"

"I'll have to see if he'll be available."

"You promised," she reminded him in a slightly irritable tone.

"Okay, okay," he said calmly. "Tonight. I promise." She gave a triumphant smile and then glanced toward the office door that led to Elliot's office.

"I'm counting on you, Warren."

Thandie watched the woman saunter away, still baffled by what had just happened. "Please tell me you're going to explain that."

Warren waved his hand and guided Thandie toward the door. "Susan's a dear friend."

"How long have you known this dear friend?"

"Ever since she started working here?" he hedged.

Thandie gave him a questioning look.

"Okay, okay, kiddo. She's been working here for nearly a month," he admitted.

"What kind of promise did you make her?"

"It's silly," he said with a shake of his white head. "Forget you ever heard that."

"Uh-uh." Thandie shook her head teasingly. "Tell me everything."

Warren blushed. "I kinda promised her I'd introduce her to Elliot."

"Kinda?"

"Ok, I did—I promised her I'd introduce her to him."

"And in return?"

He wiggled his eyebrows.

At this, she had to laugh. "You haven't changed a bit."

Warren shrugged. "Why shouldn't I profit from his good fortune? I've got to give it to the guy; he's good. He's a great business partner but an even better womanizer. Speaking of which—" he turned serious eyes on her "—heed my warning, Thandie. Stay away from him."

She cocked her head to the side. "Would it surprise you that you aren't the first person to tell me that?"

"No, but it would surprise me if I were the last." Tucking her hand into the crook of his arm, like an old-world gentleman, Warren led her to the exit. "I'm so glad you came."

"Me too."

"Excellent. I promise you won't regret it."

The drive to Warren's home was relaxing, complemented by the subtropical climate. Thandie spent most of their trip being entertained by her host. He caught her up on the latest happenings with him and Wife Number Five. He was eager for the divorce, because he was already dating potential Wife Number Six. Thandie listened, thinking Warren was a fun guy who was desperately looking for happiness. She felt a little sorry for him, but his stories were too comical not to laugh at.

Twenty minutes later, Thandie stared up at a majestic estate. She'd always known Warren was well off, but she never imagined he lived so extravagantly. His beachfront home had a million-dollar view of the ocean. Inside, it had a minimalist design, abstract art and many white walls. He gave her a tour of the home before eventually guiding her to a guest room.

Placing her bags near the door, he said, "There are empty bedrooms down the hall for your staff. Make yourself at home. If there is anything you need, just ask. The housekeeper's name is Anga. Her room is off the kitchen. She's a sweetheart. She'll be happy to assist you. I won't be at the club until later tonight; however, my driver can take you back and forth. We'll get you a rental car tomorrow."

"This is very kind of you, Warren. Are you sure I'm not putting you out?"

"Nonsense. I'm happy to have the company. Things have been pretty quiet around here lately." He looked at his watch and made a low whistling sound. "I'm going to catch up on

my sleep. You might want to do the same. I'll see you later."
He gave her a kiss on the forehead before leaving.

Too anxious to rest, Thandie began unpacking. She took
her time stowing away her toiletries, hanging up her dresses,
and taking inventory of her shoes before finally tossing herself
across the bed. She could hardly believe she was in Miami. It
was a risky move, but she didn't regret it yet. The atmosphere
was very relaxing. She could almost swear she could smell the
ocean in the air.

She stretched out and looked up at the ceiling. She still
questioned her real reasons for coming, but she was here now
and she had better make the best of it. Club Babylon was
amazing. She could really work her connections to bring in
famous faces; even if she had to put up with Ruark Randall
again, it would be worth it.

Her thoughts turned to her mother, and she felt a tinge of
guilt. She'd visited with her mother before leaving the city.
She wanted to make sure the assisted living staff had all her
contact numbers. She'd promised her mother she would be
back in a few days. She'd meant every word, but she couldn't
help but feeling as though she'd just abandoned her mother.

Unexpectedly, her mind focused on the face of Elliot Richards. It was shameful how she'd reacted to him. If a successful
business relationship was to emerge from this, she would have
to curb her attraction to him. With a little determination, it
should be easy enough to keep her distance and concentrate
on her assignment. It wasn't as if he was attracted to her. He
hadn't shown the mildest interest in her. Hell, if he'd had it
his way, she wouldn't even be in Miami.

Thandie closed her eyes and considered the matter. She
wasn't tired, but the feel of the cool linens against her skin was
refreshing. She began to make a mental list of the things she

needed to do. Unfortunately, she did not get very far. Within a few minutes, she was sound asleep.

Thandie awoke three hours later. She fussed over what to wear. This would be her first night on the job. She had to make a good impression. She had just laid her outfit on the bed when her cell phone beeped. It was Amanda.

"Hi, Amanda. How is everything going?"

"Oh, my goodness! I'm so glad you picked up. I have a crisis on my hands!"

Thandie dressed while she listened to Amanda read off a long list of emergencies that she proclaimed to be "out of control." She had to apply her makeup with her ear glued to her phone. When Amanda was finished, Thandie walked her through how to address each issue. They were things that Amanda could have resolved herself, if she'd put more thought into it rather than easily giving in to panic.

She was still giving Amanda a pep talk when Warren's driver dropped her off at Club Babylon. The club was opening in ten minutes, and there was already a line. Bruno, the bouncer Adam had introduced her to earlier, held the door open for her. The heavy throb of rap vocals could be heard from the street. It was loud and seductive. Unfortunately, Thandie could not admire Babylon in its glory. She went directly into the women's bathroom to better hear Amanda's ranting.

"I don't know if I can do this alone, Thandie. Please tell me you're coming back soon."

"Amanda, I know you can do this. Just use your best judgment. I trust you to make the right decision. If you come across another situation and you absolutely don't know what to do, call me. Now I have an important meeting to go to. Will you be all right?"

Amanda hesitated. "I—I think so. Promise me you'll answer if I call back."

"I promise."

When she ended her call, Thandie looked at her minutes. One hour and fifty-five minutes. Had she really talked to Amanda that long? She groaned and gave herself a quick once-over in the mirror, then headed for Elliot's office. She smiled at Michelle as she ascended the stairs. He nodded to her before holding the door open. She could almost feel his eyes on her backside. Obvious as it may have been, Michelle's attention was nothing compared to what she faced next. Elliot stopped mid-sentence when he looked up at her. The men lounging on the couches turned to see their visitor. For a moment, no one said anything. They just stared at her.

Elliot was outlining the next day's schedule when Thandie walked into his office. The first thing that caught his attention was her legs. She was wearing satin hot pants that were so short, they might as well be considered panties. They drew his eyes right to the space between her thighs. Her blouse was nothing more than a shiny black handkerchief, with thin strings tied around her neck and behind her back. As she stepped farther into the room, her shapely legs, slender figure and curvy hips fell under his appraisal. They were incredible. The closer she got, the more apparent it became that her shirt was nearly see-through.

She put a spell over the room. No one was able to speak. They were too busy gaping at her attributes to say anything appropriate. Elliot had to force himself to break away from her magic. He cleared his voice. "Everyone, this is Thandie Shaw of Shaw Public Relations in New York. Her firm will be helping us promote the club for the grand reopening."

Before he could say more, Adam jumped up to offer her

his seat. Markie, Tom and Eddie stumbled over each other to introduce themselves. They each fought to tell her what their responsibilities were and why they would be working closely with her. Even his assistant Romero, who rarely went out of his way to speak to anyone, made a stiff introduction. Tom Comber, his director of food and beverage, and Eddie Bloom, his efficiency expert, were struggling to get a word in, being that their positions had little relevance to her job. Thandie didn't appear to be overwhelmed by their attention. Elliot imagined she always had men chasing after her. With a body like hers, he was almost certain.

Elliot folded his arms across his chest, having grown tired of watching his management team gush. "Now that introductions have been made," he said coolly, "let's finish up, shall we? Tom, please present our sales goal tonight."

The remainder of the meeting followed suit. Every manager took turns giving updates. Reports were made quickly, to allow themselves ample time to get back to the task of drooling over Thandie. By the time Elliot called it quits, he was royally annoyed by his team's behavior. He watched Adam and Markie follow Thandie out of his office like protective puppies. They were clearly guarding her from him. It was just as well. He had a strict policy not to sleep with his employees. That is, until now. Seeing her tonight, dressed as she was, made him forget himself for a minute. She was damned sexy.

He was suddenly looking forward to the next few months.

Thandie was enjoying herself. The music was great, and everyone was lively. Adam kept her busy by introducing her guests. There was something to be said about the partygoers of South Beach. Everyone looked great and loved to dance. She now wished that Len and Raja were here with her. This would have been the perfect opportunity to become acquainted with their clients.

She moved through the different levels of the VIP area, introducing herself to as many people as she could. The lights in the room changed from blue to a glowing red. Everyone went crazy as the dancers took to the stage. The party went into full swing as the music climbed to a new pinnacle.

In spite of her good time, Thandie was ever aware of Elliot's presence. Her gaze sought him out with an impulsiveness she could not control. She mentally combed the crowd until she finally spied him. Elliot was making slow progress, moving across the VIP area. Everyone either knew him or wanted to know him. It was impossible not to marvel at his ease of socializing, and the charisma with which he did it. Men and women alike were charmed by him. Women, of course, for his good looks. Men were easily won over by his unwavering air of confidence. Elliot Richards seemed like the coolest person in the room, and everyone wanted a piece of him.

As he was leaving the upper level, two men called him over. Thandie watched this interaction and was not surprised by what she saw. Apparently, gay men were not excluded from his appeal. Unlike most heterosexual males, Elliot did not appear the least bit guarded as he mingled with the men. Instead, Elliot engaged them warmly. In fact, it bordered on mild flirtation. Of course, it was not as obvious as it was with women but it was just enough to make them walk away thinking maybe, just maybe, they stood a chance of warming a place in Elliot's bed.

With easy skill, Elliot broke away from the group and continued his rounds of greeting VIP members.

Just then, Adam sought her out in the crowd and waved her over to a table on an elevated level. From this perch he was able to point out regular customers, whom he referred to as members. Thandie listened avidly as he distinguished the rich from the hangers-on. There were telltale signs Thandie would have been able to figure out for herself, but Adam had the advantage of experience. He knew these people by name and face, oftentimes by financial records. He was vague on these details, but he revealed just enough to let her understand the clientele.

From the corner of her eye, Thandie spotted Warren entering the VIP lounge. A wave of interest swept over the rooms as he made his way through the throng. A celebrity in his own right, Warren's arrival was warmly received. He shook hands and issued nods of acknowledgment with the masterful finesse of a seasoned politician. No one was immune to Warren's charm.

A break in the mass occurred and Thandie was able to see Warren fully. His Hawaiian shirt and khaki shorts had been replaced by a fine dark suit and silk tie. His thick white hair, although stylishly brushed to the side, caught the hold of the mood lighting and now glowed a soft lavender purple. Not surprisingly, a young woman clung to his side.

Thandie waved her hand to signal him. Catching sight of her, Warren grinned and began making his way toward them. "Hey, kiddo!" he said as soon as he reached her. "I see you made it to school just fine."

Thandie hugged Warren in greeting. "Yes, I made it here in one piece."

"How did the management meeting go?"

"She made quite an impression," Adam volunteered.

Warren's white brows raised. "Oh, really?"

"I don't think the boys are excited about sharing their sandbox with a girl," Thandie suggested.

Adam gave a snort. "I beg to differ."

"No one gave you a hard time, did they?" Warren asked, a trace of concern in his eyes.

"No," she assured him. "It was painless enough."

"Well, then," Warren said happily, "no harm done." He snapped his fingers as if remembering something. "Where are my manners?" Turning to the young woman at his side, he said, "This is Thandie, an old friend of mine." He put special emphasis on the 'old friend' part. "And that's Adam," he added flatly. If Adam was offended by Warren's lack of embellishment, he did not show it. "Thandie and Adam, this is Kara."

"Tara," the woman corrected.

"Right," Warren said quickly. "Tara."

Tara made a childish pout with her lips, muttered something about wanting to dance, and then sashayed onto the dance floor. Thandie was amused by the animated way Warren and Adam swiveled their necks to watch Tara's departure. When the leering got to be too much, Thandie asked, "Warren, who is that woman?"

Warren leaned closer and whispered, "If I play my cards right, we could be looking at the next Mrs. Warren Radcliffe."

"Wife Number Six?" Thandie mused aloud.

Warren waved his hand in air. "Don't rain on my parade. Our lawyers are talking." He watched Tara dancing in the center of the dance floor. Her hands were in her hair and her hips swayed provocatively. Warren gave a sigh of awe. "Don't wait up for me, kiddo," he said. "I don't plan on coming home early." With that said, he eased his way onto the dance floor to join Tara.

"Crafty old guy," Adam muttered under his breath.

"You have no idea," she agreed.

Suddenly, without warning, Elliot appeared out of the crowd and stood at Adam's side. The expression on his face was calm, cool and collected. However, his eyes told a different story. The pale gray orbs flickered with something bright and dangerous. Thandie got the eerie feeling she was hunted prey.

Elliot locked eyes with her for a moment and then, as if nothing of significance had happened, he turned to Adam. "I trust you're keeping a close eye on Ms. Shaw."

Adam grinned. "I'm not letting her out of my sight."

"That's good to hear," Elliot said in a voice that seemed to convey just the opposite. "We wouldn't want to lose her in the crowd. Anything could happen."

Adam chuckled, but Thandie frowned at the strange comment. Was he trying to warn her, or scare her? Uncertain if the remark deserved a response, Thandie looked away. She could feel Elliot's gray gaze on her, and it was unsettling.

She stiffened when he stepped around Adam, circling behind her, to come up on her left. His movement was slow and deliberate. He came within inches of brushing against her. She could briefly feel his breath on the back of her neck as he passed her.

"I trust we're keeping you entertained," he whispered close to her ear.

"Yes," she replied skittishly; her nerves brittle from his nearness, which was too close for comfort. "I can see why Babylon is in high demand," she said lamely. "The renovations are remarkable. The views are impressive."

"I agree," he said with soft laugh. "The views are very impressive."

She looked up to find his gaze was not on the glass walls which overlooked the lower levels of the club, but trained on her. Thandie's reaction to his words played right into his hands. A flutter of arousal began to churn in her stomach, her skin puckered with goose bumps, and her nipples tightened. She did not have to look down to know her response was noticeable. She could tell by the sound of Elliot's soft chuckle.

Thankfully Adam, who'd been keeping a watchful eye on the VIP guests, thus missing their exchange, asked, "How are we doing tonight, Elliot?"

"We'll hit our liquor sales goal," Elliot replied unenthusiastically.

"Better than nothing," Adam said encouragingly.

"So you say," Elliot retorted. Without another word, he disappeared into the sea of people.

Thandie looked after him, unsure what to make of Elliot. What had been the point of that? Was he trying to bait her into saying something foolish? Or did he simply enjoy unnerving her? She watched his retreating back, his broad shoulders leaving a wide path in his wake.

"Elusive as always," a voice said.

Thandie turned around to see the speaker. Standing directly behind her was a dark-haired man with even darker eyes. He was average height, well suited, and there was an interesting lift in his voice, indicating he was not native to the area. She imagined under any other circumstance, he would strike her as handsome. However, her eyes still lingered on the spot Elliot had just vacated.

"Of course," the stranger continued, "that's why women can't get enough of him."

"Ah, you're back," Adam said, having noticed their visitor. He reached around Thandie to shake the man's hand. "I thought you would be out of town for a few more days." Adam inclined his head to Thandie. "This is Rex Barrington. He handles the marketing for Club Babylon."

Rex held out his hand to her. "And you must be the legendary Ms. Shaw everyone has been talking about."

"I am Thandie Shaw," she said as she accepted his hand. "However, I'm not sure about the legendary part."

Rex chuckled. "You're a woman on Elliot's payroll. Around here, that makes you quite famous."

"So I hear," Thandie said with a snort.

"I didn't mean to offend you," Rex confessed. "It's just that we've never had a woman on the management team. I imagine you'll have an immediate impact on the culture here."

"She's a lot nicer to look at than Eddie," Adam added with a smirk.

"Of that, I have no doubt," Rex concurred. "Elliot outdid himself this time."

At the mention of Elliot's name, Thandie instinctively sought him out in the crowd. It did not take long to spot him. In the short time since speaking to her, Elliot had maneuvered his way back to the main floor, and obtained a new companion. Even from this vantage point, Thandie could tell her enlarged breasts were fake and her pale blond hair came from a bottle. Even so, her attributes were admirable. She was yet another reason why the average male would envy Elliot.

The two were just about to head up the staircase leading to his office door, when they were distracted by someone stepping out of the crowd. It was Warren, and he was attempting to introduce Elliot to a dark-haired girl. It was not Tara. Thandie had to squint her eyes before recognizing her as the pretty Asian girl she'd met earlier that day.

Elliot smiled down at the woman, before taking her fingers in his and pressing his lips to the top of her hand. His opened his mouth to speak, but Thandie was too far away to make out the words. Whatever he'd said had been brief, because Elliot soon continued up the steps. He and the blonde disappeared into his office, the entrance to which was immediately obstructed by the giant Michelle. It was little wonder why Elliot had retreated into his office with the woman. Thandie's imagination ran wild with the possibilities.

"Thandie."

She jumped at the sound of Adam's voice. Quickly diverting her eyes, Thandie turned to face him.

"Do you want to see the DJ booth?" he asked.

She smiled. "Please lead the way."

Chapter Five

Elliot woke earlier than normal. It was a quarter to noon; practically daybreak for a person who kept his late hours. He hadn't returned home until six this morning.

All three of his clubs had been exceptionally busy the previous night. Elliot routinely split his time between his clubs, which were conveniently located within a few blocks of each other. Because Babylon was his largest enterprise, it demanded most of his attention. However, he checked in with the managers at his smaller establishments regularly. It was important that they know he was engaged in their day-to-day operations, particularly when money was involved.

Typically, Elliot began his day at Babylon, would slip away for few hours to visit Lush and Red Door, and would return to Babylon shortly before closing to help with the shutdown. He liked to be on site when the money from the cash registers was collected. Closing the club up for the night was an efficient, yet time-consuming, endeavor.

★ ★ ★

With only a few hours of sleep, Elliot was surprisingly alert and ready to start his day. He indulged himself with a long workout in his home gym, before cooling off with a few laps in the pool. He felt invigorated, lighter than normal. He knew why. It was the thrill of a new hunt. He grinned as he recalled the look on Thandie's face when he'd left her last night. She was damned cute when she was uncertain of herself. And sexy. He recalled quite vividly how those small shorts wrapped around her shapely bottom. He was looking forward to their dinner tonight.

Elliot showered and dressed for yet another long day. Romero was just parking his car in the drive when he emerged onto the front porch. His assistant looked surprised to see him up and about prior to his arrival.

Romero followed Elliot to his vehicle and got into the passenger seat. During the short drive to the Ocean Avenue bistro, they discussed his busy schedule. Predictably, the meal was cut short so not to be late for Elliot's first appointment for the day.

The two set off again, arriving at Club Babylon. It was early, and the club was slowly coming to life. Most of the lights were still off and only a handful of staff members was present. Elliot went to his office. Romero followed him, turning on the lights as they went, before using the office phone to dial into a conference call. Tapping the speaker button so that the sound of ringing filled the room, Romero quickly left the office to attend to other matters. Elliot was already behind his desk, powering up his computer while he waited for the managers of Lush and Red Door to join the call. Markie Duran entered the office looking tired, clutching a notepad and a cup of coffee. These phone calls took a harder toll on Markie than the other club managers, because Babylon kept longer hours. Knowing Markie as he did, Elliot suspected he would take a power nap in his office before their evening meeting with the entire team.

Within minutes, the managers of both clubs joined the call, and the sharing of statistical data from the previous night got underway. These meetings were cumbersome, but necessary. Each general manager was protective of his information, and the undercurrent interoffice competition was glaringly evident. The managers of Lush and Red Door strived to outdo each other with their gross revenues, and Markie was determined to upset both clubs by generating double their combined totals. These calls were highly combative and often frustrating. However, Elliot enjoyed the competition amongst his managers. He was the winner regardless of the outcome.

An hour later, Markie still looked tired, but smug. He'd decidedly outperformed his cohorts from a revenue standpoint, but he had some improvement to do. As soon as the call was over, Elliot turned to him, and said, "Our capabilities should be better. We're getting screwed on overtime hours due to all the confusion surrounding the reopening. Get our people trained up immediately. Also, I've looked at the budget for catering. We're going overboard. Get with Eddie and cross-reference those numbers with the guest list we've been working on."

There was a knock before Michelle swung open his office door. "Nico's here," the giant grunted.

Elliot turned away from Markie. "I think that will do it," he said. "Gather that information for me, and let's schedule some time together tomorrow." Scooping up his paperwork and coffee cup, Markie exited Elliot's office just as Nico entered the room.

Nico was a boy millionaire who grew his fortune by making unusual but rewarding investments. He and Elliot had known each other since their college days. Elliot had been a student at the University of Miami while Nico, who attended school in Italy, had a habit of chartering private jets to fly himself and a group of friends to South Beach for the weekend. His passion for wild parties and pretty women made him and Elliot instant friends.

Nico was Elliot's closest friend and was therefore the only person who could honestly say he knew the real Elliot Richards. They shared confidences with the knowledge that the other would tease him mercilessly but in the end would help in any way possible. When Elliot wanted to buy his first club, it was Nico who had financially backed him. Although Elliot had managed to pay him back within a year, Nico had never mentioned the favor.

Whenever Nico was in town, they were inseparable. Much like their college days, they spent most of the time discussing business, partying and sharing women. It was a routine that came as naturally to them as breathing.

Elliot stood and met Nico halfway. They slapped hands and gave a brief hug.

"You look like hell," Nico said.

Elliot grinned. "So do you."

It was a stupid greeting that they'd practiced since first meeting and for some reason had never grown out of.

"When did you get in town?" Elliot asked.

"Yesterday," his friend replied. "I won't be here long, but it was a necessary trip." Nico claimed the seat behind Elliot's desk and began fiddling with his cell phone. "I just got a new phone yesterday, and I can't figure out how to check my mail. I made a trip to the store to have them explain to me how to work the damn thing, but that kid was all of nineteen and seemed to get off pointing out to me how little I understood about technology. I should have told the little snot that I own a sizable portion of the company that designed the phone. Ah, here we go." Nico reached for the desk phone and started dialing.

"Who are you calling?" Elliot asked.

"The engineer who designed my phone." The speakerphone echoed the automated ringing. It rang exactly four times before a squeaky voice answered.

"Yeah?" answered the annoyed, high-pitched voice.

"Ralphie, this is Nico."

The person on the other end cleared his voice. "Hello, Nico—I mean, sir. How can I help you?"

"You can start by explaining how I can check my email on my phone. Several people have sent me messages, but I can't set up my browser right."

"If you send it to me, I can adjust your settings."

"Not an option," Nico said. "I'm in Miami for a few days."

"If you don't mind giving me your cell number, I can connect to your phone and do the setup for you."

Nico agreed and called off his number to the tech. Allowing him some time to work, he swiveled in the seat and looked at Elliot. "Matrix is throwing another party tonight," he said. "Are you up for it?"

"Do you only come to town for Matrix's parties?"

Nico held his hands up in mock surrender. "What else is there to do?" He shot his friend a wicked grin. The last time they'd attended one of Matrix's house parties, they'd participated in an orgy and woke up in Baltimore of all places.

Elliot laughed. "I'm working tonight."

"You're always working."

"I know."

"Lucky for you, Matrix expected you to say that. The party starts at nine. I'll pick you up."

"I can't."

"The Ripley twins will be there," Nico coaxed.

Elliot shrugged. "Tempting, but I already have plans."

Nico squinted his eyes at Elliot, looking suddenly suspicious. "Plans with whom?"

Before Elliot could answer, the phone's speaker came back to life.

"You're good to go, sir. Try to check your mail now."

Nico pulled out his phone and played with the keys. Satisfied, he grinned. "Thanks, Ralphie." Without further preamble he hung up the phone. Not one to forget his train of thought, Nico picked up the conversation where they'd left off. "Plans with whom?"

Elliot sighed, making it clear he was bored with the topic. "I'm meeting with a new employee."

"A new employee? I didn't know you were in the market."

"Stop fishing, Nico."

"Fine. Keep your secrets. I'll think fondly of you when I'm slutting it up tonight." Standing, Nico came around the desk. "Oh, before I forget, Chris is going to be in town next month. You know how quickly his schedule fills up. I was thinking we could get in a game of racquetball. The bastard has beaten me the last three times we've played."

Elliot leaned against his desk. "Tell me the date and time."

"I'll send you the info." Nico slid his phone into his pocket and prepared to leave. "I'll send your love to the Ripley girls."

Elliot chuckled. "You do that."

"Enjoy your meeting."

"I intend to."

Thandie woke up to the sound of her cell phone vibrating. She flipped it open to see it was Amanda again. She took a calming breath before answering in a groggy voice. "Hi, Amanda."

"Oh, my gosh! You won't believe what happened last night."

Thandie braced herself for the worst. She pulled the sheets over her head while she listened to Amanda's dramatic tale about the opening of Rain Bar. This should have been an easy assignment, since Thandie had set up the event before leaving for Miami. She had assumed wrong. Amanda was up in arms because several key celebrities had bypassed the red carpet in favor of a side door, and missing any chance of photographers seeing them. That was a problem when putting together a big event. It was the promoter's responsibility to make sure the press noticed the right people. Amanda was near tears.

"Amanda, calm down. We can fix this." Thandie took a moment to consider the options. "Make a list of who went in the side door. Call Nancy at *The Post,* and feed her blurbs focusing on those people. Surely you know or heard something that happened during the party. Let Nancy come up with her own assumptions; just give her enough to go off of. No embellishments. Let Nancy do that. Do you think you got that?"

"Yes, Thandie. I'm so sorry," Amanda sobbed. "I thought I had the side door handled."

"There's no need in crying over spilled milk, Amanda. Just call Nancy and give her what she wants."

As Thandie hung up the phone, she wondered if she had made a mistake leaving Amanda in the office alone. So far, she was not faring well. She hoped this was just beginner's nervousness, and Amanda would grow into her position...quickly. If not, Thandie would have to make some adjustments.

Pulling on a pair of shorts, she washed up before heading downstairs to find something to eat. Warren was already seated at the breakfast nook reading a newspaper. Anga, the housekeeper, had laid out a small spread of fruit and muffin options on the kitchen island. Thandie plucked up a shiny red apple and joined Warren for breakfast. Well, it was actually a late lunch, since Thandie hadn't woken up until well past one o'clock.

Warren was in his usual cheery mood. "Hey, kiddo. How do you feel?"

"Tired," she said sleepily.

Warren put down his newspaper, and leaned forward conspiratorially. "So what did you think about last night?"

"Babylon is amazing, Warren." And it was the truth. Aside from her run-in with Elliot Richards, her experience at Babylon had been very exciting. "You invested well."

"I knew you'd love it," he said with an enthusiastic clap of his hands. "Does this mean you're officially on board?"

"I believe so. Elliot and I are going to discuss details today."

"Very good." He picked up his newspaper, shook it out, and began scanning for the article he'd been reading. "Everything should go well. Elliot was impressed with you."

"Oh?" she said, suddenly intrigued. "What exactly did he say?"

From behind his newspaper, she could see Warren shrug his shoulders. "Not much. He's not a man of many words. He just said 'he recognized an asset when he saw one'. That's a glowing recommendation coming from him," Warren said with a nod of his white head. "Believe me, if he didn't approve of you, he would have told you so."

Thandie chewed on this scrap of information, not necessarily pleased. An asset? What was she? A horse? Not wanting to talk about Elliot anymore, she changed the subject. "I have to pick up the girls tomorrow. When will you be able to take me to the car rental?"

"You can use one of mine, Thandie. I don't mind."

She shook her head. "Warren, you're already doing enough for me. I wouldn't feel right borrowing your car on top of accepting your hospitality."

He sighed dramatically. "I try to be a nice guy."

"And you're greatly appreciated."

Giving up on reading his paper, Warren put it down and dabbed at the corners of his mouth with his napkin. "Give me half an hour and I'll be ready."

"Thanks, Warren."

"Yeah yeah," he said with wave of his hand as he left the kitchen.

Thandie finished off her apple before heading to her own room to change into more appropriate clothing. While she milled through her suitcase looking for sandals, she took the opportunity to place a call. A subdued voice answered on the first ring.

"BHP. Gage Ali's office. How may I help you?"

"This is Thandie Shaw. Is Gage available?"

"Hold on one second, Thandie."

The husky voice of Gage Ali flowed through the phone. "So it is true? You're in Miami?" Her voice was dark and exotic, softened only by the lilt of her British accent. "I called your office this morning to see if you wanted to do lunch next week."

"Sorry. I didn't get a chance to tell you I'm on assignment in Florida for the next few months."

"Months? You can't be serious."

"I know, but the pay was irresistible."

"Amanda sounds as though she's dying over there."

"I'm hoping she will simmer soon," Thandie confessed.

"Who's your contact down there?"

"Warren Radcliffe."

"Warren?" Gage laughed. "Warren is insane."

"Yes, he is."

"Well, one thing is for sure, you'll be thoroughly entertained."

"Yes, I know."

"What sort of assignment are you working on in Miami?" Gage pressed.

"I'm promoting a club down here."

"What's the name?"

"Club Babylon."

Gage paused. "Elliot Richards's club? Now that's interesting."

"What do you mean by that?"

"Nothing, really. Have you seen him?"

"Who, Elliot? Yes."

"Very tempting, isn't he?"

Thandie hesitated. "I suppose."

Gage was quiet for a second. "I've met him before, Thandie."

"So?"

"So...I know exactly what he looks like. He's fuckalious, and you know it."

"Gage!"

"Oh, Thandie," she said in a motherly tone. "I envy you just as much as I pity you."

"Thanks for the vote of confidence."

"If you don't listen to anything I say, please listen to me now. Stay away from Elliot Richards."

"I'll keep that in mind," Thandie said lamely.

"No, Thandie, I'm serious. He is a demon placed on this earth to screw women into oblivion. We thought it was that damn apple that caused Eve's fall from grace." Her voice dropped to a stage whisper. "It wasn't."

"Let me guess. It was Elliot?"

"Exactly."

Thandie burst into laughter. In all the years she'd known Gage, she'd never been so animated. "Are you finished?"

"Okay, I may be pouring it on thick, but in all sincerity, Thandie, don't go down that road. Trust me when I say if you allow yourself to get involved with Elliot, you will get your heart broken."

"Thank you, Gage—"

"The things he's into—" Her voice drifted off. "Just don't get hurt, okay?"

"Gage," Thandie said in a warning tone, "what do you know?"

The line went silent for a long time. "Nothing really," Gage hedged. "Old wives' tales, I guess."

"Just how well do you know Elliot?"

"I don't know him," Gage confessed. "No one does. He doesn't keep very close company. However, I was once friendly with an acquaintance of his."

"Friendly?"

"You know what I mean," Gage snapped. "Just be careful down there."

"I will," Thandie promised.

Long after they'd hung up, Thandie considered Gage's warnings. In the short time she'd been in Miami, Gage was the third person to caution her about Elliot.

Thandie certainly did not need further warnings to keep her distance from Elliot. In the brief conversations she'd had with him, she'd learned to be on her guard. He was beautiful to the point of unnerving, and arrogant to the point of exasperation. These were two things that, if Thandie didn't watch herself, could get her into a lot of trouble.

But those eyes. Those fascinating silver eyes of his. She'd never seen anything quite like them. They seemed to flicker with intensity, bearing into her with frightening clarity.

One thing was clear—Elliot Richards was a dangerous man.

She was definitely not looking forward to their dinner meeting tonight.

As if on cue, her phone began vibrating. She looked at the incoming number and frowned. She did not recognize it, but it had a Miami prefix. She answered hesitantly. "Hello?"

"May I speak to Thandie Shaw?" the caller asked brusquely.

"Speaking."

"Ms. Shaw, this is Romero, Elliot Richards's assistant. I was calling to confirm your meeting with him tonight at eight. Do you know how to get to Peppers?"

"Uh—no," confused by the assertiveness of his tone.

"I will send you the directions. Please be on time. Elliot is on a tight schedule."

"Er—"

"He wanted me to tell you he is looking forward to your meeting. I trust you feel the same."

Thandie's mouth fell open, and then it shut. It shut because Romero had already hung up. She looked at the phone and scowled. What was it with Floridians and decent phone manners? Did everyone hang up on each other in this town?

The sound of her phone chirping broke her silent rant. It was the sound indicator, alerting her she had a new email. She toggled the dials and discovered it was a new message from Romero. It included directions to the restaurant, and restated the importance of her arriving on time.

She hissed at the email like an angry cat. She was becoming increasingly leery of this meeting. She'd secretly harbored hopes someone from Elliot's management team might join them for dinner, possibly Adam or Markie. But she now knew that had been a foolish notion. Romero's comment about Elliot "looking forward to their meeting" was proof enough. The idea of being alone with him made her shoulders sag with the weight of a two ton anvil. Elliot was toying with her, and she knew it. He was trying to intimidate her. Well, she wouldn't allow that to happen. At least, not as easily as he might think.

Now spitting mad, Thandie resolved herself to do battle. Hastily, she finished getting dressed. After she claimed a car from the rental agency, she had errands to run. Every good warrior knew battles were not won in the heat of combat, but in the preparations. If it was a fight Elliot wanted, it was a fight he would get.

Peppers
(the foyer)
7:58PM

Thandie was twenty minutes early for dinner. It was enough time for her to second-guess her wardrobe choices. She'd packed only one suit for the trip to Miami. Upon careful inspection, it looked more appropriate for a funeral. So she'd headed to the mall to buy something more fitting.

Not normally swayed by sales consultants, Thandie found she was eager to accept the opinion of a stranger. She couldn't seem to make up her mind. The saleswoman had assured her the dress was a conservative design, but Thandie was beginning to worry if she'd been had. She tugged at the stubborn hem of her dress. It seemed to be getting shorter by the minute. She was almost certain there had been more fabric on the dress when she'd bought it two hours earlier.

Thandie pulled out her phone and checked the time. It was exactly one minute until eight o'clock. *Be on time my ass,* she grumbled to herself. Next time she saw Romero, she planned to give him a piece of her mind.

Just then, the entrance door swung open and Elliot Richards strolled into the foyer. He was wearing a pewter gray suit and crisp button-up shirt. He spotted her immediately.

As he came nearer, she could see the gray of his suit matched the color of his eyes. And the rest of him…was every bit as splendid. His thick dark hair was brushed away from his face, resembling rippling waves of black satin. The sharp features of his face were chiseled to perfection. If possible, Elliot was more handsome than she remembered. Thandie could feel her confidence begin to slip.

She watched his gaze slide over her. Even though she was fully clothed, she felt naked; stripped and completely vulnerable under his silver stare. She wished she'd chosen another dress. Something with sleeves would have been desirable. She could literally feel Elliot's eyes caressing every curve of her body. Unable to help herself, she tugged at the hem of the dress again, pulled herself up taller, and forced herself to meet his stare. It was a mistake. His eyes danced with an unspoken challenge. She could see he was amused by her discomfort.

"Elliot," she said in greeting.

"Ms. Shaw." He inclined his head slightly. "You look utterly delectable."

Thandie could feel blood rushing to her face, and knew she was turning deep red. She gripped her clutch tightly.

"Mr. Richards," an enthusiastic female voice called out.

Both Elliot and Thandie turned to see the restaurant's hostess approach them. She was practically beaming at Elliot. Thandie bit her lower lip in annoyance. The entire time she'd been waiting in the foyer, the hostess hadn't so much as spared her a passing glance.

"We're happy to have you join us today," she simpered. "Your table is ready."

Elliot flashed her a smile. "Very good. Please, lead the way." He turned to Thandie and, surprising both women, placed a possessive arm around her waist. "Shall we?" he whispered in her ear, as he ushered her forward.

Thandie walked stiffly at his side as the hostess navigated around tables before climbing a short flight of carpeted steps. They arrived at Elliot's table, a secluded booth near the rear of the upper level. It offered a superior view of the dining areas and bar below, and yet was obscured from curious eyes by layers of decorative silk curtains.

Thandie slid in first, settling herself as far on the opposite side as possible. Elliot slid in beside her, purposely eating up much of the space she'd created. His head lowered slightly, and she was momentarily surprised by the fan of dark lashes that shaded his eyes. They were long and thick—the kind women paid a small fortune to possess.

Her attention was disturbed when their waiter arrived and placed leather-bound menus before them. He greeted Elliot by name before asking for their drink requests. Without even consulting Thandie, Elliot ordered a bottle of wine. The waiter nodded his approval and disappeared. When he was well out of earshot, Thandie showed her irritation.

"I can order for myself," she said tersely.

"I'm sure you can. However, tonight I am ordering for you. So get used to it."

"I'm not accustomed to having a man treat me like this."

"That's because I'm the first man you've ever dealt with."

She laughed dryly at his statement. His cocky presumption nearly toppled her patience.

"You look nervous," Elliot remarked. "I hope I'm not the reason."

"I'm not nervous," she said frostily.

He said nothing, but the grin he gave her was wicked and knowing.

Thankfully, the waiter arrived with the wine. Elliot took the bottle, insisting he be the one to fill their glasses. As he did so, he placed their entrée order. The waiter again nodded his head.

"Please send the chef my respects," Elliot added. "And press upon him my eagerness to dine. I have a healthy appetite tonight—" he paused to let his gaze slide over Thandie once more "—and my date looks good enough to eat."

"Yes, Mr. Richards," the waiter said promptly. "I will tell the chef." He vanished without another word.

Elliot watched him leave, the hint of a smile played on his lips.

"Was that really necessary?" Thandie asked.

"It was," Elliot said as he took a sip from his wine glass, "because it's true. You look utterly edible tonight. My compliments to your dress."

Thandie had to bite down on her lip again. She reached for her own glass, in a desperate attempt to keep her hands busy, and took a sip. She was surprised to discover it was pretty good. Better than good. It was wonderful. She could feel a rush of warmth wash over her as the smooth liquid went down. She looked at Elliot, not at all surprised to see him watching her.

"You like it," he said. "I can tell. Your face is glowing."

Thandie impulsively took another sip before resting her glass on the tabletop. He'd been right of course. However, she'd die a slow death before she'd admit as much to him. She pushed her glass a few inches farther away from her. She didn't intend to get lightheaded on wine during her meeting. She would have to pace herself.

"How was your first night at Babylon?" he asked casually.

"Great," she breathed, relieved the conversation had turned to business. "I was telling Warren this morning I thought he'd made a very sound investment."

Something flickered across Elliot's face. It bordered annoyance, but she could not be sure. Whatever it was, it was gone as quickly as it had come. "Yes," he said smoothly, "it's a very sound investment."

"You mentioned yesterday you wanted me to host a series of events at the club," she said. "Did you have in mind any particular kind of events?"

"That will be entirely up to you," he said vaguely.

"Entirely?" she pressed.

Elliot smiled. "With my approval, of course."

"Of course," she said under her breath, slightly irritated by the lack of direction he was giving her. "Is there anyone specifically you wish to attend these events?" she asked. "I have a lot of contacts in New York. I planned to work my connections to get as many celebrities as your staff thinks they can handle. I know Brandon Audrey's agent. I can see how his schedule lays out."

If he was impressed by her dropping the name of a major movie star, he was a remarkable poker player. He didn't even flinch. Whether it was because he didn't care for Brandon Audrey or doubted her abilities to book him, was a mystery to her.

Elliot gave her a patronizing smile. "I see you're not familiar with how things work here. Miami is known for two things." He ticked his words off on his fingers. "Music artists and models. Wherever there are musicians, there will undoubtedly be models. And where there are models, there are wealthy men. Where there is wealth, there are more beautiful women, and where there are beautiful women, there are men. My point is, you need to focus on getting music artists here. The occasional actor is fine, but concentrate your energy on music. Am I making myself clear?"

"Absolutely," she agreed, relieved he was giving her specifics she could use. "And while we're on the subject of the target market, what about the press? Are there any syndications you want to be featured in? The Tower would make for some great photo opportunities. *Elle Décor* or even *Architectural Digest* might consider doing a story—" She broke off when he started shaking his head. "Is there a problem?"

"No press."

"Excuse me?" she asked, certain she had not heard him correctly.

"No press," he repeated, "and absolutely no photographers."

Thandie laughed. "This is a joke, right?" She stopped abruptly when he didn't join her. Instead, he sat patiently, staring at her. "You can't be serious," she said.

He flicked away an imaginary piece of lint from his suit lapel.

"You're serious?" she gasped in disbelief.

"No photos. It's a club policy."

"Who would make such an absurd policy?"

"I did."

"But this is for promotion," she stammered. "How can we motivate people to come to the club if you aren't willing to show your establishment?"

"I'm sorry, Ms. Shaw, but I'm quite firm on the matter. Guests come to Babylon for privacy, and I will not break promises just to sell a few silly fashion magazines and cheap tabloids."

"Those cheap tabloids define for many people who's hot and who's not," she said. "They set the mode for mainstream society. And if it weren't for those silly fashion magazines marketing their products, it's doubtful you would know that Purple Label suit you're wearing is the center point of Ralph Lauren's spring line."

"Versed as you are in ways of fashion, my decision hasn't changed. No photos. And if you don't like it, you can always quit. There are plenty of qualified and more…appropriate promoters who would love to be in your position right now." One dark, arched brow lifted. "The choice is yours, Ms. Shaw."

Thandie's jaw clenched closed. "It's going to take a lot more than outlandish requests to make me quit."

His handsome face split into a wicked grin. "Well then, I will have to work a little harder."

The waiter reappeared holding platters of food. How the chef ever managed to prepare the two steak dinners that quickly was beyond Thandie. She'd never been much of a beef eater, but the scent wafting from the plates was divine. The steak was thick, lean and still sizzling. She was too much of a novice to even know what cut of meat it was, but it really didn't matter. She was beginning to salivate. Painstakingly, she waited for the waiter to place their meals on the table and depart.

Elliot smiled down at his plate and, with fluid motions, he cut a small piece of his steak. He did not eat it himself. Instead, he held it up to her lips. "Please, have a bite," he said. "I promise you won't regret it."

Thandie took in his low tone and wondered if the serpent had said something very similar to Eve in the Garden of Eden. His proposal seemed to offer she take a bite of him as well as the meat. It was tempting. Very tempting. Especially when his eyes glowed a captivating hue of hypnotic silver and he wore that wicked grin of his. Thandie tore her eyes away from his lips and focused on the gleaming fork with the proffered steak nestled on its prongs. Nervously, she leaned forward and opened her mouth, aware Elliot was watching her.

The moment the meat touched her tongue, she didn't care who was looking. She was in heaven. It was the sweetest, most tender beef she'd ever tasted. She closed her eyes and enjoyed the flavors that filled her mouth. Only when she swallowed, did she remember herself. Her eyes slung open and found Elliot watching her. He did not say a word. He didn't have to. She could tell from his smug expression, he'd enjoyed watching her reaction.

Breaking the intimate moment, Elliot pulled away from her and reached for the wine bottle. Lifting the tip, he poured more of the ruby red liquid into her glass. He smiled when she eagerly grasped her goblet and took a sip. "Let's talk specifics, shall we?" He replaced the bottle and claimed his own glass. "As I mentioned before, you'll host a series of events for Babylon, leading up to our grand reopening this summer. You will be responsible for managing approximately three functions and will be paid upon the completion of each event. Your success will be measured on press coverage and sales revenue. I will communicate those objectives to you at a later date.

"Your proposed theme must be presented to me no less than seven days before the date. It will be your responsibility to communicate with my staff, to let them know your strategy. It is very important no one be left in the dark. To ensure transparency, you will present your blueprint during the managers' meeting at the beginning of every week.

"Each event will be executed on a monthly basis, performed on the premises, and must generate sales. You will be given a strict budget which must cover all entertainment, setup and travel expenses. A detailed financial log and all associated receipts must be submitted after each event. As an added incentive, at the end of your assignment, whatever has not been spent from your budget, will be presented to you in the form of a bonus check.

"In addition to these responsibilities, you will be expected to initiate and escort special guests to the club. Requests for any resources needed to ensure the comfort of these select guests must be made in advance, either to either myself or—"

Thandie held up her hand to stop him. "Exactly when am I

supposed to have time to coordinate the arrival of these special guests?" she asked. "Managing three events in three months doesn't allow me time to do much else."

"How you manage your time, will be up to you," he said matter-of-factly. "But manage it, you will." As if to make clear he had nothing more to say on the issue, he calmly took another bite of his meal.

Thandie stared at him in disbelief. Escorting guests was a nearly impossible feat. She would be pressed for time organizing the events, not to mention working with a tight budget. There would be little time to do anything else, particularly haggling with celebrity publicists.

In response to her look of incredulity, Elliot flashed her one of his perfect wicked grins. Thandie was beginning to loathe that expression.

"If at any time," he continued smoothly, "I decide to terminate our agreement, you will be compensated for hours worked on all successfully completed projects. If at any time you decide to terminate our agreement, any financial advancements issued to you must be paid in full upon notice of your resignation. As such, you surrender your eligibility to receive the bonus incentive." Elliot paused to pull out an envelope from his breast pocket and hand it to her. "Inside, you will find a contract stating the points we have just discussed. In addition, you will see a confidentiality agreement, as well as your proposed salary."

Thandie unfolded the pages, looking briefly over each item until she located the one stating her salary. When she found it, she blinked. Previously, she and Warren had discussed a few numbers, but the amount on the offer letter was nearly fifteen thousand dollars more.

"I trust you find my offer satisfactory?" Elliot asked.

"Very," she agreed. There was no need in her playing coy. They both knew she would accept the offer.

For the remainder of dinner, Elliot stated his expectations and answered her questions fully. It had not gone unnoticed by Thandie that every item worked in his favor. Specifically the termination clause. However, every club owner she'd ever known only made agreements that worked to their benefit. The only difference was, Elliot had every item clearly stated in the contract. By the time their meals were completed, Thandie was feeling significantly better about their working relationship. Elliot was an astute businessman, leaving no detail unexplored. He was brilliant in his element. Perhaps she'd wrongly prejudged him. What she'd taken as sexual overtones might just have been awkward attempts, on his part, to be more personable. It would not be the first time she'd experienced odd behavior from a clever mind.

When the check was presented, Elliot continued talking while he reviewed the bill. He pulled out his billfold and handed the waiter a Centurion Card.

After Elliot's credit card was returned, he helped Thandie to her feet and escorted her toward the restaurant's exit. Outside, Elliot approached the valet attendant and requested her car be delivered. He stood with her while someone retrieved her vehicle. A lull fell between them while they waited. Elliot glanced at his watch, apparently anticipating his next appointment.

Conversationally, Thandie said, quite clumsily, "I have to admit, you've changed my mind about you, Elliot. Now that's we've talked, I have a better feeling about my being here. Earlier, I thought you were trying to—uh—"

"Seduce you," Elliot supplied with a rakish smile.

"Yes," she breathed, relieved she hadn't had to say the words.

"Oh, but I am," he said simply. "In fact, I have every intention of seducing you, and putting you in every imaginable position."

Thandie stared at him, too astonished to speak. This was such a radical transformation compared to the no-nonsense businessman he'd portrayed minutes before.

Elliot leaned closer, pressing his lips against the sensitive flesh just below her earlobe. "Good night, Ms. Shaw," he whispered.

Thandie vaguely recalled the attendant parking her SUV at the curb, and walking around her vehicle on numb legs. Buckling up, she took a deep breath, and slowly eased into traffic. Unable to help herself, she glanced into the rearview mirror. She could see Elliot getting into a black Aston Martin parked on the sidewalk, directly in front of the Peppers restaurant. For fear of being caught staring, she quickly looked away. This was going to be a very long assignment.

Chapter Six

Thandie parked the SUV at the curb just outside the terminal. She'd given up searching for a spot in the crowded one-hour lot. Besides, she'd rather take the risk of getting a ticket than attempt to navigate her newly rented vehicle into one of the slim parking spots.

She sent a text message to Len, letting her know where she'd parked and hoped it would not take them long to locate her before airport security insisted she move her vehicle. She killed the engine and tapped on the steering wheel impatiently. She did not have to wait long. Thandie could hear the loud laughter of her assistants well before she could actually see them. The pale beauty of Len Harris and the dark elegance of Raja Travis split through the crowd. They looked more like supermodels than public relations assistants. Both tall and slender, Len had bleached blond hair with bright green eyes, whereas Raja possessed the mysterious exotic loveliness that was common of her Indian heritage. Thandie got out of the SUV to greet them. Like excited teenagers, both girls ran to hug her. As usual, they were making a scene.

"I can't believe we're in Miami!" Len exclaimed. "This is so cool!"

Raja, typically the quiet one, agreed enthusiastically. "Miami is definitely the place to be this summer. You know the Shay Thomas concert will be here soon. Do you think we can get tickets, Thandie?"

Len gasped loudly. "I totally forgot his tour included a stop in Miami. I *love* Shay," she finished dreamily.

"I heard Samara is his opening act," Raja said.

"I can hardly tolerate her," Len groaned.

"I bet if she gave you tickets to the concert you would tolerate her," Raja taunted.

"If Samara gave me tickets to see Shay Thomas, I would sleep with her."

"Calm down, girls," Thandie chided. "We're not on vacation. Let's figure out how we're going to manage the Babylon project first, and afterward all three of us can drool over seventeen-year-old rappers."

"Shay Thomas is not seventeen," Len corrected. "He just celebrated his twenty-first birthday."

"And he's a hip-hop star," Raja informed. "Not a rapper."

"Who cares?" Thandie sighed.

Raja and Len looked at each other before saying in unison, "We do!"

Thandie shook her head, no longer interested. She looked around and noticed each young woman was pulling along two oversize suitcases on rollers. It was enough luggage for five people. "Are those all your bags?" she asked.

"Oh, goodness, no," Raja said with a wave of her hand. "That's only half of it. We had to leave three of our bags in New York."

"Can you believe they have a limit on luggage?" Len said

sulkily as she checked her reflection in the tinted window of the SUV.

"We had to spend a small fortune mailing them to the office," Raja said. "Amanda promised to send them to us once we got settled."

"Great," Thandie said under her breath. She unlocked the trunk, and helped them load their luggage into the vehicle. Afterward, she slid into the driver's seat and waited until everyone was settled before putting the car into drive. At the same time, the girls pulled notepads out of their purses and were ready to take notes. They were used to Thandie delegating assignments while they were en route to one place or another.

"Okay, girls, promoting Club Babylon will be far from easy," Thandie began. "It's gorgeous, and huge. It's four stories high." Len and Raja took a sharp intake of breath at this, but Thandie talked over them. "Filling up a place with that much square footage will be difficult. We'll have to work every contact we have. The good news is the club already generates a sizable crowd. Our job is to build the club's reputation on the strip by hosting a series of promo events. In addition, we've also been tasked with coordinating the arrival of special guests. The next few weeks are going to be busy, but it's nothing we haven't handled before. We have to be organized and disciplined. Len, I want you to find out who are the big gossip columnists here. I want radio and newspaper contacts as well. Raja, I want you to work the agents of local celebrities. There are tons of stars in Miami. I want all of them to be talking about Club Babylon. I will be gathering information on every major event that is being hosted in Miami for the next three months."

"When can we see the club?" Len asked.

"I'll take you there tonight, and introduce you to the staff."

"Including the owner?" Len asked hopefully.

Thandie gave a long sigh. "Yes, including Elliot."

"Elliot Richards," Len repeated dreamily. "Even his name sounds sexy."

"I looked him up on Google this morning," Raja supplied. "There wasn't much to find. He doesn't court the press. I could only locate a handful of pictures. Most of them were taken from afar. But from what I could see, he seems delightful on the eyes. Have you met him yet?"

Thandie didn't want to talk about Elliot. In fact, she wished she had not mentioned him at all. Try as she might, what had occurred last night after dinner would not soon be forgotten. She remembered all too well the warmth of his breath on her neck and press of his lips against her skin. Even the thought of it made her shift in her seat uncomfortably. Suddenly realizing the girls were still waiting for her response, she answered in a guarded tone, "Yes, I've met him."

"So...?" Raja urged.

"He is a sharp businessman," Thandie said lamely.

Len laughed. "That's not what we want to know, and you know it."

Thandie gritted her teeth together. "Ladies, I really need you to concentrate on the project at hand. We're going to have to work ten times as hard if we intend to finish on schedule."

"Fine, fine. Be mysterious if you must," Len said with a wave of her hand. "Where are we staying?"

"With Warren Radcliffe," Thandie answered.

"Cool!" they chorused.

Thandie cast a nervous glance in the rearview mirror at them. "Please don't tell me Warren has tried to come on to either of you." Both Raja and Len were in their early twenties, Warren's preferred age range.

"No," Len huffed, "although I can't say I would stop him. Warren is a cool old guy."

Thandie pinched the bridge of her nose. "Len," she said, "Warren is old enough to be your grandfather."

"Yeah, but he's fun," Len reasoned.

Raja agreed. "He's a barrel of laughs, Thandie. I hate that he left the city. He was my favorite VIP."

Thandie stopped at a red light and turned around to face the girls. Though she was, at best, only seven years older than they, she knew they looked up to her as a role model. "Raja. Len." Fixing each girl with a serious look, she said, "I want you two to enjoy yourselves while you're here, but you're going to work. Our sole purpose for being in Miami is to promote Club Babylon. You will remain focused at all times. I won't tolerate any of your usual shenanigans. Is that understood?"

They nodded solemnly.

"And another thing," Thandie soldiered on, "the management staff is predominantly male."

Len and Raja turned to look at each other, mischievous expressions on their faces.

Thandie snapped her fingers at them. "Don't even think about it," she warned. "There will be absolutely no funny business between yourselves and the staff. I expect you to be professional, but keep your distance. If I suspect there is a trace of inappropriate behavior from either of you, I will send you back to New York. Are we clear?"

The girls grimaced before nodding their heads.

Pacified by their response, Thandie refocused her attention on the road. She knew she was being hard on them, but hopefully she had spoken just sternly enough to make herself heed her own warnings.

Warren was gone by the time they arrived at his home. The girls squealed and laughed when they walked into the grand entrance hall. Tossing their bags aside, they took a tour of Warren's house. Thandie could hear their laughter throughout. She tolerated it for a short while, before insisting they get to work. Len came up with the idea that they should sit by the pool while they worked. Not wanting to be a wet blanket, Thandie agreed to join them. They put on swimsuits and carried their paperwork onto the stone terrace leading to the pool. Len and Raja quickly entered the water, sitting on the steps of the shallow end. Len got busy calling Miami affiliates of the *New York Post* while Raja made a list of agents representing celebrities who resided in Florida.

While the girls worked on making contacts, Thandie made a list of possible event themes. It was slow going, since she was not familiar with Miami's nightlife scene just yet. She placed a call to Rex Barrington, Elliot's director of marketing. Rex was surprised to hear from her but was happy to answer her questions about previous club themes and press releases. They spoke at length and by the time she hung up, Thandie suffered from information overload.

After that, she helped the girls with making calls. She started by dialing her California contacts, making a list of celebrities who had press junket tours scheduled in the near future. She got a few hours of furious work out of the girls before they found their way to lounge chairs and stretched out like lazy feline cats. Len was sunbathing and well on her way to a much needed tan while Raja retreated to the shade to prevent getting any darker.

Thandie was still on the phone when Warren joined them. Raja and Len ran to him as if he was Santa Claus. Donned in their bikinis, Thandie could tell Warren loved their attention. He listened to them ramble on about their flight. He made the unfortunate mistake of offering to take the girls shopping on Sunday, an offer Thandie knew he would quickly regret. Raja and Len kissed him on his reddened cheeks and jumped up and down with excitement. Thandie could only roll her eyes heavenward. Deciding she'd witnessed enough, she stood and gathered her things.

"Where are you going?" Len called out to her.

"I'm going to lie down for an hour or so. You girls might want to do the same."

"No way," Len laughed. "We're in freakin' Miami! We're too excited to sleep."

Thandie shrugged. "All right, but don't come crying to me when you can barely keep your eyes open tonight."

Raja's brow perked. "What are our hours, Thandie?"

"Ten to two."

"Same rules?" Len asked.

"Of course," Thandie nodded. "No drinking, always work the room and always keep your cool."

The girls laughed as she made her way inside. Thandie gave the same rules every night before working. It had become redundant to say the words anymore, but she said them out of habit.

Thandie stretched out on her bed and prayed Warren wouldn't try anything with the girls during her absence. The last thing she needed was Len and Raja competing for the cushy position of Wife Number Six. Thandie yawned deeply and reflected back on the past few hours. The day had been productive thus far. She saw no reason why she couldn't pull together an action plan within a fairly short amount of time. Formalizing a proposal Elliot would agree to might require some persuasion. She only hoped the cost of gaining his cooperation was a price she was willing to pay.

It had taken forever to get Len and Raja to decide what to wear. Finally, they were in the car and headed toward the strip. Thandie gave them a quick rundown on the club's structure, disclosing information she'd learned from Adam, and mentioning a handful of employee names she was able to remember. After finishing, Thandie had the nagging sensation she had forgotten something important.

As Thandie drove, she and the girls went over their findings from earlier that evening. Raja had located several agents who sounded promising, and Len confirmed radio contacts and a reputable gossip columnist who lived in the area. They spent the remainder of the trip haggling over how to best utilize their new found information.

As their SUV turned onto the main street, they could see a line of cars waiting for Club Babylon's valet service. Thandie called a number Adam had given her which gave her direct access to the valet stand. After announcing her name, they directed her to drive ahead of the other cars. The attendants were all smiles when they greeted her.

"Hi, Thandie," one man said. "Have a good time tonight."

Tiny, the bouncer she'd met the previous night, made a path for them with his huge body. They ignored the curious gazes shot in their direction, aware they were the envy of everyone waiting patiently in line. Thandie heard the girls gasp in wonder as soon as they entered the club. Tonight Babylon was bathed in vibrant green lighting, and the arena took on the appearance of a tropical garden. Thandie looked skyward and was delighted to see the hanging gardens were on display. It was otherworldly, giving the heady sense of being dropped into a mystical lush garden.

Fixing a controlled smile on her face, Thandie guided the girls up the staircase that led to Elliot's office. She introduced them to the unsmiling bodyguard, Michelle, as he held the door open. When they walked inside, the men who made up Elliot's management staff turned their heads in unison. Just as before, all conversation stopped.

Thandie stepped forward. "Hello, gentlemen," she said

pleasantly. "Sorry for interrupting, but I wanted to intro-duce my assistants to you. This is Raja Travis and Len Harris. Len. Raja. This is Rex, Markie, Eddie, Adam and Tom." She paused before turning toward the handsome creature lean-ing casually against his large gleaming desk. "And this is the owner, Elliot Richards." She couldn't bear to look into his stormy silver eyes for longer than a few seconds. "Len and Raja will be helping me with the promotion plans," she said to no one in particular. "They've worked with me for years. You should find them very helpful."

Again, silence. Thandie was beginning to wonder if she was doing something wrong, but when she looked up at the men, she could see their eyes were trained on the girls' bod-ies. Meanwhile, Len and Raja were openly ogling Elliot. She could only imagine what he was looking at.

Clearing her throat, Thandie turned to the men. "Are we interrupting something important?"

Adam and Rex suddenly jumped to their feet and smiled broadly. They lightly kissed Thandie on the cheek and shook Raja and Len's hands. Tom, Eddie and Markie quickly stood and started introducing themselves. Thandie positioned her-self as far away from Elliot as she could possibly manage with-out seeming rude.

Len and Raja weren't as guarded. They gave polite nods to everyone in the room and just about threw themselves at El-liot. She watched in horror as they asked him random ques-tions about the club, each trying to outdo the other to hold his attention the longest. Elliot charmed them with his good looks and flirtatious finesse. Whether she wanted to or not, Thandie was drawn to the sound of his voice.

"You are both very lovely ladies," Elliot said silkily. "We're fortunate to have you here. I'm sure the men of Miami will soon be begging for a moment of your time."

"You think so?" Len's voice had turned unrecognizably high-pitched.

"Of course." Elliot leaned forward to pin each girl with those enchanting silver eyes of his. "Promise not to forget me when some lucky guy sweeps you off your feet."

The eruption of girlish laughter was like hearing fingernails being dragged across a chalkboard. Thandie had to turn away from the train wreck. She forced herself to listen to Adam and Rex argue over which one of them would introduce her to tonight's guest DJ. She put a halt to the dispute when she insisted that both of them should do the honors. Markie offered to give the girls a tour of the arena. However, she didn't miss that his eyes lingered on Raja when he spoke. Thandie inwardly groaned. Keeping everyone on task seemed to be a bigger undertaking than she'd expected.

She was grateful when Elliot called everyone's attention back to tomorrow's agenda. Markie and Adam spoke at length, while everyone nodded and listened attentively. Tom and Eddie made a few short comments before Rex took center stage. He was the marketing director, so Thandie was more interested in what he had to say. Even Raja and Len managed to tear their eyes away from Elliot long enough to listen to Rex recap his current projects. When the meeting was over, Adam, Markie and Rex escorted Thandie down to the arena. She had to literally call out to the girls to get them to follow her.

The club was already in high gear. Miami's most beautiful and affluent residents laughed together and swayed their hips to the steady pulsation of a bewitching tempo.

Markie held out his arm to Thandie and guided her through the crowd. The girls followed closely behind, oohing and ahhing at just about everything.

In a low voice, Markie explained the wait staff's table system and zone layout. He pointed out the hidden surveillance cameras, which were discreetly mounted above the cash registers at every bar. Markie led them backstage to meet a few of the dancers. Immediately, the dancers knew who Thandie was. Unfortunately, it was not from her reputation. Apparently, pictures of Ruark Randall kissing her at Phenomenon weeks earlier was beginning to make news. According to the dancers, *Access Hollywood* was reporting that she was Ruark's new girlfriend.

Thandie rationalized that any press a PR agent created was good, but she failed to see the joy in her connection with actor Ruark Randall. He was an idiot. At any rate, it seemed to gain her an unreasonable amount of respect from the dancers. Thandie chatted with them while Markie continued to show Len and Raja the building. The girls didn't seem to mind losing Thandie on the tour. It was their first time inside Club Babylon, and they were eager to see everything.

Thandie didn't see Raja and Len until an hour later, after Adam introduced her to Ibiza native, DJ Von. The girls appeared to be having a good time. They were working the VIP room and dancing with club members.

Thandie was more at ease when she was able to clearly see the girls and know they were not up to their usual devilry. Involuntarily, Thandie caught herself searching the crowd for Elliot. It was unexplainable. She was in a constant state of alert until she found him. It took several tries before she spied him on the upper level in the VIP lounge. He was much closer than she'd expected; no farther than twenty feet away from where she stood. He was seated in a booth chatting with a couple. Like Elliot, the man was very handsome. But where Elliot was dark-haired, the stranger at his side was blond. A flash of his intense blue eyes was enough to stamp his appeal. Even from this distance, Thandie could see the lilt of his lips give way to an arrogant expression. She recognized a man born to wealth when she saw one. It was never what they wore or what elaborate toys they owned—it was the unshaken self-confidence that radiated from them.

At the man's side was an attractive woman. She laughed prettily at the blond man, keeping a possessive hand in his lap, lest any woman mistake him for being available. Thandie wondered who the couple was. Judging by Elliot's presence at their table, and length of time he was investing, these were personal friends of his. Or at least one of them was. Clearly, Elliot knew the blond-haired man well.

Thandie continued to watch them. More specifically, she watched Elliot. There was something about him that intrigued her. She couldn't put it into words, but Elliot had a certain appeal that was enchanting. And yet as strongly as he captivated her, he frightened her. She was leery of him, not daring to get too close and yet…she was fascinated all the same.

Like a moth to a flame, she mused.

Her attention was snatched away when Adam stepped to her side. Taking her elbow in his hand, he twirled her around to introduce her to someone. Thandie was forced to turn her back on Elliot and his friends and focus on a tall, rather plain-looking gentleman. Adam presented him as the broadcaster for a leading pop radio show in Miami.

Eager to make a positive impression, Thandie dived into conversation with the man. It did not take long to figure out he was more interested in leering at her breasts than listening to her. Not that this surprised her overly much. She'd chosen to wear a mini dress, covered in simmering cheetah sequins. There was no cleavage to be seen, however the fabric pulled tight across her chest, emphasizing the fullness of her breasts. Although long sleeved, the dress was far from modest. The drastic cut of the garment exposed her entire back, before gathering together just above the rise of her buttocks.

A key factor of being a club promoter was to look the part. It was her job to make the environment look desirable. And since most clubs were owned and managed by men, she'd learned long ago to use her natural assets to her advantage. She no longer took notice when men ogled her. She expected it, at least while she was working. And putting on a flirtatious smile for Adam's guest was definitely working.

Thandie chatted with the two men for a while, soon losing track of the time. When she looked up again to check on the girls, she was startled to find they were not there. Her gaze flickered to Elliot. He was gone as well, and so were his friends. Their booth was now occupied by an ensemble of pouty model-like beauties who appeared to be on the hunt for wealthy men.

Thandie searched for Len and Raja. They were nowhere in sight. A bad sign for certain. Left unsupervised for any length of time, the girls were prone to get into trouble. Thandie stepped toward the balcony and looked over the VIP lounge. Not a hint of either girl.

She turned cautious eyes to the glass wall which overlooked the arena floor below and gave an aquarium view of the upper levels of the club. It would be impossible to spot the girls amongst the throng of dancing partygoers. She would have to walk the club in hopes of finding them. She groaned. Her feet had begun to hurt nearly an hour ago. She would not be pleased if she had to walk a mile in her beautiful, but crippling, heels.

Just as she made up her mind to do that, she caught sight of movement. The wall to her right opened up, revealing a small compartment. It was the elevator that led to the Tower.

The silent hiss as the doors slid open was like a quiet invitation. Very tempting.

Suddenly, Thandie remembered the "something" she'd forgotten to tell the girls earlier. She had not warned them to avoid the Tower. Is that where they were? Were Len and Raja touring an area of the club Elliot himself had ruled off limits? It was certainly possible. Before her imagination went into overdrive, Thandie determined she would search the lower levels first, before fretting over the Tower.

Excusing herself from Adam's side, she took the steps down to the lower levels. She saw no recognizable faces on either level. She proceeded to the arena floor. Unlike the sleek re- laxed vibe of the VIP lounges, the main arena was rowdier and dramatically more crowded. There was a buzz of frenzied excitement in the large expanse. It was the kind of atmosphere Len and Raja would escape to. Thandie walked a slow lap around the edge of the dance floor, examining the faces. It did not take long before someone took hold of her hand and asked her to dance. She was agreeable, mainly because this angle allowed her a good view of most of the arena floor and the steps leading up to the VIP entrance. After dancing through a few songs, with no luck spotting the girls, she excused herself from her dance partner and continued her pursuit.

Thandie's aching feet soon got the better of her. She quickly gave up the hunt for the girls, looking to sit down instead. The crowded arena offered few seats, and all appeared to be occupied.

With a sigh of annoyance, Thandie made her way back to VIP. She was grateful when one of the Babylon employees held his hand out to her to help her up the steps. The balls of her feet felt as if they were on fire, getting worse with every step she took. She looked around for an available seat in the packed room. She went to the next upper level, but it was just as crammed. She couldn't even find a place to lean against the bar.

She looked for Adam to ask if he knew where there was

extra seating, but he was serving club members. Thandie waited for him to wrap up, but the group didn't seem willing to let him go any time soon. After fifteen agonizing minutes, she was feeling rather desperate. She went to the hidden elevator, punched in the code she remembered Adam using and rode it up the Tower. Thandie sagged against the wall and embraced the sudden quiet the elevator provided.

When the doors opened, she had to adjust her eyes to the dimness. The room was lit only by candlelight. Blindly, she stepped forward, unable to blink anything into focus. Abruptly, the elevator doors closed behind her, and she was surrounded by darkness. The sound of music hummed in the background, filling the room with a sensuality as thick as smoke.

Suddenly, a strong arm wrapped around her waist and pulled her into the hard surface of muscled flesh. Thandie looked up to see the silver eyes of Elliot Richards. He did not look happy to see her.

He leaned his head down low enough to whisper in her ear. "I believe I told you not to come up here."

The sheer size of him was unnerving. He was even more impressive up close, not a blemish or hair out of place. It was really quite insane for one man to be so breathtakingly beautiful. Her blood felt as if it was boiling beneath her skin, and a slow ball of heat was growing in the pit of her stomach.

"Are you going to answer me?" he growled down at her.

"Huh?" Wrapped in his powerful arms, words seemed complicated to create.

"What are you doing up here?" he snapped.

"My feet."

"What?"

"I—I came up here looking for a place to sit down."

"Couldn't you find a chair downstairs?"

"The place is packed."

He frowned. "Well, there isn't much room to sit down up here, but there are plenty of places to fuck."

She turned her head to look around the room. Thandie would have fainted if it weren't for Elliot holding her up. Her eyes finally adjusted to the dim lighting to reveal a room full of naked bodies. Every corner of the room was occupied by screwing couples; some were groups satisfying each other. She gasped to see three men pleasuring a moaning woman at the same time. Horrified, Thandie buried her face into Elliot chest to block out the scene around her. Only now did she realize the whole room was moaning, grunting, and delivering cries of ecstasy.

"You deliberately ignored my request," he said in a low voice.

She shook with mortification. "I—I had no idea," she stammered. "I thought—thought—I'll leave." She tried to push away from him, but he wouldn't allow it. He pulled her closer to him.

"You can't leave," he said.

"Oh, yes, I can," she nearly shouted. If he thought he was going to hold her hostage, then he was sadly mistaken. "Let me go."

"Be still. You can't go, because someone just took the elevator down. The stairwell is on the other side of the room, and it happens to be blocked."

She followed his gaze to see he was right. Six or so people were naked and screwing each other like animals in heat. "Let me push the button to call the elevator up," she said in a weak voice.

"It won't do any good. The couple got in there to have privacy."

"What?"

"They're having sex," he said simply. "The lift is on emergency stop."

"How do you know?"

Elliot nodded toward a red light that was lit above the elevator doors. "When that is lit, it means the car has been stopped. You'll have to wait until it turns green. Until then, you're stuck here."

She tried to push away from him again, but he was far too strong. She searched the room for another source of escape, but there was none.

"I'm going to find you a seat," he said.

She shook her head. "I don't want to sit down on anything in this room."

"You don't have a choice. I'm sitting down. If you don't come with me, you'll be left standing here by yourself."

Thandie's eyes went wide with outrage.

"And at your own risk, I might add."

"At my own risk!"

Swiftly, Elliot placed his finger over her mouth to stop her from speaking any louder. He lowered his head to speak without being overheard. "The members that have access to the Tower pay good money for privacy and discretion. I can't have you making them nervous while they are enjoying themselves. Understand?"

She wanted to fight him tooth and nail, but he had a fierce frown on his face. Without another word, he took hold of her upper arm and led her to a long settee. The sight of a man's face buried between a woman's open legs at the other end of the chaise made her pale. She was seconds away from running and beating on the elevator doors when Elliot took his seat and pulled her down beside him. He placed his arm behind her and drew her into his side. Their seat gave them a voyeur's view of the room. Thandie lowered her head, not wanting to make direct eye contact with anyone. Elliot, on the other hand, seemed to be comfortable with the setting. He sat back and watched her literally die with embarrassment, an arrogant smirk on his handsome face.

"I bet you'll listen to me in the future," he taunted.

She frowned at him. "If I'd known what was up here, I wouldn't have come. So what's your excuse?"

"I don't need one."

"You come up here on a regular basis?"

Elliot grinned. "Wouldn't you love to know?"

She scowled at him. His plan to make her burn with shame was working, and she didn't like it one bit. She lashed back at him. "So this is what you're into?" Her gaze swept the room. "Voyeurism?"

He fixed her with those silver eyes. "You don't want to know what I'm into."

The seriousness of his tone robbed her of any smart retort.

Pleased he'd shocked her into silence, Elliot flashed her a devilish grin. "Or is that why you really came up here? Interested in knowing what gets me off? Curiosity killed the cat, puss."

"I don't desire to know more."

"Unfortunately for you, we're going to learn a lot about each other tonight." His large hand cupped the underside of her breast. The pad of his thumb brushed slowly across her nipple, making the bud instantly harden. "More than you can handle."

Her temper was boiling. He meant to embarrass her, overwhelm her with his presence, expected her to run and hide. Was this his way of punishing her for not leaving well enough alone? Did he plan to make her regret accepting the job? Forcing her to see why he only hired men? He would be very disappointed.

Not bothering to push his hand away, she met his gaze with a steady one of her own. "There's nothing you could throw my way that I can't handle."

"Careful, pussycat, I might take that as a challenge." His gaze dropped to her lips. "That lovely mouth of yours is about to get you into a world of trouble."

"I doubt that—oh!"

A strange hand landed on Thandie's thigh. She followed the hand to its owner; a bare-chested man with glassy eyes. He squeezed her leg affectionately and said, "Come over here and join us, sweetheart."

Elliot clasped his hand around the man's wrist and pushed it aside. "She's with me, Steinberg."

The man focused his blurred vision on him. "Elliot, is that you? I didn't know she was with you, man. My mistake. You better start fucking her before someone decides to take her away from you. She's a nice piece of ass."

Elliot nodded. "Thanks for the warning. Take it easy."

Thandie watched the man feel his way through the darkened room before looking back up at Elliot. "Would someone really try to take me by force?" Her voice quivered. She was nervous.

Elliot tightened his hold on her. "People come here to have sex. It's understood that if you're here, you want to have sex, too. So in answer to your question, yes, I suppose that could happen."

Thandie scooted closer to him. "Well, what are we going to do?"

"We're going to improvise." Without warning, he pulled her onto his lap. The hem of her dress inched dangerously up her thighs. Elliot gripped her by her forearms before she could leap off him. He pulled her forward until their lips were inches apart. "Kiss me," he breathed.

"No," she said through gritted teeth.

"Kiss me, or I'll leave you to fend for yourself. Believe me, there is a room full of horny men that would love to rip that flimsy dress right off your body."

"You wouldn't."

"Oh, yes, I would. You have no idea what I'm capable of. I'm your key to getting out of here in one piece, Thandie, so you had better pay me a little more respect."

"Fuck you," she hissed.

He grinned. "That could be arranged. We could do it right here if you prefer."

"Let go of me."

"If I do, you're on your own, puss."

"I said fuck off."

"Have it your way." He lifted her up, tossed her roughly aside and stood to cross the room.

Thandie couldn't believe he was actually leaving her, though she had told him to. She panicked and reached out to pull his arm. "I'm sorry. Don't leave."

Elliot turned around to look down at her. His dark brow lifted with playfull mischief. "Are you ready to play nice?"

Thandie licked her lips nervously and looked over at the elevator shaft; the red light was still lit. In a room full of drunk, drugged-out mating couples, Elliot was her only ally. She would prefer the devil himself over him, but by her own doing, she was stuck with him. She could not say she hadn't been warned.

Elliot slid his hands into his pockets. His eyes focused on her thighs. "Are we in agreement?"

She nodded.

He leaned down until his lips were only a breath away from her own. She expected him to kiss her, but he surprised her by placing his hands on either side of her on the sofa and lowering himself to the floor. Kneeling before her, he hooked his hands under her knees and pulled her to the edge of the seat so that her thighs were on either side of him. The hem of her dress effortlessly hiked up to her waist. If not for the black lace of her panties, she would be fully exposed to him.

Elliot's silver eyes flashed in the murkiness, hypnotizing her with their predatory power. His lips came crashing down on hers. He made her escape impossible by cupping the back of her head in his palm. His lips were cool to the touch, but his tongue was scorching hot. He swept every curve of her mouth with masterful skill. It was not long before she stopped pushing against him and leaned into his hold, her hands resting on the sides of his ribcage.

Keeping her mouth pinned beneath him, Elliot grabbed handfuls of her flesh and squeezed with the selfishness of a gluttonous man. He pulled her open legs closer to him until his groin was nestled against the crotch of her panties. He groaned. Her eyes sprang open, and she pushed hard against his chest.

Not easily detoured, Elliot dragged wet kisses along her neck. "Damn, you feel good, honey. I'm going to eat you."

"No," she gasped, warning bells going off in her head, but unable to react quickly enough. "I need to get out of here."

"*Shh,*" he cooed softly in her ear. "You'll love it. Lie back." He slid his hand from her bottom to her inner thigh. "Relax." He kissed the sensitive spot just below her earlobe as he pushed aside the fabric of her panties. Thandie gasped when he brushed his fingers over the sensitive bud of her clit as he made a slow trail southward. He groaned when the tips of his fingers became slick with her desire. "You're already wet for me," he whispered against her ear. "Tell me you want me."

"No." She could hardly breathe, let alone sound certain of herself.

Elliot lifted his head to look into her face. Her eyes were practically glowing with lust. "Tell me what I want to hear," he demanded in the husky voice. "Tell me you want this." He slipped his finger inside her again. Her folds closed around him greedily. "You don't want me to stop." He moved his fingers in and out of her with agonizing slowness. "I'm more talented with my tongue." He leaned forward and flicked his tongue against her earlobe. He chuckled when a fresh wave of her cream saturated his fingers.

It took all of Thandie's power to muster up the strength to grab his wrist. "Stop, Elliot." Her brown eyes were now shining. "Let go of me now."

He stilled his hand. She meant what she said. "As you wish." He pulled his hand away from her and held his wet fingers up between them before licking them clean. "The offer is always open."

Just then, the elevator chimed, and the doors opened. A laughing couple tumbled out, both frantically ripping the remainder of their clothes off. Thandie pushed Elliot away and headed for the elevator car, catching the doors just before they closed. She didn't dare look back at him. He represented every weakness known to women.

An hour later, Thandie fell across the bed in Warren's guest room. Her hasty retreat from Babylon had not been very graceful. She'd stumbled out of the elevator, looking disheveled and glancing over her shoulder like a frightened animal. Thankfully, there was no on around to see her.

Righting her clothes, she quickly weaved her way through the dancing crowd. It was pure luck she spotted Len and Raja standing near the bar.

Stalking up to them, Thandie announced they were leaving. Wisely, neither girl objected. They followed her, and managed to keep their babbling to a minimum while waiting for the valet to deliver their car.

On the drive home, Thandie informed the girls they were not allowed to go the Tower under any circumstances. When Len asked what was in the Tower, Thandie replied, "Unemployment."

It was not until they arrived at Warren's home, that she remembered her feet hurt. But who the hell cared? She had bigger problems now. As soon as they entered the house, Thandie retreated to the privacy of her room. She shut the door shut behind her and tossed her limp body on the bed.

Thandie buried her face into her pillow. Replaying it in her mind, she could almost feel his fingers inside her now. She groaned. That was the most disgraceful job performance ever. Yes, he had set her up, but she had rightfully put herself in that position by going to the Tower when she'd been forewarned. Under the right amount of pressure, she'd made it very apparent to him that she was attracted to him, and he'd made the most of the situation. She bet he took a lot of women up there. The sex-crazed Steinberg didn't seem surprised to see Elliot in the Tower. She groaned again. She had nearly given herself to a smooth-talking male slut. What did that make her?

She squeezed her eyes shut and tried to block out the provocative images swirling around in her head. She had to force herself to think clearly. If she stood any chance of successfully completing this project, she would have to make a point to stay as far away from Elliot Richards as possible…and find a good male masseur immediately.

Elliot lay naked across his bed. He stacked his hands behind his head, but he couldn't close his eyes just yet, because every time he did, he saw Thandie's smooth, bronzed skin.

She'd really put him in his place tonight, and that annoyed and excited him. He couldn't remember the last time a woman had turned him down. Usually, women were stepping over each other to get to him. He would have his pick of the group, using them at will before growing restless and discarding them.

But not Thandie.

She'd surprised him by snubbing him twice tonight, once by refusing to kiss him and again by refusing to let him go down on her. He had to admit he'd been toying with her, but after her first rebuff, he felt compelled to prove to her that he was the one in control. And then, she had refused him again.

That fact did not sit well with him. He had no idea why he even cared. Perhaps it was just his wounded ego, but whatever the case, he didn't like the injury his pride had sustained at the hands of Thandie Shaw. She wasn't even his typical brand of woman. In the past, he had preferred slender buxom brunettes; however, he was inclined to be attracted to the occasional blonde from time to time.

Thandie was on the opposite side of the spectrum. Yes, she was tall and slender, but had more curves than he was prone to desire. She had full hips and a wonderfully round derriere. Her long dark hair had been every bit as soft as he had imagined, and she tasted so sweet—like hot sex. Elliot had prided himself on never being easily swayed by any woman, so the idea of him sparing Thandie more than five minutes of his time was remarkable.

Thandie Shaw. She's just another woman, he thought, and there were plenty of them on the strip. But she had somehow made herself stand out. He had no interest in her beyond sex. That much he knew. Yes, she had withstood his advances. He would have to deal with that. Hell, it was only a matter of time before she would be begging him for sex, if her slick thighs were any indication. She might pretend to be the dominant one, but if there was one thing he knew about women, it was that they always came back. He could care less where her morals lay; time would eventually conquer her. And when it did, he would discipline her for tonight. But until then, he would be patient. She was only on the third day of her three-month project. He smiled. This was going to be fun.

Chapter Seven

Thandie had not slept well. Every time she slipped into some semblance of rest, she was jarred awake by erotic images of a silver-eyed stranger. She awoke groggily and highly annoyed. There was a high probably this would not be her best day ever.

Pulling her hair into a sloppy bun at the top of her head, she washed up and headed downstairs. The empty kitchen was alight with bright mid-day sunshine. Thandie pulled a glass out of the cabinet and helped herself to some orange juice. Taking a seat at the breakfast nook, she stared out the window and enjoyed the silence. She nearly choked on her juice when Warren entered the kitchen moments later. It wasn't his presence that jarred her, it was his attire. He was dressed in a T-shirt and the smallest shorts she'd ever seen on a grown man.

"Good morning, kiddo," he said cheerfully.

Thandie used the back of her hand to wipe juice from her chin. "Where are you going in those?"

"Yoga class." Warren slapped his spandex-clad bottom. "It keeps me in shape for the young ladies."

"I thought you were into biking?"

"I gave that up months ago. Yoga instructors are far more attractive."

"Warren, I don't think those shorts are legal in public," she said in what she hoped was a tactful tone. "Or that shirt," she added, having now noticed it showed several inches of pale midriff.

Warren laughed. "You need to live a little, kiddo." He grabbed a water bottle from the refrigerator and waved. "I'm off."

"Have a good workout," she said with a shake of her head.

"Ah!" Warren snapped his fingers. "I just thought of something." He looked over his shoulder to ensure they were alone before he spoke. "I'm not sure if I warned you earlier, but you'll want to stay away from the Tower during working hours. It's reserved for private parties, and they tend to get a little wild up there."

She groaned.

"Elliot doesn't allow any female servers up there," he continued. "Every so often, he has to go to the Tower to make sure they aren't doing drugs up there."

"Is that the only reason he goes up there?" she asked skeptically.

Warren laughed. "Of course. Elliot may be a womanizer, but one thing is for sure; he doesn't party like they do in the Tower." He lowered his voice to a whisper. "He prefers to party in his office, if you know what I mean."

Not wanting to talk about the Tower anymore, she changed the subject. "Thanks for the heads-up, Warren. You better get to your class."

He gave a mock salute. "Try not to stare at my ass."

Thandie giggled. "Go!"

Warren hummed happily to himself as he strolled away.

Thandie heard him all the way to the front door. Then he paused and called out, "Did you look?"

Thandie laughed aloud. "Just a little," she called back.

"I knew it!" he shouted back.

Thandie was still laughing when Len came into the kitchen. "What's so funny?" she asked sleepily.

"You don't want to know," Thandie assured her.

An hour later, Thandie and the girls hovered over their laptops. They'd converted Warren's living room into work central. Papers, pens and multicolored Post-it notes littered the heavy oak table. Since they were working from home, no one needed to get dressed or bother with makeup. Thandie was drab in a pair of cutoff jeans and Raja was wearing her favorite pair of sweatpants. Len was still in her pajamas.

"Do you think this is going to work?"

"Huh?" Thandie's head snapped up, realizing she'd been asked a question. "What did you say?"

Len stared at her from over her laptop. "I asked if you thought we could successfully complete everything in this proposal?"

"I don't see why not. Before Babylon closed for renovations, they had Lady Gaga and Jay-Z perform within the same month."

"I'm sure they had time to plan those appearances. We're attempting to lock in A-list stars in a matter of weeks." Len scrunched up her nose. "Do you really think we can book Nicki Minaj on such short notice?"

"Anything is possible."

"You always say that," Len muttered.

"That's because it's true." Thandie returned her attention back to the email she'd been typing. "My conversation with her agent went very well. I see no reason why it won't work."

"And if it doesn't work?" Raja asked.

"Then we'll move on to plan B," Thandie replied.

Raja picked up her notepad. "Lil Wayne is hardly a plan B. Why can't we go after him first?"

"Because, Raja," Thandie said in a tired voice, "his entourage is large and I'd rather not pay for all of them to travel to Miami and sleep in the most expensive hotel on the strip. We have to consider the budget." This was twice in as many minutes the girls had questioned her entertainment selections. Her patience was beginning to wear thin.

"Are we sure we can't get Shaun Cross to perform?" Raja asked in a whiny voice.

Thandie fixed her with an annoyed look. "How many times do I have to tell you we can't afford Cross? Besides, he's on tour. He's unavailable."

"Sorry," Raja muttered to her keyboard. "Someone woke up on the wrong side of the bed."

Thandie ignored her. "Len, where are we with Guetta?"

Len fumbled through her notes. "We're still haggling over the price, but it's going in our favor. It helps that his wife likes you."

Thandie nodded. Booking David Guetta would be outstanding, but she worried about the cost. The international flights would kill their budget. Thandie had already discovered the challenges of financing her grand plans. The tight budget Elliot had allowed her was a constant source of irritation.

"At least we've got Drake booked," Raja said in an effort to console herself.

"I adore him," Len chimed in. "I could definitely see myself as the next Mrs. Drake."

"Is Drake his first name or his last name?" Raja asked to no one in particular.

"Who cares?" Len protested. "He's gorgeous."

"Speaking of gorgeous," Raja whirled on Thandie. "Why didn't you tell us Elliot was such a hottie?"

The mention of Elliot's name again, so early in the day, set Thandie's teeth on edge.

"Now he is *gorgeous,*" Len said dreamily.

"I bet he has a girlfriend for everyday of the week," Raja said with more certainty than evidence.

"Do you suppose he has an opening on Wednesday?" Len asked in all seriousness.

Raja's eyes brightened. "Let's ask Google!"

Thandie had had enough. "Okay, you two," she said in a warning voice. "Get back to work."

Len and Raja ducked their heads behind their laptop screens, and began typing furiously on their keypads. The sound of a new email chimed from one of their computers, and then, like five year olds, the sound of the girls' muffled snickering filled the air. Thandie pinched the bridge of her nose. It was going to be a long day.

Thandie looked down at the Post-it and then back up at the building. The insignia read House of Glow. She was at the right place. According to Adam, it was a popular day spa. She had not asked about the massages. She planned to find out the answer to that question for herself.

Stuffing the slip of paper into the back pocket of her cut-offs, she pushed up her oversize sunglasses farther on her nose, and took a deep breath. It wasn't that she was embarrassed to be seen going inside the building, she simply didn't want to be seen period. Her hair was still piled on top of her head and she was still in the clothes she'd been wearing earlier today. Aside from the lip gloss, her face was bare of any cosmetics. She looked like a slob.

She pulled open the front door and was greeted by a pleasant looking receptionist. "Welcome to House of Glow," she said. "May I help you?"

The front door opened again and a loud voice exclaimed, "Thandie? Thandie Shaw, is that you?"

Thandie froze. Seriously? Was her luck really that bad? Hesitantly, she turned around, following the sound of the voice. That's when her gaze fell on the petite woman. Her face suddenly brightened. "Day?"

The tiny creature smirked and then gave Thandie a hug and air kisses on either cheek. "I thought that was you. I was having lunch with my cousin next door. I had to come over and make sure."

Even at full height, she barely reached Thandie's shoulder. She had to lean down to hug the woman.

Her name was Victoria Day, although most people simply knew her as Day. The product of a Jamaican father and Chinese mother, Day had striking features. With high cheekbones and small slanted eyes, she was quite pretty. Her hair was cut short in a spiky yet very becoming style.

"It's about time our paths crossed again," Day said with a bright grin. "I can't tell you how happy I am to see a familiar face down here. How the hell are you?"

Thandie couldn't help but smile at the small woman. Day had a flair all her own.

"I'm great, Day. How have you been?"

"I'm going out of my mind, as usual. I came down here to create my line in peace and quiet, and I've gotten nothing of the sort. The editors from *Vogue* and BHP want a run-through in three weeks. I keep telling them that's not gonna happen. I'll slit my wrists before I show my collection ahead of schedule. On top of everything else, I'm sweating bullets trying to secure a location for my show. It's been one shitstorm after the next. But enough about me. I heard about the breakup with Cam. Sorry to hear it."

"How did you know about that?" Thandie asked, surprised news traveled so widely.

Day's brow hiked up. "Nothing is sacred anymore."

"I guess not," Thandie said with a frown.

"And that business at Fashion Week," she wagged her finger and made a tsking sound. "I didn't know you had it in you."

Thandie gasped. "You heard about that, too? But how?"

"Don't worry, girl. I only listen to gossip. I don't spread it."

"Gage—" Thandie breathed.

"She'd never," Day promised. "I have other sources."

"Like?"

"Cam's girlfriend. "

"They're still together?" Thandie asked, too shocked to play coy.

"Do you care?"

Thandie shook her head, not trusting herself to speak. She was happy for Cam, but shocked his relationship had survived the incident.

"FYI. She doesn't want you within a mile of Cam," Day warned her. "But can you blame her?"

"No, not really," Thandie said with a sigh.

"Enough about this bleak drama. Negative energy isn't good for the soul." Day pulled a small bottle from her purse and sprayed something into the air. "It's only water," she explained. "But I feel as though it cleanses the air." She quickly tucked the bottle away. "What on earth are you doing in Miami?"

Thandie smiled to herself. Day had not changed one bit. "I'm here for work. I'm promoting a club on the strip."

"Oh? Which one?"

"Club Babylon."

"That's Elliot Richards's club, right?"

Thandie nodded. "Have you been there before?"

"Oh, no," Day said with wave of her hand. "I don't have time to go to clubs with my work and all. I've met Elliot before, but only in passing. I'm sure he wouldn't remember me, but—" she wiggled her brows "—I sure remember him." She laughed. "At any rate, everyone has heard of Elliot Richards around here. The local papers treat him like royalty. It's obnoxious." Day looked around the waiting room, as if just realizing where they were. "What are you doing in here?"

"I'm looked for a good masseur."

"Don't come here. This place is fuckin' awful!"

The receptionist, whom they'd both forgotten about, sniffed at this.

Day ignored her. "You need Fernando. He works over at Blu Moon. He's phenomenal." She snatched up a business card from the reception desk, flipped it over and jotted down a number. "Tell them Day sent you. They'll treat you like a queen." Thrusting the card at Thandie, Day checked her watch. "Yikes, I have to go. I'm interviewing an intern." She leaned up on her tiptoes and commenced to shower Thandie's face with air kisses. "Give me a call. You have my number."

She sailed out, pushing the front door wide, so that it inadvertently banged against the wall, before slamming shut. Her spiked heels could be heard snapping loudly against the sidewalk.

Day's whirlwind arrival and abrupt exit left the spa deathly quiet. Thandie smiled uncomfortably at the receptionist. Her smile was not warmly received. Sensing retreat was her best option, Thandie eased out of the building.

"Are you listening to me?"

"Not particularly," Elliot confessed. He continued to stare

out the glass wall of his office. It allowed him a perfect view of the arena floor.

He was not yet ready to admit to himself he was looking for her. He'd known there would be little chance of her coming to him. She'd run from him like a frightened cat last night. It brought a smile to his lips each time he recalled the memory. He'd enjoyed making her react to him. It had been the most delicious game.

However, it had not come without a cost. His humor was quickly replaced when he considered how soft she'd felt beneath him. The weight of her breast in his hand and the slickness of her thighs…he wanted more of her. Now that he'd sampled her, he wanted to devour her. Perhaps it was curiosity. Or perhaps it was for the simple matter she had not completely succumbed to him. But she would come to him. Preferably on her hands and knees, begging for him. The idea made him laugh softly to himself. Begging. Yes, he would make her beg for him.

"What's so funny?"

"A joke," Elliot said over his shoulder. "A private joke."

Nico smirked. "Keep your jokes. We both know you have no sense of humor."

Elliot grinned. "What did you say earlier?"

"Now you're ready to listen?"

"Nico, spit it out."

"I said I've decided to fuel up the plane and take a trip. I need a break."

"You don't work, Nico. What exactly are you taking a break from?"

"Life, I suppose. It's become quite mundane. You should join me."

"I have a job," Elliot reminded him. "I can't be away."

"It'll be a short trip," Nico assured him.

"That's what you said last August."

"That wasn't my fault," Nico retorted. "No one can go to Fiji for just one week. Besides, didn't I make that up to you?"

Elliot conceded. Nico had thrown him a birthday bash he doubted he could ever surpass. Elliot turned away from the glass wall to look at him. Nico was seated on Elliot's couch, with an attractive black woman seated beside him.

He smiled at the woman. "What was your name again?"

"Janay," she said.

"I can't keep my eyes off you."

Elliot smiled down at the lovely Janay. "I'll give you two some privacy."

Elliot left the office.

Thandie was hesitant to return to Babylon after what had happened last night. But to not go would be to lose face with Elliot. If she showed the slightest bit of weakness, there would be blood in the water. Elliot would attack like the shark he was. There was a high chance she would not come out unscathed next time.

She was still stunned by what had occurred in the Tower. She was upset with Elliot for taking advantage of the situation, and she was mortified by her reaction to him. She could not figure out the nearly hypnotic effect he had on her. She had never responded that way to any other man, and she believed Elliot knew this. He was far too confident in his effect on her. If given the chance, he would use it against her. Hadn't he already?

For once, Thandie did not rush the girls to get ready. They could take all night if they wanted. She had no intention of arriving early. So far, her plan was working well. Now that the girls had met Elliot, they were going all out to impress him. Both were dressed in their most dazzling outfits. In contrast,

Thandie chose to dress down, in black leather pants and blouse. There were no frills. She desired only to melt into the crowd.

By the time the girls were ready, it was well past midnight. The managers' meeting had been concluded hours ago. At Babylon, the music was amplified and there was a decent-size line outside the crowd. The bouncer waved them through the line and held the door open for them.

She doubted she'd ever get used to the splendor of Club Babylon. Smartly, the club's many themes altered the interior so much it was hardly recognizable from one day to the next. Tonight, the arena was darkened more than usual to give way to a brilliant laser show.

Len and Raja quickly put some distance between themselves and Thandie, which was fine with her. Thanks to their ostentatious outfits, it would be impossible for her to lose sight of them.

She surveyed the arena crowd. It did not take long before she spotted Elliot. He was easy to find. He drew people to him like a magnet. She had only to follow the small wave of people who trailed after him. At the moment, Elliot was leaning casually against the bar, entertaining a cluster of laughing sorority girls. The tallest of the girls wore a sash with Greek letters etched on both ends and the words "I'm twenty-one today" proudly scrawled in the center. The girl was a perfect distraction. Thandie was able to circle the dance floor and enter the VIP area unnoticed.

She spied Adam, but was unable to talk to him because he was attending to guests. She waved to him and headed to the upper level of the lounge. There, she found a nook along the balcony to view the lower floors. It was doubtful Elliot would notice her here. She settled into the spot and watched the crowd. There was plenty to see, and much to learn.

The Babylon waitstaff snaked in and out of the throng,

taking orders and delivering drinks. Discreetly dressed security guards patrolled the room, on the lookout for any sign of trouble. Dancers effortlessly transitioned from the backstage to their elevated platforms.

Thandie told herself she was familiarizing herself with her new work environment, but the truth was she couldn't keep her eyes off Elliot. He was truly the best show in town.

He was spending an unnecessary amount of time humoring the college girls, and he didn't look interested in leaving them. They were much prettier than the girls she remembered walking around on her college campus. At some point, the girl with the tiara had placed her crown on Elliot's head. Thandie rolled her eyes. The sonofabitch still managed to look sexy while wearing a headpiece! Didn't he have other things he should be doing? Did he intend to spend the whole night amusing these eager-to-please youngsters?

Just as the thought occurred to her, she saw Elliot crossing the dance floor, the girls following closely behind. He held his hand out for support as he guided them up the staircase to his office. Thandie watched as he and Michelle shared a quick knowing look before Michelle blocked any future entry into Elliot's office.

Thandie shook her head. Her new boss was a player, to be sure. He toyed with women as if they were amusing puppets. It was unsettling to watch how easily he charmed his way between their thighs, and they didn't seem to mind. They were all smiles hanging on to Elliot, happy to be in his presence. It was shameful. It was all the more reason to stay away from him. Elliot Richards was temptation personified.

Thandie gave a snort of resignation. Who cared if Elliot was screwing college girls in his office at this very moment? So long as she wasn't on the receiving side of his advances, she was safe. She was here to do a job, and Elliot's personal escapades were the least of her concerns.

It was a little past four o'clock in the morning. Thandie and the girls had arrived back at Warren's home barely an hour ago. When they'd left the club, Warren was enthralled with a tall, leggy blonde, whom Thandie could only guess was a model. Florida apparently grew supermodels as plentifully as citrus fruit.

Thandie burrowed deeper under the bedsheets. She stared up at the ceiling, trying to get her thoughts together. The cool confines of the bedding were soothing against her skin. Thandie considered herself lucky to have escaped from Babylon before Elliot had a chance to corner her. Thankfully, he'd been too preoccupied with his college beauties to entertain thoughts of her.

Thandie's nerves were in a state of disarray. She could not decide if she should be offended by Elliot's show of interest in someone else, so soon after their encounter in the Tower, or if she should be relieved. If he was involved with other women, then it would mean he had no serious interest in her, which was what she wanted. Then why did seeing Elliot with another woman get under her skin?

She shivered every time she thought about the Tower incident. Her body was still burning from their encounter. Not for the first time, she wondered just what would have happened if she'd lingered in his embrace only a few minutes longer. Would they have had sex? Would she have enjoyed it? *Of course you would have,* a voice inside her head screamed. A man like Elliot didn't gain a reputation like his without a little truth to it. He'd surely had enough practice.

She was far from being a virgin and normally considered herself quite proficient in the art of love. She loved the control, loved the look of desperation in her lover's eyes as she rode him. But somehow, she knew Elliot Richards would be different. He would be much more resistant to being controlled. No, Elliot thrived on power, finding a person's weakness and forcing them to submit to his desires.

She rolled over onto her side, searching for a cooler spot in the sheets. Closing her eyes, she tried to empty her mind, and rest. If she focused really hard, she might even be able to go thirty minutes without fantasizing about a tanned, silver-eyed devil in finely cut suits. Pulling her pillow into her side, she gave a deep sigh, pretending the goose-feathered duvet was Cam's sleeping form. Sweet, reliable, uncomplicated Cam. His scent, his bare skin, his soft snore.

Her muscles began to relax as fatigue crept over her. Her breathing became slower. She hugged Cam tighter—a moan of contentment escaped her lips. And then Cam's skin went dark, and well-defined muscles appeared. She looked up to see his normally handsome features had contorted into sharper angles, making him dazzle with new beauty. He blinked, and when his eyes opened they were no longer a warm shade of brown, but a hue of cool silver. His gaze burned her like shards of ice. And then he spoke.

"I'm more talented with my tongue."

Thandie bolted upright, her heart beating frantically in her chest. She looked hesitantly beside her. With a sigh of relief, there was only a pillow at her side.

"Oh, thank goodness," she whispered. "It was a nightmare."

Chapter Eight

It had been casually mentioned, and within days it had erupted into a whirlwind of activity. Over lunch, while Thandie was texting with Amanda in New York, Warren made her jump when he threw down his newspaper and snapped his fingers. "We'll have a party!" he said.

Thandie, who'd been interrupted from a rather lengthy text message, turned toward him. "A what?"

"A party," he repeated, his face gleaming with excitement. "I'll throw you and the girls a welcome party."

Len and Raja, whom Thandie hadn't even known were awake yet, ran into the dining room whooping and clapping their hands.

"A party!" Len exclaimed.

Raja jumped in jubilation. "Where?"

Warren spread his hands out. "Here, of course."

Thandie shook her head in disbelief. "Warren, why in the world would you throw a party for us?"

"Why the hell not?" He frowned at her, unable to believe anyone would question the idea of a party.

"You're insane," Thandie said. "We go to a party every time we go to Babylon."

"Yeah, but that's different." Warren waved his hand carelessly in the air. "That's business."

Again, Thandie shook her head. Warren's thinking process was beyond her. She had little time to spare these days. She was quickly learning what Miami's nightlife had to offer.

In less than a week, she and the girls had attended two red carpet events, three social galas and visited four competing nightclubs. It was exhausting work. After spending six days straight traveling from one party to the next, the last thing Thandie wanted to do was attend another party. She didn't have the energy.

"You're certifiable, Warren," she said.

"That wouldn't be the first time I've heard that," he chuckled.

"When are you going to have time to plan a party?"

"I'll make time," he laughed. "When have you ever known me not to find time for a little revelry?"

"Forgive me for being skeptical."

"We'll have it next Monday," he announced.

"That's only four days away, including today," she pointed out.

"Plenty of time," he assured her. "The club will be closed, so everybody from the staff can come. I know this great little bistro that can do the catering. It'll be perfect."

"I'm not so sure it's a good idea," she warned.

"Okay, Negative Nancy," he said with a heavy sigh. "I won't ask for your help, but you are required to come."

The girls were so taken with the idea, they looped their arms around his neck and planted loud kisses on his cheeks. His eyes lit up and she knew if Warren died this very moment, he would have done so with a smile on his face.

"Okay, okay. Plan your party, but we—" Thandie pointed to the girls and herself "—have work to do. And this work is attached to a sizable payoff. Please try not to be offended when I tell you those responsibilities outweigh your party plans."

"*Thandie,*" Len said with a dramatic whine. "Show a little gratitude. He's offering to throw you a party, not give you a root canal."

"I'm just being a voice of reason. We're here to work, not party."

Raja's hand shot up into the air. "Who votes to ignore Thandie and focus on planning our party?" Len and Warren's hands sprang into the air. "Looks as though you've been outnumbered, Thandie." And in a voice reminiscent of her boss's, Raja added. "Try not to be offended."

Len giggled and Warren clapped his hands and started listing off things he wanted to include.

Thandie shook her head and left the room. She doubted anyone noticed her absence, for they were again jumping up and down with excitement.

An hour later, Thandie and the girls piled into the SUV and headed toward South Beach. It would be another long day. They had all been long days. There never seem to be enough time to accomplish everything. There were always phone calls to make, emails to follow-up on, booking agents to persuade and hotel rates to negotiate.

And then there was the research. Not an overly difficult task, however it demanded time and a fair amount of patience. Being unfamiliar with Miami, Thandie had to invest a few days to acquaint herself with the city.

The feat would have been much easier if she could clarify the expectations. Unfortunately, she was avoiding Elliot like the plague. Not that he noticed.

Thandie's elaborate plan to be too busy with work to think about Elliot, let alone see him, was a failure. She was annoyed to learn from his smug assistant Romero, Elliot was currently out of town. When she'd discovered he was in Italy of all places, with someone named Nico, she had difficulty silencing a colorful string of profanities. Even if she had questions about the project, he would not have been available to answer them. Not that she was anxious to see the man. In fact, she felt just the opposite. Be that as it may, Elliot would have to approve her proposal before she could move forward.

Having no idea when Elliot would return, Thandie pushed onward. She was determined to complete the proposal.

Thus, she and the girls submerged themselves in the momentous task of gathering information. By day, they made endless calls, verifying the schedules of potential entertainers and high-profile guests. By night, they split up their schedules; putting in early appearances at Babylon before heading out to scout competing clubs. It was a grueling schedule. Even Raja and Len, with their bountiful energy, began to whine after a few days. By the end of the week, Thandie had a detailed project plan ready for review.

In a show of appreciation for their hard work, she gave the girls the afternoon off. This was music to their ears, as they would be free to roam the streets of Miami unsupervised.

Late Sunday evening, Thandie put the finishing touches on the proposal, dressed it in her firm's signature portfolio packaging, and arranged for the girls to deliver it to Romero, who would relay it to his employer. Thandie imagined it would sit on Elliot's desk collecting dust, anticipating his return to the city. Until then, all she could do was wait.

On the day of Warren's party, Thandie indulged herself by sleeping late. She'd managed to keep Len and Raja out of her hair by having them run miscellaneous errands, although she had the sinking suspicion they were helping Warren plan his spontaneous house party.

Warren's home had quickly become a reservoir for cleaning supplies, flower arrangements, lighting fixtures, and sound equipment. By early afternoon, there were party planners, decorators and caterers crawling all over. True to his word, Warren hadn't bothered her once for help. In fact, she'd gotten the feeling he enjoyed the project; it seemed to give an outlet to his youthful energy.

By now, Thandie was too busy to notice the constant eruptions of noise from the lower level of Warren's home. The DJ he'd hired was performing a series of sound checks, decorators were making the finishing touches, and the caterers were preparing the buffet. Len and Raja were in a state of giggles, teasing Warren whenever possible and taking turns flirting with the DJ.

Thandie, for the most part, remained locked in her room. Amanda had called earlier, and it had taken her a solid hour to calm her down. When she had finally hung up, Thandie needed a nap. She slept for two hours before being awakened by knocking on her door.

"Thandie?"

"Come in," she said sleepily.

Raja eased into her room, closing the door quickly behind her to block out the noise. Wearing a strapless black dress with her hair pulled back in a sleek ponytail, she looked very pretty.

"You should come downstairs. The decorator did a kick-ass job."

This made Thandie laugh. "A kick-ass job? Aren't you a little old for such descriptions?"

"I'm only twenty-three!"

Thandie arched her brow at the girl.

"Fine," Raja surrendered. "I'm twenty-six, but don't tell Len."

"My lips are sealed," she promised.

Raja brightened. "Thanks, boss. By the way, Warren sent me up here to ask you nicely to get ready. The party starts in two hours."

Rolling out of bed, Thandie stretched. "Okay. You've done your dirty work. I'm up."

"Want some help?"

"No, thanks. I'll be down soon."

Once Raja left, Thandie began washing up. She opened the closet and pulled out a garment that was so whisper thin, it floated in the air. Unlike the flashy outfits she wore for work, this gown would cover her from head to toe in a cool shade of gray lace. The material was lined with delicate nude fabric, giving the illusion the owner of the dress was wearing nothing beneath.

Thandie had never worn it to any of the clubs she worked because she'd always thought the coloring too delicate, and the length too formal. However, for a house party in tropical surroundings, it was perfect.

She slid into the dress and rummaged through her jewelry bag for a pair of simple stud earrings. Following Raja's lead, she pulled her hair away from her face, tucking rebellious tresses behind her ears. By the time she was applying her lipstick, she could hear the first group of guests arriving.

Now completely dressed and accessorized, she surveyed herself in the full-length mirror. She admired the way the dress clung to her body like a second skin, before falling into a pool of lace around her stilettos. There was a high slit on the right side of the gown, nearly snaking all the way up to her waist. It would be the only visible skin shown tonight. For several minutes, she debated about whether to wear panties or not.

The dress was lovely, yet very thin. She could see the slight indention of her thong along her hips. With a sigh, she lifted her skirt and pulled off her panties, grumbling to herself that no one but her would ever know.

After a final once-over, Thandie went downstairs. She was impressed. When Warren Radcliffe threw a party, he threw a party. The room was lit by hundreds of candles, and with the curtains pulled back to allow a picturesque twilight view of the ocean, the setting was beautiful. The terrace doors were open, allowing a pleasant breeze to flow through the rooms. Balanced by smooth, jazzy melodies, it was the perfect setting for seduction.

There were already fifty guests there. Miami's finest socialites had come out to play. Spotting her across the room, Warren came to her side, kissing her cheek. "There you are, Thandie. You look lovely."

"Thank you." Looking around the room, she said, "You've outdone yourself."

"You think so?"

"I love it, Warren. Forgive me for ever doubting you."

He laughed. "I aspire to impress you." Claiming two glasses of champagne from a passing waiter, he handed her the refreshment. "Here's to old friends in new places." He clinked the tip of his glass with hers and took a sip.

Just then, a large group of newcomers entered the living area. Thandie looked around the room and spotted most of the Babylon staff and a dozen pretty twenty-something girls.

"Warren, who are these women you invited?"

He shrugged. "Haven't got a clue, but God bless them for coming. Pardon me, kiddo. I see a guest who needs my attention."

She watched him rush off to flirt with a tall, thin girl who looked too young to vote. Laughing to herself, she made her way out to the terrace, where a few people had gathered. Immediately, she spotted Adam Parr. He waved her over, kissing her lightly on the cheek.

"You certainly can be counted on for the wow-factor," he said. "You look hot."

Thandie smiled. "You look pretty nice yourself."

"I try," he said with a wink. "So how has your visit been so far? Staying with Warren has got to be entertaining." They both looked across the room where Warren was doing a very suggestive salsa dance with his new lady friend.

"I'm afraid everything about Warren is entertaining," Thandie said under her breath.

"Beautiful and diplomatic," he teased.

"Careful, Adam. I'm easily swayed by flowery words."

"I'm easily swayed by loose women. But who's counting?" They laughed.

Adam stopped a passing waiter to replace their now-empty glasses with fresh, fizzing flutes of champagne. "How's the proposal coming along?"

"It's finished," she said triumphantly.

"I don't know how you did it so fast," he said with a shake of his head. "The last PR agent for Red Door took a month, and Elliot still laughed at it."

"Let me guess," she said in a forced cool voice. "The agent was a man."

Adam smiled to himself. "You wouldn't have known it from the way he started crying. Wailed like a woman. Poor fellow. He was in over his head."

Thandie gave a weak smile and fought the sensation to run back to her laptop and double-check her work.

Adam's gaze flicked to someone behind her and then he smiled. "Excuse me, Thandie. I see a friend of mine. Will you be all right by yourself?"

"Of course," she assured him.

Thandie watched Adam as he crossed the room. In all honesty, she was saddened to see him go. Aside from Warren, Adam was the only friend she had in Miami.

She was just about to introduce herself to a couple standing nearby when she heard someone call her name. She turned to see Rex Barrington making his way to her side. She smiled as he approached. He was dressed in a dark gray suit and black dress shirt which was unbuttoned at the neck. He looked very nice, she thought. Not nearly the handsome radiance of Elliot Richards, but nice all the same.

"You look splendid," he said, greeting her with a light peck on the cheek. "Of course, I'm sure every man in the room has told you so. That dress—really compliments you." He visibly blushed the moment the words left his mouth.

Thandie thought his embarrassment was endearing. "Thank you, Rex. I was just thinking how nice you look tonight."

With obvious relief, he smiled. "How are things going so far?"

"I haven't been chased off yet, if that's what you're wondering."

"That's good news. We need a pretty face around here." He gave her a nod before scanning the newest group to step onto the terrace. "I never get a chance to see you at the club. By the time I hear you're in the building, you've already left."

"Not enough time in the day," she said with an apologetic lift of her shoulders. "I've been busy working on the proposal."

"I'm afraid we've done a poor job of showing you the more exquisite pleasures of our fair city. From the moment you arrived, it's been work, work, work and more work."

"There's a lot to do," she reasoned.

"If you're not doing anything special Wednesday night—if you can manage it—I wondered if you would like to accompany me to the Yurman party. They renovated the downtown store. There will be plenty of press there. Perhaps a few helpful contacts for you."

"That would be excellent. I would love to go."

"Great. Unfortunately, I was only able to secure one additional invite. Do you suppose Len and Raja will be overly upset if they have to sit this one out?"

Thandie turned to search the girls out in the crowd. It was easy. Both girls were surrounded by a small group of men. They stood near a table, where a tall ice sculpture in the shape of a large *R,* for Radcliffe, was prominently mounted in the center.

What she saw next sent a tremor of panic up her spine. With the support of one of her admirers, Raja was assisted to stand on top of the table. In order to make sure she did not tumble backward, the stranger supported her by keeping a firm hand planted on her bottom. Raja did not seem to mind because she was too preoccupied delivering an impromptu speech. Although Thandie could not hear what was being said, the crowd of men found it humorous.

With a wave of her hand, she presented Len, who smiled and did a silly curtsy. Holding a shot glass filled with dark liquor up in the air, Raja began to slowly pour it on top of the frozen *R.* Len, having positioned her mouth on the lower tip of the sculpture, began sucking the liquor as fast as she could. The men clapped and cheered her on.

Thandie was horrified. She wanted to turn away from the scene. It was just like the girls to embarrass themselves in front of a crowd.

To make matters worse, Warren was pushing his way through the group. She held her breath for his reaction. He would either explode or do something equally irrational. When she saw his weathered face break into a wide grin and beg for his turn to be fed by Raja, Thandie turned her back on the spectacle.

Rex gave her a look of concern. "Are you all right?" he asked.

She nodded.

"Do you want me to calm things down over there?"

"No." She took a long drink from her glass. "It would only make things worse."

Rex studied the group carefully before slowly saying, "I gather they are always this enthusiastic."

"You have no idea," said with a heavy sigh.

Rex smiled. "Is their boss just as daring?"

At this, she had to laugh. "Not even close."

Thankfully, he directed her farther out onto the balcony, where the noise from the party competed with the rolling waves of the ocean. To preoccupy her thoughts, Rex entertained her with stories from his past. Israeli born, Rex was raised in Spain for most of his life, before his family migrated to London. Thandie found his story fascinating.

Whether he'd done it purposely or not, he'd managed to make her forget about the scene Len and Raja were causing indoors. Rex became distracted when a new wave of guests arrived. He pointed out various people in the crowd, careful to highlight those whom he thought would be of interest to Thandie.

"Who's that?" Thandie asked, pointing across the patio to a photographer who appeared to be quite popular with the party attendees. Instead of asking people for permission to photograph them, the guests gravitated toward him.

"Ringo Papler," Rex supplied. "Freelance photographer. Seems to work for all the Miami society papers. Everybody wants to be shot by him. His pictures always seem to land on the cover page. Warren was smart to invite him. Ringo can make or break a shindig."

"And the woman snapping directions?" she asked, nodding to a white-haired woman with oversize black glasses, snapping her boney fingers and spitting demands to a young photographer.

"Oh, that's Mira Dietrich, the editor-in-chief of *Look*. She's practically royalty around here. She can make life very easy for you if she likes you. The problem is she hates everyone. You'll get to know her soon enough. She makes a point to meet all the new talent in town."

Eventually, Rex led her back inside. By now, the girls had retired their drinking game and were attempting salsa moves with a pair of ardent dance partners. Other guests had joined in, and soon the center of the living room was clustered with dancing couples.

A group of newcomers filtered into the house. Thandie looked up and recognized a familiar face among the clutch of strangers. It was Romero. The party had now been in progress for over two hours. Thandie wasn't sure if she was more surprised by his late appearance, or by the realization that he had friends.

Smug as ever, Romero entered the room with a confidence uncommon for his young years. It was no time at all before people began circling around him, pressing in, eager to talk to him.

Thandie leaned toward Rex and asked, "What do you think they're asking him?"

"The same thing we want to know."

"Which is?"

"Where is Elliot," he said simply. "If anyone knows, it would be Romero."

Thandie observed the young man once more. Indeed, there

was a swarm of women lined up, waiting their turn to catch his attention. Romero, seemingly oblivious to their beauty, waved each one away as if she were a pesky insect. She found it hard to believe no one took offense. Nevertheless, they all appeared to accept his behavior amiably.

Thandie did not care for the man, so she was annoyed when Rex caught Romero's eye and waved him over. As if feeling her dislike, Rex chuckled under his breath.

"He's not that bad," he whispered. "Just vain to the point of delusional." His intent to make her laugh was successful.

Lifting a cocktail glass from the tray of a passing waiter, Rex offered the drink to the younger man. Romero accepted it.

"Ms. Shaw," he said with a slight incline of his head.

"Romero," Thandie said coolly.

"Long day, Romero?" Rex asked.

"Always." Romero did not immediately drink from his glass. Instead, he seemed more content to use it as a prop. "Elliot," he continued, "is, as always, a taskmaster."

"I'll drink to that," Rex agreed. "Lucky for us he's a continent away."

Romero shook his head. "Not so. His plane arrived in Miami a few hours ago." He pulled out his cell phone and scrolled through a few screens before continuing. "He's stuck in a meeting. Should be out in a few minutes. If he keeps to his schedule, he should be here soon." Romero never lifted his eyes from the phone's display while he spoke. "Time zones being as they are, these types of meetings can be a little inconvenient."

"Overseas meeting?" Rex probed.

Romero shrugged, giving nothing away, as every good assistant should.

Rex tried a different tactic. "Is everything in place for the grand opening?"

Romero took his time turning his attention back to Rex. "According to the event planner, everything is falling into place. In any case, they had better be. There's no turning back now."

"It'll be hard to top Elliot's birthday party last year."

At these words, Rex and Romero shared a conspiring smile. This surprised Thandie. For a second, Romero's young face lost its haughtiness, and he actually looked handsome. But this break from tradition was quickly restored. Romero cleared his throat and gave an apologetic nod toward Thandie.

Without warning, a loud squeal of laughter exploded from across the room. Rex and Romero both looked to see what is was. Thandie did not. She already knew it had come from Len and Raja's side of the room. She was afraid what she would see if she turned around.

Romero spotted the commotion the girls were creating and frowned. Abruptly, he said, "I see someone I need to speak to. Excuse me." As if she were an afterthought, he glanced at Thandie and nodded. "Nice dress." She never got the chance to thank him. Romero was already snaking his way through the crowd of people.

Just then, Markie rushed up to join the group. "Did Romero say anything about Elliot's whereabouts?" he asked.

Rex nodded. "Yeah, but if you want to know when he's coming, don't bother with Romero." He nodded his head toward the arched entrance of the foyer. "He's here."

All three of them turned at the same time. It was him all right. Tall, dark and beautiful. Fuckalious, Gage had called him. Simply fuckalious. From the moment Elliot Richards arrived, he seemed to suck all the air out of the room.

Elliot looked bored and seemed to be calculating how long he was required to be here before escaping. Spotting someone in the crowd, he began to weave a lazy path through the guests. He was stopped often by admirers.

Thandie watched as Romero materialized out of nowhere to stand at his employer's side. Elliot murmured a few words over his shoulder to him. Romero nodded, quickly mumbled something in response and then disappeared. When Elliot was near Warren, the old man clapped him on the back and grinned from ear to ear. Elliot was truly his crown jewel of the night. Warren's pride could not have been more evident. Rex, charming as ever, excused himself to get in a few words with Elliot. Markie followed him.

Thandie glanced toward the ice sculpture Raja and Len had sexually assaulted earlier. Thankfully, both seemed to have settled down. They hadn't moved too far from the frozen *R,* only a few feet toward the dancing area where men were taking turns being dance partners.

Thandie looked back toward the crowd surrounding Elliot. He grinned and shook hands with the ease of a politician, a very smooth politician. Without warning, he looked up and their eyes met. Thandie resisted the urge to look away. Instead, she lifted her brow slightly. He made no facial expression in return. Instead, he did something she did not expect. He came toward her.

Her stomach tightened as he approached. His grayish eyes practically hypnotized her with predatory focus. She did indeed feel like his prey. When he was only a foot away, the faint and very heady scent of his aftershave sent a wave of goose bumps up her arms. It was light, barely noticeable but distinct. Although her hormones were screaming, she managed a placid smile. "Welcome back, Mr. Richards."

His lips somehow managed to twist into a charming grin. "Thank you, Ms. Shaw." He leaned over and kissed her— not her cheek as everyone else had—he kissed her neck, just below the jawline, where the pulse was most apparent. From the look of satisfaction he now had, she could only guess her heart rate had leaped into triple digits under the gentle brush of his lips. But not entirely done with her, he cupped her chin, forcing it upward. "It's good to be back."

His hands were suddenly gone from her body, and she had the vague memory of him pressing another glass of champagne in her hand. She drank from it blindly, neither tasting nor enjoying the bubbly chill of the liquor. She had to guard herself from becoming overwhelmed by him. Elliot's presence was intoxicating, as thrilling as it was dangerous.

Three men stood just within earshot of them. Clearly, they were waiting to speak to Elliot. They seemed to be edging nearer with every passing second, hoping to win Elliot's attention. Thandie hoped they succeeded soon. Elliot, however, ignored them.

Abruptly, the music changed from an upbeat salsa number, to a soft, jazzy melody. Couples moved toward the dance floor, swaying in tune.

Without asking, Elliot captured Thandie's hand and pulled her into the throng of dancers. She tried to pull out of his grasp, but was rewarded with a firm squeeze. Elliot expertly spun her into his arms. Through a serious of quick twirls and side steps, he managed to relocate them to the opposite side of the room. In the dim lighting, matched with a depleted sunset, the house was now awash with a pale orange glow. The candlelight cast shadows everywhere, and Thandie and Elliot seem to be standing in the darkest corner of the room. If anyone was looking for Elliot, they would have a hard time finding him.

"Should I be impressed?" Thandie asked.

Elliot chuckled softly in her ear. "If you're looking to be impressed, you have only to take me to your bedroom." He grinned at her nonplussed expression. "I found your proposal to be interesting reading."

"You read my proposal?" This news shocked Thandie. "But I just submitted it yesterday. How did you—"

"It was sent to me. I reviewed it on my plane ride home."

Thandie gave a slow nod of her head. "And?" she asked, curious.

"It's approved."

"Approved?" Thandie blinked. Was he really going to make it that easy? "You don't have anything to add?"

"I thought your platform was detailed and well researched. You worked with the set budget, and abided to the timeline given. No," he said, a faint glimmer in his gray eyes, "I have nothing to add."

"And I can proceed?" she asked cautiously.

"By all means."

Thandie watched his lips as he said those last words. They looked wickedly soft, and obnoxiously tempting. They curled into a slow smile when he asked, "Did you miss me, pussycat?"

"Hardly," she said flatly.

Elliot laughed. It was a seductive sound. "I've warned you before about that pretty little mouth of yours." He pulled her closer to him, his hold tight and demanding. "Perhaps you want to push me into disciplining you. Is that it, puss? Is that your goal?" His lips brushed against her earlobe. "I should take you over my knee right now and show everyone just how badly you dissatisfy me."

"You wouldn't dare," she challenged. "Maybe in the Tower, where you're safe from prying eyes. But not in this crowd."

He chuckled. "Do you really think crowds of any sort discourage me?"

Thandie stopped dancing. She saw the seriousness in his

eyes, and tried to wiggle out of his embrace. It was no good. He was holding her entirely too tightly.

"I could tear that dress off your delicious body and devour you this very moment if I so chose," he whispered into her ear. "And you'd love every dirty minute of it."

"Let go of me, Elliot," she said a little breathlessly.

"And the plans I have for that saucy tongue of yours." He exhaled deeply. "Let's just say neither of us would walk away dissatisfied." In the blink of an eye, all humor was gone from his voice. "Be careful about how far you push me, Thandie. I don't make empty promises."

His hands were suddenly gone from her body. She had the vague memory of him collecting flutes of champagne from the tray of a passing waitress. He pressed one into her hand and watched her over the rim of his glass as he drank. Thandie sipped from her glass, neither tasting nor enjoying the bubbly chill. She was too busy trying to shield herself from becoming overwhelmed by him, but it was of little use.

Thandie was suddenly aware they were standing a few feet from the men who'd been hovering by them earlier. Elliot had maneuvered them back to the very spot they'd once stood. She had no idea how he'd accomplished it without her noticing. She glanced up at him, leery of what he might do next.

He wasn't looking at her. Elliot's gaze had drifted across the room, and landed on an exquisite woman. Their eyes met. She'd obviously been watching Elliot for some time. Thandie watched as something strong passed between Elliot and the woman. She had no idea what was exchanged, but whatever it was it had been potent. Unquestionably, this was a conversation between lovers.

Without further decorum, Elliot emptied his glass, placed the flute on a nearby tabletop and leaned close enough to whisper in Thandie's ear. "No panties, pussycat?" His hand skimmed low on her hip, not low enough to capture the attention of anyone standing nearby but just low enough to make his point. "Very sexy."

With that said, he excused himself and crossed the room to join the mystery woman. Thandie watched him, too shocked by his words, too aroused by his touch. He was too damned good, she thought. Had Thandie been made of ice, she would have been a puddle on the floor.

She could not help but follow his progress as he snaked his way through the crowd. Finally at his destination, he stared down at the woman, a look of quiet amusement on his face. Thandie considered the beauty. She was probably the most gorgeous woman she had ever seen. Standing next to each other, she and Elliot could have been twins; both were equally tanned, dark-haired and lovely. Thandie suddenly felt small and insignificant.

Without a word spoken, Elliot walked toward the front door, officially quitting the party. The stunning woman followed close behind, but not before pausing to flick her cool gaze over Thandie. Her red lips lifted into a smile. It was not a warm smile. She was curious of Thandie, but not intimidated. No, never intimidated. Her dark eyes gleamed. It was a look of total possession. She was marking her territory, making it clear to Thandie, and anyone else watching, Elliot belonged to her.

Thandie watched the departing couple disappear from sight, the front door slammed shut behind them. After having invested less than twenty minutes into the party, Elliot Richards had left the building.

Chapter Nine

The party continued well into the morning. Thanks to Warren, Thandie had been introduced to just about every guest present before retiring for the evening. With the party still going on below, it had been difficult to sleep.

Her thoughts kept drifting to Elliot's arrogant face. She'd managed to doze off into brief ten-minute naps, but never fell soundly asleep. After hours of tossing and turning, Thandie finally surrendered. There was no way she would be able to get a good night's sleep with thoughts of Elliot on her mind.

It was just after noon when she tapped on Raja and Len's bedroom doors. She'd meant only to notify them she was heading to the beach. They took the announcement as an invite. Within half an hour, they were all wearing their bathing suits and packing oversize beach bags. Thandie was grateful for their company, as it kept her mind occupied.

They lucked out by finding a parking spot on Ocean Avenue, across from South Beach's famed King & Grove Tides Hotel. After staking out a location to pitch their umbrella, they unrolled their beach blankets and began the arduous, but necessary, task of applying sunblock. Thandie and Raja lay close together, sharing the shade the umbrella offered, while Len, determined to get a deep tan, welcomed the unyielding blaze of the sun.

They'd been there less than a minute before spotting their first topless woman. At this, the girls were eager to discard their swimsuit tops. Thandie wouldn't dream of being so brazen. She was proud of her trim body and received many compliments, but that was the result of a painfully strict diet and an expensive Pilates instructor. Despite these things, Len and Raja possessed something Thandie did not, youth. It was this, the seven years of separation, that kept her bikini top firmly in place.

Pulling her hair back into a sloppy ponytail, Thandie stretched out on her beach towel. She was admittedly tired. The restless hours were catching up with her. The heat of the sun seemed to slowly massage her energy away. Her limbs felt like lead weights and she suddenly felt lazy. Sunbathing was a peaceful experience. Back home, she was always on the run. There was always someplace to go, something to do, someone to meet. Sure, she'd been to the beach before. Plenty of times, in fact. She and a group of friends rented a house in the Hamptons every summer. There was no place more fashionable than the Hamptons in July, however, Miami seemed to hold a magic all its own. Everyone was young, healthy and beautifully tanned. It was growing on her.

The girls began a deep discussion about which Hollywood stars should become the new celebrity couple. This discussion required much deliberation. As their voices became raised and whiny at certain junctions, Thandie began to regret allowing them to join her for a restful day at the beach. To avoid adding fuel to the fire, she pretended to listen, supplying nods of agreement when required. Exhausted, it did not take long before she drifted into a black and most-welcome sleep.

All too soon, she was woken by Raja, who was frantically shaking her shoulder.

"Thandie! Wake up. You have to see this!"

"Wh-what?" she said sleepily.

"Wake up now," Len squealed. "Oh, my goodness. Can you believe it?"

Thandie shook her head several times, immediately upset for having been awakened so abruptly. "This had better be good," she warned.

"It's better than good," Len laughed. "It's amazing." She nodded her head down the shore. "Talk about being in the right place at the right time."

Still groggy from her nap, Thandie tried to focus but was unable to immediately understand what had caused the girls' excitement. She yawned loudly. "Let me guess. MTV is filming a show on the beach?"

"Egh, MTV is so last year. Look!" Again, Len pointed down the beach.

"What exactly am I looking for?"

"Don't you see them?" Raja, too, jabbed her finger in the same direction. "It's Carey Charming and Nate O'Conner. The two most beautiful men in the NFL."

Thandie squinted her eyes to focus. Farther down the shoreline, she could see a photo shoot was in progress. Two men, clad in all-white suits, stood knee-deep in the bubbling waters washing in from the ocean. They each held footballs in their large hands, while makeup artists and stylists fluttered around them making last minute adjustments. The photo crew stood at an adequate distance, sun reflectors angled just so, to capture the perfect lighting. The scene was definitely eye-catching, and curious onlookers slowly crept closer, in an effort to get a better look at the two giants.

Len's smile widened. "Can you believe it? Charming and

O'Conner on the same beach with us? This is a miracle. They were both on the cover of GQ magazine last month."

"Nate is so hot," Raja murmured.

"What are they doing in Miami?" Len shaded her eyes with her hand. "Shouldn't they be in training camp, or something?"

"Training camp doesn't start until July, Len," Raja said with a sigh of resignation. "The real question isn't why are they here, but where are they going? Both Carey and Nat are free agents this season. With Carey managing to hold on to his numbers in spite of the team's mediocre year, and Nate coming off a great season, they're the most sought after players in the NFL. Carey and Nate played together in college and they've made no secret about wanting to play together again. Everyone is wondering which team can afford to sign both of them." Suddenly aware she'd said too much, Raja cleared her throat. "I dated a guy a couple of years ago who worshiped football. I was forced to learn the game." She shrugged innocently. "I kinda got into it."

"Kinda?" Len snorted. "You're practically sniffing their jockstraps."

"Shut up, Len!"

"All right, you two," Thandie warned. She was in no mood to listen to one of their colorful arguments. Thandie turned to observe the two men. They were giants in comparison to everyone standing nearby. Even from this distance, she could see their bulging biceps and tree trunk-thick thighs. Carey Charming, the leaner and taller of the two, was fair and blond. Nate O'Conner was a bit shorter, but he more than made up for it with muscle. His handsome good looks and dark skin made him instant eye candy. Coming to her feet, Thandie dusted sand off her bottom. "Well, there's no time like the present."

"Ah! What are you doing?" Len squeaked.

"I'm going to see what their plans are for tonight."

"Are you crazy?" Raja screeched. "They're NFL royalty."

"Then it won't hurt for them to mingle with their humble subjects." She gave them a parting smile before heading toward the giants. Running into Charming and O'Conner on the beach was an opportunity she could not allow to pass her by. She had every intention of inviting them to Club Babylon tonight. The worst that could happen was they would blow her off. But her chances of success far outweighed the possibility of defeat.

There was a knock on the office door before Michelle opened it wide enough to stick his head through. "Elliot, Thandie wants to speak with you."

Nico, who'd been having a whispered conversation on his cell phone for the last half hour, suddenly looked up. "Who's Thandie?"

Elliot had not had time to tell Nico any details regarding the newest addition to his staff. Before he could prepare Nico, Thandie had already crossed the threshold of his office.

Thandie was wearing a terry cloth dress. It was strapless, displaying smooth golden skin across an enticing bosom and small feminine shoulders. The dress had clearly been meant for the beach, yet it could best be described as modest, even matronly, on the sandy shores of Miami. But indoors, under the slightly dimmed lighting of his office, the silly garment tormented Elliot. The hem fell an inch or so past her buttocks, presenting a delicious view of those beautiful shapely legs of hers. Elliot had to admit, he'd had a hard time forgetting the feel of his hand between her thighs that night in the Tower. If she only knew what scenes his mind was conjuring right now, she'd probably run screaming from the building.

But she stared at him with a determined look in her eyes.

Her hip angled just so, mistranslating any attempt at appearing empowered to just looking damned sexy.

She stepped forward, bringing the scent of sunshine and fresh ocean air with her. Her hair was a bit disheveled, only adding to her appeal. She'd obviously pulled on her clothes in a rush, yet even in her casualness, she looked like a million bucks. Elliot couldn't help but admire the view.

Thandie met his stare and then shifted her gaze to his friend. Elliot noticed them sharing an appreciative appraisal of each other. Nico shot a quick glance toward him, his brow peaked. With a sigh, Elliot pushed himself away from his desk and made the introductions.

"Thandie—" sweeping a gesture toward his friend "—this is Nico."

Nico stood, wearing the same wicked grin he always wore. For some reason, it annoyed Elliot today. He shook Thandie's hand. "Actually," Nico said, "I'm Elliot's heterosexual life-partner."

"Nico," Elliot continued in a bored tone, "is one of my investors."

"I'm supposed to be a private investor," Nico offered, "but I guess the cat's out of the bag."

Thandie smiled up at him, noticeably eased by his good nature. "It's a pleasure to meet you, Nico."

He gave an airy wave of his hand. "The pleasure is completely on this side of the room."

"You have an interesting accent," Thandie observed. "Are you a local?"

"No," he smiled. "I'm visiting from the coast."

"Which coast would that be?" she asked.

"Take your pick."

She gave him a slight grin, recognizing flirtation when she saw it. "Are you in town for business or pleasure?"

"Pleasure, of course." Nico's gaze drifted over her once again. "I must say, Elliot, your hostesses are getting prettier by the minute."

"Actually," he drawled, "Thandie is a staff member. She was hired to handle Babylon's marketing prior to the reopening."

Nico looked at Elliot before openly staring at Thandie, as if seeing her for the first time. "Seriously?" his voice now devoid of its earlier humor. "But you never hire women."

"Warren insisted on it," Elliot replied.

As if that answered everything, Nico gave a resolute nod.

Piqued by their conversation, Thandie planted her hands on her hips. Elliot knew if she had any idea that the action caused her skirt to hike up several vital inches and the thin material of her dress to stretch provocatively across her breasts, she might not have chosen such a stance. It only made her look sexy as hell, rather than formidable.

"If you two are finished talking about me as if I weren't standing right here, I have some business to discuss."

Evidently still bewildered, Nico just stared at her.

"Please—" Elliot nodded "—by all means, let's discuss."

Highly annoyed, Thandie drew herself up taller. "I'm escorting Carey Charming and Nate O'Conner tonight. They'll have at least four people accompanying them. Will I have access to transportation?"

"You can have access to anything you like." Elliot's words hung in the air. He was baiting her, and she obviously hated him for it.

"I need transport," she gritted out.

He nodded. "You have it." Reaching across his desk, he pressed the numbers on his office phone, the room filled with automated ringing.

"Yes, Elliot?"

"Markie, Thandie is hosting guests this evening. She'll need two SUVs available to her. Arrange for Ricky and Christo to be her drivers. They know the routine pretty well. Also, have Adam secure VIP."

"You got it."

Elliot pressed a button on the dial pad, releasing the call. Turning to her, he bowed his head slightly. "Is there anything else I can do for you?" He could tell the words "kiss my ass" were hanging on the tip of her tongue. He gave a wicked grin. "You have only to say the word."

Her eyes went wide, and she swallowed hard. Giving a quick glance to Nico, she gave a nod and exited the room, her heels clicking with every step.

Nico laughed. "Why didn't you tell me about her?"

Elliot shrugged. "There's nothing to tell."

Nico stared after her, able to study to her retreating figure through the glass wall that encased Elliot's office. "So," he began, "are you going to share her, or what?"

Elliot followed his gaze as Thandie crossed the arena floor. He thought for a long minute before answering. "There will be no sharing of Thandie Shaw."

Nico nodded. "That's a new one."

Elliot met his knowing expression. "I'm the only one who's going to be tapping that."

Nico held up his hands in surrender. "Consider it done. I'm only appreciating the product."

"Well, appreciate it from a distance."

Nico laughed at the words. *"Touché!* Playing caveman now? I can respect that, but please remember this conversation when I discover a pretty face."

Elliot smirked.

"May I offer you some advice?"

"No."

Nico ignored the warning, and gave Elliot a brotherly clap

on the shoulder. "Keep your charms to a bare minimum. I fear it might be the deal-breaker with Ms. Shaw."

Elliot brushed off Nico's hand. "Any woman can be gotten to. You just have to know which buttons to push."

"And after you've pushed all her buttons, and she still doesn't come?"

"Oh, she'll come," Elliot said quietly. "Of that I have no doubt."

"Well, to your credit, I have yet to meet a woman who has withstood your charms."

"You never will," Elliot promised.

Several hours later Thandie found herself riding in the front seat of a gleaming black Escalade. Behind her, Nate O'Conner and Carey Charming sat casually chatting with each other. Surprisingly, they were both good-natured, and their boyish camaraderie seemed endless.

Thandie focused her attention on ensuring Carey was in good spirits. According to Raja, Carey was not big on clubs and rarely drank alcohol. Thandie had no trouble believing this. When she'd spoken to him today at the beach, she got the impression Carey would have refused to come had it not been for Nate convincing him. Nate O'Conner, however, apparently partied often. He was the more jubilant of the two and took great pleasure in flirting with Raja and Len.

A group of their friends occupied the vehicle following them. This concerned Thandie when she'd arrived at their hotel, but after being introduced to each one, they seemed harmless enough.

Their caravan pulled up to the entrance of Club Babylon a little after eleven. Nate, a natural superstar, leaped from the SUV and smiled at the crowd anxiously waiting to enter the club. Even if he were not a celebrity, he held an air about him which demanded people take notice. It did not take long for him to be recognized. The screams began, accompanied by the blinding flashes of lights. Ever the gentleman, Nate helped the ladies climb out of the vehicle. Len and Raja were all too happy to latch themselves onto each of his arms. Thandie exited the SUV just before Carey, and the crowd went crazy again. Carey Charming was not as comfortable before an audience. He did not shrink away from it, but unlike his friend, he steered away from the crowd.

Placing a reassuring hand on his back, Thandie guided their party into the building before the crowd had time to get out of control. Already, people who were standing in line at other clubs were leaving to join the long line outside Babylon.

Once inside, Thandie could not have been more impressed with the club's staff. Because she had called them before arriving, they were well prepared. Security gave them a wide berth, while Thandie and the girls navigated the group toward the VIP level.

Adam greeted her warmly before turning to welcome their party. They were ushered to a corner booth and drink orders were made. Thandie browsed the room and silently approved of Adam's work. This level of the VIP area was filled with tall, beautiful women—if possible, more attractive than the normal VIP guests.

Len coaxed a few members of their party to the dance floor. This allowed the remaining group to spread out a little on the cushioned seats. This was apparently an invitation for every platinum blonde in VIP to occupy the recently vacated seats. Within seconds, five fashionably dressed women had infiltrated the ranks. They'd pressed themselves into every nook and cranny possible. Thandie, who was positioned between the two athletes, counted herself fortunate. Because neither had moved, she was comfortably seated.

Nate and Carey seemed unfazed by the presence of the newest arrivals. Indeed, they laughed and toasted one round of beers after another, paying little attention to their smiling admirers. Nate did his share of flirting, but Thandie quickly determined he was more talk than action. Carey exercised a different tactic. Although he appeared to be ignoring their company, more than once Thandie caught him slip a sly wink to the woman seated next to Nate.

She guessed that he, like Elliot, was a predator. She frowned at the comparison and immediately pushed it out of her mind. She might have succeeded, had the devil himself not entered the lounge at that very minute. Elliot spoke briefly to Adam before crossing the crowded room to their corner. He made eye contact with Thandie, and she stood to introduce him. Smooth as ever, Elliot reached for her, giving her a light and unassuming kiss on the lips. This, she suspected, was more for the benefit of their guests. Releasing her, he turned to the group and introduced himself to both men.

Years of experience must have taught him how to iden-tify the hangers-on, as he expertly avoided the opportunis-tic women.

Thandie was amazed by his finesse. His natural confidence worked its magic over the group. He did not treat the men like celebrities. Instead, he treated them casually, as if they'd known each other for years. They immediately insisted he join them for a drink. Elliot agreed, only if they allowed him to pay for the next round. This offer was warmly accepted, and soon Adam was helping the waitresses deliver several trays of various beers and cocktails.

It struck Thandie how easily Elliot blended into the group. Even in the presence of hunky athletes, he still managed to trump them with his natural charm. He'd effortlessly shifted the group's attention from the celebrities to himself, which seemed to take the pressure off Carey and Nate, putting them more at ease. Soon, the three of them were chuckling amongst themselves like newly found frat brothers. At some point, they'd slipped into speaking in code, a secret guy language that consisted of head nods, random shrugs of the shoulders and half-sentences.

Feeling left out, Thandie excused herself from the table. It was clear they wanted guy time. She wouldn't dream of interfering, but it annoyed her that Elliot had so easily staked claim on her guests. Glancing at her recently vacant seat, she saw Elliot had stretched out, effectively eliminating her spot.

Scowling, Thandie searched out Raja and Len in the crowd. As usual, they were easy to spot. Both were laid across the bar, laughing uproariously, while guys took turns slurping body shots off their bare bellies. Right in the middle of the rowdy crush stood Warren, waiting his turn. Thandie could not quite remember if all these men were a part of the group they were hosting tonight. Even though it wasn't the most tasteful method, the girls were doing their jobs; which was to make the club as entertaining as possible.

Spotting Romero, Elliot's assistant, a few feet away Thandie inclined her head to him. He did the same, then he glanced at the girls. A look of utter disgust passed over his face, seconds before he exited the VIP area. Thandie couldn't blame him. The girls were being outrageous tonight, but Elliot, Nate and Carey were laughing at the spectacle, and Adam gave Thandie a thumbs-up.

When Thandie finally returned to their table, the group became silent, as if her presence meant they had to stop having fun. Taking the awkward silence as his cue, Elliot stood to his full height. Carey and Nate followed his lead, forming massive mountains of flesh on either side of Elliot.

"Going somewhere?" Thandie asked.

Elliot flashed her one of those cocky grins she had labeled as his "I'm in control" expression. "Actually, I'm taking the guys to Matrix's." Before she could ask who or what Matrix was, Elliot pressed his hand against the small of her back and pulled her forward. Leaning close to her ear, he whispered, "One day soon, I'm going to fuck you in those shoes."

She'd been stunned. After the initial surprise wore off, she was too angry to speak. Instead, she'd watched Elliot lead Nate O'Conner and Carey Charming out of the club. Their entourage followed closely behind. Len and Raja made a sad attempt to join the departing group, but Elliot turned on them immediately and shook his head. That froze the girls where they stood. And they, like Thandie, stood planted in place while the group exited the building.

When her senses finally returned, Thandie's face darkened. How dare he steal her guests! They'd barely been there for an hour before Elliot had whisked them away. And his whispered words…damn him. At first, she'd thought it had been part of his seduction, but the more she thought about it, the angrier she became. The words played a continuous loop in her head until she was practically shaking with fury. She now knew why he had whispered those words. He'd meant to shock her. He'd meant for her to be so completely undone she would be too paralyzed to argue. That sneaky bastard!

Her anger must have been evident on her face. Raja and Len rushed toward her with pouty faces, clearly frustrated with Nate and Carey's exit, however, one look at Thandie and they scurried away in the opposite direction. Adam Parr approached her with caution. Calmly, he took the club soda out of her hand and pushed it toward a passing waiter to deal with. Lifting her hands to his chest, he squeezed them lightly.

"I'm afraid I'm going to have to insist you smile for me," he said cheerfully. "Snarling is unbecoming on you, babe."

"What is Matrix?" she asked.

"Matrix Lang?" he asked.

"How the hell am I supposed to know?" she snapped. Taking a deep breath, she offered her apology. "I'm sorry. That wasn't meant for you."

Adam gave another sunny smile. "Not to worry. You're entitled to be upset. Your guests just got hijacked right out from under your nose."

"He said he was taking them Matrix's."

Adam's smile disappeared in a flash. "Be thankful you were not asked to go. That's no place for a lady."

"Says who?"

"Says someone who knows better." He fixed her with a serious look. "I know you're plenty pissed right now, but take my word for it when I say you came out better than you think. Had you been a man, Elliot would have expected you join them."

Again she asked, "Who is Matrix?"

"Matrix Lang is a friend of Elliot's. He owns a string of fitness clubs. He's a bit of a celebrity around here, but he's more popularly known for his house parties. Anything and everything has been known to happen there. Invite only."

"Why would Elliot take them there?"

Adam rolled his eyes when he answered her. "Do you really need me to answer that?"

No, she didn't.

Reading her face, Adam nodded. "I see it's beginning to sink in now. Matrix's parties are a pretty big deal. I take it they were suddenly interested in coming after you told them about our 'no camera' policy."

Thandie hesitated.

"That's what I thought," he said smugly. "Chances are your two football stars aren't supposed to be seen together. They probably asked Elliot where they could party in private." He shrugged. "Matrix's is the perfect place."

"Whatever," she grumbled. "He could have at least told me that."

This made Adam laugh. "Count yourself fortunate he told you as much as he did." Looking over her shoulder, he nodded. "Rex is coming. Are you up to making kissy faces with him, or do you want to have some fun?"

She scrunched her nose at him. "What did you have in mind?"

"You'll have to come with me to find out." Placing his hand over his heart, he said, "No funny business, I promise. Just a little fun amongst friends. Besides, you didn't wear those shoes only to go home early."

"What about the girls?" she asked. "I need to tell them I'm leaving."

"Call them from the car." Taking her hand, he tugged her toward the emergency exit. "Follow me, Alice. I have someplace wonderful to take you."

Pausing only for a second, Thandie allowed Adam to lead the way.

True to his word, Adam had indeed shown her another side of Miami nightlife. He'd taken her to Red Door. Thandie was immediately concerned when the bouncer pulled the entrance door open. The club was decorated completely in hues of red. From the ceiling to the floor, nothing but red...and women. Adam had neglected to remind her Red Door was a lesbian club. Not that it mattered to her, but she would have liked to have been forewarned.

Boasting about the mojitos, Adam offered her a tall, frosted cylinder of green liquid before sipping from his own cocktail. Somewhat suspicious, Thandie drank from her glass slowly. True to his word, it was good. Very good. Before long, she was on her second glass and eager to start her third. Between waiting for refills, she found herself swaying to a techno remix of Madonna's "Deeper and Deeper." She was not exactly sure when she'd stepped onto the dance floor. But none of that mattered now.

She vaguely remembered dancing with Adam. He seemed to be more entertained watching Thandie dance with other women. Their soft hands felt good on her body, making her yearn for more. She was not attracted to women, but it was a wonderful experience to be touched without feeling the pressure to give something back in return. She was soothed by the idea of being surrounded by pretty women. Elliot Richards soon became a blurred memory from the past. She felt as if she was stepping out of her body, as easily as if it were a silken garment. The desperation to put tonight's frustrations behind her was strong. If she had to use alcohol to do it, so be it.

The morning sun touched the Miami sky, painting the heavens in dusky hues of golds and lavender. It was not yet four in the morning.

And as the east coast was waking up, Thandie was preparing for bed. She stepped unsteadily out of the shower, clumsily wrapping a thick towel around her body. Her hair still smelled of smoke, but she was simply too tired to wash it now.

In the end, it had been up to Adam to take her home. When he pulled up to Warren's house, he'd been forced to carry her because she simply could not walk in her shoes. Thandie babbled incoherently into Adam's neck, while he struggled to unlock the front door. He lowered her gently to the floor, laughing when Thandie kicked off the shoes as if her feet were on fire. She listened to him make a bed for himself on Warren's sofa while she bumped her way blindly toward her bedroom.

Now, patting herself dry, Thandie folded the towel over a

chair before climbing into bed naked. She pulled the covers over her shoulders and sighed heavily. The sheets were cool, perfect for dreamless sleep, but as appealing as the idea was, her thoughts were restless. Her mind was racing in a dozen directions, and she was struggling mightily to keep her temper under control.

Tonight was supposed to have been perfect. She'd managed to wrangle two football stars into a club she was marketing. The rest should have been a cakewalk. What she hadn't counted on was…well…Elliot. Thandie pulled the sheets high over her head. For the hundredth time, she asked herself how it was possible for such a good night to go so terribly wrong? The answer was simple. Elliot.

She still could not believe he'd stolen Nate and Carey out from under her. If she'd entertained any notions before that Elliot might make her job bearable, she was wrong. This was a lesson learned. Quietly, she vowed she would not let him grandstand around her again like that. Where Elliot was involved, she would be on her guard both personally and professionally.

Chapter Ten

The first phone call came shortly after ten o'clock in the morning, and the rest soon followed.

The word was out. Everyone was talking about Carey Charming and Nate O'Conner being at Club Babylon. Before leaving the club with Adam last night, Thandie had sent tweets, Facebook updates and emails to her new local contacts, alerting them of Babylon's recent guests. It had taken a few hours before catching on, and now the news had gone viral. Aided by the buzz surrounding Carey and Nate's free agent status, it was still trending on all the top social networks.

Alternating between washing her face and brushing her teeth, Thandie was hard at work distributing the news to any journalist, gossip columnist or TV reporter willing to listen. She repackaged when needed, embellished when necessary, and mentioned the club at every opportunity. Although the evening hadn't gone the way she'd planned, Thandie was still reaping the benefits of securing the appearance.

When there was finally a lull in the phone calls, Thandie finished dressing. By the time she made her way downstairs to check on Adam, she was wide awake. She located him in the kitchen, seated at the breakfast nook with Warren, nursing a cup of coffee. Folding down a corner of his newspaper, Warren grinned at her. "Good morning, kiddo." He nudged his chin toward Adam. "Look what I found asleep on the couch."

Thandie gave him a smile. "How do you feel?"

"Well enough," Adam said sleepily.

"How was the couch?"

"Better than you might think." He dragged a hand through his untidy hair. "I think I was worse off than you. Who would have thought mojitos could be such a kick in the ass?"

Thandie slipped into the breakfast nook, opposite Adam. "Thanks for bringing me back home."

"No problem. You needed to cut loose."

"Will you get into trouble for leaving the club early?" she asked.

"Nah. Thanks to you, my boss didn't notice. I doubt he returned to Babylon last night. Matrix's parties run late into the night."

"Matrix?" Warren dropped his paper. "Matrix had a party last night? Why didn't anybody tell me?"

Adam smirked and then winced at his watch. "Is it already one o'clock?" He grimaced. "I better be going. I have a meeting with Elliot at three."

"You do?" Warren asked, suddenly very interested. "Anything I should know about?"

Adam shook his head. "Club membership business. Not overly exciting stuff."

Just then Raja and Len shuffled into the kitchen. "Hi, Adam," they said in unison.

Adam jumped, startled by their arrival. "Oh—hey, girls."

Having just woken up, Len and Raja still wore the camisoles and cotton shorts they'd worn to bed. It was innocent enough attire, but to a red blooded man like Adam, it was a lot of exposed skin so early in the day. He stared at their bare legs a second too long, before blinking and looking away. Len and Raja grinned to each other. They knew they had him.

"You aren't leaving just yet, are you?" Len asked coquettishly.

"I was just about to make breakfast," Raja added.

Adam stole another look at their legs before shaking his head. "I really need to be going, but thanks for the offer." He gave Thandie and Warren a parting grin. "I'll see you later."

"I'll show you out," Raja offered.

"Me too," Len chirped.

Thandie watched as the girls followed Adam out of the kitchen. Beneath the table, Warren nudged her. "I don't remember them ever offering to cook breakfast for me."

"Count yourself fortunate," Thandie said lazily. "Neither of them can cook."

Warren shook his head sadly. "The pretty ones never can." He shook his newspaper out and began to peruse the page.

Thandie watched him scan the paper. His brows furrowed sharply as he squinted at the words, a look of deep concentration etched on his forehead.

Warren looked up suddenly and caught her studying him. "What?"

"Nothing," she said, quickly averting her stare.

"Do you have big plans tonight?" he asked.

"Rex is taking me to the Yurman party."

"That sounds like fun. You should have a good time."

"What about you?" she asked.

"I have a dinner date."

"Someone special?"

"Very special." He said this in a low voice, as if it were a great confession. Thandie's gaze lifted to meet his. Lines she had never noticed before deepened around his eyes, making his face appear strained and shadowed. Suddenly rising, Warren tucked his newspaper under his arm. "I think I'll go for a swim," he said. Without another word, he left the kitchen. Thandie stared after Warren, wondering what was bothering him. She might have pondered it longer, but her thoughts were distracted when the girls sailed into the room, full of breathy giggles.

"He is so cute," Len sighed.

"Who?" Thandie asked.

"Adam," she said dreamily.

"Oh," Thandie said, having momentarily forgotten all about Adam.

"What was Adam doing here this morning?" Raja asked, a hint of accusation in her voice.

"He slept on the couch," Thandie said. "I hope you girls are ready to work. We have a lot to do today." Thandie poured herself a cup of coffee, and carried it into the dining area. The room was exactly how they'd left it, cluttered with papers.

"Let's talk about Adam some more," Len volunteered, having followed after her.

"Let's not, and say we did," Thandie quipped. She was saved from having to say more when her phone began vibrating. Pulling it out of her jeans, she checked the display. It was none other than Jarvis Taylor.

Thandie had worked with him in the past, hosting album release parties for his artists. Jarvis was an AR director who'd been credited with coproducing some of the top albums currently on the *Billboard* Top 10 list. This was an oddity because Jarvis could not play a single musical instrument, yet he was the biggest shaker in the music business since Clive. Because of his reclusive nature, many people had never laid eyes on him and certainly wouldn't recognize him in a lineup. Meeting him in person was rare. Speaking to him on the phone was an impossibility. Jarvis rarely, if ever, called anyone directly. He normally delegated such tasks to his assistant-slash-girlfriend.

Thandie was apprehensive about the call because it could only mean one of two things: Jarvis was either pissed off about something or he needed something. Thandie wasn't kept in suspense long. Being the businessman he was, he got right to the point.

Jarvis was representing a Spanish artist who would be traveling to Miami at the end of the week. With her first English-speaking album scheduled for release this summer, Jarvis needed to generate buzz for his artist.

"I need her in VIP," Jarvis said.

"Of course," Thandie agreed. "Who's the artist?"

"Samara."

Thandie had to search her mind. Samara wasn't a huge star in North America. If her memory served her right, Samara was better known for her modeling than her singing. And then a thought snagged—something Raja had said. Finally it clicked. Samara was the opening act for Shay Thomas. When Jarvis confirmed her suspicions with a curt yes, Thandie figured Jarvis would not be willing to contact Shay Thomas's people for her.

As soon as she hung up, she relayed her conversation to the girls. Raja and Len found little interest in escorting Samara to Babylon, but when Thandie asked them to contact Shay's publicists and extend a duel invite, their attitudes changed.

With the girls preoccupied making arrangements for Samara, Thandie was free to work on securing entertainers for the club.

There were several deals in the works, but nothing yet confirmed. So far, negotiations with Nikki Minaj's reps were proving more complicated than expected. If Thandie somehow couldn't manage to lock-in the appearance, she hoped this wasn't a chilling forecast of things to come.

Securing girl band Sugar & Spice would be a major accomplishment, however the possibility looked bleaker with each passing day. On the positive side, she was close to acquiring Will.i.am for a guest DJ spot, but was still deliberating dates with his manager.

Discussions with the agents for Pitbull and Ciara were coming along nicely, however proposed prices were more than Thandie had budgeted for. She had to consider secondary, and more cost effective, options.

Reaching out to her affiliates in New York, Thandie obtained contact information for The Freshman, the teenage DJ who'd performed at Phenomenon. Also as a backup, she'd put in a call to Celeste, the manager of The Pussy Cats, an exotic dance troupe.

She was momentarily distracted when Warren entered the room. He was dressed in a suit, and had taken obvious pains to style his hair. He fiddled with his tie nervously.

Thandie meant to ask if everything was all right, but never got the chance. Warren gave a mock salute, before shouting his farewells and heading out.

Checking the time, Thandie decided to call it quits. She'd put in more than enough work hours today. Besides, she had a few things she wanted to do before Rex arrived to pick her up. She was looking forward to their evening with anticipation and anxiety. She was unclear whether she wished to pursue anything with Rex or was simply curious about his motives. A voice inside her head warned her it was not good to become involved with a peer, but in the aftermath of her encounter with Elliot in the Tower, she was in desperate need of a distraction.

Leaving the girls to update online message boards, Thandie

retreated to her room. After searching through her suitcase, she could not decide on anything suitable for the Yurman party. She didn't want to lead Rex on by wearing something too revealing, yet she didn't want to look like a nun. She compromised by deciding to buy a new outfit, hopefully something on sale. It would be good to get away from the girls for a little while.

Dressed for comfort in a tank top, jeans and her favorite Kors sandals, Thandie slipped out of the house. Deciding to leave the car behind, just in case the girls needed to run errands, Thandie called for a taxi to pick her up. Tucked in the backseat of the cab, she watched the streets of Miami sweep by in flashes of color. She liked being alone. She needed the silence.

Thandie was dropped off at Merrick Park, an upscale shopping center in Coral Gables. She took her time roaming the boutiques, satisfied to simply stroll the walkways, drifting in and out of designer shops as she went. From Benetton to Burberry, Gucci to Furstenberg, Thandie figured she'd burned two hours and shamelessly spent seven hundred dollars on new clothes. She might have regretted her purchases had they not all fit so perfectly. This was yet another reason to earn her pay at Babylon.

Shopping was serious business, and she soon grew hungry. Locating a small café, Thandie decided to stop for quick bite to eat. While she waited for her order, she decided to call her assistant in New York. This turned out to be a mistake. Amanda was compelled to detail every difficulty she'd experienced since Thandie's departure from the city. By the time she managed to get Amanda off the phone, she'd lost all her enthusiasm for shopping.

Grabbing her shopping bags, Thandie prepared to leave. This proved to be a confusing task. She'd roamed about the mall for so long, it was difficult to retrace her steps. Deciding she could flag down a taxi from any entrance, she made her way to the nearest exit. Stepping outside, she found there were no taxis in sight. Looking down the street, she could see a busier corner. Although her bags had noticeably become heavier, it was a short walk ahead of her. Besides, there were more storefronts along the way.

Once she was on the main street, she stepped toward the curb and waved for a cab. The traffic was unusually brisk, causing the first taxi to reluctantly pass her up. Frustrated, she dropped her hand and looked down the street. There were no parked cabs available. Pushing her sunglasses on top of her head, she searched for the next cab.

She turned to check her image in the window of a trendy bar. And then she did a double take. Her eyes fluttered up, looking through her mirrored reflection toward the bar where a slumped-over figure sat. He did not seem to have made up his mind if he wanted to sit or stand, so he leaned dangerously against a barstool. Just then, a taxi pulled up to the curb and honked to get Thandie's attention.

She waved the driver away and entered the bar. She approached the man slowly, noticing the bottle of bourbon he was nursing. Placing her shopping bags on the floor, she occupied the seat next next to him. He didn't even notice.

"Is this seat taken?" she asked

"Not if you're a pretty lady." Without even looking at her, he smiled into his glass. "You can take just about anything you want if you're younger than thirty." He finished off his drink before pouring another serving. She could not help but notice his hand shook as he did so. From the smell of him, this wasn't his first glass.

Thandie placed her hand on his back. "How long have you been here?"

Warren Radcliffe gave a weak smile. "Not long." He looked at his watch and then frowned. "I got here around three."

"Shit, Warren. That was nearly four hours ago. What are you doing here?"

"I had dinner plans with my kid."

"Your kid?" she asked, confused.

"My son." His voice caught on the word, and he quickly cast down his gaze.

Thandie looked around. "Where is he?"

He shook his head. "Not here."

"What happened?"

"He blew me off." He took a sip from his glass. "Said he had other, more important, plans. He wasn't here for more than five minutes before he left."

She pointed to the bottle before him. "So you decided to have a pity party instead?"

Warren's white head perked up. "Something like that." He lifted the liquor bottle. "Care to join me?"

"No, thanks." She glanced at the wall clock. "Don't you think it's a little early to start drinking?" It wasn't until she leaned closer to him that she actually got a good look at him. His normally worry-free spirit was gone. He was visibly tired and, more shocking, he looked his age. She couldn't hide her concern.

Warren waved his hand. "Don't worry about me, kiddo. What have you been up today?"

"Do you want to talk about it?"

"No," he said quickly.

"Warren," she said in a warning tone.

"All right," he said, heaving a tiring sigh. "I'm just a little worn down. This stuff with my family is complicated." He gave a humorless laugh. "If I wasn't sure before now how they felt about me, now I know."

"And?"

"They hate me."

She could see it pained him to say the words. What was worse, he believed them. "It can't be that bad."

He turned to look her straight in the eyes. His face was serious, his eyes misty. "My son told me the only thing I was good for was my money, and now they don't even need that."

She gasped. "He didn't."

"Yes, he did." He gave a shrug of defeat. "And he's right."

"Don't talk like that." She moved closer to him. Placing her hand over his, she squeezed it. "Maybe he was just upset today."

"He's upset with me every day."

"He couldn't have meant what he said."

Warren shook his head. "Thandie, you should have seen him when he delivered the words. He was so damn calm. It was as if he was looking right through me. And I sat here and took it because he's right."

"Don't say that," she whispered.

"No, kiddo, he's right. I was a real asshole to his mother. She—" He broke off to take a long sip from his glass. "She tried to call me when she was pregnant. Said she'd had a hard time tracking me down in New York and begged me to come back to Florida to at least see my kid be born."

Thandie was scared to ask her next question. "What did you do?"

He took a longer sip from the tumbler. "I sent her money."

There was an awkward silence. She wasn't sure how she should respond. Warren was the sweetest, most thoughtful person she knew. It was hard to believe he could have done such a thing.

"I can feel your disapproval," he said.

"Warren, I would never judge you."

"Well, you should. I was awful to her. At the time, my career was skyrocketing. We were on the brink of acquiring one of Anderson's press operations. King Corporations was in our corner. Things were moving at the speed of light. The last thing I needed to worry about was a casual fling calling me about a kid." He sighed. "I sent her the money for her to deal with it. Whatever she wanted to do, she would have enough cash to do it."

"You wanted her to get rid of the baby?"

He stared down at his drink. "Honestly, I didn't care one way or the other," he said in a rough whisper. "I wanted her to make the decision. I couldn't raise a kid. I was traveling so much, I barely had enough time to see my fiancée.

"Needless to say, I didn't hear from her again once she received the money. She just vanished, and I was relieved." He waved his hand wistfully in the air. "I thought the ordeal was over. I got married to this socialite, Wife Number Two." He paused for minute. "Then, I had my skiing accident. It fucked up my leg and some other stuff. It was a nightmare. I was recuperating for six months. Wife Number Two was so shaken by the accident, she got it into her head we had to have kids. She was on a warpath. Every time we were alone, she practically tried to rape me. " He shook his head. "If I weren't such a coward, I would have told her it wasn't any use."

Thandie licked her lips nervously. "The accident," she said slowly, "the 'other stuff' you mentioned. Was it—"

"Yes." Warren emptied his glass and poured another. "Life is fucking funny, huh?"

"You told your wife eventually, right?"

He sniffed. "I think she figured it out on her own. She divorced me shortly afterward."

"Oh, Warren. I'm so sorry."

"Serves me right, kiddo." Without asking, he grabbed an empty tumbler and poured her a drink. "The strange thing was, five years later, I got a call from some private school in Florida, asking me to verify my household income."

Thandie furrowed her brows. "I don't understand."

"Neither did I. Apparently, the woman I'd knocked up a few years back kept the baby. She was requesting financial aid from some government agency to get her kid into a private school." He smiled to himself. "It was as if I had a second chance to make things right. For the first time, I knew the name of my kid. It was the sweetest thing a father could hear. I paid for the tuition in full, anonymously of course. I continued to support them from a distance. That was the happiest time of my life.

"I finally contacted the mother. She was bitter toward me, but to my relief, she didn't hate me. She told me things about my kid, stuff every father should already know. Commonsense stuff like his grades in school, which subjects he excelled in, his favorite color." His voice trailed off. "A good father knows that kind of stuff."

Thandie patted his hand. "Do you even remember those details?"

Warren held up his hand and began ticking off points. "Straight A's without even trying. He loved math. He had a head for numbers. His favorite color is white. Can you believe that? White. Most kids like blue or green. Something with spunk. But not my son. He liked white." Suddenly, he slammed his fist on bar, making Thandie jump. "I would have done anything to see him. Just to know who he was."

"Why didn't you?"

"He refused to see me." His voice cracked when he said this. "Can you believe that? He was seven years old, and he refused to see his father. That was years ago, and that little shit still hates me."

Thandie wasn't sure what to say and feared any further discussions would only agitate him. He was drunk and depressed. Not a good combination.

"Warren, I'm taking you home."

"Whatever," he mumbled.

"How did you get here?"

"I drove."

"Where are your car keys?"

"Frank has them."

"Who is Frank?"

He pointed an accusing finger at the bartender. "We made a deal. I gave him my ticket, in order to buy the bottle."

His words had begun to slur, and she feared he would be sick before long. Thandie waved the bartender over, thanked him for watching her friend and asked for help getting Warren to his car.

Luckily, Warren had valet parked. After pushing him none too gently into the car, she threw her bags in the backseat, paid the valet and sped off toward Warren's house. She called ahead to alert Anga of Warren's condition.

When they arrived, Anga was eager to help Thandie half-carry, half-drag Warren to his room. Secure in the knowledge the older woman could handle things from there, Thandie left.

She stood outside his bedroom door for a few seconds. She'd just seen Warren at his most vulnerable, and it saddened her. In all the years she'd known him, she'd not once seen him subdued. He'd always been a ball of energy. It was unsettling to see him so hurt.

Thandie retreated to her bedroom. She took note of the time and began changing for her outing with Rex. However, her heart wasn't in it. She had half a mind to call Rex and beg off their date. Warren was her friend, and being at his side was much more important than attending a party.

She dressed quickly and returned to Warren's room. She knocked softly before entering. Anga had managed to discard Warren's shirt and coax him under his bedsheet, but she'd been unsuccessful in prying the bottle of bourbon out of his hands.

"Warren, I'm worried about you," Thandie said.

"You shouldn't be," he mumbled. "I'm right as rain now."

"You're drunk off your ass," she argued.

"I like to think they're one and the same."

She grudgingly laughed.

Anga reentered the room. *"Señorita* Thandie, you have a visitor."

Thandie glanced at a nearby clock and was surprised to see Rex was right on time. She'd hoped to have a few more minutes with Warren. She gave an apologetic smile. "I'll send him away," she told him. "We can reschedule."

"Nonsense." He gave a weak smile. "You should go."

"Warren, I wouldn't feel comfortable leaving you like this."

"I'm not alone. I have Anga."

Unsatisfied, she frowned. "I'm going to tell Rex I can't go."

"Kiddo, I'm grateful for your concern, but it's not necessary. I'll be fine. Besides, you clearly have an obligation. You need to go."

"It's not that important, Warren. I can stay here and hang out with you. We could watch a movie."

He looked her over. Surveying the fitted black cocktail dress, he nodded. "You look good, kiddo."

"Thank you."

"If I had a date with a woman as pretty as you, I would not be happy to learn she blew me off to sit with a drunk old man." He waved her away. "Go. Get out of here. Enjoy yourself tonight."

She eyed the bottle in his hand.

Warren noticed the look. "Fear not. I'm done. In fact, I'm retiring for the night. Are you happy now?"

"Immensely. Now give me the bottle."

"Fine." He handed it to her. "Now go."

She smiled and kissed him on the cheek. "You're one of the best men I know. You're not perfect, but you try to be and that's all that matters."

"Thanks, kiddo."

She glanced at the door. "Will you be okay without me?"

He waved his hand again. "Go. I promise I won't get into any trouble."

"Remember you promised."

He gave a weak smile.

She wagged her finger at him. "Be good," she said, leaving the room, and going downstairs. Placing the bottle of bourbon on the kitchen counter, she headed to the front of the house to greet Rex.

When she entered the living room, he was sitting patiently flipping through a photography book. He looked up and smiled. "Wow, Thandie, you look spectacular."

She blushed. "I like those kinds of compliments."

"Good," he grinned. "There are plenty more where that came from."

She gave a weak smile. Again, she asked herself was this a business dinner or was this a date? As if reading her mind, Rex clarified his position by coming to his feet, pulling her into his arms and kissing her lightly on the lips. It had been so smoothly executed, her mind went fuzzy in the aftermath.

Holding her lightly to him, he smiled down into her face. His confidence wavered. "Is something wrong?"

"Warren," she admitted. "He's had a rough day. I'm concerned about him."

"Is he all right?" Rex asked.

She nodded. "Nothing a good night's rest can't solve."

"Should you stay and care for him?"

Thandie hesitated, and then nodded her head. "Anga is here to help. I'm sure she's far more skilled at something like this than I am, but I need to stay here with him. Warren is my friend." She gave a small shrug. "I wouldn't feel right leaving him right now...not the way he is."

"I'm sorry to hear that," Rex said with a sigh. "I was looking forward to our evening together."

"Me too," she confessed.

"However, I understand your concern," he said. "Warren is a friend of mine too. His health is important."

Thandie nodded, still wrapped in his arms. "Can I take a rain check?"

Rex's chest rumbled with a low laugh. "Yes, you may have a rain check, Thandie." He paused as he thought for a moment. "I'm not working next Monday. Do you think we can try to do this again?"

She smiled. "I'd like that."

He nodded agreeably, but there was disappointment in his face. "I'll see you tomorrow?"

She nodded.

Rex responded with a shy smile. Hand in hand, Thandie led him to the front door. Before leaving, he kissed her lightly on the cheek. She waved good-night, before closing the door.

Then she headed to Warren's room. The door was open, and lamplight spilled into the hallway. The sound of snoring could be heard as she approached.

Thandie peeked inside. Just as he'd promised, Warren was right where she'd left him. A chair had been pulled up to the bedside, a thin blanket carelessly tossed over the back. She guessed this was where Anga had stationed herself to watch over Warren. Thandie tiptoed to the bedside, and settled herself in the empty chair. Warren did not stir. Tucking her feet beneath her, Thandie watched his sleeping form. His breathing was heavy, but steady. He looked as fragile as a sleeping child, and she felt protective of him.

Though she knew he didn't deserve it, she felt a trace of animosity toward his son. If he'd known what his rejection had done to Warren, would he feel compassion? She would never know. One thing was certain, it had been heartbreaking listening to Warren's story earlier. She hoped things would improve. She knew from experience how hard it was to lose a parent. She wouldn't wish that pain on anyone.

Thandie pulled the blanket over her shoulders. It was still warm. Closing her eyes, she tried to forget Warren's past, forget the look on his broken face, forget the sound of his tortured voice, and forget the tear she'd seen escape his eyes before he could wipe it away. She wanted to forget it all.

Tomorrow, she thought, tomorrow will be better for Warren. It must be.

Chapter Eleven

Thandie woke sometime in the middle of the night.

Stretching her stiff muscles, she peered at Warren. He was still sleeping soundly. He was fine, so she returned to her own room.

She was too tired to check the time, or worry if the girls had returned safely. The lack of sleep from the previous night had finally caught up with her, and she was dead on her feet. She managed just enough strength to wash her face and toss her dress over a chair before she slipped into bed. She was asleep before her head touched the pillow.

The next morning was normal. Thandie came downstairs looking for Warren, expecting to find him still in bed, severely hung over. To her surprise he was seated at the breakfast nook reading his newspaper. Len and Raja had joined him, both prattled relentlessly about what had happened at Babylon last night. Meanwhile, Thandie studied Warren carefully. He seemed strangely fine. Better than fine. He was cheerful, flirtatious and youthful. It was as if yesterday had never happened.

Pouring herself a bowl of cereal, Thandie sat at the table

mutely. Even Anga, who was wiping down the kitchen countertop, seemed to be going about her day as usual.

Thandie ate her breakfast silently, vowing to corner Warren as soon as the girls were out of earshot. She had to know what was going on.

As it turned out, Thandie never got an opportunity to talk with Warren about his son. Every time she approached the topic, Warren would change the subject. Eventually she got the point, and stopped trying.

The Shay Thomas tour had finally arrived in Miami, and the city was alight with excitement. Tour buses had rolled into town two days before. Every radio DJ was talking about his concert, and their phone lines were flooded with sightings of the famous performer. People were willing to do just about anything to get tickets to the sold-out show. Scalpers were placing a street price of five hundred dollars, and supposedly the price was climbing.

Thandie was disappointed that they'd been unsuccessful in getting Shay's contacts to respond to their invitation to Babylon.

The night of the concert, the streets of South Beach were thick with tourists, partygoers and professional groupies. Thandie dressed for comfort. She rationalized since she was escorting a woman, there was really no need to dress provocatively. She settled for a simple white dress. It hugged her hips and fell just above her knees. It was form-fitting, but showed little skin. Sweeping her hair into a simple bun at the nape of her neck, she completed the look with a pair of chandelier earrings. Satisfied, she was ready for work.

Thandie sent Raja and Len with the drivers to collect Samara and her group from the concert hall. Traffic would be heavy tonight, so it was better to have them waiting for Samara rather than the other way around. She was feeling pretty good. She might not be hosting Shay Thomas, but she was doing the next best thing. She was escorting his opening act, Samara.

Thandie planned to be at the club before the girls arrived with the singer. Since they would be occupied with their guest, it was Thandie's job to spread the word. Once Samara was close enough, Thandie would call the local radio stations and leak the news of Samara's location. This worked well on a concert night. The artists were still full of energy and often needed to work off the adrenaline.

Thandie arrived at Babylon earlier than normal. As usual, a line was beginning to form outside the club. Tiny waved her through the crowd and held the door open for her.

"Thanks, Tiny."

He nodded.

"Is Elliot in his office?" she asked, needing to know the location of the enemy.

"He's not here."

"What?" she said with disbelief. "Where is he?"

Tiny shrugged his massive shoulders. "Don't know. I haven't seen him all day."

This was odd. Elliot was always at the club before she arrived. She'd been counting on it tonight. She'd hoped to use his office to make her phone calls.

Thandie entered the club, waved to the hostess and crossed the crowded dance floor, looking for a staff member. She spotted Markie immediately. He greeted her with a nod.

"Have you seen Elliot?" she asked.

He shook his head. "He's not in yet. He won't be here until later night." At her shocked look, he added. "He's bringing a guest."

She wanted to ask him who, but wasn't sure if she really wanted to know. If Elliot appeared with a car full of Playboy

Bunnies in tow, on loan from Hugh Hefner himself, she'd rather be unenlightened.

"I need to make some phone calls before the girls get here," she said. "Is there a quiet place around here?"

Markie nodded. "My office is behind the bar." He led her to a door just off the main bar. The door was painted black and blended perfectly with the wall. You would have to know it was there in order to open it.

They entered the office. It was small but neat, every inch designed to be used for files, shelving, media, etc. There was a large one-way window that looked over the bar. From here, Markie would be able to see every drink transaction. She quickly noticed there were several cameras positioned at various angles to record everything.

When Markie closed the door behind him, it was impossible to hear anything from the arena floor. Thandie arched her brow at him. "Let me guess," she said. "Soundproof?"

"Of course." He nodded to the phone on his desk. "Dial nine for an outside line. If you need me for anything, press two. That goes straight to my headset."

"Got it. Thanks, Markie."

He nodded and left the room.

Thandie called Raja for an update. Raja answered on the first call. She informed her they were a few blocks away, but were stuck in traffic. Samara had a group of three people accompanying her. Thandie asked a few more questions before ending the call. She then began dialing her contacts at two local radio stations. They promised not to make the announcement for the next thirty minutes. She then pressed two and was immediately speaking to Markie. She informed him of Samara's arrival time, and asked for him to notify security.

When she was done, she left Markie's office and went in search of Adam. Surveying the club, she noticed tonight had a gothic theme. The dancers were wearing black leather and waving fringed whips. The acrobats had not begun their show, but she could see they were beginning to harness themselves in.

Thandie climbed up the steps that led to the first VIP level. She saw Adam in the far corner, shaking hands with someone distantly familiar. Seeing her, Adam waved her over.

"Where are the girls?" he asked.

"On their way. They have a guest." She filled him in on the details.

Adam listened carefully and was soon speaking rapidly into his headset, alerting the waitstaff. "By the way," he said while half-heartedly listening to Markie bark commands into his ear. "I'm not sure how you did it, but Tiny says the line outside is wrapped around the corner. Markie has increased security."

"What about the girls?" she asked. "Will they have any problems getting in?"

"They shouldn't," he answered. "Their car just pulled up."

From this level, Thandie had a great view of the entrance. She turned just in time to see Len and Raja enter the arena. Turning back to Adam she asked, "Are you ready?"

He held up his hands, as if saying, "I'm always ready."

Thandie smirked. Adam had proven himself more than competent. In the short time she'd known him, she could honestly say he was the best VIP manager she'd worked with.

Then her attention was snagged by Tiny's wide form parting the crowd on the arena dance floor. Thandie focused on the group following in his wake. Raja and Len were easily noticeable. Tall, statuesque and very confident. Latin singer Samara, however, could have gone completely unnoticed standing next to Len and Raja. She was considerably shorter and curvier than her escorts. The soon-to-be-famous Samara wore a Red Sox baseball cap, tank top and ripped jeans. It was fashionable enough when paired with her long hair extensions and a dozen bangles hanging from each wrist, but it wasn't glamorous. Samara's lack of presence caused onlookers to stare at Raja and Len. Curious dancers craned their necks to get a better look. They could not identify who they were, but were determined to guess. Certain Len and Raja were the real celebrities, the two of them attracted the bulk of attention.

Upon entering the VIP area, Samara looked smaller than before, her clothing baggier. Her bushy hair, which Thandie was sure looked great on a concert stage, was too big for her body.

In spite of her presentation misstep, Thandie knew she was looking at a future star. Jarvis saw something in her that was worth cultivating, and everyone knew Jarvis Taylor had yet to associate himself with a failed project.

Not exactly comfortable with her new stardom, Samara seemed unsure of her surroundings, as if they would suddenly be cast out of VIP at any moment. Determined to make their guest feel welcome, Thandie greeted the singer like an old friend. "Samara, I'm so glad you're finally here. How was the show?"

Samara nodded. "Cool enough. Of course, everyone comes to see Shay. But Jarvis says it's good for my career."

The ball cap was pulled low over her eyes, making them impossible to see. Thandie guessed that if she could see them, there would be a lot of uncertainty swimming in those brown pools.

Thandie gave her a reassuring smile. "Well, you've worked hard and now it's time to play." Taking Samara's hand, Thandie led her to the reserved booth Adam had selected earlier that evening. "We're going to take care of you tonight." Raja and Len flanked her sides. "But first, let's have a drink."

As if on cue, Adam appeared with a waitress in tow. A bottle of chilled champagne and flutes. This went over well with Samara's entourage. Assured he had impressed her group, in one showy motion, Adam poured a glass and presented it to Samara with a wink. This act of mild flirtation made everyone in their party laugh. Everyone except Len who, for reasons Thandie did not understand, grimaced.

As the conversation became livelier, Samara began to loosen up. Half an hour later, the girls were finally able to coax Samara onto the dance floor. Confident their guests were in good hands, Thandie stepped away from the group to check her phone. Jarvis had called her twice. Unable to make a phone call with the noise around her, she escaped to Markie's office. She tried to reach Jarvis, but the call rolled right into his message center.

Thandie returned to the VIP area. It was becoming increasingly congested. Craning her neck, she caught sight of Adam through the crowd. She moved to him. "Is everything all right?" she asked.

"Better than that," he said. "We're doing pretty well for a Sunday night."

Thandie nodded and checked her phone again. She did not want to miss Jarvis's call if he tried her back. She assumed he was calling to check on Samara, but why now? And why twice? He knew it would be nearly impossible for her to hear in the club.

"I'll be damned," Adam whispered.

"Hmm." Thandie was in the middle of sending Jarvis a quick text message. Suddenly, there was a loud gasp from the crowd, before the sound of cheers and whistles erupted. Curious, Thandie looked up. "What's going on?"

Adam pierced his lip, staring intently at something across the arena floor. "I believe our little celebrity just got eclipsed by another star."

She frowned at his words. "What star?"

"That star."

Thandie followed his gaze across the room. To her astonishment, a large group of men were crossing the arena floor. Babylon bouncers and several beefy men she'd never seen before ensured the group had a wide berth. In front of the marching army was Markie, who herded them toward the VIP level. Romero followed closely behind. Stationed in the center of the group were two unmistakable faces. Elliot Richards was talking earnestly with singer Shay Thomas.

The sight of the two of them being so friendly made Thandie momentarily speechless. Was this where Elliot had been all night? Had he been at the concert? If so, why hadn't he told her he knew Shay Thomas? Bringing such a big celebrity to the club demanded planning and security.

Their entourage arrived on the second level. The temperature seemed to heat up the moment Elliot entered the VIP area. He was wearing a gray suit tonight, with a black satin shirt. The shiny material of his shirt seemed to match the glossy tresses of his hair. She found it impossible to tear her eyes away from him. Even standing next to the handsome superstar Shay Thomas, who set a new standard for the term "bling-bling", Elliot more than held his own.

Adam welcomed the group into the VIP area by guiding them to corner sofas, the best seats in the house. Their booth was large and excellently positioned to be easily seen by the crowd below and the many terraces hovering over the arena floor.

Shay and Elliot took their seats and began ordering drinks. The two men talked and laughed together like old friends. They might not have been true friends, but one thing was evident: they had known each other long before tonight.

Cutting her way through the crowd, Thandie made a direct

path toward the large group. Shay, whom she'd met briefly a few times before, noticed her.

He stood to hug her. "Hey, girl, how are you?"

"I'm great, Shay. I heard the concert was amazing."

"We can only hope so."

Thandie turned to Elliot. She gave him a tight smile. "Elliot," she said, acknowledging him but refusing to say anything else.

In response, Elliot stood and gave her a brief kiss on the cheek. He said nothing, but allowed his eyes to slowly sweep her body. This was purposely done. He knew she would not make her anger visible in front of Shay. To prove his point, he winked at her before reclaiming his seat.

Returning her attention to Shay, Thandie was able to get a few words out before they were interrupted. As if conjured by magic, Raja and Len appeared at her elbow. Thandie introduced them to their idol. Raja played it cool, but Len practically implied she would do anything for him. Shay gave them a mild smile before turning back to his entourage.

Elliot was clearly amused. Romero gave a heavy sigh, not caring to mask his annoyance with Raja and Len. Not to be ignored, the girls hovered close to Shay's group, inserting themselves into the fray. Shay didn't outright ignore them, but he didn't exactly welcome their presence. He did this not with the same grace Elliot always managed, but he got his message across. He might be a free agent, but he wasn't interested.

Satisfied the girls would keep a close eye on Shay, Thandie searched for Samara. The Latin singer was quietly sipping a club soda when Thandie found her. Her eyes lit up when Thandie sat down next to her.

Since the girls were occupied, it was now her responsibility to keep their guest entertained. It took a great deal of effort to ignore Elliot and Shay. Everyone seemed to be interested in their group. Beautiful women were circling around their table like predatory sharks. The prettier amongst them were invited to sit at their booth. Raja and Len sat on opposite sides of Shay, while two unknown women pressed themselves close to Elliot.

Frustrated with everyone residing on that side of the room, Thandie forced herself to focus on the task at hand, which was to ensure Samara enjoyed herself. It was irksome having her guest upstaged by Elliot's superstar.

Finally, she got Len and Raja's attention and motioned them over to keep Samara entertained.

Thandie then started communicating with every gossip columnist and local journalist she could manage. Through a series of text messages, emails and online message boards, she made sure everyone knew Club Babylon was the party to be at tonight. For safety reasons, she'd withheld mentioning Shay Thomas's name. Thandie planned to broadcast this news at the most opportune moment.

It came time when Elliot normally made his rounds to mingle with the club guests. Like clockwork, Thandie saw him rise and shake Shay Thomas's hand before leaving the VIP area. She couldn't resist watching him step onto the arena floor below and ease into the mass of dancing people. He quickly became a magnet for attention. People sought him out, encircled him, embraced him; as if he were some majestic being. Thandie huffed. With everyone always treating him like God's gift to women, it's no wonder he was so arrogant. Thandie turned away, no longer interested in the Elliot Richards show. She had more messages to send.

About an hour later, Thandie was admittedly tired. The women were becoming aggressive in their efforts to meet Shay, and he did little to deter their affections. Shay enjoyed dancing, and for the most part, people gave him plenty of room to do so. With hours of professional choreography under his belt, no one was eager to dance too closely. Needless to say, he was entertaining to watch.

Samara wasn't as thrilling. Len and Raja made attempts to lure her onto the dance floor, but she was reluctant. She swayed in placed halfheartedly, and showed little interest in doing much else. When Shay pulled Samara next to him and began dancing with her, she actually managed to smile. They danced to the cheers of the crowd. The DJ was accommodating, playing one of Shay's songs followed by Samara's. The dancers moved in unison.

Tonight would have been a perfect time for Elliot to reconsider his "no camera" rule. Thandie could have kicked herself for not pressing him harder on the issue. Pictures of Shay and Samara dancing together would have been priceless.

Eventually, Shay was ready to move on to the next club. He said his goodbyes to the room at large and made a noticeable exit. Thandie knew it had taken a great deal of self-control for Len and Raja not to push Samara into the nearest corner and take off running after Shay Thomas's motorcade. When they found out Samara was staying at the same hotel as Shay—right down the hall, to be exact—they immediately considered her their new BFF.

Having weaved his way around a clutch of dancers, Adam came up on Thandie's left, and whispered loud enough to be heard over the music, "Whatever you're doing is working." At her puzzled expression, he added, "Everyone in the city seems to know Shay Thomas is here. The reporters are out in full force. Ed wants to call the police to direct traffic."

"That's not such a bad idea," Thandie said, keeping a leery eye on the girls as she spoke.

"I noticed you didn't take credit for the crowd," he teased.

"I didn't realize I had to."

Adam laughed.

Predictably, Raja and Len soon cornered Thandie to ask if they could take the car. With exaggerated sincerity, they explained how fond they were of Samara and, being the good friends they were, desired to show her more of Miami. According to them, Babylon was too much for her. She needed to go somewhere more intimate. Adam, who'd overheard the entire tale, offered to call his friend at Opium Garden.

The idea of leaving Samara alone with Len and Raja made her nervous. She consented with reluctance.

"Okay, you can go. But—"

"Don't get into trouble," Raja finished for her.

"Right," Thandie nodded, "And—"

"Don't drink and drive," Len supplied.

Thandie frowned. Was she really that predictable? "Well, for heaven's sake—"

"Don't get caught doing anything illegal," both girls chorused in a parody of her voice.

Unsettled, Thandie presented the keys to the Expedition. Adam offered to take her home, but she was in no mood to hang around the club until eight in the morning, waiting for Adam to get off work. She'd happily take a taxi back to Warren's home.

When there was nothing left to see, Thandie said her goodbyes, warned the girls to behave and descended from the VIP level.

Miami weather was a strange thing, Thandie thought as she stepped outside. It felt the same as it did ten hours before, when the sun shone bright and fat white clouds dotted the sky. There was a slight breeze, but it wasn't cold. The many lights that lit South Beach made it appear as if it were still daytime. She could truly understand why Warren enjoyed it so much down here.

Apparently, her thoughts had jinxed the moment, for it was at that very second she felt the first drop of rain fall on her shoulder. The reaction was quick. The sparse few droplets instantly began a shower of fine white tears. Thandie screeched. She could hail a cab under any weather conditions, but rain created a problem. Competition for a taxi increased considerably. Looking up the street, she saw several cabs flying in both directions. She would have to move decisively.

Thandie stepped toward the curb and lifted her arm to gain the attention of the next passing taxi, but she was brought up short when a hand took an iron hold on her upper arm

"What are you doing?" he snapped.

At the sight of Elliot, Thandie groaned. Annoyed he kept appearing unexpectedly, she rolled her eyes. "I'm going home."

"Where's your car?"

"I loaned it to the girls." She pulled out of his hold. "Good night." She hoped she had put an end to the conversation, but found she was wrong.

"I'll take you home," he said determinedly.

Desperate to get away from him, Thandie shook her head. "I can hail a cab."

"No, I'm taking you home."

"No, you aren't," she insisted.

"You're arguing with me in the rain?"

Suddenly she realized that the downpour was drenching them both. His dark suit was being pelted with raindrops. His neatly combed hair fell in dark, loose locks about his temples, giving him a devastatingly sexy look. "Yes," she said in a stronger voice. "I'm arguing with you in the rain."

Elliot gave her an incredulous look. "You're going to take a cab in a strange city, rather than allow me to drive you home?"

"Yes," Thandie said. Spotting an available taxi, she skipped hurriedly over to the vehicle and pried the door open. To her horror, she was once again yanked by the arm, and the cab door was slammed closed. "What the hell?" she sputtered.

"I'm taking you home." As if on cue, Elliot's car slid up to the curb, stopping just feet from them. Michelle got out of the driver's side and jogged over to Elliot, holding an umbrella over him.

Looking between the two men, Thandie shook her head. "I'm a big girl. I can take care of myself."

"Thandie," he said in a warning tone, "get in the damn car."

Not waiting for her reply, he took the umbrella from Michelle and held it above her. All but pulling her to his car, he roughly helped her into the passenger seat of his Range Rover and walked to the other side to claim the driver's seat.

Elliot locked the car doors. "Just so you don't get any bright ideas."

Reaching around her, he fastened her seatbelt before adjusting his own. Dragging his fingers through his hair, he cleared his vision from wet wayward tendrils. Winking at her, he pulled into South Beach traffic, flicking on the radio in the same motion.

Thandie was surprised to hear soft jazz fill the car's interior. It was a far departure from the heavy hip-hop beats often played in his club. Grudgingly, she had to admit this style suited him well.

To avoid staring at him, Thandie turned so she faced the window. Elliot's nearness truly put her nerves on edge. They hadn't been alone since their encounter in the Tower. Although being seduced in the middle of an orgy didn't necessarily qualify as alone, it had been intimate nonetheless. Thandie crossed her legs to prevent herself from fidgeting. Why did she act like an anxious schoolgirl whenever she was around him?

"Cold?" His deep voice broke through the silence.

"Yes," she lied.

Elliot turned up the heat, casting her a sideways look as he did so. "Your dress doesn't seem to have withstood the rain."

"I'm sorry?"

He answered her by sweeping his gaze over her body. Thandie looked down at her dress and gasped. The thin fabric was plastered to her skin, making her dark nipples glow lewdly against the white material. She crossed her arms over her breasts, in a vain attempt to reclaim her modesty.

Elliot snorted. "Please don't do that for my benefit. I was enjoying the view."

Thandie hugged her arms tighter around her breasts. She ignored him.

"That's what I get for being a Good Samaritan," he said with a laugh.

Unable to resist the taunt, she snapped. "You call dragging me against my will into your car and ogling me an act of a goodwill?"

"Absolutely," he said. "A simple 'thank you' is always welcome. But in your case, I'm willing to accept sexual favors."

"You are unbelievable," she hissed.

"I prefer to think misunderstood." Looking in his rearview mirror, he merged onto the freeway. "I insisted on driving you home, because it's three o'clock in the morning and you're traveling alone. You were standing in the rain on a busy corner, filled with drunken men, wearing a dress that concealed nothing. Have I mentioned South Beach is known for prostitution? And you, my sweet little pussycat, made it pretty easy to create confusion. Whether you're aware of it or not, guys were circling around you like dogs. If I hadn't been there to take you home, I assure you some horny idiot would have followed you. Now, if you prefer me to take you back, just say the word."

Thandie sat there feeling properly put in her place. As much as she hated to admit it, he was right. She blushed with embarrassment. She wasn't in New York, where there were hundreds of people everywhere and perverts could be scared off by a creative string of swear words. She could have very well gotten herself into some serious trouble.

"Put in that context," she murmured, "thank you."

"Uh-uh, pussycat. Remember we agreed on sexual favors."

"Do you talk to all your employees like this?"

"Just the females."

"I'm the only female."

"Then you shouldn't feel special."

Ready to be rid of him, Thandie stared out the window. The man had the ability to get under her skin in the worst way. And the maddening thing was she got the feeling that her anger only amused him.

They drove several minutes in complete silence. The music spiraling to a climatic crescendo was annoyingly in sync with the tension in the car. Elliot's next words surprised her.

"Did you enjoy your date with Rex?" Although he wore a slight smile, his tone was glacial.

"How do you know about that?" she asked.

"I make it my business to know."

"How does my seeing Rex concern you?"

"You'd be surprised how much it concerns me. Now answer my question, Thandie. How was your date?"

Thandie pulled her arms tighter across her body, refusing to respond. Although she was surprised that Elliot knew about her and Rex, she refused to let the shock show. She wouldn't give him the satisfaction.

"I doubt he could keep his hands off you," Elliot mused.

Thandie's temper got the best of her, and she was compelled to correct him. "I'll have you know Rex was a perfect gentleman. Unfortunately, something came up and I was unable to go."

"That's interesting," was all he said.

Unable to help herself, she snapped, "What's that supposed to mean?"

"You standing Rex up," he said conversationally. "I find that rather interesting."

"I didn't stand him up," she snapped. "I just couldn't go."

"Why not?"

Thandie scowled at him. There was no way she was going to tell him Warren's personal business. It was none of his affair.

"I had my reasons," she said in a low voice.

"That's too bad," Elliot said with mock sympathy. "Rex was looking forward to your little night on the town. I imagine he was crushed when you told him."

Thandie squirmed in her seat. Rex had been disappointed when she'd told him she was staying home to look after Warren. She thought she'd delivered the blow gently enough, but what if he hadn't seen it that way?

"I'm making it up him," Thandie heard herself say.

"Oh?"

She bit back a hasty retort, and said in an even flat tone, "We've rescheduled for next Monday night."

A smile played across Elliot's lips. "Good for Rex," he said. "He could use the attention. Regrettably, you'll have to break your plans. You'll be busy."

"Busy? Busy doing what?"

"You'll be busy being fucked by me."

His vulgarity caught her completely unaware. Thandie had no response to such a statement.

"I see you're speechless," Elliot cooed. "Try not to make a habit out of it. I prefer my women to be a bit more vocal."

Thandie could feel blood rushing to her face. "What makes you think I want to sleep with you?"

Elliot gave her a chastising look. "Come now, Thandie. Surely we aren't playing that game again."

She gave a humorless laugh. "You're cute, Elliot, but not that cute."

He gave her a disbelieving snort. "So you say."

Arriving at Warren's home at last, Elliot pulled into the circular driveway and parked the car. Swiveling in his seat, he stared at her until she met his gaze. "I think we should get a few things straight, Thandie. I have every intention of screwing you. Keep up this act, and I promise you'll find yourself in a lot of trouble with me."

"I'm not interested," she said through gritted teeth.

Placing his hand on her headrest, Elliot leaned forward. "I could make you." His finger brushed a wet lock of hair behind her ear. "Quite easily."

With a swiftness that left her breathless, Elliot cupped the back of her head and moved her forward until her lips were mere inches from his own. His gaze was heated as he stared at her mouth. And then his lips came crashing down on hers.

Momentarily stunned, Thandie struggled to remember to breathe. Her fury assailed her at the exact second her senses returned. A strangled screech of outrage vibrated in her throat. Bringing her hands up, she pushed against his chest with all her might. In response, he dug his fist into the hair at the nape of her head and pulled. Thandie wanted to fight him, wanted to scratch his eyes out with her nails, but his dominance over her body and intoxicating scent overwhelmed her.

Sensing her surrender, his tongue swept into her mouth, plundering every corner with relentless possession.

Elliot pushed aside the material of her dress shielding her breast, groaning the moment he cupped her bare flesh in his hand. He rubbed the pad of his thumb across her nipple until it puckered under his touch. Although she wanted to be disgusted by him, Thandie was quickly melting under his seduction. The more he pressed, the more she wanted to submit. A throaty purr escaped her lips. Her blood was boiling, and her skin tingled. No longer pulling away from him, but moving toward him, Thandie pressed into him, savoring the taste of him.

Just as suddenly as his passionate assault began, Elliot pushed away, his eyes glowing with desire as his gaze focused on the junction of her thighs. "You're wet for me," he said. His eyes lifted to meet hers. "I can smell you." He caressed her breast one final time before stroking his groin. "Sweet dreams, pussycat."

"Huh?" His words unbalanced her. "I—"

"Good night," his voice was shockingly stern.

Anger flared inside her. How dare he force himself on her and then kick her out? If this was how he normally treated women, she wanted nothing to do with him. "Good night," she said through gritted teeth before all but jumping out of his car. Using her purse to cover her head from the downpour, she ran to Warren's front door and quickly let herself in.

Resting her head against the cool surface of the door, Thandie fought to calm her racing heartbeat. Elliot Richards was truly a bastard. He'd known she was attracted to him, had probably planned that scene days ago. And she had fallen for it. Hook line and sinker. That bastard! Did he think himself so superior that he could toy with women at his will?

"Just who the hell do you think you are?" she whispered into the darkness.

Thandie vowed she would not play the fool again. Elliot Richards might easily be able to control other females, but she would not fall into that trap. He might be sexy, but not unbreakable. She would fight fire with fire. She would bring The Great Elliot Richards to his knees.

There was only one thing an arrogant man could not withstand. Rejection. His ego would be his downfall. A smile snaked across Thandie's lips. Elliot Richards would never be invited into her bed. *Never.*

Chapter Twelve

"I hear you're the talk of the town in Miami. Cheers."

"Thanks, Gage," Thandie said as she switched the phone to her other ear. "I appreciate the vote of confidence."

Gage gave a heavy sigh. "Don't get all mushy. I haven't the stomach for it, you know?"

Thandie laughed. Gage never changed.

"I understand *Us Weekly* is doing a mention on Club Babylon in their next issue," Gage informed her.

"So are *People* and *OK! Magazine,*" Thandie said. She was thrilled and exhausted by all the attention the club had been receiving over the last few days. They'd finally managed to secure a performance date for Will.i.am. Even though the appearance was only for an hour and a half DJ spot, and on a Thursday night, the place had been packed with partygoers. It helped that a handful of local celebrities chose that evening to visit the VIP rooms. Security had their hands full holding curious guests at bay.

Long after Thandie had seen to Will's safe exit from the club, she'd stayed behind to help Adam cater to their special visitors. The night had been long, and her rest had been short.

Thandie was up extra early taking calls from columnists and TV reporters.

"You're quite the little worker bee," Gage mused. "If I didn't know any better, I'd think you were trying to prove something."

Gage was taunting her, but the comment held more truth than her friend knew. Thandie had been trying to make a point to someone. Elliot. Ever since their conversation in his car, she'd skirted around Elliot at every opportunity. As much as she disliked the company of his assistant Romero, lately she'd relied on him to pass on messages to his employer. Likewise, she filled her days with work, even taking on responsibilities she normally delegated to the girls.

Thankfully, Elliot seemed to have lost interest in her. He did not make any effort to seek her out.

Rex, the person she might have spent her extra time with, had unfortunately taken a trip to California to visit some advertising company Elliot did business with. At first, Thandie had assumed this had been a ploy by Elliot to prevent her and Rex from dating. However, when Elliot made no advances toward her during Rex's absence, she figured she'd been wrong.

She had to face the fact Elliot might simply be all talk. Or he'd become bored by the idea of seducing her. If nothing else, life appeared to be business as usual for Elliot. He and his partner-in-crime Nico, a man who seemed to have nothing better to do than indulge himself, took care to flirt with the prettiest women in the room and eventually sneak away to some secluded place. Without question, not having to encounter Elliot made Thandie's job less nerve-racking. It was exactly what she needed.

So why did the idea piss her off?

Her unexplainable attraction to Elliot was not the only thing that Thandie lost sleep over. For the last week, she'd been keeping a suspicious eye on Warren. He had yet to mention his family to her again. In fact, he was careful not to mention anything remotely related to what had happened earlier this week. As far as Thandie could tell, Warren was fully restored to his old self. There was no trace of the broken old man she'd witnessed that night. He never betrayed any trace of embarrassment or vulnerability. The burst of emotion had either been a random occurrence due to his drunken state, or Warren was masterful at concealing his pain. Whatever the case, he appeared to have blocked out his drunken confession entirely.

About the most exciting thing to happen at the Radcliffe residence were visits from Warren's divorce lawyer, visits that had become more frequent lately. Apparently, things were heating up in the legal proceedings.

Nibbling on her bottom lip, Thandie sat on the edge of the bed to slip on her heels. "Gage, I'm hurrying off to a meeting. Can I call you back later?"

"Who are you meeting with?"

"Mira Dietrich."

"Hmm," was all Gage said.

Thandie stopped fiddling with her shoes. "What does that mean?"

"Nothing really." Casually, Gage asked. "Have you ever met Mira?"

"No, her secretary set up the appointment." Actually, it had been more of a summons.

Gage tsked. "Well, I have met her. My advice is don't let her gray hair fool you. Mira Dietrich is a shark. She'll swallow you whole and pick her teeth with your bones."

"That's a comforting picture," Thandie grumbled.

"The good thing about Mira is she's direct. If she wants a piece of you, she'll let you know. Better to know where the knife is coming from, rather than guess. Be careful what you say."

"Noted." Thandie looked around the cluttered bedroom, searching for her purse. "Is there anything else you want to add before I jump into shark infested waters?"

"Nothing comes to mind," Gage chirped. "Have a good meeting."

"Thanks for the heads-up."

"No problem. I—ah! I forget to mention my sighting."

"Sighting?" Thandie, tossed aside a garment, still looking for her purse. "Who did you see?"

"Cam."

This news made Thandie pause. "Cam?"

"The one and only," Gage said with a laugh. "I ran into him the other night."

"You did?" she asked. "Where?"

"At the premiere for the new Brandon Audrey movie." As if reading her mind, Gage added, "He was there with a group of people from BHP. No female companion, just in case you were wondering."

"I wasn't," Thandie said quickly.

"Of course not," she said. "Well, better be hurrying along. I have a phone call coming through."

Thandie stared into space long after she hung up with Gage. Hearing Cam's name caused a fresh wave of guilt to wash over her. Gage had seen Cam out alone. That was curious. She'd been led to believe Cam's relationship had survived what had happened during Fashion Week. Had Cam and his girlfriend broken up?

Spotting her clutch purse on the dresser, Thandie snatched it up and headed out the door. When she was downstairs, she stepped into the living room, and found Len working on her laptop. Len looked up and beamed at Thandie.

"Mira?"

Thandie nodded. "I should be back within an hour. Will you and Raja be all right without the car?"

"Sure," she said lazily.

Pulling her keys out of her purse, Thandie waved. "I'll let you know how it goes—"

Both women jumped when Raja burst into the room. Without saying a word, she pulled Thandie and Len with her to the farthest corner of the room. Her face was bright with excitement. "I have gossip!" she whispered loudly.

"What do you got?" Len demanded, suddenly all business.

Raja looked around the three of them, ensuring they were indeed alone. She leaned forward. "Warren cancelled all Wife Number Five's credit cards two days ago."

Thandie and Len gasped.

Raja nodded her head, agreeing with their shock. "Supposedly, she's livid. She was still in Rio, living it up and now she's stuck there with nothing."

"Why now?" Thandie asked. "Warren's been hesitant to do anything to upset her."

"Because," Len said with a dramatic sigh, "the divorce negotiations have been going so badly lately. Warren's lawyer insisted she be cut off to put pressure on her to cooperate."

"That's right," Raja said thoughtfully. "I forgot about that. Well, she's pissed off now."

"Serves her right," Len declared.

Thandie looked between the two girls. She did not want to know how Len and Raja had come by this newest information. Deciding it was better she leave now before things got too interesting, Thandie slipped from the room. She doubted the girls realized her absence. They were too busy coming up with new theories for the outcome of Warren's divorce.

Turning her thoughts away from Warren, Thandie focused

on what was to come. She had dinner plans with Mira Dietrich, the reigning editor of *Look,* a premier social newspaper in the Miami-Dade metropolis. *Look* was a weekly syndicate which played double duty of reporting high society events, fashion updates, and spreading gossip about Hollywood celebs. It was a one stop shop to get the pulse of Miami nightlife. Making it therefore imperative that Thandie gain Mira's favor to promote Club Babylon.

Thandie arrived at the Tides Hotel at exactly one minute 'til seven. Handing her car keys to the valet, she smoothed her suddenly clammy palms over her skirt. She had dressed carefully, accessorizing herself conservatively. She did not want to risk offending the temperamental editor. Since Warren's house party, Thandie had tried to get in touch with Mira. Every attempt had been unanswered. Mira clearly did not see Thandie as a credible contact. But that had been over two weeks ago. Now, due to a string of successful performances, Club Babylon was the talk of the town. The call from Mira's office had been welcome.

Giving her name to the hostess, Thandie was led to the terrace where Mira Dietrich sat at a bistro table. Dressed in all black, with pale wrinkled skin, and oversize eyeglasses she looked formidable. Her long fingernails and thin lips were painted blood red. She seemed as welcoming as an ill-tempered witch. Clutching a cigarette between her boney fingers, she stared at Thandie, unsmiling and unapproachable.

"You're late," was the first thing she said.

"I'm sorry I kept you waiting," Thandie said, nonplussed. She slid into the seat opposite Mira. Thankfully, the wind was blowing against her back, making the cigarette smoke float away from her.

"My time is valuable," Mira snapped.

"I'm sure it is."

Mira narrowed her gaze at Thandie, making the wrinkles at the corners of her eyes deepen. The setting sun glinted off her oversize glasses, intensifying her stare. She clicked her tongue and then gave a snort of laughter. Tapping the ash of her cigarette into the wind, Mira said, "I like your spunk. I've decided I'm going to like you." She tilted her head to the side. "It's hard to impress me."

Thandie raised her brow. "I've impressed you?"

"For the moment," Mira agreed. "You should know I'm easily disappointed."

She gave a tight smile in response.

Thankfully, their server chose that moment to come and take their orders. Once they were alone again, Thandie tried to engage her in light conversation. Mira did not attempt to hide her boredom. Finally, after five painful minutes of forced civility, Mira decided to put Thandie out of her misery. She explained why she'd invited her to dinner.

"I want pictures inside the club," Mira said, pointing her cigarette at her. "And you're going to get them for me."

Thandie smiled pleasantly. "I'm sure you know as well as I do that Elliot enforces a 'no camera' policy."

"Your job is to change his mind," Mira informed her. "You're the publicist for goodness' sake."

"Yes, Mira, I'm aware of that fact, but Elliot still needs persuasion."

"Well, then," the older woman made a shooing motion with her hands. "Persuade him. Meanwhile, I want pictures of VIP guests. See if you can get me some of Shaun Cross. He's a personal favorite of mine."

Thandie shook her head. "I'm not committing to anything, Mira. Not until Elliot gives the okay. And it doesn't look like that will happen anytime soon."

Mira pursed her lips and then extinguished her cigarette stub in her water goblet. "I want those pictures."

By the time dinner was over, Thandie did not feel her chances of working with *Look* were good. Mira needed more convincing to give Babylon a mention. She would have to talk to Elliot about the "no camera" policy.

When Thandie arrived at Warren's home, the windows were brightly lit. Just as she was letting herself in, Len and Raja were coming down the stairs. They were dressed in nearly indistinguishable strapless mini dresses and sparkling stilettos.

Len smiled when she saw her. "How did it go with Mira?"

"Well enough," she replied.

"I knew you would work your magic," she boasted. The comment was watered down by the inattentive trailing of Len's voice. She'd found a mirror in the foyer and set about playing with her hair.

"Where is Warren?" Thandie asked.

"He left for the club about an hour ago," Len said distractedly.

"Are you coming with us?" Raja asked.

Thandie shook her head. She had not planned on going to Babylon, or anywhere else tonight. She was too tired. Reaching into her purse, she held up the car keys, and said. "Here you go. Have fun tonight."

Len clapped her hands together. "Can we drink?"

"Absolutely not," she said firmly.

Len gave a pout worthy of a two-year-old.

Thandie sighed. "I can't afford for one of you to get a DUI down here. It wouldn't look good."

Raja snatched the keys out of her hands. "That's fair. Are you sure you don't want to come?"

"I'm sure," she said. An image of Elliot Richards flashed in her head. "In fact, I'm positive I want to stay here."

"Okay," Len chirped. "Don't wait up."

"I won't," she assured her. "Be careful," she called after them as they made their way out the front door.

"We will," Len promised.

"And don't get into trouble," she said.

"We won't," Raja shouted back.

"We won't drink and drive," Len added.

"And we won't get caught doing anything illegal," both girls chanted in unison.

Thandie shook her head. It was doubtful they would be back before sunrise. She was well aware the girls ventured to the club as often as possible to party with the locals and drool over Elliot. Any other time, Thandie would have been nervous to let them roam free, but tonight she couldn't care less. Her dinner meeting with Mira had drained her.

Thandie headed straight to her room. Taking a quick shower, she crawled into bed and checked her emails on her phone. For a fleeting moment, she considered calling Cam. Just as before, she rejected the idea. It was too late to call.

Tossing her phone onto the comforter, Thandie nestled beneath the covers. The days of constant work had finally caught up with her.

Thandie woke up screaming.

There was a woman standing over her with a wild look in her eyes. Thandie leaped out of bed and grabbed the bedside lamp for defense. Outrage spread over the woman's face.

"How dare you pull a weapon on me in my own house!" she screeched.

Thandie took a nervous step back. The woman's scream literally bounced off the walls. "Who are you?"

The stranger scoffed. "You'll know soon enough," she hissed.

If need be, Thandie was prepared to defend herself, but the woman surprisingly turned and stomped out of the room.

Her ears perked, listening for any sound. In the distance, she could just make out the woman moving. Thandie cursed. Adrenaline was coursing through her, but her mind was still fuzzy. Was the crazy person on the other side of the house? Or was she down the hall, waiting to pounce on her? Thandie could not be certain.

What the hell was going on? Then, a dreaded thought occurred to her that the kitchen was on the other side of the house. And where there was a kitchen, there were weapons. Hurriedly, Thandie dressed and packed her things as quickly as she could. She wasn't sure what Warren had gotten her into, but she knew she had to get out of there.

Elliot was dropping Warren off at home from another night of heavy partying. The man was too drunk to drive himself, and he didn't feel right asking one of the other guys to do him the favor. Besides, he had an obligation to Warren. He was after all one of his biggest investors. If Warren wanted to party until he fell asleep in the VIP area, that was his business. The guy certainly proved that you were never too old to have a good time.

The night had been a really good night. There had not been an entertainer scheduled to perform, but the place had been packed. Having surpassed their liquor goal sometime around two in the morning, the bar had run out of glass tumblers and plastic cups. They'd had to wait for Markie to make an emergency run to the store, and the bartenders had kept the crowd entertained by spraying them with water. Elliot hadn't known Warren had been carried to his office and was sleeping soundly on his couch until he returned to shut down his computer for the night.

It was nearing six o'clock in the morning, and Elliot was still fired up. It would take a while before he was relaxed enough to go to sleep. A good workout should tire him out.

With a snoring passenger seated at his right, Elliot had plenty of time to consider how he planned to spend the rest of his morning. However, he was abruptly jarred out of his musing when he pulled into the driveway of Warren's home.

He slowed the car, and stared at the scene in front of him. Thandie and another woman were standing in the front yard, yelling at each other. And to make matters worse, the other woman was holding a long butcher knife.

Elliot slammed on his brakes. "Warren, wake up," he barked.

"Wha–what?" Warren's head rolled to the side. He blinked rapidly before his eyes focused on the situation beyond the windshield. "Oh, shit!"

Thandie was too busy screaming at the woman to notice the car pulling up the drive. Vaguely, she heard footsteps rushing toward them, but she was unwilling to turn away from the knife in the woman's hands.

Then a haggard Warren stepped forward. Thandie had never been happier to see him. He glanced at her to make sure she was all right, and then turned to the woman. His eyes widened with shock. He opened his mouth to speak, but nothing came out.

She had a sinking feeling she was going to have to continue to fend for herself.

Reassuring hands cupped her shoulders. Without even looking, Thandie knew it was Elliot. She chanced a glance at him. He was not looking at her. Instead, his cool gray eyes were trained on the woman with the knife. He knew her. Thandie shifted her gaze to the woman. She was staring intently at Elliot. A look of silent fury froze her features. But it was not Elliot who bore the wrath of her anger—Warren would receive that honor.

She whirled on the older man. "I bet you thought that was pretty fucking funny, didn't you? Canceling my credit cards while I was out of the country, Warren. How dare you? I bet that sleazy lawyer of yours put you up to it, didn't he?"

"Sophia—" Warren said.

She cut him off with a simple lift of her manicured hand. "I finally come home and this is what I find—" she waved the knife in Thandie's direction "—one of your whores sleeping in my house."

"Now wait a minute—" Warren tried again.

"My lawyer is going to have a field day with this," Sophia jeered. "And *you*," she swiveled her dark eyes to glare at Thandie. Before she could conjure a cutting insult, Elliot pushed Thandie behind his broad shoulders blocking her from view.

"Leave her out of this, Sophia," he said. "She works for me."

"Bullshit!" she spat. "You don't hire women."

"This is different," Elliot explained, with more calm than Thandie would have thought possible. "She's handling promotions for the club. Warren was doing me a favor by hosting her stay. Now," he said in a suddenly menacing voice, "you need to calm down and put the knife away."

Sophia looked at Elliot's protective stance. Her eyes went wide. "Are you sleeping with her?"

Instead of answering her directly, he said, "I protect what belongs to me."

Sophia laughed in his face. "Do you expect me to believe you're involved with one woman?"

Elliot stepped forward, pinning her with his silver eyes. "You haven't been around, Sophia. A lot has changed."

Sophia stiffened, measuring him. Thandie noticed a change in her body language. Something strange and unsettling passed between Sophia and Elliot. His words didn't seem harsh, but they must have held another meaning, because she suddenly looked wounded. She looked at Thandie. If possible, her eyes were filled with more hatred.

"You and I both know you grow bored too easily," Sophia hissed. "No woman can keep you for long." Her eyes flickered over Thandie. "Least of all her. She's not even your type."

"Neither are you," he said flatly. "So stay out of my business."

"Sophia, put the knife down," Warren called out. The sound of his voice broke the staring contest between Elliot and Sophia.

Looking down at the knife, Sophia seemed surprised to see it was in her hand. She threw it on the ground. It clanged noisily against the concrete of the driveway. Warren used the tip of his shoe to kick it aside, out of reach.

If Sophia realized the terror she had caused, she was unfazed. She cast a thoughtful glance at Elliot, before turning scornful eyes on Warren. "Wait until my lawyer hears about this."

That being said, she marched toward a bright red Ferrari Thandie had not noticed earlier. Sophia slid into the driver's seat, slammed the door, revved the engine loudly and sped away from the house.

Thandie waited until the car was out of sight before she took a calm breath. She had thought the woman was going to stab her. She hadn't realized tears were flowing down her face until Elliot reached out and brushed her cheek dry with his palm. Still stunned by the encounter, she didn't object when he pulled her to him and wrapped his arms around her.

Warren cursed. "Thandie, I'm so sorry. I can't believe she did that. Are you hurt? Do we need to take you to a hospital?"

She shook her head but was unable to look at Warren. She was furious with him. If she'd known the true situation between him and his wife, she would have never agreed to stay with him. What if Warren's wife had harmed Raja or Len? She would have never been able to forgive Warren. Or herself.

Elliot must have sensed her growing fury. He rubbed her back until her trembling legs felt strong enough to support her weight again.

"Get your things," he whispered into her ear.

When all her things, as well as the girls', had been loaded into Elliot's Range Rover, he helped her into the car. She was still not speaking to Warren, and he took her rejection hard. He didn't press her to talk, but it was clear Warren felt responsible for what had happened. He promised to redirect Raja and Len to Thandie's new location.

Wherever that might be.

They were fifteen minutes into the drive, before Thandie trusted herself to speak. "Do you care to explain to me what happened back there?" she asked.

"Warren and his wives," Elliot said casually.

"That was Wife Number Five," she said, much for her own confirmation.

"In the flesh."

"She seemed to know you very well."

Elliot looked over at her, burning her with those cool gray eyes. "We have a past." He shrugged, and then added, "Before Warren."

"Was she your girlfriend?"

"No," he said with a light laugh. "I don't have girlfriends."

"Just fuck buddies?"

If he was surprised by her lewd language, he didn't show it. "If that's what you want to call it."

Thandie waited for him to elaborate, but he said nothing more. "Where are you taking me?"

"It looks like you're coming home with me."

She shook her head. "I would feel more comfortable staying at a hotel."

"Then I guess you're going to be on edge for the remainder of your trip."

"Elliot," she said with thin patience, "I appreciate your hospitality, but the girls and I can't stay at your home."

He glanced at her. "Thandie, I admire your attempts at professionalism, but let me be blunt with you. Warren is going through a messy divorce. Sophia finding you in their home doesn't look good for him. Even though there is nothing going on between you two, Warren is given her and her lawyer a lot of ammunition. If playing host to you, and your assistants for a few weeks helps Warren, then that's a small sacrifice. I know you're upset with Warren, but he didn't mean for any of that to happen."

"We're not staying with you," she said firmly.

"You don't have a say in this."

"Oh, yes, I do. You can't imprison me."

"You don't know me very well," he chuckled. "You will stay with me. And if you think for a second you can run from me, guess again. I know every hotel manager in the city. You have nowhere else to go."

"You can't do that."

"I can, and I will." Elliot focused back on the road. "For reasons I won't explain, I actually care what this divorce will do to Warren. He doesn't need you around his home right now. You'll only complicate things for him. So sit back."

Thandie huffed. The situation was bleak. She had barely escaped being killed, and now she would be forced to endure Elliot's hospitality. Being under the same roof with him would be agony. She wouldn't be able to ignore him.

Ten minutes later, they were passing through the guarded gates of Star Island. Even though Thandie was resolute in giving Elliot the silent treatment, she couldn't hide her astonishment at their location. Only the cream of the crop resided on this narrow strip of land. "You live on Star Island?" she asked.

Elliot nodded, keeping his eyes on the road.

"How in the world did you manage that?"

"I have a buddy who was looking to relocate, and he knew I was looking." He shrugged. "He phoned me, and I bought his house. It took me a year's worth of renovation to get it the way I wanted, but now I'm satisfied."

"Still, to live on Star Island—" She openly gawked at the luxurious estates they drove by. "Your buddy must have really done well for himself."

He looked over at her and shrugged.

"We're here." He pulled into the curvy drive of a spiraling Mediterranean-style home. He parked in front of an enormous porch held up by massive stone columns. He helped her out of her seat, holding her longer than necessary against him.

The front doors opened, and a petite Cuban woman stepped onto the porch. She was gracefully aged, with thick dark hair and pleasant laugh lines around her mouth. She smiled brightly at Elliot before casting curious brown eyes on Thandie.

Elliot surprised Thandie by introducing her to the woman in impeccable Spanish. He must have explained why she was visiting, because the woman muffled a laugh before smiling kindly at Thandie. The only thing Thandie made out of the conversation was that her name was Lucinda. They were soon joined by a tall man, whom Lucinda quickly ordered to unload the Range Rover. Elliot took Thandie's hand and led her inside.

"I didn't know you spoke Spanish," Thandie mused aloud.

Elliot did not answer her. Instead he guided her deeper into his home. Thandie quickly lost her train of thought when she stepped into the grand entryway. The scent of sunshine and fresh linens licked the air. The calming sound of trickling water, hanging plants and rotating ceiling fans overwhelmed her senses. She was astounded by the beauty surrounding her.

Elliot walked through the house, pointing out where the pool and exercise room were located. By the time he directed her to the guest rooms, her bags were lined up in the hall.

"There are five rooms down this hallway," he said. "You can take your pick of which ones you want."

She peeked into the rooms. "This is a remarkable home, Elliot. It looks just like—"

"The Tower," he finished. "I know. Does it meet your approval? Is it enough to make you change your mind about running away?"

She frowned. "I never said I would run away."

"But you were thinking it." He retrieved a key from his key ring and pressed it into her hand. "You'll need this. Don't lose it. I'm particular about lost keys."

She looked at the key. "What's this for?"

"My house."

"Huh?" Her mind was still spinning from the event that had stranded her here.

"My house," he repeated. *"Mi casa es su casa."* And he turned and started down the hallway. "Make yourself at home," he called out over his shoulder. "If you need anything, look for Lucinda."

"Wait," she shouted nervously. "I can't speak Spanish."

Elliot stopped and turned around. "Lucinda speaks English, just not very well. Keep it simple, and be respectful."

Thandie frowned at his last comment. As if she would ever be disrespectful to his housekeeper. When Elliot turned away again and began moving down the hall, she called out to him. "Where are you going?"

Elliot grinned at her over his shoulder. "I'm going to take a shower and then I'm going to bed. Would you like to join me?"

Thandie rolled her eyes. "No."

He shrugged. "So you say." He turned and disappeared around the corner.

Thandie knew immediately when Len and Raja arrived at Elliot's home. Their screams shook the paintings on the walls.

"This is so hot! Raja, look at this...and that over there."

"Len, look at this TV. This guy is loaded!"

Having claimed a guest bedroom for herself, Thandie had quickly climbed into bed. But after an hour of staring at the ceiling, she was ready to admit sleep would not come easily. She welcomed the arrival of Len and Raja. She found the girls exploring, and still dressed in what they had worn the night before.

"You two haven't slept yet?"

Len spun around. "You should have been at Babylon last night, Thandie. It was freakin' awesome!"

Raja leaned against the couch while she slipped off her heels. "I would say you missed out on all the fireworks, but it sounds as though you had a pretty interesting morning."

Len shook her head. "Warren told us what happened, Thandie. He was pretty bummed that you're mad at him."

"Are you all right?" Raja's eyes scanned the vaulted ceiling of the room. "This place is really cool."

"I'm fine," she offered, even though both girls were occupied with examining a sculpture piece. It was pointless, retelling her brush with death. They were much too absorbed in their new surroundings to pay attention. "We'll have to stay here until our project is over," Thandie said. "Warren needs a little space, due to his divorce. It might be a good idea to keep your distance while working at the club. His wife might decide to drop by, and we don't want to create a scene."

"You mean like the one you two made this morning?"

Thandie threw a dirty look at Raja. "We all need to be respectful of Warren's situation." She told them. The girls were again examining the room. "Your bags are upstairs in the hall on the left. If you need me, I'll be in my room."

Both girls nodded absentmindedly, neither caring nor listening. Thandie eyed them closely. Although they were clearly excited to be in Elliot's home, there were dark circles under their eyes. "You two should get some rest," she added. "We have a lot to do tomorrow. You'll need your energy."

"Yes, Thandie," they chorused.

Feeling like a taskmaster, Thandie mumbled a "good night" and returned to her room.

Chapter Thirteen

Thandie awoke well past noon. Rolling out of bed, she pulled on a pair of cotton shorts and began to wash up. Brushing her hair away from her face, she studied her reflection. Her pale brown skin looked ashen, making her look ill. For an instant, she considered climbing back into bed and sleeping a few hours longer. She didn't give herself time to consider it. She had phone work to do. Rest would have to come later.

With the help of her cosmetic arsenal, she made up for the lack of color in face before heading downstairs in search of caffeine. She'd been slightly frantic when she'd first arrived at Elliot's house. She hadn't taken the time to appreciate the home's details, nor establish some sense of orientation. After two wrong turns, she found her destination. Elliot's kitchen was vast and well-stocked. Not exactly what she'd had in mind for a thirty-something bachelor. She spotted the coffee pot, and filled it. She was determined to enjoy one cup alone before she woke the girls. She could use the quiet time to get her head together.

While she waited for the water to percolate, Thandie amused herself by studying their new surroundings. It was nothing like Warren's place. It was much more modern. The home was an open layout, allowing natural sunlight from its many windows to fill the rooms. The kitchen was conveniently pocketed just off the main living area, and accessible to the dining room. There were two large entryways into the kitchen, offering a sense of welcome and privacy at the same time. The countertops were black granite, which complemented the stainless steel appliances. Situated in the center of the room was a massive island, which acted as a prep station and kitchen table. Six sleekly designed barstools lined the island on one side.

Thandie's observations were interrupted by the hissing sound of the coffee maker. She poured herself a mug and took one long sip. It was perfect. It was probably the best coffee she remembered making. She leaned over to study the brand name of the machine. Perhaps she should buy one for her office?

"Good morning."

Thandie turned around at the sound of Elliot's voice. He was barefoot and wearing a pair of sweatpants. His bare chest was hairless, rippled with muscles and wonderfully golden skin. He had a light five o'clock shadow along his jawline, and his eyes were smoky. For a guy who had just woken up, he was exceptionally breathtaking.

"Good morning," she said, unable to help herself from staring at him over the rim of her mug.

Elliot flashed her a sinfully charming smile. "You realize you're a woman after my heart, don't you?"

"Wh-what?" she stammered, nearly choking on her words.

He stood before her, so near she could smell the fresh scent of his skin. He placed his hand on the countertop behind her and leaned close. His chest was inches from brushing hers. "Coffee."

"Huh?" she squeaked.

He smiled. "You made coffee. It's a luxury for me." He reached around her and pulled the carafe free. He smelled the aroma. "Hazelnut?"

Thandie nodded, watching him pour a cup. He poured creamer and sugar in, and when he was satisfied with his creation, he tasted it. Elliot exhaled deeply before resting his mug on the counter. He reached out and pulled her toward him before dropping a kiss on the tip of her nose.

"You've discovered my weakness," he said.

Elliot stared down at her with those damned glowing eyes, completely at ease with touching her. She was too paralyzed by his nearness to protest.

Thankfully, Romero took that moment to enter the kitchen.

"Hello, Thandie," he said as he stepped past her. He took a seat at the counter, appearing quite at ease. Without a word of greeting to his employer, he held out a cell phone. Elliot accepted it and, pressing the phone to his ear, immediately dived into a serious conversation. Thandie watched as Elliot's whole demeanor changed from a sleepy-eyed flirt to a no-nonsense businessman in a matter of seconds. It was interesting to watch the seamless transformation. Thandie wondered how many personas Elliot possessed.

Forcing herself to leave, she headed upstairs to retrieve her laptop, and find a quiet place to work. Thankfully, Elliot wasn't the type to laze about the house.

Thandie and the girls spent the day responding to emails. It was a slow evening. Without Elliot around to distract them, the day managed to be fairly productive. The dining room was currently their office. The long dining table gave them ample room to spread out their materials.

Just before dusk was upon them, Thandie retreated to her bedroom to change clothes. She'd made plans to meet Victoria Day at her studio. She pulled on a pair of jeans, a tank, and sandals. While she was looking for her lip gloss, she heard Len shout, "Thandie! Your phone is ringing."

Hoping it wasn't Warren calling again, she trotted down the stairs. Len held her cell phone up. Thandie took it from her and answered, "Thandie Shaw speaking."

"Thandie, it's Gage."

"Two days in a row?" Thandie teased. "Is everything all right?"

"Things are fine for me. Bad for you."

"Meaning?"

"I was curious, so I decided to call your office today. Amanda is in over her head. You do know this, right?"

"Oh, dear." Thandie pinched the bridge of her nose. "Cam said as much."

"Oh?" Gage's interest was suddenly piqued. "You and Cam are talking again?"

"Calm down. We're not dating. I called him the night before."

"What for?"

"I needed to hear—it doesn't matter. We only talked for a few minutes. Nothing serious."

"Are you going to give me details?"

"You're very nosy, Gage."

"I work in PR. It's my business to know details."

"Getting back to your point." Thandie sighed. "Cam visited the office recently. He mentioned that Amanda might have a little too much on her plate. I was hoping to talk with her and give her another week to get her feet wet."

"That's a bit risky."

"Amanda is my best assistant."

"That's sad," Gage said under her breath.

"She deserves a second chance."

"You're a lot braver than I. I'd be afraid that she'd scare off my clients."

Gage was right. It had taken Thandie years to establish herself on the Manhattan club scene. Amanda was a great employee, but if she didn't watch her carefully, she could easily lose a valuable client. "She's learning. If she fails, it's because I didn't train her well. Her workload isn't too heavy for the next few days. Just playing host to a few B-list stars. However, the Simmons's party is fast approaching. If Amanda hasn't learned the ropes by then, I'll have to fly up to handle the assignment with her. At any rate, I'll check in with her more often."

"I'll do the same."

"I really appreciate that, Gage."

"You're welcome. So…anything new with Elliot Richards?"

She grimaced at the sound of his name. "No, nothing new," she said quickly.

Thandie had spent the better part of the night thinking about him, and her first waking hours being unnerved by him. The last thing she wanted to do was talk about him.

"Liar."

"As much as I'd love to entertain you, I'm afraid I can't today. You caught me on my way out."

"Oh, yes, you're meeting with Day."

"How did you know about that?"

"I know everything," Gage said. "Promise me you'll call if something happens."

"Something like what?"

"Surprise me."

Warren strolled into Elliot's office unannounced. Somewhat annoyed, Elliot looked up from his computer screen. Michelle, who normally guarded his office as if it were Fort Knox, hadn't stopped him. He knew Michelle was at the door, but for some reason he'd chosen to display a generous amount of tolerance toward Warren.

Elliot was not pleased. This was becoming a bothersome habit amongst his staff. Everyone extended favors to Warren. Perhaps they did it because he was an investor, because of his age, or because they simply liked him. Whatever the reason, Elliot would have to put a stop to it.

Warren threw himself on the couch and ran a hand through his white hair. "Are Thandie and the girls all right?"

For a moment, Elliot considered amusing himself by dragging this out. However, he could see Warren's discomfort. Even Elliot wasn't that cruel. "They are fine."

"Which hotel did you take them to?"

"I didn't take them to a hotel." Answering the curious look on Warren's face, he said, "They're staying with me."

Warren's face froze in shock. "With *you?*"

Elliot raised his brow, not caring for the hint of accusation in the older man's tone.

"These are my friends, Elliot," Warren said solemnly. "Their well-being is important to me."

"If that were true, you would have taken better care of Thandie," Elliot retorted. "I imagine it's not every day she has a knife pulled on her."

Warren grimaced, his shame evident. "I know I screwed up, Elliot. I'm not perfect."

"I'm well aware of that fact." Elliot's eyes flashed. "You should have never allowed them to stay with you. Someone could have gotten hurt."

"You're right." Warren dragged his hand through his hair again.

"I have everything under control."

"I'd feel better if they stayed at a hotel," Warren said in a low voice. "I'll pay for the expenses."

"They'll stay with me for the duration of their assignment," he said with finality.

Warren looked away sheepishly. "How bad is it?"

"I imagine it's pretty bad."

"I've called Thandie numerous times," Warren said helplessly.

Elliot stiffened at the thought. "And?"

"She won't take my calls," Warren finished miserably. "Do you think you could—"

"No."

"But I haven't even asked—"

"No," Elliot said, slicing his hand in the air. "You got yourself into this mess. You can certainly figure a way to get yourself out."

"I'm asking for your help, Elliot. I messed things up. I need to apologize to the ladies properly."

Thandie looked around Victoria Day's studio. Bundles of brightly colored fabric were stacked into tall piles on almost every flat surface. In the center of the room was a small platform, with a pedestal used to display garments. Situated on the stage was a voluminous ball gown fitted to a dress form. The gown was dyed the richest shade of blue, with a train that blossomed out from the back, creating a waterfall of foamy tulle. It was an exquisite gown. Nevertheless, Day was not satisfied. She knelt over the hem of the gown, examining the stitching; shaking her head and swearing to herself.

"My life is filled with one disaster after another," she declared.

"Don't you think that's a bit dramatic?" Thandie asked.

"Not if it's true," Day said with a groan. She stood up and walked around the gown, examining every angle. "I know something is wrong with this design, but I can't quite..." She tapped her chin with the tip of her finger. "I can't see it, I feel it." Day dug her fists into the pockets of her cutoff jeans, and continued to stare at the dress.

Thandie watched Day concentrate. She'd done little else since Thandie's arrival. Her obsession to discover the unseen flaw in her creation was interesting to watch. That Day could create something so elegant and classic was amazing, especially since it was so different from her personal style.

Day had always been a free spirit. Even today, dressed in a tank top and stilettos, with a heel so thin it seemed ready to snap under serious pressure, Day looked terribly trendy. Having styled her short hair into a spiky Mohawk, few could compete with her effortless edginess. Standing next to the lavish splendor of the gown, it was hard to believe she was the designer behind the masterpiece.

Day stomped her foot and said, "I still can't find what I'm looking for. This is bothering the hell out of me. How can I do a show in a few short weeks when my finale dress looks like garbage?"

Not daring to contradict Day, Thandie changed the subject. "How are the plans for your show going?"

Day made a sound of disapproval. "My show will most likely be a calamity of epic proportions." When Thandie raised her brows, Day groaned in surrender. "Nothing is going right. There's never enough money. Ever since I was a little girl, I always had dreams of starting my own fashion line. No one ever prepared me for the monetary challenges. Even with my family helping me pull everything together, I'm barely able to do it. We finally found a location for a price I can afford, but the place is too far from downtown. Every vendor is demanding an up-charge for travel expenses. And then, the manager of the site informed me yesterday that 'due to management changes' I'll be required to pay a premium rate for…oh…I don't even know anymore!" Day released another groan. "And now *this*." She pointed to the ball gown. "Even if I find the problem, I hardly have the time to fix it. I'm creatively tapped out."

Thandie could see frustration roll off Day's shoulders like vapor.

"Have you made an appointment with Fernando yet?"

"Who?" Day's question jarred Thandie. It was such an abrupt change in topic, it took several minutes to register the question.

"Fernando, the masseur."

"Oh, not yet. Things have been a little crazy about the club lately."

"So I hear." Day tossed the fabric aside and claimed another. "Is it true Deadmau5 is scheduled to perform there this month?"

Thandie nodded. "We're excited about it, but there is a lot of work to do. Deadmau5 does this cool laser show during his performances, and we're trying to come up with themes to complement his style. It's hard think up ideas when the club will be darker than normal."

"Why don't you do a glow-in-the-dark theme?" Day said with a shrug.

The idea instantly clicked with Thandie.

"It should be rather simple," Day said with another lift of her small shoulders. "People love to wear costumes like that."

Thandie pulled out a scrap of paper from her purse and began quickly writing down an idea. "I need to look online for a place that makes glow in the dark outfits for myself and the girls."

"I can do it."

"I could never consider it, Day. You have too much on your plate with your show."

Day waved her hand. "I think about my collection every minute of the day. I could use a temporary distraction. Besides, it's not as if it'll be rocket science. I could sketch designs and make samples within a matter of days." Invigorated by the idea of a new project, Day pulled her measuring tape from around her neck and motioned for Thandie to stand. "Let's get your measurements."

Thandie stood and allowed Day to take her measurements. And then a thought occurred to her.

"Day," she said, "I think I have a solution to your show's location problem."

By the time Thandie returned to Elliot's home, her mind was racing with details. If she could pull this off, it would bring noteworthy attention to Babylon and help a friend. But her plans would require convincing Elliot. That might prove tricky, given she hadn't yet had the discussion with him about his "no camera" policy in the club. She would have to persuade him to bend on that rule in order to consider her newest idea.

Approaching both topics would demand finesse on her part, something she'd been lacking in all her earlier encounters with Elliot.

Chapter Fourteen

Thandie would have loved nothing more than to stay in bed all day, but she was rendered helpless when Raja and Len came into her room the next morning, barely able to form a complete sentences without giggling.

"Thandie, you have to wake up," Len squealed. "We have exciting news!"

Thandie rolled over to look at the time. "Len, it's not even eleven o'clock. What are you doing up?"

"We have a surprise for you," she giggled excitedly. "And you'll never guess what it is."

Thandie growled. "Len, you know I hate surprises."

"But you'll love this," Raja said. "Trust us."

Thandie pulled the covers over her head. "Tell me your surprise after noon."

"But it can't wait, Thandie," Len whined. "You're gonna miss it if you don't get up now."

Thandie peeked her head out from beneath the covers. "Miss what?"

Raja and Len looked at each other before wordlessly deciding that Raja should handle the situation.

"Thandie, we've planned something for you. You'll want to get dressed for this."

"I'm not getting out of bed until somebody explains what is going on."

Out of the blue, Thandie's bedroom door swung open, and Elliot came into the room. Dressed in a navy polo shirt and white shorts, he looked refreshingly handsome. There wasn't a single wrinkle or dark circle under his eyes. The man looked effortlessly perfect. His glowing morning beauty made Thandie painfully aware of her haggard appearance. Her hair was all over her head, and she was only wearing an old T-shirt, her bra and panties. She yanked the covers over her shoulders and scowled at him.

"Excuse me," she snapped. "I don't remember inviting you in."

Elliot looked at Len and Raja, clearly irritated. "What the hell is taking so long?"

Both girls pointed at Thandie.

"She won't budge without us spoiling the surprise," Len explained. "Warren said he wanted this to be a surprise."

"Len!" Raja nudged her friend.

Thandie sat up straight. "What does Warren have to do with this?" She turned on Elliot. "Again, what are you doing in my room?"

Elliot placed his hands on his hips. "We're waiting on you. Hurry up and get out of bed." He turned to Len. "Get her clothes. We don't have much time. We need to head out early if we want to enjoy the cool weather."

"I'm not going anywhere," Thandie practically growled.

Elliot fixed her with a serious stare. "You can either get out of that bed of your own accord, or I'll dress you myself."

"You wouldn't!"

He approached the bed slowly and then yanked the covers

off. Thandie screamed, grabbing a pillow to shield her body. Raja and Len stood like deer in headlights, too shocked to offer any help.

"Okay! Okay!" Thandie told him. "I'm getting up."

"We're waiting," he said calmly.

Elliot walked out as abruptly as he had arrived. Len laid Thandie's bikini and sundress on the edge of the bed before hurriedly following Raja out of the room.

She washed up and dressed as quickly as she could and headed downstairs. She honestly didn't think she could endure another Elliot Richards encounter.

Warren and a large bouquet of white lilies greeted her.

"Good morning, Thandie." He smiled brightly. "You look great."

"What are you doing here, Warren?" She hadn't meant for her voice to sound so cold.

"I'm here to apologize about what happened and beg for your forgiveness." He pushed the flowers into her hands. "I'm so sorry you had to go through that. I've been beating myself up with guilt. I would have been over yesterday, but I was giving you time to cool down."

Thandie could barely see him over the fragrant flowers. "I—I don't know what to say."

"Say you'll forgive me."

Thandie set the flowers aside. "Warren, you're not off the hook, but I'll stop giving you the silent treatment."

He smiled. "I guessed as much, so I convinced everyone to join us on a boat trip. Well, actually, it's Elliot's boat, but I figured both of you could use some relaxation."

Thandie had little interest in boating. Large masses of water had always unnerved her, and she'd seen enough episodes of Animal Planet's Shark Week to make her appreciate living on land. Stalling, Thandie looked around the room. "Where's Lucinda?" she asked.

Warren frowned, as if that very question had been plaguing him.

"She's not here," Elliot announced, shooting Warren a cool stare. Leaving no room for anyone to ask questions, he asked, "Is everyone ready?"

Warren held out his hand to Thandie. "Will you come?"

"Please say yes," Raja begged.

"Please," Len chirped. "Elliot's boat looks really awesome."

Thandie shifted her gaze between the girls' pleading expressions, and Warren's anxious one. Then she sighed. With such odds against her, how could she say no?

Elliot's boat was tied to the private boat slip behind his home. It was a sleek, all-white sailing yacht. Graceful in design, the yacht was perfect for entertaining. Len and Raja's gasps of amazement echoed Thandie's own sentiments. It was beautiful.

They loaded up supplies, and thirty minutes later they were drifting away from the dock. Elliot took control of the helm and steered them toward open water. Raja and Len kept themselves busy laughing about anything and everything. Warren joined in on the fun, quickly becoming more animated the farther they got out to sea.

Thandie was still grumpy from her rude awakening this morning but she couldn't help but enjoy the pleasant weather. The crisp smell of the morning air and calm lull of the ocean soon enticed her. She was tired, but the scenic view of the coast was remarkable. She gazed out at the water and marveled at the natural beauty surrounding them. Drinks were passed around almost as soon as they set sail.

They sailed for about an hour before Elliot lowered the sails and dropped the anchor. Warren turned on the radio while Len and Raja stripped down to their swimsuits. Within minutes, the girls were overboard, swimming in clear blue water, with Warren following eagerly behind. This left Thandie and Elliot on board alone.

They hadn't spoken since yesterday morning in the kitchen. Thandie felt a little tense, being alone with him now. Casting him a cool glance, she said, "You really didn't have to storm into my room this morning."

Elliot gave the briefest of shrugs. "I figured the longer Raja and Len made explanations, the less a surprise it would be."

"It was rude."

He gave another careless shrug. "What can I say? I'm an asshole."

"And you're very good at it."

"I'm good at a lot of things, Thandie."

"Hmm," was all she said. Thandie turned her face toward the ocean, where Warren and the girls were frolicking in the water. They were too far away for her to hear anything aside from the occasional squeal of laughter.

Feeling Elliot's gaze on her, Thandie shot him a quick glance. He was at the helm, one hand casually rested on the wheel while the other pressed a bottle of Corona to his lips. His cool gray eyes were set on her.

Unable to resist him, Thandie looked away. She immediately berated herself. Why did she always act like a frightened cat around him? She bit on her bottom lip, feeling the burden of silence begin to weigh on her. Deciding now was just as good as any to broach the conversation about her plans to help Day, Thandie turned to face him before she lost her gumption. "Elliot, I have something I'd like to discuss with you."

He lifted one dark brow in question.

"It about the club," she began.

"Go on," he said, his voice a delightful low rumble.

"I would like to add an additional event to the agenda."

Again, he raised his brow.

"I know a local designer who'll be launching her own fashion line this summer. Her name is Victoria Day—"

"I know Day," he cut in.

Thandie paused to consider this. She couldn't help but wonder how well Elliot knew Day. According to Day, she barely knew Elliot. Had Thandie been misinformed?

The question must have played itself out in her expression because Elliot added, "Miami is a small town, and I have a long memory."

There, she thought. That should have satisfied her curiosity, but it didn't. "Yes, well…" Thandie struggled to move on. "Like I was saying, Day needs a central location to display her collection. I would like to recommend Babylon for the event."

Elliot seemed to turn over the idea in his head.

"It would attract some of the top journalists in the country," Thandie said quickly. "The press coverage could be highly beneficial."

She watched Elliot as he took another slow sip of beer, his eyes never leaving hers. Finally he asked, "Can you make it profitable?"

"I believe so."

"All right."

"All right?"

"You have my approval," he said.

Thandie had to bite down on her lower lip to prevent a sigh of relief. Fighting to school her features, she said, "Thank you."

"Outline the financial benefits in a proposal and submit it by the end of the week."

"Again, thank you."

"Deliver it to me personally," he said.

"Personally?"

Elliot gave a slow nod of his head.

Thandie opened her mouth to argue, but quickly stopped herself. "Gladly," she said with a stiff smile, deciding this was not a fight worth picking. She had another issue to put to him, and it was much more important. "There's something else I'd like to cover with you."

"Oh?" he said, sounding amused.

"It's regarding your camera policy," she said carefully. "I was wondering if you would be willing to—"

"No."

"But—"

"No," he said again, this time his tone left no room for doubt.

Thandie could see from the stern set of his jaw this was not a discussion she would win today. She would have to attempt the topic at a later date. But not too late, she reminded herself. She did not have a lot of time to play with.

A shout of laughter came from the water, causing both Thandie and Elliot to look toward the spot where Warren and the girls were swimming. The sounds of water splashing and more laughter erupted. The three of them were having a good time. From the corner of her eye, Thandie could see Elliot turn away from their playfulness and resettle his gaze on her. It was alarming how easily she could sense his attention.

Feeling another lull falling between them, Thandie said, "I wouldn't have taken you for a sailboat guy."

"Why is that?" he asked softly.

"I suppose it's because you seem to constantly be on the go. I would have figured you for a speedboat."

Elliot chuckled. "It's because I live a busy lifestyle that I chose a sailboat," he explained. "Sailing seems slower. Besides, I practically grew up on the water."

Thandie turned to him, seeing something warm and safe in his eyes for the first time. "Where did you learn to sail?"

"From my father," he said, not appearing to be surprised by her question. "Luis...he loved the ocean. He taught me everything he knew."

"You speak in past tense."

"He passed away a few years ago," he said matter-of-factly. "Heart attack."

"I'm sorry to hear that," she said, remembering her own mother with a pang. "Were you close to your father?"

"Very close." Elliot took another sip of his beer. "And you? Are you close to your parents?"

Thandie shrugged, beginning to feel uncomfortable with the conversation. "I suppose I am," she said. "In all honesty, I'm not sure." She looked away, debating how much to convey. "My mother suffers from dementia. She was diagnosed when I was very young. Her memory is tricky." Thandie clinched her hand into a fist beneath the folds of her dress. "I visit her often. She rarely recognizes me."

Elliot must have caught the increasingly clipped tone of her voice, because he didn't press her for details. "And your father?"

"Gone." Explaining to him that her father had abandoned her and her mother years before was too painful. She would not talk about her father, or the hellish years that followed. That was a past she was trying to leave far behind her.

"Are you getting in?"

"Huh?" she asked, confused by the subject change.

"I asked if you were going to get in the water?" he said causally, as if this is what they'd been talking about all along.

"Oh, uh—no." Thandie cast her eyes downward before he

could see the look on her face. "Please don't let me stop you from joining the others."

"I'd rather keep you company."

Thandie's eyes flitted up to his. "It's not necessary. I insist you go."

Elliot came from behind the wheel and sat on the davenport across from Thandie. "Would it make you feel less nervous if I did?"

"I'm not nervous."

"So you say."

"I'm not," she snapped.

His brow lifted in challenge.

"What?" she grimaced. "I don't have to prove anything to you."

"Take off your dress."

"Excuse me?"

"You're wearing your swimsuit underneath."

"I know, but I'm not undressing just because you want me to."

"Are you self-conscious?"

"No," she said quickly.

"You shouldn't be. You have a great body. Let me see it."

"No."

"Is no your favorite word?"

"No." She groaned, knowing she'd fallen right into his trap. Elliot grinned. "Take it off."

"How many times do I have to say—ah!"

Without warning, Elliot had grabbed the hem of her dress and yanked it high over her head, exposing her cherry-red bikini. Desperately, Thandie tried to cover her breasts with her hands.

"Don't bother," he laughed. "You have lovely breasts."

"You—you maniac!"

"Turn around. Let me see your ass."

"Fuck you."

He winked. "How about *I* fuck you instead?"

Thandie turned her head away from him. She was amazed at how quickly the tone of the conversation had changed. It had gone from business, to somewhat sympathetic, to now this. She no longer saw the hint of warmth in his eyes, only icy determination. "I know what you're trying to do, Elliot."

"What might that be?"

"You're trying to bait me."

"That may be," he consented. "But what exactly do you think I'm trying to bait you to do?"

"I don't know, and I don't care. But know this, Elliot, my answer is no."

He tsked. "You're no fun, Thandie. At least ask me what I want."

"I said I don't care."

"Yes, you do. Why else would you be so nervous around me?"

"For the last time, I'm not nervous!"

"Then stop trying to hide yourself from me."

"You're toying with me."

"Yes, I am. Now let me see you." He reached out for her, but Thandie slapped his hand away. Elliot only chuckled. "What's the matter? Bad nerves?"

With a frustrated huff, Thandie dropped her hands from her bikini-clad breasts. "There! Are you happy now?"

"Immensely." Elliot's grin disappeared as his eyes narrowed. He stared at her breasts for what felt like hours before speaking again. "Turn around."

"No." She set her hands on her hips. "Now that you've seen me, will you leave me alone?"

"Ask me what I want."

"What?" She was surprised by his comment.

"I'm baiting you, remember? Ask me what I want."

Thandie rolled her eyes. "Fine, Elliot." She released a heavy sigh. "What do you want?"

His voice turned smooth as his silver gaze ravaged her body. "I want you on your back with your ankles behind your head, screaming my name."

She gasped. An unwanted rush of hot lust dampened her thighs. "You can't be serious," she sputtered. "Do you talk to all your women like that?"

He pulled his eyes from her breasts to meet her gaze. "I've never been one to lead a woman on." His eyes dropped down to her bikini bottoms. "I'm not interested in a relationship, Thandie. I just want sex with you."

"No, thank you."

"You'll change your mind."

"No, I won't."

His voice was dead serious when he said, "I'll make you."

Thandie gathered what remained of her pride. "I know you're used to women obeying your every whim, but I—"

"You try so hard not to be attracted to me. Why?"

"This is a working relationship," she said sternly.

"It could be more, Thandie. It could be a lot more."

"I said no."

"Is it so hard to admit you want me?" He leaned forward, cupping her face in his hands. "I can smell your desire, pussy-cat. I know you want me. You want me near you, inside you, on top of you. Stop denying yourself the pleasures I can provide." His gray eyes were intense. "Stop denying us, Thandie."

She shivered. His words were washing over her skin like smooth silk. Her legs shook under his silver stare. She could feel her defenses crumbling. She was breathless. "You give yourself a lot of credit, Mr. Richards."

"I have the experience to back it up." He grinned. "Trust me. I'm as good as they say."

"Why me?"

"You interest me."

"What happens when I'm no longer interesting?"

Elliot shrugged. "I'll find someone else."

"This is all a game to you," she whispered.

He stared at her for a long while before nodding his head. "Everything is a game, Thandie. And I play to win."

The sudden drop in his voice made her uneasy. She meant to turn away from him, but his body moved over her, trapping her on the chaise. Her eyes grew wide as he lowered his face to her breasts. She could barely catch her breath. "Don't—"

When Elliot's silver eyes flashed up to meet hers, Thandie knew she was in trouble. She should have moved out of his reach, but she couldn't. Her body was frozen in place, unwilling to obey what her brain was demanding. Instead, she sat there, powerless, watching as he lowered his head to nuzzle her cleavage with his nose. He inhaled the scent of her skin. His nearness was causing havoc on her nerves. Every cell in her body was screaming for more.

Thandie gasped when his tongue flicked over the thin material covering her nipple. She watched in horror as her body betrayed her, the sensitive flesh instantly growing pebble-hard. He ran his tongue around the covered bud. Thandie's breath quickened as she watched his perfect white teeth pull the fabric of her top away; exposing her bare breast to the cool ocean air.

Elliot sucked in a breath at the sight of her dusky dark nipple. His lips latched onto the chocolate-dipped dessert. Thandie's flesh was soft in his mouth. His tongue lapped the bud hungrily, nearly overwhelmed by the need to taste her. He nibbled and tugged until they were both breathless with desire.

He wanted to brand her with his touch. So that every man after him would know he had possessed her. He smothered his face into her softness as his hands caressed the sides of her ribcage. Thandie moaned. Her back arched up to offer him more. Elliot pushed aside her top to free her breasts completely. His mouth devoured one while his fingers squeezed the other. His unoccupied hand skimmed down her stomach to cup her womanhood. Thandie released a throaty groan. Before she could register what was happening, Elliot lowered himself to his knees, positioning himself between her legs.

Blinded with desire, he pushed her legs apart and placed his face between her thighs. He licked the crotch of her bikini bottoms. Thandie's legs shook under his touch. His tongue circled the moist fabric, his hunger for her growing. He slid his fingers into the waistband of her bikini bottoms. He was in mid-action of pulling them down her legs when she gasped and went stock-still.

"Elliot, get up!" she rasped.

He was too far gone to care what had changed her mind. Confident he could get her back in the mood, Elliot flicked his tongue over her crotch again.

"They're coming back," Thandie said hoarsely. "Get up."

He blinked. "What?"

"They're coming."

Elliot lifted his head just in time before Thandie slammed her legs closed. She pushed against his shoulders so she could sit up, and fix her swimsuit. She fumbled with the ties of her top nervously, struggling to make her fingers obey simple commands.

Elliot took hold of her wrists, bringing her frantic movements to a halt. "I'm not finished with you, Thandie."

"Oh, yes you are," she snapped.

"No, I'm not. Not by a long shot."

The sound of a loud splash of water signaled the approach of the group. Thandie gasped, slapped Elliot's hands away, and finished adjusting her suit. She righted herself just as Len climbed into the boat, followed by Raja and then Warren. They were so busy laughing, they didn't notice Elliot scowling at Thandie before pushing himself to his feet.

"The water is wonderful, Thandie!" Len said as she wrung out her hair over the side of the boat. "You're missing all the fun."

Thandie flashed a nervous smile at Len, trying her best to ignore Elliot's fierce frown. "Did you have a good swim?"

"Absolutely." Len laughed. "The water feels great." She glanced at Elliot and gave him a sexy smile. "Elliot, you have to join us next time."

He forced a tight grin. "I would enjoy that, Len."

By now Raja had finished wringing her long black hair free from ocean water. She joined Len to flirt with Elliot. Warren watched the girls, his eyes glued to their wet bodies.

Warren sighed as he sat down beside Thandie. "Those two get more beautiful every time I see them."

Thandie nodded. "I'm glad you think so, Warren."

He blushed.

"Of course, they don't compare to you, Thandie."

"You're a natural charmer," she said distractedly, too busy trying to ignore Len and Raja's advances on Elliot.

"I'm serious," Warren said. "I always expressed my interest in you when we were both in New York. But you were dating that photographer. Rotten luck, I have."

"Sounds as though you have pretty good luck," Thandie said, finally turning to look at the older man. "You got married to Wife Number Five soon after moving to Miami. Despite my encounter with her, she's pretty."

"Yeah, she's pretty. I just wish I had looked beyond—" his voice trailed off.

Thandie smiled. She couldn't help but soften toward him. In spite his antics, Warren was a good guy. She nudged him with her shoulder. "What doesn't kill you makes you stronger, right?"

Warren tossed his arm around her shoulders and gave her a light hug. "Right."

The weather was on their side. They sailed along the coastline for a greater part of the day. The gentle sway of the boat cradled them to relaxation. Len, Raja and Warren entertained themselves with periodic swims in the ocean and silly drinking games. Lunch consisted of cold sandwiches, fruit and bottled water. No one seemed to notice Thandie was keeping an almost comical distance from Elliot.

Nor the fact that Elliot was nursing a hard-on for most of the afternoon.

By the time they neared the boat's dock, it was half an hour until sunset. They watched the sun disappear over the horizon. It was a dazzling display of warm golden hues, soft pinks and cool violets.

When they finally tied up, there was a welcoming party waiting for them. Romero stood just a little ahead of the group, and was therefore the first to welcome Elliot as he stepped off the boat. The two had a quick whispered exchange before Romero offered him a cell phone.

Elliot accepted it, took a few steps away from everyone for privacy, and started talking to someone on the other end of the line.

Adam, Markie and Rex patiently stood nearby, waiting for their chance to speak with Elliot. The sight of Len, Raja and Thandie stepping on deck captured their attention. Instantly, there was shuffle of activity as the men elbowed each other to help the ladies. Warren barely jumped out of the way to prevent being knocked overboard. Rex reached out to help Thandie get safely to the gravel.

After a brief hug, Thandie asked, "When did you get back?"

"Last night," he said. "I went over to Warren's house looking for you, but Anga told me you were here." Rex's eyes tilted in the direction of Elliot's home. "I heard there was an interesting event."

Thandie smiled up at him. "You have no idea."

He tucked her hand into the crook of his arm. "You'll have to tell me about it."

Embracing his arm, Thandie allowed herself to be led back to the house by Rex.

Chapter Fifteen

Elliot gave a merciless swing at the rubber ball and then swore.

"When you're done pouting," Nico taunted as he returned the pass, "do you want to tell me what's wrong?"

"I'm not pouting," Elliot snapped.

"Whatever, man."

"Can you stop trying to distract me from the horrible game you're playing?"

Nico gave a loud snort. "It can't be too horrible. I'm winning, if you hadn't noticed."

To Elliot's disbelief, he missed the next pass. He was annoyed to see his friend grinning at him.

Breathing hard, Nico rested his hands on his knees. "What's up, Elliot? That was an easy serve."

Elliot contemplated whether he should tell Nico what was bothering him. They had been friends for years, but he struggled with the idea of sharing his recent obsession. Nico would only tease him mercilessly, which would be well-deserved, as he would treat his friend in kind. The problem was his feelings were beginning to consume him. In the past, when he had a problem to talk out, he contacted Nico. Although Nico was one of the last people he wanted to confide in right now, he had to admit he had few options. If not Nico, it was nobody.

Choosing his words carefully, he shot Nico a hard stare. "I'm having difficulty figuring something out."

Nico looked at him in all seriousness. "Do you need my help?"

"Hell, no," he growled.

Nico eyed him suspiciously before a slow grin spread across his face, followed by a howl of laughter. "It's a woman." He laughed again.

Elliot rolled his eyes in annoyance.

"It's the woman you hired." He pointed an accusing finger at him. "Thandie, right?" Not waiting for a response, he howled again, his boisterous laughter echoing off the racquetball court walls. "I knew it! The moment I saw her, I knew she was going to be trouble for you."

"Fuck you."

"No, my friend, fuck you. Serves you right. You've always had women served to you on silver platters. This time, you'll actually have to work for one. I think my respect for Thandie just soared through the roof."

"Are you finished?"

"Not yet." A fresh bout of laughter assailed him. "I never thought I'd see the day."

"You're not helping, Nico."

"Oh, now you want my help?"

"Okay, forget it. Serve the ball."

"Oh, no," he said with a lazy drawl. "We have to savor this moment." He looked at his watch. "Let's see here. It's exactly 3:43 p.m. on this beautiful Sunday afternoon—"

"Let's just play the damn game."

"If I had my phone right now, I'd take a picture of you."

Elliot frowned, more than annoyed with Nico's attitude. "Now that you've made your point, can you drop it?"

Brushing his hair out of his eyes, Nico wiped at the sweat from his forehead. "Like you would treat me any differently." Bouncing the ball in preparation for his serve, Nico doled out a hard swing, putting the game back in motion. "Why her?"

Elliot returned the serve easily. "Not sure."

"Of course you know. She's not making it easy for you."

"So?"

"When have you ever backed down from a challenge, Elliot?"

He answered him by returning a difficult pass.

"I rest my case," Nico snorted.

"I don't get her. I don't understand the connection I feel with her." Elliot was beginning to pant as he charged for one return after another. "She won't give in to me."

"Maybe she's not interested."

"She's interested," he said confidently.

"Maybe she already has a man."

Elliot came to an abrupt stop, letting the ball fly past him and roll quietly to a corner of the court.

Nico paused as well. "You never asked if she was spoken for?"

Elliot grimaced, mentally turning over a possibility that had never crossed his mind. An image of Rex Barrington flashed in his head, causing him to glower.

Nico retrieved the ball and began bouncing it in place on his racket. "You know, Elliot, this could be the reason she's immune to you. If she's hot for some other guy, your invitations may very well be a nuisance rather than a blessing."

Elliot's frown darkened. "Are you going to serve the damn ball?"

Unfazed, Nico continued bouncing the ball. "Seriously,

Elliot, you may just have found the only woman who doesn't go faint whenever you give her a little attention. Not that I'm doubting your powers of persuasion, but your affections just might be misplaced on this one."

"Nico," Elliot warned in a low growl. The thought that Thandie might be attached to someone else awoke a beast in his chest that he hadn't known existed.

"Oh, dear," Nico drawled. "I see your mind at work. You're intent on starting trouble, aren't you?"

"Stay out of it."

"Has it occurred to you that you might be in over your head? That finally there's a woman who just might tame you?"

Elliot greeted that comment with a snort. "That will never happen."

"Okay, *amigo*. So what are you going to do about your predicament? I know you're no stranger to wooing women away from their significant others, but what do you have in mind?"

"If she has someone, he will quickly be a thing of the past."

Nico laughed. "Does your ego ever get a rest?"

"No." Snatching the ball in mid-bounce over Nico's racket, Elliot gave a brutal serve toward the far wall, causing the ball to whip back quickly and dart at Nico's head.

"Damn!" Nico swore, countering the serve just in time. "That almost took my head off."

Elliot swung at the ball. "That was the point."

"Oh, I get it." Nico swung at the ball. "You're back to pouting again. It's not my fault you aren't sleeping with the woman of your choice."

Elliot gave another hard serve. "Only a bump in the road," he said, releasing a loud grunt as he hustled to counter a clever backhand from Nico. "A problem I will quickly remedy."

"Whatever you say, Elliot."

"When have I ever disappointed you?"

"I'm not saying you have. But if there's one thing I know about women, when they have their minds made up, that's the end of that."

"Well, I happen to know a lot about women, and I'm telling you I'll get my way."

"Okay, Casanova. Just remember I'm not the one taking out my sexual frustrations on a rubber ball."

"Who's sexually frustrated?" a voice called out.

Elliot and Nico turned to see their friend Matrix Lang had entered the court. Cradling his racket under one arm, Matrix began tying back his long dark hair with an elastic band.

"Nice of you to join us," Elliot said sardonically.

Matrix gave a mock bow. "The pleasure is all mine."

"You're late," Nico announced.

"So it would seem," Matrix drawled.

"Where's Chris?" Elliot asked. "We'd like to start our game."

"Not coming," Matrix said matter-of-fact. "He had to fly back to New York for a family meeting."

"We're going to be uneven," Nico mused aloud.

"Never stopped us before," Matrix said untroubled. Having secured his hair into a knot at the nape of his neck, he pulled his T-shirt over his head, revealing ripples of tight muscles. Elliot and Nico smirked. They were fit men, however Matrix took his health to the extreme. As the owner of a string of fitness clubs within the Miami–Dade area, Matrix was almost as busy as Elliot. When he was not preoccupied with instructing advanced workout classes at his clubs, he was providing private sessions for his celebrity clients. In his spare time, he did what he was most renowned for—hosting exclusive sex parties.

"You should have been over the other night," Matrix announced. "Quality guest list."

"Such as?" Nico asked.

"Playlon for starters," he said with a slow grin. There was little need for Matrix to mention anyone else in attendance. Playlon DeleTorre, an Italian duke and heir apparent to the throne of Sardinia, was heavily sought after by the media masses. The fact that he was extremely handsome, to the point of feminine beauty, made him a human magnet to both men and women.

Elliot arched his brow in interest. "And?"

"You know how it is when word gets out DeleTorre is in town." He gave a helpless shrug. "Women come out of the woodwork. Cream of the crop."

Nico's brows hiked up. "Any one we know?"

"*Everyone* you know," Matrix said with a satisfied smile. He punctuated his words by releasing a long yawn, as if to insinuate he'd only just left his party to join them. "The ladies were very friendly." Turning to Elliot, he added, "The Ripley Twins were there." When Elliot shrugged at the mention, Matrix focused his dark gaze on his friend. "That's interesting."

Elliot ignored the comment and asked. "Busy tonight?" Elliot scooped up the rubber ball from the floor and served it, putting the game back in motion.

"Depends." Matrix stepped forward to exercise a masterful forehand swing with the precision one only got after many hours of practice. "What did you have in mind?"

"Are you able to swing by the club tonight?"

Matrix glanced at Elliot. "If I come, you must do something for me." He winked at Nico. "Explain to me why you're sexually frustrated."

Nico burst into laughter.

"Fuck both of you," Elliot grumbled.

"I can't believe this!" Thandie shouted to the ceiling. "This has got to be the worst day of my life."

Victoria Day sat cross-legged atop the dining room table at Elliot's house, and watched her pace back and forth. She'd been doing it for the last half hour.

Not too long after Thandie had woken up, she received a message with distressing news. Nicki Minaj, her headliner for the weekend performance, had pulled out. Thandie couldn't place the blame on her. Everything had been done on such short notice. Negotiations had been shaky from the start. Learning days before showtime she had to find a substitute entertainer was a daunting task. Thandie and the girls had spent the better part of the day considering their options. There were not many.

In the end, Thandie had to make the decision to call the only person she knew who could respond on such short notice. She wasn't thrilled about the resolution. She'd have to call Markie, Rex and Adam about the emergency change, and make corrections for all the media announcements they'd scheduled. It hadn't been pretty. And so, this Saturday night, instead of hosting Nicki Minaj, Club Babylon would be presenting a burlesque show featuring The Pussy Cats.

And now this!

"Okay, I've been more than patient," Victoria said. "Are you going to tell me what bee crawled up your butt?"

Thandie tok a deep breath before saying, "Ruark Randall's agent just called me."

Victoria's eyes lit up. "The actor?"

"The jerk, is more like it," Thandie grumbled.

"Jerk or not, he's a cutie. What did they want?"

"Ruark is in town tonight and he wants to come to Babylon. Which means, I'll have to escort him."

"That sounds exciting, Thandie. Why the long face?"

Thandie shook her head. "It's hard to explain."

"Well, I have something that should put you in a better mood."

"What's that?"

Victoria slid off the table, and retrieved a garment bag she'd brought in with her. She held it up with pride. "Your glow-in-the-dark outfits." She wiggled her eyebrows playfully. "Want to try yours on?"

Fifteen minutes later, Thandie was staring at her image in the floor length mirror. She turned one way and then the other, examining the dress. Finally, she asked, "Where's the rest of it?"

The dress in question was really not a dress at all. It was a sheer ghost of a dress pulled over a bra and matching panties.

Victoria's eyes shone with excitement. "The beauty of this little number is when the lights are off, you'll only see the lingerie beneath. It glows bright orange."

Thandie scrunched up her nose. "How do Len and Raja's outfits look?"

Victoria grinned. "I made something very special for them." She placed a protective hand on the garment bag. "You'll have to wait and see."

Thandie sighed and looked down at her dress. "Don't you think it's a tad risqué?" she asked.

Victoria rolled her eyes. "It's supposed to be risqué. You're wearing it to a club, not a nunnery." She pulled out a small plastic bag and handed it to Thandie. "I brought you some cosmetics and accessories. All glow-in-the-dark, of course."

"You bought these?"

Victoria laughed. "Oh no. I had them at my house. You never know when you'll need stuff like that."

"Thanks," Thandie said, placing the bag on the dresser. She turned to the mirror and examined herself once more. She was a little concerned about the cut of the panties.

"Thongs are in. Trust me on this."

Thandie shot her a worried expression.

Victoria missed it because she was too busy looking around the spacious guest bedroom. "Does Elliot normally invite contract employees to live with him?"

"Actually, we were staying with Warren at first."

"Warren Radcliffe?" Victoria said, her expression registering shock.

"The one and only."

"What happened?"

"An unfortunate event," Thandie said vaguely.

Victoria held up her hands. "Say no more. If it involves Warren, it's guaranteed to be unbelievable." She scanned the grand expanse of Elliot's home. "I can't say I pity you, Thandie. It would seem you got the better end of the deal. This isn't a bad place to hole up for a few months. Not to mention the breathtaking view you get to enjoy."

Thandie looked out the dining room windows. The view of the sunshine glistening off the ocean was indeed breathtaking.

"I was talking about Elliot," Victoria said with a smile.

Thandie laughed.

Victoria looked at her watch and made a face. "Wow, I didn't think is was so late. I have to go. When is the glow-in-the-dark thingy?"

"Tomorrow night," Thandie answered, already beginning to change back into her shorts.

"Cool. Add me to the list."

"You're coming?" The question came out harsher than she'd meant it. Thandie had honestly been hoping she wouldn't want to go. She didn't know if she had enough nerve to pull off a dress so provocative.

"Of course, I'll be there," Victoria said. "I wouldn't miss it for the world."

★ ★ ★

Elliot waved past the security guard at the entrance to Star Island. He and Nico were currently arguing about the outcome of today's racquetball game. Matrix, as usual, bested both of them. Nico was sore over the loss. Meanwhile, Elliot was in a state of denial, being that he'd also lost a rematch against Nico.

They turned into the drive leading to the house. Elliot slowed the car, parking directly in front. Killing the engine, he was just about to get out of the car when Nico stayed his action by asking, "Who's car is that?" He pointed to the black Expedition in his drive way.

"The Expedition belongs to Thandie." Elliot frowned, when he said, "I'm not sure who the other car belongs to."

"Thandie is at your house?"

"She's staying with me for a short while," Elliot confessed.

Nico looked at him and laughed. "You have Thandie living with you?"

"I was helping out Warren," he said. Elliot was forced to explain the whole sordid tale about Sophia's sudden return to Miami and the knife incident. When he was done, Nico simply stared at him.

"Why didn't you tell me this earlier?"

Elliot shrugged. "What was there to tell?"

"And her assistants?"

Elliot gave a slow nod of his head.

Nico considered this news, and then asked, "Do you think it's wise to have all that…talent under one roof?"

Elliot gave a snort. "Are you offering to house them?"

Nico threw his hands up, as if pushed into a corner. "If you insist."

"Not a chance."

Grinning, Nico wagged his finger at him. "Now I understand why you were so confident in your powers of persuasion."

"Proximity has nothing to do with it."

"Tell me that after she's been here for a week."

The sound of the house's front door opened, and without warning, Nico's grin slipped. Something caught his eye. Elliot followed his stare. It lead straight to the petite form of Victoria Day. She was crossing the front porch. She was so absorbed in her thoughts, she hadn't noticed them there.

Flashy as ever, Victoria was wearing a leopard print mini dress and strange high heels covered with multicolored feathers. Using her key fob, she popped the trunk of a bright yellow VW Beetle. Rounding the car, she leaned over to stuff a garment bag inside. The action caused her skirt to rise, offering both men a generous glimpse of her thighs.

As if she felt that she was being watched, Victoria's head popped up. Looking over her shoulder, she spotted them. It was easy to tell what held their attention. Smiling, she pulled the hem of her dress down slowly, and then she flipped them her middle finger. Both men were too shocked to say anything as she drove off.

Finally, Nico said, "What was that?"

"That, my friend, was Victoria Day."

Nico turned in his seat, to watch the tiny car speed off. "Who is she?"

"A local fashion designer," Elliot said as he got out. "Delightful little thing, isn't she?"

A thoughtful grin claimed Nico's face. "To say the least."

Within a few short hours, Thandie would once again be in the company of Ruark Randall. She was not looking to their reunion.

According to his agent, Ruark had left numerous messages

at her office hoping to persuade Thandie to join him for dinner. Because of Amanda's frazzled mind, she had not relayed the messages to Thandie. It wouldn't have mattered either way. Thandie felt nothing but annoyance toward the actor. She would love to tell him to kiss off, but she was mindful of the fact his attendance at Babylon was great publicity. So, swallowing her disdain, Thandie prepared for her night with Ruark.

She dressed carefully, avoiding anything overly provocative. Not wanting Ruark to get the wrong impression, she donned the most unassuming outfit in her possession: black leather pants and a long sleeve blouse.

In the limo on the way to Ruark's hotel, she called Amanda to see if everything was all right. As before, her assistant was beside herself. She begged Thandie to come back to New York or at least send Len or Raja. Thandie calmed her down by listening to her current disaster and offering a solution. She promised she would consider sending help but was still uncertain how she would manage it. It didn't take a rocket scientist to know that Len would be completely useless, and Raja was needed here in Miami.

She disconnected her call with Amanda. It was inevitable that she would have to get on a plane and return to the city. Not for Amanda's sake, but for her own.

Ruark Randall was exactly as Thandie remembered him—obnoxious. Somehow, he thought that they were on some sort of date. He was all hands the entire ride to the club. Thandie was elated when the limo finally pulled in front of Babylon. Doing their job quite well, Len and Raja had ensured paparazzi would be present to capture Ruark's entrance. Not surprisingly, Ruark was a complete ham in front of the cameras. The crowd of bystanders pressed forward to see him, while the more fanatical females started screaming.

Ruark posed for a dozen pictures before Tiny, the bouncer,

ushered them inside. Ruark had no problem throwing his arm around Thandie's waist as they moved through the crowd. She added this to the long list of reasons why she despised him.

Adam welcomed them into VIP and escorted them to a private booth. Ruark made quick work of groping and kissing her. Thandie pushed him away as best she could, but it was to no avail. He was tenacious in his efforts. He ordered a procession of drinks, taking the liberty to order for her as well. Adam delivered their drinks, always passing her what he referred to as "the usual," which was nothing more than cranberry juice and club soda. Ruark had come to Babylon to have a good time. Mercifully Adam made sure she wasn't dragged along for the ride. The more intoxicated Ruark became, the more affectionate he was. Strangely enough, it was easier to reprimand him. He continued to attempt to cup her breasts, only to have Thandie slap his hands away. He didn't seem to notice that she was hitting him with much more force than earlier. She plastered a smile on her face for publicity's sake, but she couldn't wait until the night was over.

Club Babylon was as energetic as ever. Tonight's theme was Dominatrix. The dancers wore black leather outfits and high-heeled boots, complete with whips. Elliot imagined that he would have enjoyed tonight's show, but as it was, he was hard at work. The staff meeting ran long. Afterward, he had a phone conference with potential investors. Markie had to come up to remind him to make his rounds with the guests.

Elliot descended to the arena floor. He greeted guests and offered complementary drinks, welcoming the distraction from his work. He smiled and charmed all who approached him. From across the room, he spied Thandie in the crowd. Just as he'd been warned, she was escorting Ruark Randall tonight. Presently, he was signing an autograph for a fan, but he was too close to Thandie. He frowned.

"Elliot."

Mrs. Sophia Radcliffe, Wife Number Five, suddenly appeared. Her hair and clothing were styled to perfection.

"What can I do for you, Sophia?"

"I've called you a dozen times," she said brusquely. "Why haven't you returned my messages?"

Elliot looked back toward Thandie. Frowning, he looked at the woman before him. "Sophia, I have no desire to talk to you. You should call your husband if you want companionship."

"Screw you," she hissed.

"Yes, we've covered that, haven't we?" He gave a final glance toward Thandie. "You'll have to excuse me, Sophia. I need to finish my rounds."

She grabbed his arm. "How long are you going to do this?"

"Do what?"

"You know what, damn you. Why won't you return my calls?"

He pulled her hand away from him. "Why would I?"

"You hate me for marrying him."

Elliot fixed her with a serious stare. "Yes, Sophia, I do hate you for marrying Warren. You're using him for his money, and the poor bastard is so blinded he can't see you for what you really are."

She lifted her chin. "And what am I?"

"You're a cheap whore who struck gold."

She faltered a step, taken aback by the menace in his voice. "You'll never forgive me, will you?" she whispered.

"The only thing I would be unforgiving about is that you used my club to prey on wealthy fools."

"I can't help that Warren's rich," she argued.

"And his connection to me never crossed your mind?" He smirked when he saw a guilty look in her eyes. "That's what I thought," he breathed. "You're using Warren just like you use every man."

Her eyes stung with sudden tears. "I never used you."

"Only because I wouldn't let you." His eyes turned glacial. He'd had enough of Sophia. He decided to hurt her where it mattered most. Hopefully, she would get the point, and would leave him alone for good. "Guys like me only sleep with you just to break up the monotony. And once we realize you're more trouble than you're worth, we quickly move on."

"You really are an asshole, Elliot.

He bowed his head. "I've never pretended otherwise." He began to walk away.

"And to think I actually thought—" she stopped when her voice quivered.

Elliot whirled around on her. "You thought what?" he snapped. Observing a flicker of genuine vulnerability in her face, he laughed. "Please spare me the dramatics. You're not the type to fall in love." Noticing Nico and Matrix entering the arena, he gave a slight nod. "Do me a favor, Sophia, and get the hell out of my club."

He could hear her spitting a string of profanity at his back, but he paid her no mind. He was happy she was leaving. The idea of Sophia roaming his club annoyed him. She had always been a thorn in his side. He'd thought he'd finally gotten rid of her, but Warren just had to marry the woman without a prenup. How stupid could he be?

He met his friends at the bar. Matrix was already spreading his charms on a tall redhead.

Nico grinned in greeting. "I saw you in conversation with the viper," he said.

"Unfortunately."

"Is she looking for Warren?"

"Who knows?" Elliot said.

"It looks as if you're getting great returns on your investment." Nico nodded toward the VIP area where Thandie's silhouette was currently wrapped in the arms of actor Ruark Randall. "Lovely couple, wouldn't you say?"

Elliot glanced at his friend. "Are you trying to make me jealous?"

Nico shrugged.

"What are you expecting me to do?" Elliot asked. "Go up there and throw her over my shoulder?"

"Something like that," Nico drawled.

"I'm not the jealous type."

"I certainly hope not." His toned implied Elliot should be concerned with the amount of attention Ruark was raining on Thandie.

Elliot looked up at Thandie and Ruark in VIP. He heard Nico chuckle, clearly amused with himself. Just as he'd hoped, he'd planted a thought in Elliot's head. It did not sit well with him.

An hour after their arrival, Ruark dragged Thandie onto the dance floor. Pulling her close, he took a firm hold of her bottom. Surrounded by curious onlookers, she gave up the fight to ward off his advances. Women danced close to them, trying to ensnare Ruark's attention, but much to Thandie's annoyance, he was focused solely on her, not letting her go for a second. Ruark mumbled incoherent advances in her ear, but over the loud music, it was impossible to hear him. For that, she was thankful.

They danced through a few songs before Ruark tired. He invited a handful of women to their table, clearly enjoying their star-struck awe. Thandie waved a waitress over and slipped her a note, instructing her to deliver it to Adam. With any luck, this nightmare might yet correct itself.

Apparently, she'd gotten her hopes up too soon. Elliot approached their table. He looked cool and handsome as ever. He grinned at them. "Ruark, it's a pleasure to have you at Club Babylon. I'm Elliot Richards." He held out his hand. "Anything you need, please feel free to let my staff know."

Thandie watched Ruark's chest puff up as he shook Elliot's hand. "Thanks, man." He threw his free arm around Thandie's shoulders. "I've heard a lot about you. Nice place."

"Thank you." Thandie could tell Elliot didn't like him. "Is there anything I can get you?"

Ruark squeezed Thandie into his side. "How about a hotel room?" He winked at him to punctuate his meaning.

Elliot didn't smile. Instead he coolly replied, "How about a round of drinks for your party instead? On me, of course."

Ruark flashed him a movie star smile in agreement. Thandie groaned in mortification. If she thought Ruark had embarrassed her on the dance floor, his display in front of Elliot was humiliating.

Luckily, her prayers had been answered. Her message to Adam had obviously been received. The Babylon dancers she had met weeks before arrived at their table. They smiled brightly at Thandie, thankful she had remembered their infatuation with the actor. She moved over to allow them room to sit.

The dancers were in awe of Ruark, asking him a dozen questions, all of which he was happy to answer. Thandie excused herself from the table without anyone noticing. After a trip to the ladies' room, she was on her way back to the VIP room when she was confronted by the sight of Warren trying to calm down Sophia. Thandie managed to slip by, undetected. But not completely. Someone touched her arm. Thandie turned to see Adam standing near.

"Are you all right?" he asked.

She smiled. "Yes, I'm fine."

"You're a real trooper, Thandie. Ruark was practically mauling you. I stayed close by to see if you needed my help. Thankfully, Elliot sent Tiny over to make sure things didn't get out of hand."

"Tiny?" Thandie shifted her daze toward the booth Ruark was seated at. Next to it, stood Tiny, looming over everyone like a dark shadow. Strange she hadn't noticed him before. "I'll have to remember to thank Elliot."

Thandie searched the crowd for Elliot. As usual, he was easily found. He was on the arena floor, standing near a secluded alcove. His arms were crossed, and he was leaning forward to allow a dark-haired woman to whisper in his ear. His face was impassive, but it was clear he was listening to every word she said.

She turned slightly, allowing Thandie to view her profile. Thandie recognized her. It was the same woman from Warren's party, the beautiful dark-haired woman who'd left with Elliot. Who was she? Thandie turned to ask Adam, but he was gone.

Turning back to Elliot, Thandie saw him whisper something in the woman's ear. The closeness of their bodies looked intimate, and natural. Just as the first time she'd seen them together, Thandie knew this was different from the empty flirtations he usually showered on women visiting the club.

This was personal.

A burst of ridiculous jealousy assailed Thandie. She couldn't explain it, but it was there all the same. While she was still replaying images of their kiss on the boat, Elliot was back to playing musical beds. Thandie turned her back on Elliot and the mystery woman. As she made her way back to the VIP area, she vowed she would not make the mistake of being lured by Elliot again.

Thandie staggered into Elliot's home late. It was five minutes until six o'clock in the morning.

Ruark had been a handful. Even with the dancers to keep him company, he was ever aware of her presence. Even though he had five Babylon dancers on his arm, he still tried to persuade Thandie to join them in his hotel suite. She'd firmly refused, then wished the drunken crowd farewell.

It had been a nightmare, but in the end she had succeeded in creating press for the club and that was all that mattered. She would have to call later this morning to ensure the newspapers mentioned Ruark's appearance.

She managed to muster enough energy to take a shower and brush her teeth. She looked at the dresser clock and figured she had seven hours before she would have to begin making calls. She set the alarm on her cell phone before easing herself into bed. As soon as she slid beneath the sheets, drowsiness overwhelmed her. She fell asleep soon after.

What seemed the next moment, Thandie awoke with a jerk. A sheen of sweat covered her, and she felt like she was burning up.

She pulled the sheets away, welcoming the cool air that the overhead fan offered. But it wasn't enough. Swinging her feet to the floor, she went to the window. Pushing open the plantation shutters, she sighed with relief as a gust of cool air rolled in from the ocean. Her skin cooled immediately, but the relief was momentary.

She pressed her hand to her forehead. It felt clammy, yet

her forearms were covered in goose bumps. Feeling her breath quicken, she forced herself to take inhale deeply. The temperature of the room had nothing to do with her discomfort. She was hyperventilating.

Sitting on the edge of the bed, she mumbled, *calm down*. She whispered the words over and over until her breathing returned to its normal pace. She sighed deeply, feeling control over her nerves once again. It had been weeks since she'd had a panic attack. They'd only occurred when she was under tremendous stress. Until now, she'd believed she'd had everything under control for the Babylon events. So why was she reacting like this? Had she forgotten something important? Was this her subconscious warning her that something was wrong?

Fear assailed her. She jumped up to search for her binder. For a brief second, she couldn't find it, but she finally spotted the black monogrammed binder on the dresser. She tore it open and flipped through the pages, scanning quickly over her event plans, agent correspondences, receipts and handwritten notes. At first glance, it all appeared to be in order. Determined that there was an unchecked issue, she went back over her notes. She studied every document, memorizing them. Again, nothing looked wrong.

Convinced she was losing her mind, Thandie snapped the binder shut and pushed it away. *Calm down. Calm down.* She closed her eyes and tried to force herself to continue breathing slowly. Thinking of party plans all day was beginning to overwhelm her. She had to get out of this room.

Quickly pulling off her clothes, she grabbed a swimsuit. It was a bright yellow bikini with a provocative cut. The top bralette could better be called pasties. It offered just enough fabric to cover her nipples. She would have never mustered enough courage to wear the bikini in public. She could scarcely believe she'd even packed it. But she quickly shrugged off her modesty. It wasn't as though anyone would see her.

Grabbing a towel from the adjoining bath, Thandie padded barefoot toward the indoor pool. The house was silent. No doubt Raja and Len were asleep, worn out from another heavy night of partying. Elliot wasn't expected home for another few hours. She would have the pool all to herself.

She was grateful for the solitude. She was in no condition to chat. A late-night swim would distract her from the constant planning and, with luck, tire her out.

Thandie opened the heavy oak door that led to the pool. The room was dimly lit. Moonlight filtered in from the oversize widows, reflecting off the water and bathing the room in shimmering crystals. Someone had turned on the pool lights, causing the water to glow with a soft pale blue.

Thandie unwrapped the towel from around her body, tossed it onto a nearby chaise, and dove into the deep end of the pool. After a few seconds, her head broke the surface of the water. She filled her lungs with air, and savored the weightless sensation of floating. The water temperature wasn't nearly as cold as she'd expected. Dipping her head below the surface, Thandie swam to the opposite end.

Just as she reached the pool's edge, she was brought up short by a hard wall of flesh. Frightened, she screamed. Forgetting to keep herself afloat, her head went under. She fought to swim, but the sudden shock made her gasp for air while still submerged. Water shot up her nose, and panicked, she flailed her arms, splashing water in every direction.

Without warning, a pair of strong arms encircled her, bringing her up against a muscled chest. Blinking away droplets of water, and coughing, Thandie focused on the handsome face of Elliot Richards.

He grinned down at her. "Hello, pussycat."

For a moment, she was speechless. He was so handsome, she felt frozen. His dark hair was plastered to his forehead. His long, wet eyelashes shaded those glowing silver eyes which had the power to pierce her soul with a simple glance.

"What are you doing here?" she snapped.

"Where else would I be?" Elliot's gray eyes danced with humor. "This is my home."

"You know what I meant." She tried to push away from him, but his hold was firm. "Shouldn't you be closing the club?"

"I left early."

Thandie pushed against him again, and this time he released her. Putting a little space between them, she asked, "Okay, well—why are you in here?"

"I could ask you the same question. Isn't it past your bedtime?"

"I couldn't sleep."

Elliot gave her a devilish grin. "I have an idea of how to wear you out."

"Does it amuse you to talk to me like that?"

"Immensely."

"You have a poor sense of humor."

"I was about to say the same to you."

"I'm leaving."

"You just got here." His eyes turned a dangerous shade of gray. "And I believe you and I have some unfinished business."

"About that—"

"I've decided I'm going to make you beg for it," he said conversationally. His gaze skimmed over her. "By the by, I love your bikini. It's very stimulating." As if to prove his point, she could feel him grow hard against her.

Thandie gasped. "You aren't wearing any clothes."

Elliot flashed her that bedazzling smile of his. "You're very perceptive." He moved closer. "Does it give you any ideas?"

"The only idea that comes to mind would involve a great deal of pain for you." She underlined her meaning by raising her knee just below his groin.

"You're a very naughty girl," he said.

"You could say I've learned to adapt to my surroundings."

He tsked. "You're no fun, pussycat. I mean only to bring you great pleasure." He tilted his head to the side, in a thoughtful gesture. "And myself as well, of course." Moving even closer, he brushed a lock of wet hair off her shoulder. "Where is your actor friend?"

She slapped his hand away. "How should I know?"

Elliot lifted his eyebrow. "He isn't waiting for you in your room?"

Thandie lifted her chin. "Regardless of the answer, it would be none of your business."

He grinned at her. "I beg to differ." He moved forward, slowly inching her closer to the pool's edge. "He was quite taken with you, wasn't he? Did you oblige him tonight?"

"What's that supposed to mean?"

"I think you know damn well what I mean."

Thandie looked away. "My personal life is none of your concern, Elliot. Besides, I don't see why it would interest you." An image of the lovely dark-haired woman flashed before her eyes. "Don't you have a pretty bed partner waiting for you?"

His brows rose in question.

"Oh, never mind," she muttered in disgust. "Just stay out of my personal business. My affairs have nothing to do with you."

"What if I wished to change that?" Elliot inched closer, invading her personal space. He leaned down to kiss her just below her earlobe. His chuckled when he felt her shiver from his touch. "Tell me, Thandie, were you as hot for him as you are for me?" He nuzzled her ear with the tip of his nose. "Did you ache to have him deep inside you, the way you ache for me?" He nipped at her shoulder with his teeth. "Did you give in to him as passionately as you will for me?"

"Elliot—" she said in a shaky breath, unable to think straight with him so close.

"Tell me, Thandie, did you come as loudly and as hard for him as you will for me?" The question lacked the soft pander his earlier quips had possessed. His voice now held an icy edge to it. "Tell me everything you let him do to you."

"Nothing," she gasped. "We did nothing."

"No?"

"No," she breathed.

His grip on her tightened. "Tell me the truth."

"I am," she panted. "We did nothing." She licked her lips. "Elliot, please." Her voice sounded distant to her own ears. Her frail plea for him was the last thing she heard before his mouth came down on hers. Her lips gave way under the pressure.

She closed her eyes and let herself be carried away on a cloud of reckless desire. She could feel his cock grow hard against her. She stepped forward to feel his throbbing heat. He groaned at her touch and pulled her against his naked chest. His hands ran along the sides of her legs, caressing her buttocks and thighs. It wasn't the same as when Ruark had touched her. Elliot wasn't groping her as if she was simply flesh. No. He worshipped her with his touch, acquainting his body with hers. If this was anything like how he was with his other women, she now sympathized with them.

He was worth chasing after. He was worth begging for.

He pulled her closer, deepening his kiss. Thandie moaned, enjoying the feel of his muscular body against her. Reaching around her, he effortlessly pulled the strings that held her bikini top together. The action was quick and expertly engineered. The sound of her top splashing against the water resonated in her ears and then disappeared into nothing. She could think of little else but Elliot and sensation of her bare breasts against the smooth surface of his chest.

With a strength she didn't know she had, Thandie managed to wedge her hands against him and push him away. They fell apart easily. Too easily. Horrified, she realized it was not he who held her prisoner, it was she who'd been holding him. She'd been hanging on to him for dear life.

A blush rushed to her cheeks, setting her face aflame. She could feel his gaze on her, intense as ever. She was too embarrassed to look at him. Too frightened at her own reaction when they were this close. And then he took the choice out of her hands. Using his thumb and forefinger, he took hold of her chin, and lifted her face so that her gaze met his. His eyes were the color of smoke. Thandie knew then she was hooked.

Fearful of where this was surely headed, she backed away from him. "Well," she said nervously, "I guess I'll be going back to my room—" She attempted to move away from him, but he placed his hands on the pool's ledge, imprisoning her between his arms.

"And what should I do in the meantime?" he asked.

They both looked down at his engorged cock.

"Umm," Thandie appeared to give the question serious consideration. "I suppose you could take care of that yourself."

"You're suggesting I masturbate?" Elliot smirked. "I haven't done that since—perhaps high school." His eyes suddenly turned dark. "Let's see if I still have the hang of it."

Elliot pressed her back against the cool surface of the pool wall, trapping her there with his broad form. Lifting her legs, he wrapped them around his waist. Thandie struggled to move away, but she had no leverage. Using his height to his advantage, he'd purposely moved them to a location where her toes could not touch bottom.

With nowhere to swim, she was forced to either grab hold of his shoulders or reach high above her to clutch the edge of the pool. Touching Elliot was a last alternative, but the smooth stone surface of the ledge was slick with water and slippery.

Feeling herself sinking, she clasped her hands onto Elliot's strong shoulders. She was helpless. Trapped. And he knew it.

Thandie watched in horror as he grinned down at her, satisfied with the turn of events. He reached down between them and took hold of his cock. Pressing the tip of the head against the crotch of her bikini bottoms, he stroked himself. With every thrust of his hand, the head of his cock rubbed intimately against her. Only the thin material of her swimsuit was preventing them from having sex.

She watched his facial features become serious with passionate concentration. He pressed his cheek alongside hers as he pressed forward. His free hand pressed against her lower back, preventing her from moving away.

His hand worked swiftly, stroking his shaft while his head prodded her. The water swished around them, moving to his rhythm. His breath became harder with every thrust of his hand. Unable to keep a good grip on him with the constant movement, Thandie wrapped her arms around his neck, uncertain if she was pulling herself closer or pushing him away. The feel of Elliot's bare skin against hers was sinfully irresistible. She could no longer deny her desire to feel him plunge deep inside her.

Instincts took over. Thandie lowered her hips and moved against him, attempting to brush her clit against his groin. Her fingers slid through the wet locks of his hair. Her moans filled the air. She felt his back tense, and his hips thrust forward for a final time. He released a soft shudder and then the water beneath her buttocks went warm.

Their breathing echoed in each other's ears. His hands palmed her bottom, squeezing her flesh possessively. It was a long moment before he spoke. His voice was just above a whisper. "I haven't lost my touch." He fell silent until she finally met his gaze. "But I prefer the real thing."

Keeping his hold on her, he eased them toward the arched steps at the shallow end of the pool. With her legs still wrapped about his hips, he stepped out of the water, carrying them to a nearby chaise longue. There, he laid her down, stretching himself out on top of her. His mouth covered hers. Thandie pulled him closer, inviting his kiss.

Elliot lowered his head to her breasts and hungrily pushed one dark nipple into his mouth. The feel of him untying the laces of her bikini bottoms furthered her passionate haze. As if just waking up from a deep sleep, her eyes widened. Elliot's lips and tongue teased her nipple until it stood erect. With a flick of his wrist, her bikini bottoms were tossed aside.

He came up on his knees, and looked down at her. Pushing her thighs apart, he took hold of his cock and stroked himself. His eyes lowered as he focused on the treasure that lay between her quivering thighs.

Through heavy lids, Thandie stared up at his deliciously naked body. He was beautiful, and generously erect. His body was amazingly perfect in every way. She might have obsessed over the fact, had he not begun to smile.

"Now," he said in a voice that was as cool as it was impassive, "you may go back to your room."

"What?" Thandie blinked slowly, confused. "What's happening?"

"Absolutely nothing, pussycat."

She blinked again. "We—we aren't going to—?"

Elliot shook his head.

Embarrassed, she rolled out from under him, reached for her towel and quickly wrapped it around her.

"It's a bit late for that," he said casually.

Thandie screeched in outrage. "You're a real bastard, Elliot," she hissed.

"That's actually truer than you know, but at least I'm a fair bastard." He took hold of her, gripping her forearms tightly. "You had your chance, now we're going to do things my way." Leaning close, so that his words were whisper-soft. "I'll fuck you when I'm good and ready. And not now."

Abruptly, he let her go. Thandie stumbled back before catching her balance. She could literally feel the steam coming out of her ears and the tightening of her lungs. She gasped for breath. It was not enough. Not nearly enough. Her hands formed into tight fists at her sides. She strained to keep her focus, but bright stars burst before her eyes.

Oh, no, not here. Please not here. Not in front of him.

Frantic, she stormed out of the room, pausing only to burn him with an enraged glare. She marched to her room and slammed the door. She'd made it just in time. Right before the doubled over with uncontrollable quakes. She wanted to be as far away from him as possible. Elliot Richards had lived up to his infamous reputation. She cursed his name. He'd made a fool out of her. Painful as if was, she'd learned a powerful lesson tonight. Thankfully, she'd learned it before she'd made a bigger mistake.

Chapter Sixteen

Thandie fumbled to find her phone among the bedsheets. She felt as if she had just laid her head down on her pillow before the annoying ringtone woke her up.

"Huh?" she grunted.

"Have you seen the papers?" an exasperated voice asked.

"Gage?"

"When you wake up, I'd advise you read the morning paper."

"Which one?"

"Take your pick."

Thandie muffled a yawn. "What is this all about?"

"You'll know soon enough. Look, I'm going into a meeting. Give me a call later." The line went dead.

Thandie pushed her phone beneath the covers. She was too tired to give much thought to Gage's cryptic message. Whatever it was, it could wait until she had at least six hours of sleep. Until then, she didn't care if the sky came crashing down and killed them all.

Unfortunately, no one seemed to share her view. What felt like only minutes later, Thandie found herself sitting in the dining room, nursing a cup of black coffee. She was sleep-deprived and irritable, but nevertheless duty was calling.

After Gage's call, she'd barely slept an hour before Raja was knocking on her door to join them for press calls. Thandie had dragged herself every step of the way. Her late-night encounter with Elliot weighed heavily on her mind. He'd intentionally meant to humiliate her. When she thought back to how easily she'd welcomed his advances, she wanted to crawl into a hole. She was mortified by her behavior. If he still entertained any ideas of being welcomed into her bed after his performance, he had another think coming. She didn't want to be within ten feet of him.

Thandie was brought out of her thoughts when Len tapped her knee. She forced herself to concentrate on the situation at hand. Word about Ruark Randall visiting Club Babylon had spread fast. Due to a slow day in celebrity news, Ruark's visit to Miami made unnecessary headlines in the gossip papers. Pictures of him entering the club were accompanied by articles that were as short as they were vague. Thandie's job would be to call her contacts and give them a full account of Ruark's time at Babylon.

It did not take long for Thandie to figure out the reason for Gage's call. In a handful of the pictures, a glimpse of Thandie could be seen in the background. Unfortunately, they showed a pompous Ruark with his arm tossed around her waist.

The pictures would require explaining.

Mira was their final call for the morning, and she was literally saving the best for last. Apparently, the gossip mill was strong in Miami. Having somehow learned ahead of time that Thandie would be escorting Ruark to Babylon, Mira managed to plant a photographer inside the club. The results were a series of pictures of Thandie and Ruark cuddled together in a booth. Depending on the picture, some of their positions were questionable. Mira had delighted in emailing Thandie sample shots. Thandie called her as soon as she viewed the email attachments.

When Mira answered the line, her cackling echoed through the phone. "What do you think, Thandie?" Her voice was practically gleeful.

"I think you need to delete the pictures," Thandie said. "I was very clear regarding Babylon's camera policy."

"Oh, you were clear," Mira agreed, "I just decided not to listen to you."

Thandie pinched the bridge of her nose again, staving off a headache. As much as she disliked the idea, she would have to report this to Elliot. He would not receive the news well. "What do you plan to do with the pictures?"

"Run them, obviously."

"All of them?" Thandie asked.

"A select few," she said vaguely.

"Which ones?"

Mira took her time answering. "You'll see soon enough."

"What does that mean?"

"The issue is already out."

"Out?" Thandie repeated in a dry croak.

"Yes," Mira practically sang. "Thanks to good timing, we received the pictures before we went to print. It was a rush job, but well worth the trouble. The issue hit newsstands a few hours ago. You should pick up a copy, Thandie. I think you'll find it quite flattering."

Checking her email, Thandie reviewed the pictures again. She groaned. Every one of them implied more was happening between her and Ruark than was true. Thandie now regretted having worn a ponytail. With her hair pulled back, there was nothing to obscure her face. She could be identified from the moon. She swore under her breath, then asked, "Did we at least get a spread in *Look?*"

"I did better than that."

"Can you be more specific?"

"You've got the cover."

Thandie felt stunned. Because of the success of his TV show, *LA Homicide,* Ruark Randall was a popular celebrity at the moment. Having him photographed in Babylon was exactly the kind of attention Thandie had been hoping for. What she hadn't planned on was her being trapped in the spotlight.

"I'm impressed, Thandie," Mira drawled. "Is this really you kissing Ruark Randall?"

Thandie sighed. "Yes, Mira, that's me." It would serve no good to deny what the woman already knew. "And for the record, he was the one doing all the kissing."

Mira grunted in disbelief. "I can't tell from the pictures."

"Take my word for it. By the way, how did you get a photographer into the club?"

"I have my sources."

"Elliot is going to hit the roof when he hears about this."

Mira laughed. "Elliot Richards will be fine. He'll have no choice but to be. I'm running the cover story with or without his consent."

Thandie rubbed her temples. "No more photographers in the club, Mira. Seriously."

"I know you're obligated to say that, dear, but let's be realistic. I'm the chief editor of *Look.* I'll do my job any way I want."

"I know," Thandie conceded. "I just have to give you a heads-up that camera access inside Babylon will not be as easy next time."

"I've been warned," Mira snorted. "And so have you."

There was no reason to argue. Mira Dietrich was the press. She would do whatever she could to get a good story. Incidentally, Mira's tactics provided a silver lining for Thandie. Since Elliot had not been willing to bend on his camera policy, Thandie could inadvertently achieve her goal of getting pictures of VIP guests through her media contacts. Hopefully, by warning Mira of the camera policy, Thandie had piqued her interest to send more photographers. Babylon needed all the publicity it could get.

Made curious by Mira's taunts, Thandie sent the girls out to shop the newsstands. They returned fifteen minutes later, their arms laden with purchases. They spread out the gossip papers to see what the headline stories were. Len and Raja got a kick out of the *Look* cover story. True to her word, Mira had made sure the story was front and center. In big, bold letters the banner read Ruark Randall Finds Love in Babylon!!!

Len excitedly volunteered to read the article aloud. "Actor Ruark Randall," she began, "from the hit show *LA Homicide,* did very little dancing while partying at South Beach's popular Club Babylon Thursday night. Instead, Ruark kept himself busy locking lips with a mystery woman. Who is Ruark's new girlfriend?"

Raja laughed. "This is hilarious, Thandie!"

"You're famous now," Len teased.

"I think you mean infamous," Raja corrected her.

Len gaped at the large picture of Thandie wrapped in Ruark's arms, receiving an open-mouthed kiss from the famed actor. "Where was I when this was happening?"

"Chasing Elliot," Raja sang.

"Raja!" Len cried, clearly embarrassed.

Thandie shook her head. "Believe me, I would have switched places with either one of you."

Raja frowned at her. "You didn't like it?"

"Not even a little," Thandie muttered, starring at the picture in disbelief. She'd known Mira would see to it that *Look* used the pictures to paint the most interesting story, but she hadn't thought she'd be slammed in the process.

"This is going to be a big deal," Len whispered more to herself.

"I think you're right." Raja looked at Thandie. "It's only a matter of time before someone realizes you're the same woman Ruark was seen with in New York."

Thandie couldn't offer an answer. Even though she'd already previewed the pictures, it was ten times worse seeing them in print. The vision of Ruark forcing his tongue into her mouth was horrifying.

"This might be a good thing, guys." Len's voice turned high-pitched. "The press will be eager to see you, Thandie. That means you can bring more press to the club."

Raja looked up at her. "Do you want me to tip off the press? We could have them at the club tonight. Thandie? Hello?"

Thandie had to jerk herself out of her stupor. "Yes," she said in a hoarse voice. "That would be nice."

"Are you concerned about this article?"

"Of course not," she lied. "Len's right. This gives Babylon publicity. That's all I care about." She rubbed her temples with her fingertips. The headache she'd been hoping to avoid had arrived in full force. "Now that we've seen the worst of it," she said, waving her hand to the newspapers. "Let's make the most of it."

With their scheduled press calls out of the way, they had time to manipulate the situation. Even if Thandie didn't want to be on the receiving end of the media scrutiny, she had to take advantage of the opportunity. If played right, they could bring invaluable attention to Babylon.

After making a quick call to Markie about stepping up the security in the upcoming weeks, Len and Raja got to work rallying media interest in the club.

Meanwhile, Thandie busied herself preparing for tonight. Deadmau5 would be performing, and the details going into his show were the most elaborate they'd attempted so far. Lunch was a hurried affair, eaten between more phone calls and email exchanges. The entire time, Thandie had been bracing herself for when Elliot finally emerged from his wing of the house. She'd expected a showdown.

As it turned out, her worry was pointless. She learned from Lucinda that Elliot had left an hour before she'd awoken, to tend to something at one of his other clubs.

At any rate, his departure saved her from having to break the news to him about Mira's photos. She was now able to take the less confrontational route. She'd send him an email.

Chapter Seventeen

Her massage appointment at Blu Moon was set for an evening three days from now. Still troubled by the recent developments between her and Elliot, Thandie had left the responsibility of handling press calls to Len and Raja. The Ruark Randall story was alive and well, and Elliot was furious. He called her into his office and was quite terse on his edict about photographers and the press.

There were gossip columnists out there who still craved details. And then there was the matter of her costume last night. Based on a text message from Gage, Thandie had been photographed.

Another reason for her to delegate was she had no desire to run into Elliot in the house. To ensure this, Thandie stayed in bed. Pulling the sheets over her head, she closed her eyes and listened to the sounds of the water outside.

Ring. Ring.

Blindly, Thandie answered her phone. "Huh?"

"Sorry to wake you."

"Cam?" she said groggily.

"Good guess."

"What time is it?"

"9:00 a.m. I know it's early for you, but it's the only chance I had to call. I'm in Rome and about to go on set. Gage left me a message to call you and tease you mercilessly about Ruark Randall."

Thandie sighed. "Okay," she said wearily. "Go for it."

"I would if I could," he admitted. "Who the hell is Ruark Randall?"

She paused and then burst into a fit of laughter.

"Did I say something funny?" he asked.

"No, Cam," she answered between breaths. "You said something right." She had been so frustrated by being linked to Ruark, it was a relief to know there were people who didn't know or care about the actor.

"So who's this Randall guy?" he asked. "Is he the guy in Miami you've been telling me about?"

"No." She rolled over and snuggled deeper into the comforts of the mattress. "He's an actor who visited the club this week. A real character."

"Why was Gage laughing when she told me to call you?"

"She has a twisted sense of humor."

"So everything is okay?" he asked slowly.

"Yes," she said. "How's Rome?"

"Ridiculously amazing, of course. Hold on a sec." He muffled the phone with his hand while someone spoke to him briefly. When he returned to the phone, he sounded regretful. "Look, Than, I hate to cut this short, but I really have to go. They've loaded the van, and the group is waiting for me. I'll try to call back later."

"All right. Thanks for checking on me."

"I can't help it. Sweet dreams."

She disconnected the calle, feeling much better. The sound of Cam's voice calmed her. After her encounter with Elliot last night, she feared she would have a panic attack she was so badly shaken. She had only a few more weeks in Miami. If she could only hold her own until then, she could return to New York in one piece.

She was considering getting out of bed, when her phone chirped. A new text message had come through. It was from Rex.

Are you busy tonight?
-Rex

Thandie sent him a reply, confirming she had no plans. Rex's response came within seconds.

May I take you up on our rain check?

She smiled. She'd nearly forgotten about their cancelled dinner. There had been precious little time to think about Rex. Lately, her thoughts had been consumed by a gray-eyed devil. It would be nice to spend time with Rex, and away from Elliot. She agreed to dinner. Rex sent one final message with his arrival time. He ended it by simply saying, "I can't wait to see you."

It had been a long day. By the time Elliot arrived at Zuma, he was in a foul mood. One of the financiers was dragging his feet on expanding the budget for a new investment opportunity. To add to his annoyance, Thandie was back to hiding from him. She'd been huddled in her room all evening until he'd finally left for the club. She meant to avoid him, but she'd made it impossible for him to do the same.

There had been more photos of Thandie in the paper today. Thankfully, none were taken inside Babylon, but they weren't much better. They'd gotten pictures of Thandie in that damned dress. Normally, he thought her sexy attire was amusing, entertaining even. Something you looked forward to with the heady delight of a holiday. But that damned dress, with its glowing bra and panties, had simply been too much. He'd relished sending her home early, if for no other reason than to put an end to men gawking at her.

Sure, there had been plenty of women there last night in all forms of nakedness, but somehow seeing Thandie baring it all, grated on him. She'd hardly been there two hours, and he wanted her gone, out of his sight, and away from prying eyes. Even if the photographers hadn't been so aggressive, he would have sent her home anyway.

Why did everything about Thandie needle him? They'd crossed some invisible line that no longer made his attraction to her simple to explain. This thing between them was far more complicated than he could have predicted, or needed. Why the hell did it matter to him that she was avoiding him today?

No longer interested, my ass, he thought to himself.

There was a small line of eager patrons, patiently waiting to be seated. The hostess looked up, and like a majority of people who working in Miami's entertainment industry, she recognized him. Her smile was warm as she welcomed him. Confirming his dinner guests were already seated, she moved to escort him. Elliot held up his hand, insisting he locate their table.

As soon as he was past the host stand, he saw Matrix leaning against the bar, grinning wolfishly at an attractive female bartender. He whispered something to the woman, and the smile she gave him was inviting. Looking around them, she grinned at him once more before slipping away toward the employee entrance. Matrix watched her go, grinning to himself.

Turning his attention to the crowded expanse, Elliot spotted Nico in the main dining area. Their table was in the center of the room. Elliot knew this was Nico's doing. He enjoyed being on display. Elliot however, outside of the club, preferred more secluded environments. Stifling a sigh, he cut a path through the tables toward his friend.

Nico was studying his watch when Elliot arrived at their table. "Prompt as always," he said.

Still in a bad mood, Elliot pulled out his chair and seated himself without fanfare. A waiter materialized at his elbow, asking for his drink order. Elliot ordered a highball. Nico gave him a quizzical look, well aware Elliot was not a serious drinker. Elliot ignored his curious gaze. Instead, he nudged his head toward the bar. "Matrix?"

"Settling a bet," was all Nico said in answer.

Both men turned to see Matrix leaning against the bar. The pretty bartender reappeared, and wordlessly slid something small to Matrix. He accepted it and moved away from the bar. He was grinning as he made his way to their table.

Nico gave a snort, and then turned to Elliot. "Warren called me today."

Elliot groaned inwardly. Next to Thandie, Warren was the last thing he wanted to talk about. But he couldn't help asking, "What did he want?"

"He wanted to know if my sordid connections involved a private investigator." He shrugged. "I suppose things are heating up between him and the viper."

"He shouldn't have called you."

Nico fixed him with a telling look. "Who else should he have called for help?"

The jab did nothing to improve Elliot's mood. Luckily, the waiter arrived at that moment, sliding his drink in front of him. His seamless departure was followed by Matrix's appearance. There was a confident smirk on his face as he took his seat.

"Thirty-two C," Matrix announced proudly. "Just like I said."

Nico looked suspicious. "Proof, please."

Beneath the table, Matrix handed him something small and lacy. Nico turned it over in his hand. It was a woman's bra. Nico searched the tag and then swore.

"Pay up." Matrix said.

Releasing a heavy sigh, Nico reached into his jacket breast pocket to pull out his wallet. He pulled out several bills, laying them before his friend. Matrix gave a grunt of satisfaction, and then added, "Aren't you forgetting something?" He held out his hand.

Nico smiled and unearthed the bra he'd slyly pocketed. He shoved it into Matrix's palm. "Greedy bastard."

Finding little amusement in his friends' antics tonight, Elliot looked around the room. However, he was conscious of Nico studying him again. Before he could ask, Elliot snapped, "Stay out of it."

Matrix gave a low whistle. "Careful, Nico. Elliot is practically growling."

"More like foaming at the mouth," Nico offered.

"Which means," Matrix said casually, "he's pissed about something to do with his clubs."

"I'd wager it has more to do with a woman," Nico said with a slow grin.

"Thandie Shaw?" Matrix asked.

"I sent you a picture of her last night," he said with a nudge of his elbow.

"You sent him a picture?" Elliot asked with exasperation.

"Ah, Thandie!" Matrix said with a broad smile. "I recall

quite vividly now. Quality work, Elliot. She certainly makes things interesting."

"That's her job," he said stiffly. "She's supposed to make the club interesting."

"Well, in that case, she succeeded." Matrix held up his glass in a mock toast. "To Thandie...."

Nico joined him in the toast, barely able to rein in his laughter.

Elliot ignored them, pretending to be immensely engrossed in the menu.

"You know, Elliot," Matrix began, "since your Thandie comes so highly recommended, perhaps I might extend her an invite to one of my parties."

Elliot's answer was immediate. "No."

Matrix had the good sense to retreat. Holding up his hands in surrender, he said, *"Touché."*

Nico leaned back in his seat, a look of disbelief on his face. "You still haven't—"

Before he could get the question out entirely, Elliot gave the smallest shake of his head.

Nico sat up straighter. "Seriously?"

"What are you talking about?" Matrix asked, wounded to have been left out of the discussion.

"Nothing," Nico said quickly. "I told you she wouldn't be as easy as the others."

Matrix looked between the two of them. "I'm still waiting for an explanation."

Elliot scowled at Nico, regretting having ever let slip his frustrations with Thandie. "Perfection requires patience," he said, with a roll of his shoulders.

"I've never known you to show this much patience," Nico retorted.

It was true, Elliot was nearing his limit. The only thing

that calmed him was the simple reminder of the grand plans he had for Thandie. It was this alone that stopped him from pressing her too far, too soon. He was biding his time for the moment that best suited him.

"And this business with the actor?" Nico asked.

"Ruark Randall is of little consequence to me," Elliot said with certainty. He remembered all too well how quickly Thandie melted under his stare, and how passionately she'd returned his kisses. He knew Ruark had never been a contender for Thandie. His presence had been brief and unimpressionable.

"Did you ever find out if she's seeing someone?" Nico asked.

"It wouldn't matter," he said with a shrug. "My mind is made up."

"I think you've met your match."

"Rest assured, I have everything under control." Elliot signaled the waiter for another round of drinks.

"Um, hello," Matrix said irritably. "I'm still here and still uninformed."

Thandie was excited about her date with Rex. He was easy to talk to, and their conversations never seemed forced. Being around him felt comfortable.

Additionally, he was a charming man, whose interest in her seemed genuine. He was kind, thoughtful and handsome (in a Macy's catalog book way). He'd played no games. In short, he was everything Elliot wasn't.

So it was with great pleasure she'd allowed Rex to sweep her into his car and drive them toward the city lights.

"You look spectacular, Thandie."

"Thank you," she said, smiling warmly at him. She was wearing a long black dress with a high slit on her left side.

Rex made no attempt to hide his fascination with her. He often turned to gaze at her. Thandie was pleased by his attention. It was flattering in its quiet gentleness. Thandie badly desired a relaxing night out. She needed time away from the club, all the party planning, and especially time away from Elliot.

"I'm glad you accepted my offer tonight," Rex said, pulling her out of her thoughts.

"I'm glad you asked," she confessed. "I'm sorry about the last time."

Rex shrugged. "You did the right thing. Warren is your friend. You had every right to be concerned about him."

"Thanks for understanding."

"Anytime," he said, grinning. "How is Warren?"

She scrunched her nose. "I'm not quite sure. I try to keep an eye on him, but he isn't the easiest person to keep tabs on. Obviously, since we've…relocated to Elliot's home, I see less of Warren." Thandie had not told Rex exactly what had happened that dreadful morning when she'd been confronted by Wife Number Five. "I need to call him," she mused aloud. "I kinda miss Warren."

Rex chuckled. There was something in the sound of his voice that made Thandie laugh too. Before they knew it, their laughter overwhelmed them. It was loud, lighthearted and a little uncontrollable. By the time they arrived at their destination, any hint of tension was erased. While Rex handed his keys to the valet, Thandie looked up at the exterior of the chic restaurant. It was small but impressive. She had little time to consider her surroundings, before Rex opened her door and helped her out of the car.

Pressing his hand on her back, he leaned close and whispered, "Have I mentioned how phenomenal you look to-night?"

She laughed and was surprised to see his face light up in a most attractive way. Guiding her through the crowd, they made a direct path to the hostess's stand. After giving his name, they waited while the young woman looked up his reservation. Some minutes later, they were led to a booth. Thandie slid in first, looking around the room as she did so. Rex settled himself beside her. "I hope you like Japanese food," he said.

"Actually, I do."

Their waiter presented himself and offered menus. Rex ordered a bottle of wine and an appetizer Thandie couldn't pronounce. After the waiter was gone, Thandie leaned forward to be heard over the noise.

"You know how to read Japanese?"

Rex laughed. "Oh, goodness, no! Purely repetition. I come here often." He waved his hand at the atmosphere. "The food is great, and the ambiance is romantic." He reached out to place his hand over hers. "I'm glad you came," he said in a low voice.

"Me, too."

The intimacy of the moment was disturbed when the waiter returned with the bottle of wine. He poured two glasses for them, and not wanting to get lost in the shuffle of a busy night, Rex insisted they place their dinner orders.

When the waiter had once again disappeared, Thandie looked up to see Rex watching her. Once again, she marveled at how comfortable she felt around him. Doubt and tension simply did not exist when she was around him.

"So," she said, reaching for her wine glass, "how long have you been working for Elliot?"

"A few years," he said with a warm smile. "But I don't actually work for Elliot. I mean, not entirely." When she frowned, he continued. "I do marketing work for several clubs. I search the industry, identify new trends, and report back to my employers. They sort of 'pool' their finances for my services. It's the most efficient way to go about it if you don't want to pay for a full-time marketer. I mean, let's face it. Unless you have a chain of locations, the market is fairly cyclicle. And whatever tactics the guy down the street is using to rally interest in his business, you'll try it to see if it works for your company. It's rather different from what you do for Babylon."

"Oh," was all Thandie could say. This explained why Elliot simply hadn't assigned Rex to do what she'd been hired for.

"One of the perks of my job is it requires I travel from time to time."

"Such as?" she asked, genuinely interested.

"Anywhere, I suppose. I've been to New York, L.A., Dubai, Rio and London. I've even been to Shanghai a few times." He lifted his shoulders. "It depends on where the client is competing. Miami is a strange beast. The club owners here want to compete with Vegas. So, lately I've been traveling there more often."

"Is that where you were a few weeks ago?"

He nodded. "Unfortunately, I have to go back. Short trip, but necessary." Again he placed his hand over hers. "I'm afraid I'm going to miss your next presentation."

Thandie was reminded of the Nicki Minaj debacle, and her hasty booking of The Pussy Cats. She'd had such high hopes for pulling off a large show, and now she was forced to promote an erotic dance group few people in Miami had ever heard of. The only advantage she saw was she was saving a large portion of the tight budget Elliot had set.

"I leave tomorrow evening," he said. "That's why I wanted to see you tonight. You're always busy with work at the club, and I hardly get to see you. But tonight, I have you all to myself." He smiled shyly. "I hope you don't mind if I monopolize your time."

Thandie smiled up at him through thick lashes. "By all means."

With their dinner dishes taken away, the three friends leaned back in their seats, laughing as they finished off their drinks. The mood had lightened significantly, aided by good food, and an attentive bartender.

Signing his name with a flourish, Nico asked, "How did I get stuck with the bill?"

"Because I paid for dinner the last time," Elliot reminded him.

"And I paid the time before that," Matrix chimed in.

"Fine, fine," Nico muttered as he tucked his copy of the receipt into his wallet. Their waiter appeared to refill water glasses. When they were once again alone, Nico turned to Elliot and said, "I ran into a friend of yours last night. The tiny little angel who flipped us the bird."

"Victoria," Elliot offered.

"Yes, Victoria," Nico said. "I saw her at the club, and decided to introduce myself. I thought she might be nicer in person."

"Oh?" Elliot asked with a raise of his brow.

"She wasn't," Nico confessed. "She's a hellion, that one."

This actually made Elliot laugh. He could only imagine the creative string of expletives Victoria had spit at Nico. "You were warned," was all he could say.

Matrix, who'd been checking his cell phone, looked up. "What about a hellion?"

"Victoria Day," Elliot answered. "Local designer."

"Designer?" Matrix asked.

"Thandie is expanding our horizons," he explained. "Victoria will be hosting her fashion show at Babylon in a few weeks."

Matrix leaned back in his seat. "Sounds very high brow."

"I suppose," Elliot mumbled, uninterested.

"When is it?" Nico asked.

"When is what?"

"The show," Nico said impatiently. "When is it?"

The question made Elliot turn to look at his friend. "I can't recall off the top of my head. Would you like me to send you details?"

Matrix leaned forward. "Why the interest, Nico? Are you thinking about getting into the fashion business?"

Before Nico could answer, their waiter returned, asking if there was anything else they would like to order. When Nico declined the offer, the young man graciously bid them good-night, before deftly taking possession of the leather binder containing the bill. Taking this as their cue to leave, the men got up.

"Headed to the club?" Matrix asked.

"Perhaps," Elliot said with a nonchalant shrug, even though he was certain that was his destination.

Matrix elbowed Nico. "And you?"

Nico did not immediately speak. Instead, he came to an abrupt halt, and stared off into the distance with keen interest. Elliot and Matrix paused to look after their friend. When Nico gave a wicked smile, Elliot frowned.

"What are you grinning about?"

"Are you sure you've got everything under control?" he said, nudging his chin toward the tables across the room, where couples sat intimately close while sharing dinner.

At first, Elliot hadn't understood. There was movement all around the restaurant, and several dimly lit dinner booths. And then, with a clarity of a bird of prey, he saw them. Rex and Thandie, nestled together. Candlelight threw shadows across their faces, but it was her. He was certain of it. As if he needed further clarification, Thandie threw her head back, and her laughter punctuated the air.

How had he missed her? Had his back been turned when they'd entered the restaurant? Had his attention been focused on Matrix at the time? Few things escaped his gaze. And yet, there they were. Thandie and Rex, sharing a romantic dinner together.

Elliot knew without seeing, he hated her dress. It was a dark color and formfitting. Even from this distance, he could see the seductive swell of her breasts. No doubt Rex was getting a healthy view of Thandie's golden skin.

"It looks like your kitten has come out to play," he heard Nico whisper beside him.

Elliot straightened his tie and smiled slowly. "I think we should go and say hello."

Nico grinned. "After you."

Thandie was laughing when she suddenly went rigid. Like a guilty child, she jumped, intentionally putting several inches of space between her and her companion.

Rex noticed her change, and looked up. Unlike her, his grin brightened when he saw their employer approaching their table. Elliot was flanked by his good friend Nico and another man she'd never laid eyes on before.

Thandie could not believe her luck. Of all the nights, all the places, and of all the people...why did they have to run into Elliot Richards on the one evening she was desperate to not think about him?

Thandie tried to stand, forgetting they were seated in a booth. Her knees banged painfully against the table, forcing her to fall back onto the leather console. But not before she saw Elliot's cool gray gaze zero in on the flash of upper thigh, made visible by the high slit of her dress.

"Are you all right?" Rex asked, concern marking his face.

"I'm fine," she said quickly, embarrassed.

"Are you sure—"

"Yes, very sure," she said, softening her hasty reply with a tentative smile. Any chance of escape was gone. Thandie whispered a curse under her breath as Elliot and his friends surrounded their table. There was a look in his eyes she didn't trust. And the smile he wore definitely could not be trusted.

"Well, if it isn't the two lovebirds," Elliot said in a low voice. "Imagine my delight when I saw you across the room."

Thandie gritted her teeth together, and Rex smiled. What he took as a compliment, she registered as a taunt.

Sliding out of the booth, Rex stood to greet their visitors "Good to see you, gentlemen." His surprise at running into them was evident as he shook the hand of each man, but he was pleased nonetheless.

Intent on ignoring Elliot and Nico's cheerful smile, Thandie turned her attention to the other man. He was a tall, dark figure. Even dressed in a suit, Thandie could tell he was incredibly fit. He was all tanned skin, thick dark brows, dark goatee, and long dark hair. He could have been a pirate in another life.

Noticing her fascination with Matrix, Elliot inclined his head. "I don't believe you two have met before." He held out his hand to his friend. "Thandie, this is Matrix Lang. Matrix, this is Thandie Shaw."

Matrix held out his hand to Thandie. When her hand settled into his palm, he bent over it and kissed the smooth skin. "I've heard a lot about you. It's refreshing to see the rumors were true."

Thandie blushed a little under Matrix's dark gaze, but retracted her hand as soon as she could without being offensive. Matrix spelled trouble, in all capital letters.

"And I'm sure you remember Nico," Elliot went on smoothly.

Nico did not reach for hand. Instead, he chose to wink at her.

Thandie couldn't help but notice the similarities between the three men. All of them dark and handsome. Elliot with his serious yet aloof nature, brightened by his pale gray eyes. Nico with his dark charm and devil-may-care attitude. And Matrix, with his dark good looks and even darker mystic. She imagined the havoc they caused to the women of South Beach.

As usual, Elliot's beauty eclipsed everything in the room. Against her will, her gaze was drawn to him. And there it stayed.

"I trust you're having a lovely evening so far?" Elliot probed.

"We are," Rex answered with an affectionate glance in her direction.

Thandie noticed with some alarm, Elliot's observation of Rex's reaction. Something flashed across his features. It was so quick, she couldn't make it out, but she was wise enough to be on alert.

"Are you coming or going?" Rex asked the men.

"Going, I'm afraid," Elliot said with a derisive smile. "Otherwise, we would love to join you."

Thandie released a sigh of relief. Her celebration was premature, because at that moment their eyes met. Something foreboding loomed in those cool gray orbs. Thandie shook her head ever so slightly, willing him to understand her desire to have him out of here and far, far away from her. The tips of his lips lifted, and she saw him give the barest shake of his head.

"However," Elliot said smoothly, "it would be rude of us to pass without at least joining you for a drink."

"Uh—yes, of course," Rex stammered, clearly thrilled by the suggestion. "We'd love you to—"

Without waiting for him to finish, Elliot slid into the booth next to Thandie, moving so close their thighs were pressed together. She attempted to slide over to put a little space between them, but her efforts were pointless when she felt Elliot's large hand land on her leg.

Powerless to stop the train wreck that was sure to happen, Thandie watched as Rex slid into the booth beside her, followed by Nico. Matrix pulled out one of two chairs facing their booth, and took his seat. With dread, Thandie knew what was happening. Like trained assassins, Nico and Matrix had settled themselves on the opposite side of Rex, making it easy to distract his attention away from Elliot and Thandie.

Rex chanced a glance at Thandie, but before he could turn his head entirely in her direction, Nico said, "You have excellent taste, Rex." He lifted up the wine bottle. "This is one of my favorites."

Rex turned to Nico. "A special wine for a special lady," he said.

"So you say," was Elliot's reply.

Thandie reached for her wine goblet, and murmured "asshole" into her glass. Apparently, Elliot heard her, resulting in a squeeze of her leg. She fidgeted uncomfortably in her seat. The movement caught Rex's attention. Again, he turned to look at her. And yet again, his attention was stolen away. This time by Matrix.

"So what else do you have planned tonight?" he asked conversationally.

Rex turned to Matrix and explained how, if time permitted, he hoped to take Thandie to Bleau Bar for after dinner drinks. The conversation got complex when Matrix began suggesting a list of lounges he preferred over Rex's destination. He even offered to call his contacts to place Rex on the VIP list.

Thandie lost the thread of the discussion almost immediately, when she felt Elliot's hand expertly slide past the folds of her gown, and find bare flesh. She gasped when she felt his hand make an unhurried path up her thigh. He stroked the tender flesh, his fingers edging dangerously close to her sex. She slammed her thighs closed, but was momentarily paralyzed when he pinched her tender flesh, causing her to muffle a cry of pain. Instinctively, her thighs fell back apart, just as he had planned.

With her date so easily occupied, the dimness of the lighting, and the dark folds of her dress offering ample coverage, Elliot was free to do whatever he wanted beneath the table. And he took great pleasure and time doing just that.

With erotic slowness, his finger flicked across the thin material of her panties. Thandie was now shivering with anger and anticipation. The pads of his fingers were so dangerously close to her womanhood, her thighs were shaking with keen arousal.

As if nothing were amiss, Elliot signaled the waiter over with his free hand and announced he was buying another bottle of wine for the table in celebration of Rex and Thandie's special night out.

As the waiter ticked off their long list of selections to Rex, Elliot took the opportunity to gather the crotch of her panties into his palm, and with one firm tug, ripped the material right off her body. The cacophony of whispered conversations and usual restaurant noises, compounded by Rex's inattention, made the sound of ripping material go unnoticed. Elliot transferred her panties into his other hand and pocketed them into his suit jacket.

Now vulnerable to his eager hand, Thandie licked her lower

lip nervously when she felt his finger slide into her dripping wet folds. She tensed and her stomach gave a lurch. He inserted another finger into her hot center.

Thandie's natural juices poured over his fingers like thick honey. He enjoyed the feeling of her body trembling at his touch, and delighted in watching her fight to keep composure. Turning her face away from him, she pretended interest in the discussion between Rex and Matrix. He knew she was feigning it; her eyes were glassy and unfocused.

Elliot enjoyed his affect on her so much, he allowed his fingers to play with her for tortuously long minutes. In and out. In and out. His fingers dipped, teased and stroked her until Thandie had no choice but to give up the pretense of following the table conversation and attempting to eat. She resorted to staring down into her plate, her fork dangling precariously from numb fingers.

Smoothly, his palm along her inner thigh, he caressed her skin until he cupped the underside of her knee. Effortlessly, he lifted her leg, hooking her knee over his thigh. She did not fight him. She was too far gone, too defeated, to put up any resistance. With her thighs now spread wide, he was free to roam and discover ever intimate corner of her sex. This time, when he slid his fingers inside her, he went possessively deeper. Thandie began to chew on her bottom lip in what he suspected was an effort to stop from moaning aloud.

In spite of the sensual torment he was inflicting on her, Elliot was suffering from his own arousal. His throbbing groin pressed against the zipper of his slacks. He wanted to pull himself free and place the weight of his engorged cock into her palm. The thought alone made his testicles tighten painfully.

And yet, for all his imagination, what he wanted most of all was to simply kiss her. He wanted to feel her lips beneath his own, tasting her sweet, sweet mouth, until her lips were wet and puffy from his kisses. But he could not. At least, not right here. Not with Rex seated so close, and so clueless, beside her. He wanted her badly. So badly, the line between social decorum and savagery was beginning to blur. What would happen if he pulled her into his lap right now? The thought had merit.

While he pondered this, he watched the rise and fall of her breasts. He was enchanted by the way the candlelight danced across her golden skin, as her breath came and went in short gasps, in rhythm to his fingers.

Eventually, Elliot's fingers slid up and began making slow torturous circles around her sensitive bud, applying just enough pressure to keep her highly aroused but not giving her release. From time to time, Elliot would insert himself into the ridiculous conversation. He did not say enough to overtake the exchange, but just enough to tie him to the discussion. His tone however was disinterested, giving him the appearance of a bored participant. Meanwhile, beneath the table, he was driving Thandie closer and closer to the brink of insanity. Her orgasm was just within reach. And just when she thought he was going to take her over the edge, he slowed the progression of his finger, bringing her down slowly. After she calmed, he would begin his seduction again.

Thandie's legs were shaking so badly she feared she would start vibrating the table. And her thighs were so slick with moisture, she was certain she'd formed a puddle beneath her. She could smell her arousal and knew Elliot could as well. What she feared was Rex discovering what was happening under the table.

The waiter returned with the bottle of wine and additional goblets. He made quick work of filling their glasses before quietly departing. Without warning, Elliot held up his glass in a gracious gesture.

"I'd like to toast this moment," he said.

Rex, Nico and Matrix held up their glasses, forcing Thandie to follow suit. Her fingers shook as she held up her glass. Elliot was applying more pressure between her thighs. With the pad of his middle finger, he plied the taut bud with soft sliding motions. Thandie was now seeing red and blue stars. Her breathing was choppy and her pelvic muscles began to pump against his hand, making her stomach contract.

"To new beginnings," Elliot said, with an air of detachment. "I wish you both one climactic turn after another."

Rex tipped his glass and drank, although he wore a quizzical look at Elliot's words. Nico grinned and drained his glass. Elliot sipped from his glass as he watched Thandie. Fighting the beginning sparks of ecstasy, she held her glass to her lips and took a calming breath. She had just begun to sip when the first wave of rapture washed over her. Her body went completely still and then began to shudder. The wine she'd been drinking flowed down the wrong tube, causing her to go into a fit of coughs, interrupted by more body-ripping contractions of elation. She clapped her hand over her mouth to prevent herself from screaming. It was the strangest coughing spell any of them had ever seen.

She didn't have enough time to recover before Rex turned wide eyes on her, asking if she was all right. Elliot followed suit by asking the same question, although his words held no sympathy. His fingers were now buried inside her, pulling in and out of her as her inner walls squeezed him.

"Here, drink your water." Rex insisted.

"Yes, Thandie," Elliot said in his mocking voice, "drink some water."

Without warning, she jumped to her feet, bumping the table again. "Excuse me," she said in a near panic.

"Are you okay?" Rex asked. He moved to get up, but Nico blocked his exit, and seemed slow to register his attempt.

"Yes," she squeaked. "Ladies' room." All but stepping over Elliot in her haste to get away from him, she slid out of the booth.

She could feel everyone's gaze on her, making her escape all the more desperate. But her legs felt rubbery and were unwilling to cooperate. She stumbled once, only to catch herself by planting a steady hand on a fellow diner's chair. Pulling herself up tall, she shot Elliot a hateful look before stomping off to the restroom.

Several hours later, Thandie let herself into Elliot's house. Rex had offered to walk her inside but, still tense after what had happened earlier at Zuma, she'd politely declined.

After her hasty flight to the ladies' room, Thandie had to deal with cleaning herself up. It had not been easy and, thanks to Elliot, she did not have panties. Thandie had stayed in the bathroom as long as manners would allow.

Luckily, Elliot and his friends were gone before she returned to the dining area. The only person at their table was her worried date.

Aware that their uninvited guests might have dampened the romantic dinner he'd planned, Rex made a gallant effort to redeem the evening. He'd been charming and well-mannered. Reacting to her sudden lack of conversation, Rex seemed eager to regale her with tales about the places he'd traveled and the people he'd met. At any other time, Thandie might have been entertained, but tonight she was not. Her enthusiasm for the evening was gone. It wasn't Rex's fault. It was Elliot's, and Elliot's alone.

True to his word, Matrix had indeed put them on the guest list at a series of private lounges. Thandie had half expected to see Elliot at one of the venues. Mercifully, she had not. If he meant to spoil her night, he had succeeded. Thanks to him, she was jumpy, irritable and uncomfortable.

He'd even managed to ruin her and Rex's good-night kiss. Thandie could tell Rex had been anticipating this moment with about as much as excitement as she had been dreading it. Thandie'd had about all the intimacy she could stand for one night.

Elliot had coaxed an orgasm out of her that was so strong, she was still recovering from it. And like any woman who'd recently experienced the best climax of her life, she was drained of all energy. The only thing that kept her lucid was the turbulent argument she planned to have with Elliot as soon as she got home. And if he wasn't there, she intended to drive to club and find him. Her anger had been boiling for hours, waiting for a chance to erupt on the silver-eyed devil who'd earned her enmity.

Locking the front door behind her, Thandie walked through the foyer and crossed the formal dining room. She found the culprit exiting his private gym. He was wearing a pair of sweatpants cut off just below the knee; his chest was bare and slick with sweat. He had the audacity to smile when he saw her.

"How was your date?" he casually asked.

"Sonofabitch!" she spat at him.

"That bad, huh?"

She stomped her foot. "How dare you do that to me!"

"You enjoyed it," he retorted.

She tossed her purse at him, which he easily dodged. "You intentionally embarrassed me tonight."

"I'm not going to apologize for touching you. I've given you ample opportunity to handle our affairs privately." He grinned.

She could not hide her disbelief. "You humiliated me in front of a crowd, Elliot."

"You have only yourself to blame for this escalation."

She screeched with anger. "Damn you, Elliot!"

He crossed the room with that predatory stalk of his, stopping only when he hovered over her. His voice was steely when he spoke. "No one knew what took place except for you and me, and I certainly won't apologize for touching you."

"Are you crazy? "

"If my memory serves me correctly, you came quite willingly—and loudly, I might add."

"You're certifiable," she whispered.

"So you say," he said with a grin.

She shook her head in disbelief. She was on the brink of screaming from sheer frustration. "Why do you insist on putting me in such awkward positions?" She held up her hand to prevent him from speaking. The wicked grin that had just snaked across his mouth told her he would turn her words into something juvenile. "I'm a businesswoman who happens to have peers who look to me for guidance. I can't mentor them properly if I'm constantly struggling to keep your hands off me."

Visibly annoyed, he crossed his arms over his broad chest. "Stop using Raja and Len as a shield. I'm not buying it. Your assistants are adults, if you hadn't noticed."

"They're barely out of college."

"They're old enough."

She planted her hand on her hip. "Old enough for what?"

"Old enough for everything that matters."

The look he gave her was one of sinister intent. She gasped. "Don't you dare touch one of them."

He only lifted his brow in challenge.

"I'm serious, Elliot. Leave the girls alone."

"What makes you so sure the girls want to be left alone? I happen to personally know that Len and Raja would love nothing more than to get me in bed."

Her face stiffened. "Elliot, I swear if you so much as touch—"

"Are you sleeping with Rex?"

"What?" The question caught her completely off guard.

"You heard me," he snapped.

"What does that matter to you?"

"Answer the question, Thandie."

She jutted her chin up determinedly. "Who are you sleeping with?"

"Would you like me to make you a list?"

She snarled at him and turned away, meaning to put an end to the discussion. She got no farther than an arm's length in distance before Elliot grabbed hold of her and pulled her around to face him.

"I asked you a question," he said through gritted teeth.

"No," she seethed. "I'm not sleeping with Rex."

"Good," he said. "Keep it that way."

"How dare you tell me—"

Her words were cut off by his kiss. It was hot, hard and punishing. Planting her palms on his chest, she pushed against him, trying to break his embrace. But it was no good. Elliot was too determined. He broke off the kiss abruptly. His silver gaze raked her before saying, "Run along to bed, before I completely lose my patience with you."

She was stunned by his callousness, and astonished by his offhand reference to Rex. He showed no traces of jealousy when he spoke about the man. His tone seemed to imply he saw Rex as no more than an inconvenience to him. Infuriated by his lack of respect, she planted one hand on her hip and jabbed an index finger at him. "You have no right to tell me what I can and can't do. What happens between Rex and me is none of your—"

He effectively cut her off by holding his hand up. "Push me on this and you will see a side of me you won't like."

His words were delivered with such malice, she almost recoiled. But refusing to be intimidated, she glared at him instead. "Behave yourself, Elliot, or I'll quit and I'll take all my contacts with me."

"Drop the shit," he snapped. "You and I both know you got more enjoyment under that dinner table than you could ever hope for with Rex."

"Don't touch me again."

His silver eyes seem to light with fire. "I'll do whatever I please, and if your body is included in those plans, then you had better sit back and enjoy it, puss."

"I mean it, Elliot. Stay away from me or else." She'd meant to walk away, with every intention of delivering her threats and leaving him to ponder the ramifications. Her hopes of a grand exit lasted only two steps. Elliot took her arm and pulled her back to him. She winced, her hand instinctively reaching up to detach his hold, but his grip was firm, and the harder she fought, the tighter he held.

His lips were only inches from her ear. The warmth of his breath against her skin sent ripples of shivers over her body. Her nipples were immediately erect, pressed against his bare chest.

"Let me give some words of wisdom." His flirtatious smile vanished, only to be replaced by determination. "You're only setting Rex up for disappointment and getting yourself into a lot of trouble. Don't ever think you can give away what's mine."

She shoved hard away from him, breaking his hold on her. Thandie was so angry, she was shaking uncontrollably. Then something fragile broke inside her. She felt it instantly, and knew she was in trouble. Gooseflesh puckered her skin at the same time as cold sweat rushed over her. She flinched her fists into balls, willing herself to stop trembling, to focus on what was real and steady. However, her body would not obey. She was so upset, she could not keep focus.

"Shit!" Turning abruptly, she made for a quick escape. She almost made it out of the room before her legs went stiff on her. She slumped against the wall. Distantly, she heard someone call her name, but she ignored it. Desperate, she labored across the room in shaky but determined motions. She felt as if she was wading through quicksand. It soon became apparent she would not make it to her room. She doubled over, in great pain.

Taking quick unsteady breaths, she pressed herself against the wall. The fireworks exploding before her were so bright, she had to squeeze her eyes shut. The attack was so acute, so abrupt, she could not regain control of herself fast enough.

She gasped at her chest, as if trying to remove some heavy weight that was planted there. She flinched when a pair of hands took hold of her shoulders. Unable to open her eyes fully, she was able to make out the faint outline of a man hovering over her. Knowing it could only be one person, she began to struggle out of his touch, but her movements were a mixture of sluggish tugs and sudden jerks.

"Listen to me, honey," he said in a strong yet soothing voice. "I need you to calm down and breathe. Are you listening to me? Breathe."

She squeezed her eyes shut again, trying to push him out of her thoughts. *Calm down. Calm down. Calm down,* she repeated again and again in her head.

"Thandie." Elliot's deep and steady voice cut through her thoughts like a blade. "I need you to look at me and focus."

Unwilling, but desperate, she did as he said.

"You must breathe slower. Take deep breaths." While he spoke, he pulled her hands toward him, using his thumbs and strong fingers to work them out of the tight fists. When her hands were relaxed, he pressed her palms together. "Take deep breaths," he said. "Deep slow breaths." As he spoke, he covered her hands with his own and applied pressure. "Squeeze your palms together," he instructed. "Squeeze them as hard as you can." She obeyed. The harder she squeezed, the harder he pressed. "Squeeze harder," he urged. "Breathe from your abdomen. Yes, that's better."

He kept up a barrage of directions, instructing her to continue pressing her palms together. "Breathe deeply…" and "You're safe.…" But it always came back to making her press her hands together.

His voice was low and trancelike. Easy to follow, easy to depend on. After a while Thandie understood what he was doing. Elliot was using her distraction of pressing her palms together to help her capture her breathing. Surprisingly, it worked much faster than her usual tactics. Her breathing became steady once again.

When she opened her eyes, she saw Elliot was staring at her but this time the arrogant smile was gone. Only a blank expression remained. Elliot was kneeling before her, his weight balanced on his knees.

"Feeling better now?" he asked.

She nodded, not trusting herself to speak just yet.

He looked deep into her eyes, and asked, "How long have you suffered from panic attacks?"

"Get away from me," she rasped.

"I asked you a question."

"Why do you want to know?" She was ashamed and defensive.

"Because I do," he said calmly. "Now tell me."

"I've always had them. Ever since I was a child. There! Are you happy now?"

"Yes," he said quietly.

Silence fell between them, making her outburst seem all the more loud and unnecessary.

She shifted her weight, only now realizing she was slumped against the wall, her legs crumpled beneath her. How had she gotten like this? Had she done it herself, or had Elliot moved her?

"How—how did you know?" she asked cautiously. "How did you recognize...my condition?"

For a long while he seemed to measure her with his eyes. Finally he said, "Let's just say I've had plenty of practice."

Before she could ask what he meant by that, the sound of a car pulling up to the house could be heard in the distance. Minutes later, the front door opened, and the sound of laughter and clumsy steps could be heard. Len and Raja had apparently returned home for the evening. Shrill giggles erupted, followed by loud *shhhhing*. The two laughed again, before stomping noisily up the stairs.

Thandie turned her head in the direction of the voices, a frantic look on her face.

"They don't know, do they?" Elliot said in a low voice.

She shook her head.

"No one knows," he surmised.

Thandie looked at the ground, embarrassed for having been found out.

"You should have told me."

"Why?" she snapped, anger bubbling up inside her. "So you could use it against me?"

"Perhaps," he said truthfully. "Or maybe I would have gone about things a little differently."

"And tonight?" she hissed. "Would you have gone about that differently as well?"

"No," he said flatly. "I make no apologies for what happened. I meant every word and every action. This—" he fanned his hand over her collapsed body "—changes nothing."

Thandie moved to get up, but froze when his hand reached out to cup her chin. Lifting her face so he could peer into it, he said, "Because I'm not completely unscrupulous, I'll do you a kindness." He waited until she met his gaze. "Consider this a truce between lovers."

"We are not lovers, Elliot."

He smiled. "We will be, pussycat. Very soon."

"Let go of me."

And he did. Like an exotic cat, Elliot rose smoothly, turned his back on her, and left the room without another word.

Thandie watched him disappear around the corner. When he was out of sight, she listened to his footfalls, which had become softer the farther he went. Eventually the sound of his bedroom door slammed shut. And then there was nothing.

Thandie allowed herself to weaken. Hot tears streamed down her face. She had to force herself to keep taking deep breaths. She was not fully recovered from her episode.

Damn him!

Why did he have to be the one to see her fall apart? She'd kept her panic attacks a secret for so long. Why did he, of all people, have to be the one to expose her? And how had he known how to calm her down? Why had his face expressed genuine concern, and his voice have to sound so soft and comforting? Why did his kindness make her soften toward him? And why did she allow him to get under her skin?

Damn him!

Angrily, she wiped her wet face. She still had two months left on her contract. It didn't take a genius to point out what the successful completion of the Babylon project would do for her reputation. But, her faith had been shaken. For the first time ever, she questioned if she could get through this.

Damn him!

Chapter Eighteen

Victoria Day had been right.

Upon meeting Fernando Fonseca for the first time, she added a few more attributes to his résumé: young, Cuban and handsome. As she followed him to the dressing rooms, she was convinced this was just the distraction she needed to keep her mind off Elliot.

Surprisingly, Elliot had held true to their truce. He'd kept a modest distance from her over the last two days. In truth, she'd seen very little of him at all. Evening glimpses of him and Romero coming and going from the house was the extent of her interactions with him. And due to her scrambling to secure arrangements for The Pussy Cats performance, she hadn't had the energy to visit Babylon recently.

Turning off her phone, Thandie began to undress. She took her time clipping her hair up and removing all her jewelry. When she was swathed in only the fluffy white spa robe, Thandie was escorted from the stylish ladies' dressing area to Fernando's room. The lights were turned low, and a soft Spanish guitar ballad was playing in the background.

"I'm going to step outside while you disrobe." His voice

was a soft whisper which easily relaxed her, as well as stimulated her erogenous zones. "Lie facedown on the table. I'll knock before I come back in."

Thandie tossed her robe aside and climbed on the table naked. She was pleased to find it was heated. She closed her eyes, released a deep sigh and tried to clear her mind. Fernando returned, giving her a quick explanation of his method before beginning their session. She welcomed his strong, skillful hands on her attention-starved body. She knew why Fernando was highly recommended. His attention to detail was beyond reproach. He zeroed in on the places where she had tension, and kneaded the muscles until they were smooth and supple.

Afterward, Thandie felt refreshed and completely relaxed. She did not want to leave. She changed into her clothes with sluggish ease, and marveled at the effects a proper massage could do not only for a person's physical state, but their mental being.

Thandie strolled out of Blu Moon ready to take on the world. Basking in her sunny disposition, she waited until she was in the car before turning her cell phone on. Immediately, the phone rang. It was Len.

"Oh, thank God you answered! Where have you been?" Her assistant sounded hysterical.

"I had my massage today," Thandie reminded her. "Why? What's wrong?"

"We have a big problem," Len announced. "The Pussy Cats refuse to perform and want to cancel."

"What?"

"Three of their girls are sick at the hotel. They think it's food poisoning from some hole-in-the-wall restaurant they ate at last night. Apparently, they've been in taking turns puking their brains out all morning."

"They can't do the show without them?"

"Raja has been trying to talk them into it, but Celeste won't budge. I think you need to come down here."

Dammit. Thandie had a luncheon with Mira Dietrich in half an hour. There was no way she could make it down to the club, resolve The Pussy Cats crisis and be downtown to meet with Mira in time. Shit, she hated being rushed. "Okay, Len," she heard herself saying. "I'm on my way, but you need to cover me by meeting with Mira."

"Okay, just hurry."

When Thandie arrived at Babylon, Len was waiting outside for her. She tossed the car keys to Len and dashed into the club while Len started the engine and headed toward downtown. It was early, and there were few staff members roaming about the building. Thandie did not bother to glance up toward Elliot's office. She knew without looking he was up there. Instead, she made a direct path for the backstage entrance. Climbing the steps, she rounded the corner just in time to hear Raja attempting to reason with the Pussy Cats' leader, Celeste.

"There are roughly two hours before opening," Raja was saying. "Surely you can adjust the routine to fit four dancers instead of seven."

"No, I can't," Celeste said emphatically. "How many times do I have to tell you, Raja?"

Thandie walked up behind Raja and placed her hand on her shoulder. "Celeste, what is going on? Len tells me you're having trouble performing."

Everyone seemed to give a sigh of relief, happy to see Thandie. Even though Celeste was breathing fire, she seemed pleased not to have to deal with Raja anymore.

"I've told your girls a hundred times this isn't going to work. Thandie, we can't do the show without half the team.

You know that. Maybe if we had one more person, we could rebalance the routine, but that's a long shot."

Thandie nodded her head, thinking. "Have you asked someone else to step in?"

Celeste was already shaking her head. "It's not that easy. They have to be taught the steps. No one can learn a routine in a few hours. Save for a professional dancer."

Thandie looked to Raja. "Call the Babylon dancers. See if any of them are willing to work tonight."

"I've already tried that," Raja whined. "When we couldn't get hold of you, we asked Markie for the dancers call list. They're all booked."

Thandie pinched the bridge of her nose. "You can't be serious," she groaned.

Raja threw up her hands. "What can I do? There's some open casting call for a music video today. The girls I was able to get on the phone told me they didn't know how long they would be there."

"There you go," Celeste said with a shrug of her shoulders. "There's no one available to learn the routine. And these aren't exactly easy steps."

"Blowing off this performance isn't an option," Thandie informed everyone within earshot. "We paid for your travel expenses and the agreed upon retainer."

"Yes, I know. But—"

Thandie continued as if Celeste hadn't interrupted her. "Unless you plan to pay back those funds, a backup plan needs to be presented right now." From the corner of her eyes, Thandie could see Raja edge behind her, lest she be in the way when the fireworks commenced.

"What do you expect me to do?" Celeste fired back. "The only people who have seen our routines enough times to grasp the steps in record time would be you and your girls." She meant her words to be an absurd notion, but the moment the idea was out it began to resonate. Celeste and Thandie held eye contact, both thinking the same thing.

Raja hadn't yet caught on and blurted out, "Len can't dance. She has *no* rhythm." She felt rather than saw Thandie look at her with a pleading expression. "No way!" Raja shook her head vehemently. "Not on your life. I'm not dressing in one of those costumes. They barely qualify as clothing."

Thandie felt like pulling her hair out. Why wasn't anyone willing to help her out? The past week had been a nightmare of one bad event to another.

Celeste disappeared into the dressing room and reemerged carrying a hanger with what looked like a tiny piece of leather dangling from the hook. She pushed the hanger toward Thandie. "You can either do it with us or be prepared to tell your boss that we had to cancel. You'll only be on the pole. It's not that big of a deal."

"A pole!" Thandie felt sick. "I can't do that, Celeste. I'm sorry."

"Then I'm sorry to tell you that we'll have to cancel our performance."

Thandie knew she was going to be sick for sure. She massaged her temples. "Celeste, surely you can find a way to do your show without your full team."

"If I could, I would, and I wouldn't be wasting your time."

"Can't you call someone else—anyone else—to stand in?"

"We don't have enough time for that. You're the only person here who has seen our performance a dozen times. You know the routines."

"But I—"

"Yes or no, Thandie. You need to make a decision." Again, Celeste pushed the outfit toward her.

Thandie groaned before snatching the hanger out of her

hands. "But I'm wearing a mask, or something, right? I can't have people seeing my face."

Celeste nodded. "Then we'll all wear one. Now let me give you a few quick tips."

Elliot had been locked away in his office most of the day. His only break had been a brief trip home to shower and change clothes. His return to the office had been slowed by Lucinda forcing a meal in front of him, and demanding he eat everything on his plate. He'd been in a rush to get back and complained he did not have time.

But, as usual, Lucinda won the argument.

While he ate, he listened to her ramble about trivial matters around his house, relatives she planned to visit and places where she'd like to vacation. Elliot listened patiently while he ate and found himself inadvertently getting sucked into the conversation. He hardly noticed when she gave him a second helping.

By the time Lucinda cleared away the dishes, Elliot was vastly informed on every detail of her life, and well fed. He was pleased with both outcomes. He'd always enjoyed her company and he adored her cooking. But he was running behind schedule. Getting up from his seat, he brushed a hasty kiss against her cheek and headed out of the house.

The meal had done wonders to his attitude. He'd been tense lately. He refused to believe this had anything to do with the fact that he had not seen Thandie in two days. He intended to keep his word about their truce. It was the least he could do. He'd been harboring a lot of guilt over causing her panic attack.

Elliot was fifteen minutes late to the investor meeting he'd scheduled today. Romero looked him over curiously when Elliot finally sailed through his office door. The room was crowded with eight men, all looking eager to begin. Even Warren, who often arrived late, was in present company. Elliot was rarely late for an appointment, especially a business meeting. Ignoring his assistants' imploring gazes, Elliot immediately got the meeting underway.

Two hours later, after the meeting had concluded, Elliot stood and said, "Warren, a word please."

Warren jerked at the sound of his name but stepped back to allow the other men to step past him. When the room was empty, save for the two of them, Elliot retrieved an envelope out of his breast pocket and handed it to the older man.

Frowning, Warren looked down at the paper. "What's this?"

"I understand you may be in the market for an investigator." Elliot tapped the envelope. "This is a short list of professionals. Their references are included."

Warren opened his mouth to say something, but seemed unable to vocalize his thoughts.

Elliot waved away the attempt. There was no kindness in his voice when he said, "In the future, if you need assistance, come to me. Not Nico."

"I didn't think you would be willing to help," he said.

"I'm not," Elliot retorted. "But I'd prefer you not to involve my friends into your legal matters."

When Warren nodded sheepishly, Elliot considered the matter closed. However, Warren did not immediately leave. To Elliot's frustration, the older man took a seat and said, "We need to talk."

Thandie could feel herself shaking, even though she was wearing a hoodie one of the dancers had kindly loaned her. Abandoning one of her own rules, she had Raja get her a shot of vodka from the bar. If she was going to do a Pussy Cat pole routine in front of a South Beach crowd, she damned well wasn't going to be completely sober for the disaster. Lord knew she didn't have the body to be dancing nearly nude on stage beside professional dancers. The more she thought about it, the sicker she felt.

Celeste did all of their makeup. With a delicate hand, she artfully drew what could easily be mistaken as dark lacy veils across their eyes, effectively masking their faces. They all wore identical black wigs that stopped just below their earlobes.

When everyone was fully dressed, even Thandie had to admit she wasn't easily distinguishable from the other dancers. But this did not calm the butterflies in her stomach. She could feel the dull numbness of the alcohol begin to hit her. She felt a little safer, unfeeling and inhuman. Celeste tried to keep her calm by talking to her, stepping her through the routine, offering her tips on how to work the pole.

It was almost twelve o'clock, and Thandie was counting down the minutes to their midnight act. She slowly discarded the safety of the hoodie and slipped on the pointy leather boots that zipped up to her thighs. When she stepped in front of the mirror, she barely recognized herself. The wig and the makeup had done wonders to hide her identity, but the outfit…there were no words. It was simply appalling. Thandie knew she wore revealing clothing when she worked, but what she was currently wearing made her speechless. It was a two piece outfit, with bikini bottoms that sat low on her hips. The back of the shorts were cut so high they exposed the entire underside of her ass. The top was nothing more than a strapless bra. This was where she had the most hesitation. Thandie wouldn't necessarily consider herself top-heavy, but the outfit was at least a size too small. She was literally spilling out of it. Yes, there was a thin string that tied around her neck, but it offered little support, and looked ready to snap if put under serious stress. Thandie felt as though she might as well be naked.

Celeste walked into the dressing room and slapped her bare ass cheek. "Wow, you look great! You have an amazing body, Thandie."

"I think I'm going to be sick," Thandie said, meaning every word.

Celeste shook her head. "That's just nervousness. You'll be fine. I'll be close to you. We'll do a little girl-girl action to get the guys crazy." She laughed when she saw Thandie's ill expression. "It's meant to take your attention off the men in the crowd. They're going to go crazy when they see you."

"I doubt it."

Celeste winked at her. "You'll see soon enough. They're cueing up our music."

She took Thandie by the hand and led her to join the rest of the girls standing stage left, waiting to go on. Thandie watched with dread as the house lights went down and the house DJ began making a rousing introduction. The vibrating beat of Britney Spears's "Breathe on Me" rumbled to life, and The Pussy Cats took the stage.

Elliot was not in the best of moods. He bristled when he recalled his earlier conversation with Warren. It had single-handedly destroyed his good mood. Elliot had no desire to be privy to the details surrounding Warren's divorce, particularly because of his own history with Sophia. Any involvement on his part would only complicate matters. And yet, against his better judgment, he'd allowed Warren to divulge every bloody blow his and Sophia's lawyers were pummeling each other with. When it was all said and done, it was doubtful either would be satisfied.

Elliot had no idea why he even cared. He was disgusted with Warren for getting involved with Sophia in the first place. He'd tried to forewarn him; but the asshole could only see the pretty face and alluring body. Only Warren could be held responsible for his actions. So why did Elliot keep catching himself pondering Warren's situation, considering how he could best help?

Elliot was so distracted, he hardly recalled the details of the management meeting he'd just sat through. Not that it had been significant by any stretch of the imagination. Today's meeting had been a short one, and he was glad it was over.

Elliot checked his cell phone as the men filed out. Just as the last straggler left his office, Nico strolled through the door. Making himself at home, he flung himself into one of the chairs facing Elliot's desk. "Why is everyone hovering around the stage?" he asked lazily.

Not bothering to look up from his phone, Elliot said, "An exotic dance troupe is performing tonight."

"Really?" Nico's grin brightened. "In that case, let's not drag our feet." He sprang from his seat with the animation of a cartoon. "After you."

Elliot had little interest in watching the show, but it was time for him to make his rounds. Better he do it now, than later. Coming to his feet, Elliot straightened his tie and headed for the door. Nico followed closely behind.

Together, the two descended the stairs leading from Elliot's office. The crowd was particularly dense tonight. With a glance, he could see the male populace rivaled the females, which was unusual.

Before long, the house lights dimmed and scantily clad dancers advanced on the stage. The sight of half naked women and the positioning of stripper poles, caused the males in the room to begin pressing forward for a better look. After a dramatic introduction from the DJ, the music began and dancers commenced to swaying their hips provocatively.

Elliot scanned the room as he and Nico moved through

the crowd. Suddenly, Nico nudged him roughly and pointed toward the stage. "Is that—?"

Nico never got a chance to finish his sentence. Elliot was already shoving his way through the crowd.

Thandie could hardly believe she could remember the steps. Under the protection of the makeup, she felt as though she was another person. She moved in sync with the other dancers, albeit not as seamlessly, but doing her best to blend in. Shaking her bottom, she crawled along the catwalk wantonly. A guy from the crowd slapped her ass as she passed by, and surprising even herself, Thandie stayed in character.

Finally making her way to her pole, she swung around it, just as she'd been instructed. From the corner of her eye, she was impressed to see that the other girls were climbing to the tops of their poles, contorting themselves into provocative positions, before slowly sliding downward. It was done with acrobatic precision, and easily won the audience's attention.

Wisely, Thandie was positioned to the far right-hand side of the stage. Celeste had taught her a few pole tricks, but for the most part her role was to simply even out the routine formation, stay in sync with the others, and try not to fall down. So far she was holding her own. The more complicated steps were not until the end of the performance. Thandie prayed she could last that long.

Just as they'd practiced, Thandie wrapped her leg around her pole, and began to grind her body suggestively against it. The audience was cheering her on. The vodka was giving Thandie courage she might not have had on her own. She swayed to the music, dancing with shameless abandonment. Because of the bright stage lights, she could hardly make out faces in the crowd. This made her more daring. Details became hazy as she gave herself over to the rhythm of the music. So fuzzy were her thoughts, she didn't immediately react when one the rowdy spectators managed to propel himself over the edge of the stage and push his face into her crotch.

He was gone, disappearing back into the sea of shadowy faces, before Thandie registered what had happened. The sound of ruckus laughter and catcalls from the crowd seemed to roar in her head. Thandie hesitated for only a second, and then threw her head back and laughed as she eased herself away from the edge of the catwalk.

Somewhere in the shadowy crowd, she could make out bulky figures approaching the stage. Without recognizing them, she somehow knew they were club bouncers coming to settle the mob.

Celeste was suddenly dancing behind her, her hands on Thandie's shoulders. Her head fell back against Celeste's shoulder. She felt hands rubbing her thighs, and lips on her. And, for a moment, she had no idea what was going on.

Somehow, Celeste lay her on her back and was now hovering above Thandie. Hands reached out to touch her. Celeste attempted to shield Thandie with her body, but the frenzy of the crowd got to be too much for her to handle.

She pulled Thandie to her feet to prevent further groping, but the crush around them continued to press forward. Thandie felt even more hands on her, sweaty palms reaching to fondle the flesh of her thighs. She flinched away from their touch, but not before someone got a good hold on her and actually pulled her off the stage. Celeste tried to reach for her, but couldn't grab her in time.

Thandie screamed as she went down.

The horde of people surrounding the stage seemed to melt away from her abductor. Thandie didn't know what was happening until she looked up into Elliot's eyes. He was furious. His silver gaze flashed like lightening.

She tried to push him away, but he effortlessly tossed her over his shoulder and crossed the dance floor. She looked around for help, but saw that there was none. There was only a barrier of big bouncers guarding Elliot's way through the crowd, ensuring no horny men were able to touch her.

"What are you doing?" a voice called out. Nico appeared at Elliot's side. His voice sounded strained, although his features were relaxed. It was clear, however, he did not like what was happening. "Have you completely lost it?"

Elliot brushed past Nico, ignoring him completely.

"Elliot," he said more sternly, "drop the girl and come to the bar with me. You need to cool off before you do something stupid."

Elliot whirled around on him. "Get the hell out of my way before I put my fist in your face."

Nico's concern instantly turned into anger. "Put her down," he demanded, his lazy drawl replaced with a dangerously quiet one.

Blinded by his own anger and completely unfazed by Nico's threat, Elliot turned away from his friend. Nico lunged for Elliot and, to Thandie's horror, Tiny placed a beefy hand on his chest and held him back. Furious, Nico slapped his hand away and glared at the giant.

Fearful of a brawl, Thandie fought harder to get out Elliot's hold. She soon discovered it was no use. His grip on her was iron-strong. A crowd soon gathered around Nico and Tiny, hiding them from her sight.

She could see Elliot was taking her to his office, and that was the last place she wanted to go. She begged him to let her down, but he wouldn't answer her.

As he headed up the stairs to his office, Michelle gave her a worried look. She tried to reach his hand for help, but she couldn't quite make it. He looked as if he was on the brink of helping her, but Elliot swung around and yelled for him to close the door. Michelle hesitated only for a second before closing the door.

Stalking across the room, Elliot threw her onto the couch as if she was a bag of laundry. She could see the enraged look in his eyes.

"What the hell did you think you were doing out there?" he asked in a terrifyingly low voice.

Thandie flinched. She would have preferred he'd shouted at her. That way she could have responded in kind. But this, she had no idea how to handle. Again, she licked her lips. "I—"

"Did you enjoy flaunting that lovely body of yours to a club full of drunk men?" he asked. "If I hadn't intervened when I did, you might have gotten raped out there. Is that even registering with you?" The look in his eyes was that of disgust and something…unknown.

"I can explain—"

He didn't respond to her, just picked up his phone and pushed in a number.

"This is Elliot. I'll be leaving shortly. Have my car ready.

"We're going home," he said. "You're sleeping with me tonight." Carefully, he scooped her up in his arms and carried her into a private bathroom she had never known existed. As with all things concerning Elliot, it was nicely decorated, equipped with a shower stall, armoire and open shelves stocked with fluffy wide towels. He gently lowered her to her feet and turned the shower faucet. Within minutes thick curls of steam began to fill the air. Elliot turned to her and wordlessly pulled the wig off her head before tossing it into the wastebasket. "I hate this, your makeup, this whole outfit"

He ripped off the skimpy material and threw it into the wastebasket with the wig.

"It was meant to hide my identity."

He lifted his brow. "It didn't do a very good job." He stood closer to her, piercing her with his intense gray eyes. "Don't do it again."

Thandie wasn't given an opportunity to respond before he reached out and pulled clean towels from the shelf. "I'll give you some privacy. There are supplies in the armoire. Help yourself to anything you need." And then he was gone, closing the door softly behind him.

Relieved to have a moment to herself, Thandie released a heavy sigh. When she turned to look at her reflection in the foggy mirror, she gasped. She looked a fright. The heavy stage makeup Celeste had labored over was ruined with smudges.

Thandie made quick work of cleaning herself up. After a thorough, but brief, shower, she emerged from the bathroom wrapped in one of the fluffy white towels and the sexy thigh high boots she'd worn. Elliot was leaning against the edge of his desk, waiting for her. He looked impeccably put together, not a hair out of place. One would never guess from the look of him what had gone on earlier.

She tugged at the towel. "I don't have anything to wear."

For a moment he just stared at her bare legs. His face was impassive, making it impossible to know what he was thinking. Finally, he pushed himself away from his desk and stepped into the bathroom. He opened the armoire doors to reveal several suit jackets, slacks and dress shirts. He curled his finger at her. "Come here."

Thandie stepped into the bathroom behind him. Without appearing to be selective, Elliot reached for the nearest shirt and handed it to her. Thandie accepted it and, out of habit, glanced at the label. Since he'd already seen everything there was to possibly see of her body, she did not protest when he took hold of her towel and pulled it free. Under his watchful stare, she slipped her arms through the shirt sleeves. As she fastened the buttons, she couldn't help but wonder how often he dressed women in his Prada shirts.

When she was done, she looked up at him. Something flashed across his face. In that instant she could tell he was still livid with her. She half expected him to start an argument, but instead he quietly shrugged out of his jacket and offered it to her for extra covering.

Thandie was surprised to learn Elliot had his own private exit. He guided her through a series of short corridors and down a stairwell until they arrived in a well-lit parking garage. A valet had Elliot's Range Rover running and ready. He discreetly disappeared as soon as he saw Elliot approach.

Elliot helped Thandie into her seat before climbing into his own seat. He appeared to be in deep thought as he buckled his seatbelt. His hands braced the stirring wheel tightly. "What happened tonight will never happen again, Thandie." He stared straight ahead, refusing to look at her. "I won't allow you to parade yourself in front of my staff or any other man. Understood?"

Thandie nodded. She'd hoped her quick agreement would ease his anger, but as he sat there unmoving, it was becoming clear that his anger was far beyond her. The man was struggling to calm himself. She feared if she didn't do something, he would explode.

Pulling her knees into her seat, she crawled across the console. Her bottom was lifted in the air as she reached for the fly of his pants. She looked nervously at him as she worked to release his cock. His silver eyes sliced into her. Hesitantly, she leaned forward to kiss his mouth. The passion he possessed consumed her. At the touch of his lips, she could feel herself being pulled into him.

His wonderful, hot tongue no longer teased her. He was focused on the pressure of his mouth against hers. She wanted to melt into him, let him take control of her. Finally, she freed his cock. His hot flesh, stood magnificently erect. She pulled her lips away from Elliot's to stare at the long, thick flesh. Its velvety head glistened with a pearl of moisture. Its beauty made her mouth water. She wrapped her hands around him, stroking his shaft, enjoying the weight of him in her hands. Her excitement grew as he nibbled on her neck; the sound of his soft groans vibrated his chest.

She lowered her head to run her tongue along the underside of his cock. His balls tightened at her touch. If possible, she could feel him grow larger. Her tongue and hands caressed him, taking pleasure in the taste of him. She looked up at him as she sank her lips over the head of his cock. They held an intense stare as she worked her mouth up and down his shaft, her tongue making slow swirls over the sensitive hole at the tip.

Unable to resist the hunger for him, she closed her eyes and sank her mouth over him, taking as much of him as she possibly could. The taste of him was so deliciously male. Her moans of pleasure joined his as she quickened her motions.

She groaned roughly when she felt his hand caress her lower back, then ease lower until a finger slid inside her. Her back arched, throwing her ass higher in the air. She wiggled her bottom as he explored her, then lowered her mouth deeper over him, savoring the feel of him. He groaned loudly.

She could feel him coming, but he didn't plan to go alone. He inserted another finger into her and began to carass her vigorously. She struggled to catch her breath. Her rising orgasm would push her over the edge. He was touching places that a cock could never explore. Her inner walls pressed against him, desperate for his touch.

With a quick intake of breath, she knew he was close. She sucked hard as he filled her mouth with his hot sperm. She pumped his shaft tightly with her hands, forcing as much of his cum as she could get into her waiting mouth.

She was licking his shiny head when a jolt of electricity jerked her body forward. A strangled moan escaped her as the waves of climactic sensations washed over her. She rested her head against his strong shoulder as she waited for the calm to claim her. Taking hold of her shoulders, he pulled her up to face him. He kissed her long and hard. Their tongues mated, uniting their joined flavors.

She opened her eyes to see him staring at her. There was still a distant look in his eyes, but they were less cold than before.

"We're not done, you know," he said, his voice a rough timbre.

She nodded and tried to look away, but he caught her face between his hands and forced her to look at him.

"When we get home, I'm going to come in you over and over again."

A warm flush covered her face. Anticipation overwhelmed her. Luckily, he didn't feel the need to say more. She allowed him to help her back into her seat to drive home.

He waited until they were well on their way before calling Romero and instructing him to locate Thandie's assistants and tell them she had left early. He listened intently for several minutes, frowned, and then said, "Take care of it."

Minutes later, they were pulling into Elliot's driveway. He helped her out of his vehicle and guided her down the hallway that led to his room. Thandie watched in quiet awe as his world unfolded before her.

His bedroom was masculine, yet beautiful in its simplicity. It was calm and relaxing in comparison to the rest of the house or his office at the club. The fresh scent of linen assailed her. All the tension that had built up during the quiet drive home was melting away.

She stood still as Elliot pulled his jacket from her shoulders, freed her of the shirt, and lay her on the bed. He burned her with those silver eyes as he undressed. She watched him with fascination.

He unbuttoned his shirt, revealing that wonderfully muscled torso. Even though he unfastened his slacks with ease, it felt like an eternity until he freed himself of the garment. And as he stepped out of his pants, Thandie's whole body tingled with excitement. The man was beautiful. Physically perfect.

She knew she was in big trouble. How would she ever be able to turn away from this man? It wasn't possible.

He came to her, his eyes devouring every curve of her body. "Turn around," he whispered. "I want you on your hands and knees." She complied. "Arch your back, sweetheart. I want to see that lovely ass of yours. Don't be shy. By the end of the night, I will know every inch of your body. You've made me wait for it long enough."

He plunged into her wet warmth, burying his cock inside her. He withdrew and then sheathed himself inside her again. On and on, he moved in her, her body feeling as though she were sizzling from the inside out.

Just when she thought she could take no more, he flipped her onto her back and crawled between her legs. He began to slowly, lovingly, lick her inner lips. His touch was soft and torturously slow. The hungry lust he had shown before had disappeared, replaced by the gentle touch of a lover. She was on the brink of coming in his mouth, but he pulled back just in time.

"No," she pleaded. "Please don't stop."

He looked up to watch her flushed face. "Not yet." He rubbed the tender flesh of her inner thigh. "Calm down," he said in a soft whisper. "Tell me when you're ready."

Easing himself on top of her, he settled himself between her thighs. Balancing the bulk of his weight on his forearms, he thrust himself into her warmth. His pelvis slammed against hers, but he softened his assault by kissing her softly along the neck. He made a trail of hot kisses that led to her mouth. He moved rhythmically inside her, plunging deeply and withdrawing slowly.

Thandie did not last long. She came on a cry against his mouth. He kissed her soundly and moved slowly within her; allowing her to enjoy her climax.

He thought he could withstand her writhing beneath him, but as her walls closed around him and began milking him for his seed, he knew his precious control was slipping away. Unable to hold back any longer, he surrendered.

His cum burst forward, filling her until it spilled onto the sheets. His breath was heavy. His eyes were closed tight from the pure rapture. He lowered his head to nuzzle her neck with his nose, taking pleasure in her scent.

Thandie held on to his shoulders tightly. She could feel the slight ache her body would endure tomorrow, but as he gently nestled her neck, her desire for him grew. The feel of his beautiful body pressing lightly over her made her yearn to have more of him. Finally being this close to him, sharing this level of intimacy made her lightheaded. It was him! It was his damned charm that drew her into him. That damned smile. The smell of his skin. The texture of his raven black hair between her fingers. The slick feel of his skin against hers. It was too much. She was intoxicated with him. And she longed for more. Much more.

Her legs tightened around his slim waist. He groaned in her ear. He lifted his head to look into her eyes. His silver eyes flickered with light. He wasn't smiling. He wore a very serious frown.

His voice rumbled in his chest, vibrating the peaks of her breasts. "I'm going to pull your legs up, Thandie."

Even as he said the words, she could feel his hands encircle her ankles and pull them slowly upward. She braced her arms beneath her as he pulled her legs parallel to her torso. Her knees hovered inches above her shoulders. He pulled out of her before burying himself inside her slick folds. He made a tense grunt at the snug fit. His hands closed tighter around her ankles as he moved inside her. Held prisoner beneath him, she bore every thrust he rendered. With her body lifted to his pleasure, each plunge was intensified.

She climaxed hard and fast. Elliot did not pause. He continued to take her until, eventually, he too joined her completeness. Without saying a word, he lowered her legs, pushed himself off the bed, and disappeared into the bathroom. He returned with a damp towel. Parting her legs, he gently wiped her.

Thandie was stunned by how tender his touch was. Her breath still came in short gulps. She was fighting to regain control of her emotions. The weightless abandonment he demanded from her was both exhilarating and terrifying. Tears flowed from her eyes unchecked. She turned her face away from him to hide from his silver glare.

"Look at me," he demanded in a harsh voice.

She looked down at him with unsure eyes.

He was looking up at her from between her open thighs. His eyes burned into her. "I want you to watch me." His voice felt like silk over her naked skin. "Watch me, Thandie." He tossed the towel over his shoulder. "I want you to watch me lick you and tell me where it hurts."

Her eyes stayed trained on him, as if hypnotized by his gray orbs. She watched him lower his lips to her cunt, lightly trailing his tongue along her soft folds. He lightly licked her, teasing her with his slow seduction. His devilish tongue dipped beneath her folds, to briefly taste her, before withdrawing to caress her. He was giving her a chance to recover from any early foreplay, and yet wanted her desire for him to remain. By demanding that she watch him, he was giving her no choice but to acknowledge their intimacy. He was branding the image of him eating her into her mind.

"Where do you hurt?" he asked.

His voice tickled her flesh. She was unable to form words. Under her careful observation, she watched his eyes cloud with lust. He lowered his head and delivered a breathtaking kiss. Thandie shuddered. He pushed her legs farther apart, his desire to taste her not nearly quenched. He sucked on her puffy lips, drawing them into his mouth, and stroking them with his tongue. She bucked against him, and began swaying her hips. He groaned into her. Using the tip of his tongue, he traced the exquisite furrows of her nether lips before dipping low to savor the hot juices welling inside her.

When he moved upward to slide the flat of his tongue over her most sensitive nub, Thandie nearly came off the bed. Her eyelids became heavy with passion, and her head fell back on her shoulders. An image of Elliot staring up at her with stormy eyes was branded into her thoughts. She began to thrash beneath him. Her thighs shook as another climax claimed her. He licked at her sweet honey until her last rush of elation passed.

Elliot pulled away from her, watching her with immense pleasure. Her breasts rose and fell as she struggled to capture a calm breath. He stroked his cock as he regarded her. She was so enticing. Damn, if she wasn't the most delectable woman he'd ever tasted. His hunger for her was insatiable. If he wasn't careful, this could create a problem in the near future.

When finally she looked up at him, her almond eyes looked wide and innocent.

"You enjoyed it," he said.

She nodded. "Yes, you were right. You're very talented with your tongue."

"I know." His voice was still devoid of its normal playfulness. His eyes bore into her with all seriousness. Elliot's brow arched. "Are you ready?"

She bit her lower lip nervously. "For what?"

He gave a dry laugh. "I hope you don't think we're done." He moved between her thighs. "I have much more planned for us."

They did not rest until a long time later. The man was true to his word. She felt like a piece of rubber; he'd stretched and turned her every way imaginable, seeking his pleasure. He ensured she would not have much energy to do anything beyond resting.

And true, she desired rest more than anything right now. Her limbs felt like lead weights. She didn't dare move, for the ache she knew she would feel. He made her work just as hard as he had. She rode him tirelessly. When she feared she would fall off, he held her above him, lifting her up and down his engorged shaft as if she weighed no more than a feather. Her thighs throbbed from the experience. But oh, how wonderful it felt!

Now, finally free from Elliot's affections, she was unable to drift into slumber. Though thoroughly exhausted, her mind raced at a maddening speed. The reality of sleeping in his bed overwhelmed her. She held her breath, able to feel the rise and fall of his muscular chest against her back. Turned on their sides, they slept in "spoon" fashion. His heavy arm wrapped around her to cup her breast, occasionally squeezing it in his sleep.

She silently cursed herself. How could she have allowed herself to sleep with Elliot? Having sex with Elliot was the worst thing she could have done. True, she had been weak under his powerful silver eyes and devilish good looks. But that wasn't an excuse for her falling into his bed.

Yes, he had pretty much dragged her here, but she hadn't given him much of a fight. From the moment he had carried her into his office, she'd hoped he would take her. Despite her words of protest, she desperately wanted to feel what so many women before her had experienced in his capable arms. And did he take her? He took her very well. Treating her as nothing more than a woman. No sweet words, no longing caresses. No, in his eyes, they were simply male and female coming together for nature's oldest dance. She could not remember ever coming that often. Even now, her skin tingled with memory of his touch.

But that time had passed. Now she was left with a sudden emptiness. She was annoyed that she had finally become just another one of his women. The very group of women she had secretly despised for their constant pursuit of his attention. The very women she had pitied for chasing after him while he chased after a newer and prettier conquest. And now, she was one of them. For even as she loathed her recent actions, she knew he had but to reach for her and she would welcome his touch.

She frowned. What had she been thinking? It didn't take a genius to realize that Elliot wasn't a guy for the long-term. A woman only slept with him to enjoy the pleasures that he offered and nothing more. Elliot wasn't a lover. He was only interested in the challenge. Now that he had conquered her, she would no longer be desirable. He would find another target to shower his attentions on tomorrow. She had better be smart about this. This was only a one-night stand. She needed to salvage her pride and recoup quickly.

Chapter Nineteen

To avoid seeing Elliot over morning coffee, Thandie awoke early. She'd meant to tiptoe out of his room quietly and unnoticed, but she'd stubbed her toe on the upholstered bench at the end of his bed and she had to clamp her hand over her mouth to muffle the scream.

For several torturous seconds she didn't dare breathe, fearing she had roused Elliot from sleep. She limped back to her room and quickly washed and dressed.

Thandie woke the girls by bribing them with breakfast at a swanky bistro off the beach. Neither was excited about waking up early, however, the lure of being seen on the patio of a ritzy bistro was enough motivation. She was patient, waiting for them to get ready. Not having to suffer the shame of being under the same roof with Elliot when he awoke was worth its weight in gold. She was not yet ready to face his heated stare.

She'd decided to wear a polo shirt and a pair of old cotton shorts that hung loosely on her hips. Even if she wanted to forget her encounter with Elliot, her body wouldn't let her. She was sore everywhere.

She breathed a sigh of relief when the girls were finally

ready. "Early" for them was "late" in the real world. When they were craving breakfast, everyone else was finishing late lunches. It wasn't difficult to get a patio table at a popular beachfront bistro. The rush had gone, and the girls had their pick of seating. Though obviously tired, Len and Raja were excited to be out. They chattered nonstop about the latest fashions before turning their attentions on Thandie.

"Are you all right?"

Thandie forced herself to smile at Raja. "I'm great. Why?"

Raja looked nervously at Len. "We were really scared for you last night. When Elliot pulled you off the stage, my heart stopped."

Len touched Thandie's hand. "He didn't hurt you, did he?"

That's a loaded question. Giving her a reassuring smile, she said, "Len, I'm fine. Elliot was upset over my conduct, that's true. But we worked everything out. It was a misunderstanding."

"We tried to get in Elliot's office to check on you, but Michelle wouldn't let us pass."

Raja nodded. "We even begged Adam and Markie to help, but Michelle wasn't letting anybody in. When Romero told us you were leaving early, we assumed you were okay."

"Yeah," Len giggled. "So we stayed until the club closed. We figured you'd want us to keep working VIP."

Thandie grinned. Any other time, she would have been annoyed by their over-the-top partying, but considering what she and Elliot had been doing at his home, she was relieved to know Raja and Len hadn't been there.

"You did well," she said. "I'm glad I can count on you two." Thandie focused her gaze on the food on her plate. "What happened with The Pussy Cats after I—"

Taking turns, Len and Raja painted a dismal picture of the evening. After the mishap, which involved Thandie being carried away, several shoving matches ensued. The bouncers had their hands full breaking up arguments and removing the troublemakers. According to Len, there was an usually high number of bachelor parties being celebrated that evening.

"Rotten luck we have," Raja mused aloud. "Of all the times to do a pole dancing routine, we do it on stag night."

"Celeste and the dancers?" Thandie asked. "What happened with them?"

"Oh, they're fine." Len said. "Better than fine, actually. After you…left the stage…Markie pulled the plug on The Pussy Cat performance. The dancers were paid for their time and escorted out of the building. Things simmered down after that."

Thandie pinched the bridge of her nose. "Mira Dietrich," she said with a heavy sigh. "How did your meeting go with her, Len."

Len averted eye contact and began fiddling with her hair.

"Len," Thandie said in a warning voice.

"It's not my fault," she blurted out. "You should have told me she was a witch."

"Why? What happened?"

"Nothing happened," Len scowled. "She was pissed off you sent me as a stand-in."

"Did she say that?" Thandie pressed.

"She didn't have to. She got one good look at me, blew cigarette smoke into my face, and left." Len scrunched her nose. "I tried to explain, but she wouldn't listen."

Great. Thandie thought. *That's just flipping great.* She'd dressed like a stripper, embarrassed herself by being dragged off stage, was the direct result of people being thrown out of the club, paid for entertainers who could not perform, and now she was on Mira Dietrich's shit list. *Great!*

Wanting nothing more than to forget about last night as

quickly as possible, Thandie tossed her napkin onto her plate and announced they were going shopping. This statement won the hearts of the girls. They squealed like teenagers, and hastily gathered their things.

When they were back in the car, they headed eastbound to Bal Harbour Shops. They roamed many of the stores, but took great pleasure wandering about Carolina Herrera, Miu Miu and Dolce & Gabbana. All of them found something to enjoy. Thandie took a particular interest in La Perla's wide selection of delicate lingerie, being that Elliot had ripped off two of her favorite pairs of panties. If this kept up, she would run out of panties long before it was time for her to return to New York.

Amazingly, Thandie wasn't annoyed that they spent several hours shopping. She was thankful to be away from Elliot's Star Island home. The longer they were away, the more confident she was that he would be gone upon their return.

When they finally arrived home, their arms were laden with shopping bags. Though Thandie was eager to get to work, she agreed to patiently sit and wait for the girls to display all their new buys. She surprised herself by joining in their excitement, marveling at her own purchases.

By the time they were finished, Thandie needed a nap. She excused herself from Raja and Len's fashion show and retreated to her room. She fell across her bed and was asleep before her head touched the pillow.

She awoke a few hours later. Not willing to risk running into Elliot, she remained in her room, sending emails and placing calls. Len and Raja, however, had donned their swimsuits and were working by the pool. Thandie doubted that either of them was getting much done, but as long as they were busy and she had her privacy, she was content.

Today it was difficult to focus on work when her mind kept

straying toward Elliot's glowing, silver eyes. Several times, she had to shake her head to escape the heated thoughts that assailed her.

Elliot had been amazing last night. But chances were he would either ignore her today, or he would try to seduce her again just to prove he could. The troubling thought was that she doubted she could resist him anymore. She had sampled his lovemaking, and even as she sat before her laptop, her body went warm, yearning for more. This was going to be an uphill battle. She would do well to come out of this with her sanity in check. Somehow, she would have to restrain herself. She needed to focus on her job.

She had no time to concern herself with Elliot Richards.

It was only sex, she told herself. Mind-blowing sex, but it was still just sex. She would do well to accept it for what it was and move on. Keeping that in mind, she would continue to stay clear of him and do her job. She would show him she could be an adult. She would rise above this.

She decided not to go to Club Babylon, instead sending the girls and getting some much-needed rest herself.

And staying away from Elliot.

Elliot couldn't quite put his emotions into words. Thandie was avoiding him again. For what reason, he did not know. She had played the coy routine far too long with him. He intended to have sex with her until he grew tired of her.

But Elliot's problems of the evening didn't stop there. Sophia Radcliffe, Wife Number Five, appeared out of thin air with a young man in tow. He held her hand possessively, making his position in Sophia's life clear. Elliot could only laugh. "New pet, Sophia?"

"He's my new lawyer," she snarled.

"Good for you," he told her, and tried to walk around

them. Sophia blocked his path. Apparently, she was in the mood for war.

Elliot glanced toward Thandie and Adam again before focusing on Sophia. "Call me outside working hours if you want to talk, Mrs. Radcliffe."

She shook off her lawyer's hand and pointed a long manicured finger at him. "I've left several messages for you, Elliot, and you know it. So, since you won't talk to me on the phone, you'll talk to me now."

He rolled his eyes. "Try some other time, Sophia. I'm not in the mood to tolerate you."

She tossed her mane of dark waves over her shoulder. "If you don't talk to me now, I'll make things very difficult for Warren." She'd played her trump card. She was confident it would work. "You're not a complete bastard, Elliot. You'll do anything to help Warren."

He fought to keep his voice casual. "Where you're concerned, Sophia, I have my limits."

She smiled sweetly. "Do you?"

Elliot scowled at her.

"That's what I thought," she said with a laugh. "Shall we follow you to your office?"

He hated the arrogant grin she wore. She had him between a rock and hard place, and she knew it. He nodded. "Follow me."

Once the three of them were alone in his office, Elliot turned on her. "Out with it. What do you want?"

Elliot was in a dark mood the rest of the night. Sophia's visit had drained him. She'd offered to be more agreeable with her divorce settlement if he, Elliot, provided her with a cash agreement. The subtle hint that she and he could rekindle a relationship he had long since forgotten was maddening. For a moment Elliot could not believe what he was being propositioned. And in the presence of her young, love-struck lawyer.

The meeting ended abruptly when Elliot had Michelle escort the pair out of the club. Elliot's anger for having been dragged into this mess rested solely on Warren's shoulders. Elliot cursed the old man. Why couldn't Warren be smarter about the women he chose to wed? Couldn't he see this had been her plan all along? Now he would have to clean up after Warren's mess.

After Club Babylon's doors were closed for the night, Elliot helped Markie count the tips and allot the dancers and waitresses their pay. They asked him to join them for breakfast, but Elliot was determined to go home and sleep.

He arrived home a little after eight o'clock in the morning. The house was silent. Lucinda would be about her chores soon. He entered his bedroom, calmed by the decor. No elaborate designs or colors. It was soothing.

He showered and slid into bed. Sophia's outrageous offer replayed in his head. Never had be been more annoyed with her. Frustrated, he turned on his side. Even in his bad mood, he was horny.

He considered going to Thandie's room. Her soft curves would feel heavenly beneath him. Her full breasts, small waist and round bottom quickly filled his mind. But would she welcome him into her bed? He was confident he could eventually persuade her to accept his company.

It was clear she was greatly troubled by his effect on her. But he was in no mood to speak the sweet words she needed to hear. He only wanted to sleep beside her. The more he thought about it, the more that surprised him. Thandie was getting too close for his comfort.

Chapter Twenty

Thandie, Len, Raja and Victoria hovered over the dining room table. They were staring down at a detailed diagram the set designer had rendered for the fashion show. The show was already draining more resources than Thandie had anticipated. However, after the disastrous Pussy Cat production, Thandie was determined to make Victoria's show a success.

Thandie was not the only one who would not soon forget the Pussy Cat performance that had ended so abruptly. Mira Dietrich was reveling in the debacle.

She'd taken Thandie's absence at their luncheon as a personal insult. And judging by the latest issue of *Look,* Mira was not the forgiving type. That week the cover story showed a close-up of Thandie wrapped around a pole. Above the picture read "Randall's lover fails to please."

The article went on to detail how Thandie took part in a failed pole dancing routine that ended badly, leaving a dissatisfied audience. The story was reported so accurately, the reporter must have been there. However, some of the minor details were so outlandishly false they overshadowed everything.

Followed by pictures of Thandie and Celeste on stage, and unrelated to the incident, pictures of Ruark Randall boarding an airplane. It was still unclear to Thandie exactly what Ruark's pictures were supposed to imply. However, the article showed Thandie as an out of control party girl whose wild behavior was embarrassing her movie star boyfriend.

Recognizing the jab for what it was, Thandie tried to ignore the article. Nevertheless, it needled her to have her failed venture publicized. Being linked to Ruark was an added insult. Thandie figured she would give Mira a few days to calm down before calling her. Until then, she had a fashion show to help coordinate.

"You need a scientist to figure out this diagram," Len complained.

Thandie nodded. The intricate lines that crisscrossed the artist's drawing of the Babylon arena floor were dotted with measurements and illegible handwritten notes. It was confusing to look at, and impossible to understand.

From her perch on the dining room table, where she could swing her legs lazily from side-to-side, Victoria frowned and said, "I can't make heads or tails out of any of this stuff, and I make designs for a living." As always, Victoria was dressed in one of her unusual outfits, a ruffled shorts-set with a leopard print camisole draped over her shoulders. Her wrists were loaded with chunky gold bangles. "Didn't we already decide on white benches in lieu of chairs?" Her many bracelets clinked loudly against one another as she pointed out the error on the sketch. "Won't that throw off the seating arrangement?"

"She's right," Raja said with a lazy yawn. "We've been at this for hours. I say we take a break."

Thandie checked the time. Raja had not been exaggerating. They'd been laboring over the layout for a while. "A brief break," Thandie conceded. "We still need to discuss the sound equipment."

No sooner had the words left her mouth, than she heard the front door open. Thandie's breath hitched in her chest. She had the sinking feeling it was Elliot returning home. She was not certain how she and he were supposed to behave around each other.

After having sex in his bedroom the night before, they hadn't so much as said a passing word to each other. True, she hadn't stuck around the club much longer. She was frustrated by the desire to study him from across the room. Although she hadn't seen him disappear into his office with anyone, she'd grown tired watching women cue up to talk to him, smile up at him with glossy lips and flirtatious eyes. It rubbed her wrong way. She'd waited half an hour before taking her leave. She doubted he'd noticed.

And now she could hear heavy footfalls in the foyer, her stomach muscles tightened. There was a pause before Romero's dark head emerged from the hall. He was alone, but not empty handed. He was carrying a bulky black box. From his easy handling of the box, it appeared to be lightweight.

Romero saw the women surrounding the table and joined them. "Ladies," he said in a flat tone. Thandie gave him a slight nod in greeting while Day made a lax salute motion. Raja and Len seemed incapable of feigning politeness. In unison, they crossed their arms and smirked at him.

Nonplussed by their reaction to him, Romero addressed Thandie. "I have something for you," he said.

"For me?" Thandie asked.

Romero placed the large box on the table before handing her an envelope. Cautiously, she accepted the paper, aware everyone was watching her. Unsure what might be inside, she took a step back, just far enough so no one could read over her shoulder, and opened the envelope. Inside was a single sheet of stationary paper. In the center was a short note. "6:00 p.m. tonight. Wear nothing else. —E."

She read the note three more time before slipping it back into the envelope. Thandie could feel four pairs of eyes trained on her, but she focused on the box. "What is it?" she asked, glancing at Romero.

"See for yourself," he gently urged.

Thandie lifted the lid and pushed aside the layers of tissue paper. She gasped as she pulled out a beautiful evening gown. It was made of gray lace and had delicate beading. A long chiffon train spilled onto the floor. It was breathtaking.

Raja gasped. Len squealed. Victoria became teary-eyed.

"Shall I confirm you will be available this evening?" Romero asked, apparently the only person in the room capable of speaking.

Thandie nodded weakly, unable to tear her eyes away from the gown. Afterward, none of the women could remember exactly when Romero had taken his exit, or if he'd said anything in the form of a farewell.

Ten minutes to six o'clock, Thandie studied her reflection in the mirror as she affixed her earrings. When she was finished, she stepped back to examine her figure. The dress. It really was a work of art. The plunging neckline was offset by lovely lacework that covered bodice and sleeves. A length of pale silk wrapped delicately around her waist before cascading to the floor like a ribbon of water. The length of the train contrasted wonderfully with the short hem. It perfectly balanced elegance and sensuality. And the fit was perfect.

She recalled Elliot's message instructing her to not "wear anything else." She doubted that would have been possible. The dress was so lightweight, she felt naked. Wearing a bra had been quickly ruled out. The thong she was wearing was slightly noticeable, but she refused to take it off.

"So exactly where are you going?"

Thandie looked over her shoulder toward the bed, where Len and Raja lounged. Day had been forced to leave an hour earlier to attend a model casting call for her show. Since then, the girls had been helping Thandie select accessories and offering up useless comments.

"I'm not sure," Thandie said in answer to Raja's question. "The note didn't say."

"Is this a date?" Len asked.

This was not the first time this question had been asked. It would not be the last time Thandie ignored it. In truth, she couldn't answer the question. She had no idea what Elliot had in mind. It would be dicey to assume anything. For all she knew, this could be a business event.

She checked the time. It was six. She checked her makeup one last time, before gathering a tiny clutch purse. "Wish me luck," she said.

"Luck?" Raja snorted. "You won't need luck in that dress."

Thandie laughed as she walked down the hall. Len and Raja followed close behind. Just as Thandie reached the top of the staircase, she came up short. Standing in the middle of the foyer was Elliot, wearing an exquisitely cut dark suit, black dress shirt, no tie. His hands were in the pockets of his slacks, a posture she'd come to recognize as his "thinking" stance.

He looked up and spotted her. For a moment Thandie was struck mute by how handsome he was. Elliot truly had to be one of the most attractive men she'd ever met. And the way he was looking at her now…brought erotic memories to mind.

Thandie carefully made her way down the steps, aware Elliot's eyes followed her every move. When she was within reach, he placed his hand on her hip and kissed her cheek. "You look breathtaking," he said against her ear.

His whispered words made the hair on the back of her neck and arms stand straight up. "Thank you for the dress. It's lovely."

Elliot looked her over slowly and gave a small smile. "I'm glad you like it."

Their eyes met and the air around them seemed to heat up. The moment was lost when the sound of girlish giggles could be heard.

Without taking his eyes off her, Elliot said, "Hello, ladies."

"Hi, Elliot," two voices chorused.

Not breaking eye contact with her, Elliot placed his hand on Thandie's lower back and guided her toward the front door. He led her to the Aston Martin and helped her inside. Thandie had never been a car enthusiast, nor had she ever sat inside a car valued over a million dollars. She was quickly beginning to understand why people drooled over these luxury vehicles. Elliot hadn't even started the engine and Thandie could feel the opulence.

He slid into the driver's seat beside her and revved the engine. The car purred with life. He turned his head and admired at her body. The hem of the skirt snaked high up her leg, revealing a lot of thigh.

Making some inaudible sound, he put the car in Drive. They sped out of the neighborhood at breakneck speed. Thandie was thankful for her seatbelt.

They'd been riding for nearly ten minutes when Thandie broke the silence. "Elliot, I need to talk to you about something important."

"I need to talk to you as well."

"You do?"

He gave a solemn nod of his head. "I realize I've been careless with you," he began. "We haven't used protection during the times we've been together. I'm clean, though, I'm normally more cautious, but I find my eagerness to have you clouds my judgment. For that, I apologize."

Thandie was stunned into silence. He'd gotten right to the heart of the matter. She was thankful for that.

"Thandie, is there something you'd like to contribute to the conversation?"

"I'm on birth control."

"The pill?"

"No, I take shots."

"And you're on schedule?"

"Yes," she confirmed. "I took my last shot just before leaving New York." After another long pause, Thandie asked. "Where are we going?"

Elliot took his time answering. "A movie."

Thandie's brows hiked up in surprise. "We're going to a movie? What kind of movie?"

He grinned. "I'm not exactly certain. I believe it's an action film."

"You don't know for certain?" she asked, suspiciously.

"The tickets were sort of a gift."

"From whom?"

"Would it matter?"

"I suppose not," she admitted. She was quiet for a minute and then, unable to stop herself, she stated the obvious. "We're overdressed."

"Are we?" he asked with a grin.

Thandie liked the sight of his smile. She smiled too, and then she yelped. Elliot swerved the car sharply to the right, and came to an abrupt stop in the emergency lane.

Thandie looked out the window, searching for the potential problem. "What's wrong?"

"This." Elliot reached over the console, placed his hands on her knees and pushed her thighs apart. Before Thandie could slap his hands away, he'd hiked her dress up and until the crotch of her panties was visible.

"Are you insane?" She shoved his hands away and tried to pull her dress down.

Elliot held her dress up, preventing her efforts. "I thought my note was quite clear," he reasoned.

"I'm wearing them," she told him.

"Take them off."

"No."

"Take them off, or I will rip them off."

"You better not. I just bought—ah!" Hooking his fingers on either side of the thin elastic strips, he yanked. The fabric snapped as if made of smoke. To the sound of Thandie's curses, Elliot tucked the panties into his suit jacket.

"There," he said pleasantly. "Don't you feel better?"

"I—can't—believe—you—did—that!"

"Follow the rules next time."

Thandie scowled at him. "You…you…"

"Keep your legs open please. I want to smell you."

Scowling, Thandie pressed her thighs firmly together.

Elliot chuckled. "You're cute when you're upset with me. But try to curb your anger for a spell. We're here."

Thandie looked up and, for the first time, noticed the traffic. A line of chauffeured cars was pressing into one lane. Less than half a mile ahead, crowds of screaming fans could be heard. Forgetting to be upset with Elliot, Thandie asked, "We're going to a movie premiere?"

"I believe it's more of a private screening."

"What's the movie?"

Elliot looked thoughtful, and then flipped open the console and pulled out a glossy folder. Inside were two tickets for

Dread Commission: Ghost File starring Paris St. John. Thandie gaped at the tickets. *Dread* was a highly anticipated movie for the summer and Paris St. John was Hollywood's golden child. Access to *Dread* tickets would be hard to come by.

"These were a gift?" she mused aloud.

He gave a lift of his shoulders. "I receive a lot of invites to attend events in the city. I typically don't go."

"Why are you going tonight?"

A sexy smile slid across his lips. "And miss an opportunity to see you in that dress?" He tsked. "I wouldn't be able to live with myself."

Thandie smiled and turned to look out the window to hide her blush. She was both pleased by his answer and uncertain. Was this a date? Or was this business? She was still unclear.

Fifteen minute later, they were checking in with the name board. Ten minutes after that, Elliot had rolled to a stop in front of the theater. Red carpet covered the sidewalk, photographers readied their cameras and eager fans craned their necks. Thandie sucked in a breath as Elliot got out to open her door. A gust of warm air brushed over her skin as the passenger door opened. Elliot smiled down at her, looking every bit a movie star himself. He held out his hand to her. "Shall we?"

Attending a movie with Elliot was amazing. As soon as they'd stepped onto the red carpet, they were barraged by camera flashes. Thandie had been to movie showings in the past, however she'd always been on the outskirts of the fanfare, never the center of attention. Elliot took everything in stride. He held her close as they posed for pictures, guided her through the crush and applied the slightest pressure to her hip every so often. Multiple times, local journalists stopped to ask him for an interview. He declined them all with a suave sophistication that was enviable.

Thandie was not a fan of action movies but, as it turned out, *Dread Commission: Ghost File* was a decent film. She doubted it would win any awards but it had been entertaining. The star, Paris St. John, was present and he was a contributing factor to the many distractions that accompanied movie premieres. A tanned blond with an easy smile, Paris caused many female attendees to make the hard decision between staring at him or the movie screen. As far as Thandie could tell, Paris, the man, was winning the competition with his on-screen persona. Those who weren't gaping at Paris were busy staring at his lovely companion and co-star, Natalia di Rossi. The two had recently scandalized the media with an off-screen romance and hurried marriage announcement. Thandie could tell by the whispers in the room, the gossip was still fresh on everybody's mind.

When the movie was finally over, Elliot guided her toward a less traveled exit, avoiding the fans, photographers, publicists and party promoters. With a majority of the attendees mingling in the lobby, Elliot was able to have the valet retrieve his car in record time. As soon as he was behind the wheel, Elliot accelerated away from the theater.

"Do you always drive so fast?" Thandie asked.

Instead of answering the question, Elliot asked a question of his own. "Are you hungry?"

Actually, she was famished, but she said, "I could nibble."

He acknowledged her words with a nod of his head. "I asked Lucinda to put something in the oven for us. Can you wait until we get home?"

Thandie nodded and turned to look out the window. The brightly lit streets of Miami passed her in flashes of color and muffled sounds. The city was so different from New York. The comparison made her a little homesick. She missed her home, her closet, her wide collection of expensive shoes, her bed, but mostly her mother. However, Miami had its perks. The weather was one. The laid-back energy, the vibrant night life.

Elliot.

"You have a sex room," she said. The comment had come out of nowhere. She'd meant to ease into this topic, but it seemed to pop out.

If Elliot was surprised by her comment, he did not show it. He gave a slow nod of his head, before saying, "I do."

A heavy silence fell between them. Clearly, Elliot felt no need to elaborate. He was not going to make this subject easy for her. So, she soldiered on.

"Have you...did you plan on..." She was suddenly unsure how to broach the question.

"Yes?" A small smile tugged at his lips. "Cat got your tongue?"

She looked away, trying to collect her thoughts.

Elliot rolled to a stop at a red light. Turning to her, he gently took hold of her chin, forcing her to look up at him. "If the question is do I plan to take you to my little room, the answer is no. I enjoy having you in my bed."

"And your office," she reminded him.

He chuckled. "Yes, I rather enjoy sex in my office."

The light turned green and Elliot returned his attention to treating every straightway like a racetrack. When they arrive at Star Island, he waved past the security guard and zoomed into his neighborhood. Aside from the purr of the Aston Martin, the air was quiet. The night was young and many residents seemed to have just left their homes for dinner on South Beach. Pulling up to the house, Thandie noticed the black Expedition was gone. A clear indicator Len and Raja were out. But in the spot where their car was normally positioned, a car Thandie did not recognize was parked there. Lucinda's car was positioned next to it.

"We have a crowd," Elliot said with a bemused smile.

Taking Thandie's hand, he led her inside the house. She followed him through the foyer and into the kitchen. Lucinda was there, humming softly to herself as she put a pot away. Her face split into a beautiful grin when she saw Elliot. She smiled warmly at Thandie, and gave an approving nod to her dress.

Elliot came to her side, kissed her lightly on the cheek in greeting. Lucinda's rich brown eyes danced with delight over his show of affection. The two conversed in Spanish. It occurred to Thandie she'd rarely seen them in the same room together. Elliot kept such odd work hours, and Thandie was usually asleep or working on her own projects to interact much with Lucinda herself. Now, watching them talk, their dark heads bowed toward each other, Thandie could see they got along rather well. She couldn't catch any of the words, but she could tell there was a mutual fondness between them.

As Lucinda pointed out what she'd prepared, Thandie noticed a large basket placed neatly on the kitchen bar. She looked toward the stove, where a tightly wrapped casserole dish was cooling. She watched as Elliot carefully placed it into the basket, and nodded his head occasionally as Lucinda ticked off instructions. Finally, he scooped up the wicker container and patted her on the bottom.

"Ready?" he asked.

"Where are we going?"

Without answering, he took Thandie's hand, pulling her toward the back of the house. They were just crossing the living area when out of nowhere, Warren's silver head popped around the corner. "Hey, you two," he said with a broad grin. "What are you kids up to?"

Not bothering to look at Warren, Elliot walked right past him as he mumbled, "I'm taking Thandie out on the boat."

"Excellent idea." Warren clapped his hands together. "Mind if I come along?"

"Yes," Elliot said sternly. "I do mind."

Warren looked at him curiously, his smile faltering just a little, but he quickly recovered. "Just as well. Can we talk later, Elliot? I have a few things I'd like to go over with you."

Elliot shrugged. "Fine."

Warren looked between them, and took a cautious step back. "Are you sure I can't tag along?"

"Goodbye, Warren."

Warren gave a momentary pause. Awkwardly, he forced a smile on his face. "In that case, I'll give you two kids some privacy."

Elliot stopped abruptly. "Where are you going?" he snapped.

Warren shrugged. "I'll go give Lucinda a hand in the kitchen."

"I'm sure she can handle it on her own." His voice was cold, but Warren either didn't notice or didn't care.

"Well, it can't hurt to ask." And with that said, Warren left the room.

Elliot watched until the older man disappeared down the hall. He cursed under his breath before turning to look at Thandie and urging her out the patio doors. They walked toward the boat dock in silence. Thandie could tell Warren had put Elliot in a bad mood, but she could not understand why. Warren had been harmless enough.

With Elliot's help, Thandie stepped gingerly onto the boat deck. She looked around her. "Shouldn't we change into more casual clothes?" she asked.

"There are spare clothes downstairs," he said through gritted teeth.

One glance at his stern expression and Thandie could tell he needed a little time to get over whatever was bothering him. She was happy to give him his solitude. Slipping off her heels, Thandie seated herself on a lounge, and pulled her feet beneath her. From there, she watched Elliot skillfully loosen the ropes binding the boat to the dock.

In a few minutes, they were drifting ever so slightly away from the boat dock. Elliot stood behind the controls, turned on the motor and eased out to open water. Unlike his high-speed driving on the city streets, Elliot was a much calmer navigator behind the wheel of a boat. The farther they got away from land, the more his tension seemed to melt away. By the time they were a quarter of a mile out, Elliot looked remarkably more relaxed.

He took off his suit jacket and offered it to Thandie. She placed it over her shoulders, slipping her arms into the sleeves. She could smell his aftershave. It was rich, masculine and heady. She liked it very much.

Elliot kept guiding the boat so that they were parallel to the coast, only a mile or so out. The city lights danced in a darkening sky. The sun had already set, and the sky was now fading from hues of pinkish gold to deep violet purple. When they'd reached the location he desired, Elliot dropped the anchor. He laid out cushions and a blanket on the wide deck floor, creating a comfy makeshift bed. Loosening his tie, he curled his finger in her direction. She rose from the lounge and joined him.

For a while they sat there, staring out over the water and enjoying the gentle breeze. The wind ruffled his hair, softening the chiseled angles of his handsome face. Thandie knew now why he enjoyed being out here. It was so peaceful.

Glancing at him, she decided to voice a question that had been nagging her for some time. "The night after we came back from Zuma. The night I had…my episode….” Her voice trailed off.

Elliot turned to look at her, his silver gaze imploring her. “Yes?”

“How did you recognize—” She stopped, and tried to think of a different tactic. “How did you know? You said you had plenty of practice.”

Elliot shrugged. “I did say that, didn’t I?”

“Yes, you did,” she urged. “What did you mean by that?”

He was quiet for a long while, before saying. “My mother suffers from panic attacks.”

Thandie jerked away from him, as if suddenly seeing him for the first time. She searched his face, wondering if this might all be some bad joke at her expense. She did not see any hint of deception in his cool pale eyes. Licking her bottom lip, she asked, “Is that how you knew what to do? That thing you did with your hands?”

He nodded.

“You did it for your mother?”

“Often. It was the only thing that calmed her down. It made her feel safe.”

“Oh,” was all she could say.

“Her attacks came and went in waves. She’d do fine for weeks, months even, and then—” he snapped his fingers “—she’d have one out of the blue.” He turned to study her face. “How did you keep your condition a secret from Len and Raja?”

Thandie shrugged. “It doesn’t happen often. Only when I’m extremely…taxed.”

“How long?” he asked.

“What?”

“You told me before you’ve had the attacks since you were a child. How long ago was that?”

She shrugged uncomfortably.

"How long?" he asked again.

"Since I was eight or nine years old," she confessed.

"What happened to start the attacks?"

"Elliot...."

"Tell me."

Thandie looked away, debating whether she should say anything at all. Finally, she gave a heavy sigh. "My mother's medical issues were taking a toll on my family."

"Her dementia," he recalled.

Thandie could not keep the look of surprise from her face.

"I remember everything," he said in answer. "Go on."

"My father couldn't handle it. He walked out on us." She paused to pinch the bridge of her nose. "My mother was devastated. Her illness took a drastic turn for the worse." She splayed her hands out. "My panic attacks started shortly after." Keeping her eyes downcast, she focused on her hands. Thandie had never spoken of her condition to anyone. She felt strangely liberated and yet vulnerable at the same time.

Elliot tucked his finger under her chin, lifting it until she met his eyes. "There's nothing wrong with that," he said. "We all deal with our issues in our own way."

"And your mother?" she asked. "When did her attacks start?"

Elliot let his hands fall away from her, as he considered the question. "I'm not exactly sure," he said thoughtfully. "She's had them as long as I can remember."

Thandie envisioned Elliot as a small child. Olive-skinned, dark-haired and skinny. She imagined what it must have been like for a young kid to watch a parent suffer from a panic attack. She saw her own image; doubled over, shivering and straining to control herself. It was scary to endure. She imagined it was even scarier to watch.

Somehow, pressing into this area of her life felt too raw.

Suddenly desperate to change the subject, she asked the first thing that popped into her head.

"How did you learn to speak Spanish?"

Elliot actually laughed. "I grew up with it. Learned it while I was learning English." Seeing the confusion on her face, his grin widened. "My mother is Cuban, Thandie. Didn't you know?"

"No," she whispered. "I had no idea."

He laughed agains as he watched her observe his bronzed skin. "Surely you didn't think I tanned."

"Actually," she laughed, "I did."

He snorted. "You're more naive than I thought."

"Is your mother still alive?" she asked.

"You tell me. You've met her." He flashed her a mischievous grin. "Lucinda."

Thandie couldn't hide her utter shock. "Lucinda is your mother?" she said. "But I thought—"

"I know what you thought."

"But you never—"

"You never asked," he cut in.

Lucinda was Elliot's mother? That answered many questions. She now understood why Lucinda had so much power over his household and the caring manner in which Elliot always addressed her. This also explained why the woman didn't appear to have set hours, or how Romero and rest of his staff seemed to go out of their way to appease her. It also accounted for how such a controlling man could deposit so much trust in what Thandie had previously believed to be only his housekeeper.

How could she not have seen it? Recalling Lucinda's flawless skin, her thick shining black hair and her high cheekbones, it should have been a dead giveaway. Not that Elliot was the mirror image of Lucinda, but it was those small things that tied them to the same lineage. Elliot's sharper features, his height, eyes and body frame must have come from his father.

"And your father."

"What about him?" His voice suddenly became guarded.

"Tell me about him." She stretched out on her side. Propping herself up on one elbow, she rested her head in her hand, and looked up at him. "He taught you how to sail."

Elliot lifted his brow.

Thandie smiled slyly. "I don't forget much either."

A flicker of great sadness flashed across his eyes when he stared down at her. "He taught me to sail, swim, and do just about everything a little boy craves to learn from his father."

Thandie considered him. "He was a big part of your life. I'm sure you miss him."

Elliot's demeanor had rapidly changed in the few short minutes they'd been speaking. He went from being gentle and considerate to being acutely irritated. He'd startled her by showing a more vulnerable side. Something about that tugged at her heart so painfully it stung her eyes with tears.

But now he was back to the Elliot she knew.

"Fuck this," he grunted. "We're not talking about this anymore." He stood and ran his hand through his hair, paused for a moment and then stared at her, his controlling calm now masterfully restored. "We're never going to talk about it again, understood?" When she nodded, he slid his hands into the pockets of his slacks. "Now take off your dress for me."

She was momentarily dumbstruck. Was this his way of dealing with his issues? Did he use sex as a way of creating a barrier around himself? Was this the way he kept people out, using his enormous sex appeal to control them? If so, how did anyone ever get close to him? Was Elliot even capable of letting someone in? Was he so haunted by his past he saw nothing desirable in compassion or love?

She wanted to understand him. She wanted to break through that cool shell he'd spent years erecting. She wanted to be the person to see him completely naked of his arrogant control.

She wanted him. And more importantly, she wanted him to want her.

She slid off his suit jacket before coming to her feet. Thandie held his gaze as her fingers slowly undid the buttons at the back of the dress. His gaze became heated with her progression. When the gown was loose enough, she pulled her arms free of the lacy sleeves. The dress slithered down her legs and cascaded onto the cushions. She was completely naked. A gust of air tousled her hair, causing it to splay over her bare shoulders.

It had become darker while they'd talked. The sky was a cloudless blanket of black velvet. The South Beach shore glowed brightly against the dark heavens. With her back facing the shoreline, Thandie knew her body was outlined in shadows. However, Elliot's face was lit. In his eyes, she could see the depth of his sexual desire. It was so raw and voracious, it seemed to settle around him like steam.

Stepping toward her, Elliot cupped either side of her face and lowered his lips to hers. The kiss was deep and passionate. His mouth was warm to the touch, his tongue eager to taste. Thandie leaned into him, wanted to give him everything his kiss demanded of her. Wrapping her arms around his waist, she pressed forward, her curves molding to the wide planes of his body. Her thighs cupped his sex, which was now hard and prominent.

When Thandie nipped at his lower lip, a low rumble shook his chest. His large strong hands glided over her shoulders, down the smooth surface of her back, past the slope of her waist, and lower still. He cupped her bottom in his hands, squeezed greedily. His palms grasped, pressed, smacked and hugged her lush flesh with impatient admiration. Clutch-ing her bottom, he pulled her up and against him. Her legs wrapped easily around his waist.

Still kissing her, Elliot made steps toward the door leading to below the cabin. Well-acquainted with the layout of his boat, he navigated the steps, crossed the plush living area, and walked directly into the owner's suite. A large bed awaited them. Elliot laid her down on the downy covering, his body quickly covering hers. For long minutes they delighted them-selves with ardent kisses, breathless moans and intimate ca-resses. Finally, Elliot pulled his head back and looked down on her. Her lips were puffy from their kisses and her eyes were glassy with lust.

"You feel so good," he murmured. "And so warm." He leaned forward to let his mouth barely brush against hers. "You have a long night ahead of you," he whispered against her lips.

"So do you," she whispered back.

He chuckled as he eased himself off the bed. He stared at her lovely nakedness, enjoying the rise and fall of her breasts and their puckered nipples. Slowly, he pulled his tie free, and began to unbutton his shirt. "Do you know why I brought you on the boat tonight?" he asked.

With her eyes transfixed on the sliver of flesh he was re-vealing with the freeing of each button, Thandie was able to do little else than shake her head. The sight of his flawless skin pulled tightly over firm stomach muscles caused Thandie to sink her teeth into her bottom lip to stop from moaning. She rubbed her legs together in anticipation.

Letting his shirt fall to the floor, Elliot placed his hands on his hips and gazed down at her. "I brought you out here, be-cause I don't want anyone but me to hear you scream when you come."

He began to unzip his pants.

Chapter Twenty-One

Thandie awoke to the warmth of Elliot's arms wrapped around her. Beneath her, the boat swayed gently, lulling her to go back to sleep.

Last night had been wonderful. Elliot's lovemaking had been slow, exact and exhausting. He'd been gentle and attentive to her every need. Having worked up quite an appetite, they devoured the food Lucinda had prepared. Once sated, they returned to exploring each other's bodies.

Thandie's breasts and inner thighs were still raw from whisker burns. Her cheeks were still sore from sucking Elliot's cock with ravenous abandonment. The memory of it made her mouth water with the desire to do it again.

She knew instantly when he stirred beside her. Elliot flinched, made a faint sound, and then pulled himself up to lean on his elbow. He squinted his eyes against the sunlight streaming into the cabin, and then looked down at her. Thandie's stomach erupted with butterflies. Even early in the morning, he was magnificent. His mussed hair fell in lazy locks over his forehead. Combined with his intense gray eyes and kissable lips, Thandie thought she was in heaven.

Wordlessly, he pulled her beneath him, parted her legs and eased himself inside her. He gave a groan of pleasure when he sank into her wetness. His cock jumped, lengthened, and then instinct took over. They moved against each other slowly and fervently. Each thrust met one of equal strength and desire. Hot kisses stamped their lips, necks and shoulders. It did not take long before they were quivering and gasping for breath. Spent and sweaty, they collapsed onto the bed. Elliot pulled her against his chest while they slowly came back to Earth.

They might have lain there longer had not Elliot's phone begun vibrating insistently. He ignored the first call, but it was immediately followed by another. And then another. And then another after that.

Their quiet refuge now disrupted, Elliot rolled onto his back and began taking calls.

With the day upon them, Elliot and Thandie began gathering their things. They shared a shower and changed into clean clothes. With no clothes to change into, Thandie rummaged through Elliot's dresser drawers. She pulled on a faded University of Miami T-shirt and a pair of his boxer shorts. Finding her lack of bra or panties convenient, Elliot kept his hands busy on the boat ride back to the house. It was early and the house looked tranquil in the morning light.

After depositing the food containers into the galley sink, they walked hand in hand toward the house. In the foyer, Elliot gave Thandie one last mind-numbing kiss before handing her the gown she'd worn the night before and heading to his wing of the house.

Thandie drifted up the staircase and down the hall to her room on a cloud of bliss. Her bed seemed highly inadequate compared to the one she'd shared with Elliot. Any bed with Elliot was desired over one without him. She wondered what he was doing right this very minute. Was he thinking about her? Shaking her head over her silly schoolgirl thoughts, Thandie climbed into the bed. Releasing a satisfied sigh, she laid her head down on the pillow.

No sooner had she closed her eyes, her phone began vibrating. Picking it up, she checked the time. She did a double take. Thandie had been asleep for two hours. She could hardly believe it. Still wheeling over the time lapse, she answered the phone. Romero's haughty voice greeted her.

"My employer would like to see you immediately." His voice did not exude friendliness.

"Employer?" she asked dumbly, still waking up.

"Elliot," he said slowly. "How soon can you come to the club?"

"Er, an hour." she guessed. "Is something wrong?"

"I'd advise you to check the latest issue of *Look*," he said in answer. "In the meantime, I will advise Elliot of your ETA."

Thandie opened her mouth and then closed it. If she'd had a question, it was pointless to ask it now. Romero had already hung up. *Geez,* she disliked him.

Sliding out of bed, she hurriedly washed up. While brushing her teeth, she searched the internet from her phone. She saw nothing out of the ordinary. Whatever Romero was concerned about was apparently so fresh it had not been updated to the magazine's website.

Deciding to go straight to the source, Thandie called Mira's office number. She'd hoped to ease herself back into the woman's good graces before the woman retaliated. Obviously, she'd been beaten to the punch.

The call was answered on the fifth ring. A chipper voice announced she'd reached Mira Dietrich's office. When Thandie gave her name and insisted she be put through, the young secretary was not ruffled by Thandie's tone. In fact, she sounded like she'd been expecting her call.

"I'm sorry, Ms. Shaw, but Mira is not in the office at the moment. She's out for a late lunch."

Without even having to ask, the woman gave Thandie the name of the restaurant and the address.

Checking the time, Thandie dressed quickly, grabbed her purse and headed out the door.

It took only fifteen minutes to get to the bistro. Thandie handed the valet her car keys and strolled into the restaurant. She spotted Mira seated on the back patio. Dressed in all black and puffing a cigarette, she looked about as friendly as a shark.

Sunlight glinted off Mira's thick glasses when she looked up to watch Thandie approach her table. The paper-like creases of her face pulled back into a semblance of a smile. She'd been waiting for Thandie like a spider patiently waiting for prey to wander into its trap.

When Thandie was seated in the chair opposite her, Mira handed her a folded newspaper. "We're running the story in our gossip column today."

Thandie's brow rose suspiciously.

In response, Mira shrugged her boney shoulders. "Consider yourself fortunate. I should be given a damn Nobel Prize for this act of generosity."

Taking the paper from Mira's outstretched hand, Thandie read the article slowly.

Randall out...Richards in.

Elliot Richards and new girlfriend, Thandie Shaw, were recently spotted together at last night's movie screening of *Dread Commission: Ghost File*. Shaw, recently known for her public affair with actor Ruark Randall, has apparently stolen the heart of Miami's own Elliot Richards. Will Shaw treat

Richards better than her last love? Or will she dump him for the next celebrity stud that crosses her path? The *Look* will keep you posted.

Stunned by the assault, Thandie's eyes rolled up to the picture above the article. It was a photo of her and Elliot at the *Dread* event the previous night. He was holding her hand, guiding her down the red carpet. He looked handsome as always, grinning that wicked smile he was famous for. Thandie nearly gasped at her own image. She wasn't smiling. She appeared to be pouting and extremely smug. She looked like a snob. For added appeal, a screen shot of Ruark Randall dressed as his TV personality, was positioned in a small box right next to her head. His expression implied deep sadness.

Appalled, Thandie threw down the paper. "This is bullshit, Mira. You can't possibly be serious about printing this story."

Mira, unfazed, flipped her cigarette with a fluid motion. "This is how you thank me?"

"Thank you? Exactly why should I be thanking you?"

Mira rolled her eyes. "I'm preparing you for my slam."

"Why in the world are you slamming me in the first place? I'm your business associate."

Shaking her head, Mira said, "You're also news," she said sensibly. "And news sells papers."

"I'm not news," Thandie defended. "If you're going to print nonsense, the least you could do is focus on Elliot. I'm promoting his club, not my personal life."

"Wake up, Thandie," Mira snapped. "I've been printing Elliot's affairs for years. Don't convince yourself for a second this story makes you special. The only reason people remember your name is because you locked lips with Ruark Randall. You want to bring attention to Richards? Well, you did. You're both in the picture, aren't you? We spelled his name right, didn't we? Get over yourself. Any news is good news. In another week, Elliot will be spotted in public with some pretty model hanging on his arm. She'll be prettier than you and much younger. Suck it up, for heaven's sake. This is business, not playground antics. You should know better than that."

On the drive to the club, Thandie had been trying to think of a way to spin the *Look* story in their favor. So far, she was coming up blank. When she pulled up to Babylon, she was still stumped. It was hours before the club was scheduled to open for business. In the evening sun, the exterior of Club Babylon looked rather modest. A drastic difference from its nighttime appearance.

Pushing through the entrance, she glanced up at Elliot's office. The door was closed; a good sign he was in a meeting. She actually gave a sigh of relief. That is, until Michelle saw her. He smiled and waved her forward. Thandie had no choice but to follow.

Pushing the door open, Thandie could see there was indeed a meeting in progress. Elliot was standing in front of his desk, addressing the group. Adam, Markie, Ed, the accountant and Tom were seated in the couches hanging on to his every word. Romero lounged in the corner, busily hovering over his cell phone. The motion of the door opening caused them all to turn in her direction.

Focusing her gaze on Elliot, Thandie was surprised by what she found. He did not radiate the warmth and passion he'd shown her hours before. His face was impassive, and his eyes were distant. He was all business, and noticeably annoyed.

"Let's take a break," he announced to his audience. "We'll reconvene in an hour."

The group gathered their things and slowly stood. None

of the men had crossed the threshold before Elliot lit into Thandie.

"What the hell is this?" he asked cooly. He held up a fresh copy of *Look*. Even from a distance, Thandie could see outlines of their images in full color. As if disgusted, Elliot tossed the paper onto his desk. "I don't want gossip to be the only news I'm generating," he informed. "I own three of the hottest clubs on the strip and the best *Look* could report is who I escort around town? This is bullshit, Thandie."

Thandie waited until the last man left the office before saying, "I agree with you."

"So you'll yell at Mira?"

"I already have."

"Do it again," he quipped.

She approached him, placing her purse and planner into a chair, ready to make her argument. "Perhaps it's time we revisit the camera policy again." The instant the words left her mouth, she knew she'd lost his interest. She rushed on. "If we could give Mira something to sink her teeth into, feed her curiosity about what goes on here during business hours, she may be appeased enough to give us some slack."

"No." It was said with finality.

Thandie knew there was no point in pressing the matter, at least not for the moment. She decided to pick up the original conversation. Pointing at the *Look* article, she said, "This not necessarily a bad thing," she said reasonably. "You have to look at this from a publicity point of view. The more people see you, the better. This is free press, Elliot, on a relatively slow week. We should be so lucky."

"So you say."

She wasn't exactly sure if he agreed with her or not. In an effort to satisfy him, she added, "I'll talk to Mira again."

He gave a curt nod.

"Is there anything else?" she asked.

"No." He shook his head, although he was already preoc-cupied with scanning another article in the newspaper. "That's all," he said quietly, having already mentally excused her from the room.

Thandie fumbled with pushing her planner back into her oversize purse. She was desperate to get away from him. His moods were so erratic, she couldn't begin to understand him.

Pulling her purse onto her shoulder, she was mid-step in taking her leave when his arm circled her waist and pulled her close. She found herself staring at his chest, his lips graz-ing her ear.

"I had a great time last night," he said. "Wear something sexy tonight. Just for me." As suddenly as he'd ensnared her, his hold vanished.

After enduring a painfully long and very strained phone call with Mira, Thandie and the girls spent the remainder of the day finalizing plans for the fashion show and confirming travel arrangements for upcoming club performers. By the time they were done working for the day, it was time to get dressed for the evening.

Tonight, Len and Raja weren't the only ones employing great care in their appearances. Twice Thandie had changed her mind about what to wear. She felt a certain amount of pressure to impress Elliot. Regardless whether he was still upset over Mira slamming them in the paper, Thandie wanted to look desirable tonight. But not too overdone. Thus her in-decision over what to wear. Frustrated, she selected a shimmer-ing backless mini dress, but played down her hair and makeup.

When everyone was finally ready, they piled into the car and headed for the strip. The streets were crowded with avid partygoers dressed in brightly colored outfits. Len and Raja prattled nonstop about organizing a trip to Key West.

There were a small number of photographers milling about in front of the club. Having become familiar with her vehicle, they positioned themselves as soon as she pulled up. Thandie leaped from the car and hastened toward the club entrance. Seeing her approach, Tiny lifted the velvet rope and waved her forward.

Thandie, Raja and Len weaved their way through the crowd, smiling and greeting guests as they went. They eventually arrived at the VIP level. Warren Radcliffe could be seen seated at one of the tables surrounded by women half his age. He was holding a bottle of champagne, laughing as he filled the ladies' flutes to the brim. Len and Raja made their way to his table.

Left alone, Thandie looked around the room, observing the well-dressed crowd. She spotted Adam leaning over the bar, talking to a waitress. He turned around, scanned the faces, and seeing Thandie, Adam made his way to her side.

He made a low whistle at her dress. "Very nice. I see why the press can't get enough of you."

Thandie grinned as she gave him a kiss on the cheek. "How is the crowd tonight?"

"Very tame," he announced. "I like it when people act as though they know how to behave."

"Photographers?" she asked.

"The typical," he said with a shrug. "One or two have been caught and tossed. Security has been tight tonight. Boss's orders, of course."

Thandie nodded. No doubt Elliot had insisted on it because of the *Look* article.

There was a shuffle in the crush, and Markie appeared. Catching sight of Thandie and Adam, he joined them.

Leaning forward, he informed Adam of the approaching arrival of a club member, some professional athlete who had very specific tastes when it came to his nighttime entertainment. Excusing herself, Thandie left the men to their discussion.

Instinctively, she looked out over the crowd. Elliot was nowhere in sight. Her eyes flitted up to his office door. Behind Michelle's bulky form was a closed door. Somehow, she knew he was inside, running his empire. Not for the first time today, she considered his earlier about-face. When he'd complained about Mira's slam, he'd been a completely different person from the man who'd slowly stroked her to orgasm that morning on the boat. His abrupt change happened too rapidly for her to separate business matters from personal emotions. Try as she might to conceal it, her feelings had been slightly wounded. And then he'd pulled her to him and reminded her of their time together the previous night. He did not attempt to hide his desire for her. Again his sudden change befuddled her, turning her thoughts into mush as quickly as her panties began to dampen.

She was nowhere near understanding him. During their time on the boat, Thandie had thought she'd glimpsed a flicker of the real Elliot Richards. She envisioned the handsome dark-haired boy who idolized his father and adored his mother. But that image clashed drastically with the aloof business-man she knew.

Shaking her head, she decided to check her makeup. Taking the steps to the lower level, Thandie crossed the arena floor and entered the ladies' room. Like the rest of the club, the decor was sleek and modern.

Making her way to the sink, Thandie stared at her reflection. Nothing had changed. She looked exactly the same, but her eyes were troubled. An image of Elliot floated before her, and something tightened in her chest. Even thinking about him caused a wave of desire to wash over her. And then guilt. The guilt came from embracing pleasure over reason. Elliot was not the sort of man who settled down for long. He would eventually grow bored and find someone else to amuse him.

Thandie wondered what she expected to come from this affair? And how did she expect this to end?

Forgetting the reason she'd come in here in the first place, Thandie strode out of the washroom. As she stepped into the darkened arena, the opening cords of Nine Inch Nails' "Closer" began to play. As if on cue, Elliot's office door opened. He stepped into the flickering blue and green lights, looking every bit as striking as a mythical Greek god. He stepped aside, and the lovely dark-haired woman Thandie noticed days before emerged from the office. She came level with Elliot. The two made eye contact before the woman turned to climb down the steps outside his office door. Elliot's eyes followed her the entire way, a thoughtful expression on his face. As if bored, he turned his gaze on the crowd of dancers before him. His cool gray gaze made contact with Thandie's almost instantly.

As if in slow motion, Thandie watched him descend the steps and weave a graceful, yet direct, path toward her. He moved like a surefooted panther. She took in his dark suit and flawless hair. If he had fooled around with the mysterious dark-haired woman, there were no obvious signs. He was immaculately put together.

Arriving at her side, he greeted her with a kiss. It was soft and slow. And when his eyes opened to look into her own, every barrier she'd begun to erect around her heart melted away. Unable to help herself, Thandie looked over his shoulder and sought out the lovely woman. She found her standing near the bar. She was staring at Thandie and Elliot. Her gaze was so intense, for a moment Thandie was frozen in place.

Elliot followed the path of Thandie's stare and gave a bemused chuckle. "If possible," he said in a low voice, "she's more curious about you than you could ever be about her." With that said, he placed his hand on her hip and guided her toward his office. "Come," he whispered. "I have a strong desire to taste you."

Without hesitation, Thandie let herself be led through the mass of dancers. As he guided her up the steps, Thandie could once again feel invisible eyes trained on her back. It was as heavy as a firm hand pressing against her spine. Her familiarity with Elliot was not going unnoticed by anyone. She inwardly berated herself. How many times had she loathed the women who followed after Elliot like sex-starved zombies to get a brief pleasure session with the man? The desire to feel his beautifully tanned body pressed against their naked flesh, if only for one night? She flushed at the thought, knowing at this very minute she'd become the thing she despised most.

Thandie chanced a glance over her shoulder. The beautiful dark-haired woman was standing on the opposite side of the bar, almost directly across from them. She was staring at Thandie and Elliot with a look of unveiled envy. Thandie wondered how soon would it be before she, Thandie, were doing the same to Elliot's next favorite.

As the Victoria Day fashion show approached, the days and nights began to run together. Thandie and the girls barely had time to sleep, let alone retreat to Babylon in the evenings. The show was causing extra work for everyone. Adam and Markie came to the house daily to discuss strategy. Of everyone, Victoria was the most taxed. Aside from the constant growing pains involved with putting on a production, she had to keep up with last minute model fittings, guest invitations and overseeing the finishing touches on her collection.

Meanwhile, Thandie and the girls had their hands full managing a temperamental stage designer, a knowledgable but unorganized lighting specialist and helping with gift baskets.

There were many hands to hold, and multiple ways to get lost. There never seemed to be enough hours in the days to tackle the ever-changing workload.

For three days straight, Thandie and Elliot rarely saw each other. Their fledgling affair had all but come to an abrupt halt. Fortunately, she was too busy to dwell on the matter. Otherwise she would have driven herself crazy.

The day of the fashion show, there was a nervous vibe in the air. Everyone held their breath, waiting for the first disaster to occur.

It happened just short of nine o'clock that morning. The red carpet rental had not been delivered. Then the draping expert had shown up with over three hundred feet less draping than needed. The benches that arrived had to be sent back to the warehouse because they were the wrong color. And finally, the workmen setting up the stage had to redo their work when they realized they misread the layout diagram. And this was everything that happened in front of the curtain. According to Len, Victoria had unleashed on one of the models and two of the makeup artists had nearly come to blows.

Two hours before showtime, Thandie and the girls stepped away from the activity to change clothes and freshen up in the dressing room often used by the Babylon dancers.

An hour later, Thandie, Raja and Len were seated in the front row. They'd reserved two benches for their party, plenty of room to invite four additional people. Somehow, with all the preparations, they'd forgotten to extend invitations. So they sat with plenty of room between themselves, happy to finally be off their feet.

Fifteen minutes before the show was scheduled to start,

Thandie saw Elliot stride toward them. He had not come alone. Over his shoulder, Nico and Matrix could be seen several paces behind him. Thandie stood up to greet them.

Watching Elliot approach, Thandie was amazed by how happy she felt at the sight of him. She could feel the smile on her face spreading, her joy nearly radiant. She was too overjoyed to care that his arrival was drawing attention to them. All she cared about was being near him.

When he was close enough, he reached out to place a hand on her hip and brushed his lips lightly against hers. It was nowhere near the ardent reception she'd been hoping for, but when he whispered, "Hello, pussycat," in a low whisper next to her ear, a shiver of naked delight shot up her spin.

Resisting the urge to melt into him, Thandie smiled up at his friends. "Nico. Matrix. I'm glad you could make it." She paused long enough to give each man a brief hug. "I don't believe either of you have met my assistants. This is—"

"Hi! I'm Len," Len said brightly.

"And I'm Raja."

The two girls beamed up at the men with looks of instant adoration. Thandie could feel Raja and Len drinking in Nico's easy smile and Matrix's dark looks. Thankfully, the overhead lights began to dim, indicating the show was about to start.

The lights having finally settled into place, the words "V. Day" illuminated the stage backdrop as the soulful voice of Chet Faker singing "No Diggity" blasted from every speaker in the building. A single spotlight touched the center of the stage, and large shadows appeared. A shadowy figure walked closer to the white curtain; her figure became smaller and shapelier. The curtain split, and out walked Victoria Day.

Thandie immediately approved of her outfit. When she'd seen Victoria earlier, she'd been donning sneakers, cutoffs and no makeup. She could have passed for a teenager. However now, she looked fierce in hues of orange, yellow and pink. Clearly dressed in an original creation, Victoria had a certain style that was definitely hers alone. Her outfit complemented her body perfectly.

The crowd went crazy as Victoria took the stage. Her many bangles and red heels clicked with every step. Her pace was quick and direct. Holding a microphone at her side, she paused when she was midway on the runway. Planting a small hand on her hip, she put the crowd at ease when she flashed a brilliant white smile, and took a minute to wave at someone in the crowd.

"Thank you for coming," she began. Her New York accent more pronounced. "They told me I had to make a speech about my line, but I refused. I don't want anyone to talk about my clothes. I want them to fuckin' wear them." The crowd chortled, obviously put at ease by her down to earth persona.

"As many of you know," she said once the laughter had died down, "I have been waiting for this day for a long time. I've always dreamt of designing a line that expressed my love for the two places I call home, New York and Miami. I wanted to see women wear something fun and functional. I hope you agree." Another bright smile. "So let's stop with the speeches and get on with the effin' show."

The crowd applauded politely as Victoria exited the stage. Her departure was immediately replaced by the arrival of a tall, blonde model strutting down the catwalk in tempo to loud reggae rap. The critics leaned forward and began the age-old ritual of critiquing and gossiping.

Thirty minutes went by at lightening speed. Thandie could hardly believe so much work had been compressed into such a short time. The good thing was the show had gone without a hitch. By the time the last model had left the stage, everyone agreed: the V. Day collection would be a success.

While Victoria scandalized the journalists with racy quotes, Thandie's group made their way backstage. Thandie pretended not to notice the attention Elliot, Nico and Matrix were drawing from the females in the room. Indeed, it was hard not to notice them.

Eventually, Victoria burst through the stage curtain. A crowd of journalists stuffed recorders in her face, while photographers followed closely behind. Cameras flashed with her every step. Thandie couldn't help but smile at the designer. She deserved the attention being showered on her.

After thanking her staff, Victoria spotted Thandie and waved her over. Her smile was brilliant when she hugged her. Their celebration was cut short when a handsome reporter introduced himself and asked for an interview. Before Victoria could respond, someone said, "Get lost."

Both Thandie and Victoria turned to see Nico, snarling at the man.

Victoria's eyes widened with outrage. "Can't you see I'm having a conversation?" she hissed.

"I don't care if you're talking to the Queen of England," he said through gritted teeth. "Get over here." Taking a firm hold on her upper arm, he all but dragged her behind a rack of clothes. The two quickly dived into a whispered, and very animated argument which drew a lot of attention.

Thandie did not know what to make of this. As far as she knew, Nico and Victoria were strangers. She was distracted when she heard someone shout, "Tammie!" She turned to see the very last person she hoped never to lay eyes on again. It was Ruark Randall.

"Hey, babe," he said, kissing her on the lips before she had the chance to pull away and run. "I've been looking everywhere for you. I called your office, but your assistant wasn't much help." He leaned closer. "Between you and me, I think she's spazzed out." He gave a goofy grin that was meant to be charming, but instead Thandie wanted to punch out all his perfectly capped teeth.

"It's nice to see you, Ruark," she said, looking around for a plausible escape. "What are you doing here?"

He leaned his head to the side, tossing hair out of his eyes. "My agent has me doing a string of publicity junk. It's been a complete drag." He gave a careless sweep of his hand around the room. "What the hell am I doing in a place like this? I'm not buying this stuff."

Thandie nodded, pretending to sympathize. "Well, that's nice. I'd love to chat, but I have to go."

A photographer appeared out of nowhere, and being the product of well-trained publicity protocol, Ruark pulled her into his side and gave a flirtatious smile to the camera. Thandie had no choice but to do the same. After momentarily blinding them, the photographer vanished just as quickly as he'd appeared.

By this time, Thandie was annoyed Ruark thought it necessary to keep his hand planted on her butt. She would have gladly pushed him away, but she was keenly aware that since being captured by the photographer, they were the focus of several furtive looks. It was clear several of the women considered her fortunate. They obviously had not spent more than five seconds in Ruark Randall's presence.

"What are you doing later?" he asked.

You wish, she thought. Instead of telling him what she felt, she smiled up at him. "I have several appointments today." Actually, her priority for the evening was to catch up on much needed sleep.

"Ah, come on, Mandy," he whined. "I'm not going to be

in town long. I was sort of hoping we could pick up things where we left off."

"She's busy," a steely voice said.

Thandie could feel Elliot's presence behind her.

Ruark looked up, frowned and said, "Excuse me?"

Elliot came up beside Thandie and, without asking, brushed Ruark's hand off her bottom. "I said, she's busy." He encircled her waist with his arm, drawing her to him possessively. The act was gentle, but belied the icy gaze he was giving the other man.

Seeing he might have a problem on his hands, Ruark retreated slightly.

Without another word, Elliot guided her through the crowd. Pushing aside the draping, he held it open for Thandie to pass through. Here, they were shielded from curious eyes. Elliot looked down at her, his gaze sweeping her face. "Are you all right?"

In spite of his kind words, Thandie got the impression he was upset with her. "I'm fine."

He stared at her a moment longer, before saying rather tersely, "I have a long night ahead of me. I'm sure you're tired from the work you've put in."

Thandie nodded, unable to deny her fatigue.

"Go home and get your rest." He cupped her face between his hands. "I want you in my bed when I get there." He lowered his lips and kissed her hard.

Fixing her with a hard stare, he slipped out from behind the curtains, leaving her confused and aroused.

Thandie awoke when he entered the room. She'd never seen Elliot come home from work. He was still handsome, but he was tired. His shoulders were slumped, and he appeared to be fighting to keep his eyes open. He slid his jacket off, carefully folding it over a chair. Yawning, he unbuckled his belt. She hoped he would undress in front of her, but he turned toward the bathroom. He didn't seem to notice she was awake.

Having left the door ajar, Thandie was able to see his reflection in the vanity mirror. She watched as he adjusted the water temperature and stripped out of his clothes. He picked up his phone, and furrowed his brows in a particular way, squinting at the small screen. There was something about his expression that seemed oddly familiar to her. As if she'd seen it hundreds of times before, but she knew this couldn't be right. She'd never seen Elliot like this. And yet...

She lost track of her thoughts when Elliot rested his phone on the countertop and stepped into the glass-enclosed shower stall. From the bed, Thandie watched his mirror image. She was captivated by what she saw.

He lathered and washed, shampooing his hair quickly but thoroughly. Then, he braced his hands on the shower wall and hung his head between his shoulders, letting the hot water spray over his back and past his bronzed buttocks. He was in obvious deep thought. She'd never seen this side of him. He was always totally composed, as if overseeing his businesses and a large staff were a passionate hobby rather than work. But she could see that it did wear on him, and she had the strangest sensation of sympathy and she wanted to ease his burden.

When he was done showering, he exited the stall and for a moment moved out of sight to retrieve something. Thandie counted the moments until he stepped back into view. It seemed to take forever. When he was back in sight, a towel was tossed over his shoulder and his dark hair was tousled.

After brushing his teeth, he came to bed. He slid next to her. Wrapping his arm around her, he pulled her closer. She felt him grow hard against her thigh. She rolled over to place her head on his shoulder.

For a second, she wondered if he'd been with another woman tonight, but her worry vanished just as quickly as it had appeared. The man was exhausted. And his immediate reaction to her made her feel special. She leaned up to kiss him. He reacted by caressing her back. Thandie liked the feel of his large, warm hands touching her skin. She inched closer to him, deepening their kiss. He allowed her to be the aggressor. Her hands clutched his shoulders while their tongues mated. She moaned when his hands skimmed down her back to settle on her butt.

Her breath was lost. She wanted more of him. It seemed impossible to believe he could be so tender. His touch was soft, making her body yearn for more. Unable to stand the intimate distance, Thandie pulled her nightgown up. She shimmed out of her panties and straddled him, her body pocketing his manhood perfectly. Rising above him, she took hold of his thick shaft. He held his breath as she guided him inside her, inch by inch. She was warm, wet and tight.

Elliot groaned loudly. She felt so right. So painfully perfect. He fought to hold himself back from rolling her over and burying himself inside her again and again. As much as he wanted to take her, he enjoyed watching her when she was in control. Her small hands pressed on his chest as he lifted her hips up and down his cock. Her eyes closed as she abandoned all reality in search of complete fulfillment. She was beautiful. Her back arched, her lips parted, her hips riding him. She tossed her hair back, moaning thickly. The simple movement made the thin straps of her gown slip from her shoulders, exposing her heavy brown breasts. Unable to stop himself, his hands reached for her, cupping her breasts, enjoying the weighty handsful. She moaned again. Her back arched farther. His body tensed but held strong. He wanted to come with her. He needed to feel her warmth squeeze his cock until he couldn't think or breathe.

Within minutes, her body jerked, and she screamed. Her juices washed over his shaft, and he exploded. His hands held fast to her waist, and his hips jutted up uncontrollably. A hoarse cough escaped his lips. His seed was hot and thick as it burst inside her. For an instant he cursed himself for not using a condom. He'd promised to be more careful with her. But as the aftershock of his climax shook him, he knew he would not have done it differently. She felt too good like this. The way her body pocketed his manhood so snugly was paradise. And damn if he wasn't getting hard again.

He'd been tired when he'd arrived home, but his appetite was not yet sated with her. Cupping his hand behind her neck, he pulled her down on top of him to kiss her soundly. He slapped her bare bottom. She gasped the first time but moaned the second time. They kissed for a long time. He moved slowly inside her. The lovemaking that followed was slow and erotic.

They did not go to sleep for a long time.

Chapter Twenty-Two

In the early morning light, Thandie slowly opened her eyes. The sound of Elliot's soft breathing rustled her hair. A secret smile touched Thandie's lips as she snuggled closer to him. She liked the feeling of being wrapped in Elliot's arms more than she would like to admit. His embrace was strong, enveloping her in his warmth. It was the sort of thing a woman could quickly get used to.

A dangerous notion to have when Elliot Richards was part of the equation.

He had not mentioned, nor hinted, at an exclusive relationship. And why would he? Beautiful women swarmed around him every night, each more willing than the last. How could she compete with that? *Was* she competing? Or was she simply enjoying an exciting fling?

Yes, she was mesmerized by Elliot, but was she emotionally attached to him? She did not believe so. At least, not yet. But how would she feel when she saw him taking lovers at the club? She'd like to believe she could be a mature adult about their sexual encounters, able to separate sex from matters of the heart. But if they kept making slow, mind-blowing love in his bed, she wasn't sure about how long her guard would remain intact.

And then the day would come when Thandie's time in Miami would be up, and she would be on a plane back to New York. What then? Would their affair simply end? How would she feel about that?

Did she even want to know?

It soon became apparent to the entire Babylon staff that Elliot and Thandie were involved in some sort of relationship. Over the span of a few short days, Thandie noticed she was given free reign at the club. The staff went out of their way to cater to her, and the management team became even friendlier. Michelle allowed her unlimited access to Elliot's office, regardless if he was in a meeting or not. Valet service was done promptly and with urgency. She was treated as their most coveted guest.

Following the Victoria Day fashion show, Thandie had a mess on her hands. *Gossip Extra* featured a story about the show, but put a great emphasis on the backstage antics. Not surprisingly, a picture of Thandie and Ruark Randall was on display. Below it, a blurb asked "Have the two kissed and made up?" Not to be left out, another less-known newspaper posted the same picture of Thandie and Ruark, proclaiming the two had reconciled.

Of course, it was *Look* which took a completely different route. Having been the only gossip column to capture a grainy picture of Thandie, Ruark and Elliot standing together, the *Look* reporter's take had been a complicated love triangle that made Ruark a victim, portrayed Elliot as gullible, and colored Thandie a heartless slut.

The headlines had not been well received by Elliot.

It was not yet clear if *Look* was to blame for the subsequent news articles that appeared throughout the week in competing gossip columns. Or perhaps it was the fact that Thandie and Elliot disappeared into his office every night, sometimes more than once, for lengthy amounts of time. Throughout these vanishing acts, it was understood Elliot was not to be disturbed under any circumstances.

It was during these entanglements that Thandie enjoyed the most delicious adventures. She'd found herself sitting atop Elliot's desk, lying flat on her back, her legs spread wide, and Elliot's face buried between her thighs. Elliot had taken her doggy style several times on just about every piece of furniture in the office. And during those times when neither could wait long enough to strip off their clothes, they'd engaged in sex standing upright. Most of the time, they were so impatient for each other, clothes were torn and pushed aside in haste. And then there were times when they took things slow, caresses were plentiful and kisses were passionate.

At the end of the night, Thandie would sleep in her own bed. Elliot's work hours were long and unpredictable. On occasion, she would wake to find him lying beside her, but often she slept alone.

It was during these times doubt crept in. She would lie in bed wondering where Elliot was and whom he might be with. It drove her crazy, especially since she could not see any evidence of unfaithfulness. But the questions gnawed at her like a cancer, slowly eating away at her sanity.

A relationship with Elliot Richards, even in the loosest sense of the word, was not normal. It was unlike anything she had ever experienced, and yet exactly what she expected of him. Elliot was a notorious flirt and appeared to be quite unattached when he was among the set. Thandie told herself this was a persona he put on for his guests, but she still felt a pang of hurt every time she saw another woman's arm around his waist or leaning forward to kiss him on the cheek. The only time she truly felt as though he belonged to her was when he sought her out in the crowd, whispered something tantalizing in her ear, and led her to his office.

Tonight, was a night no different from the others. Thandie stood in the center of Babylon's VIP lounge, helping Adam amuse his club members. Len and Raja were doing their part to save tables and entertain male guests.

Thandie had been there for a little over an hour, and so far had only glimpsed Elliot once. He'd been at the arena's main bar when she'd first entered the club. Leaning against the railing, he was smiling down at two identical blondes. Wearing similar dresses that were equally short and tight, the twins could have passed for life-size Barbie dolls. Over their shoulders, Elliot had looked up and caught her eye. He slyly nodded his head and returned his attention back to the women. Thandie had not seen him since.

Having grown tired of dealing with their guests, Thandie decided to take a break. She left the lounge and climbed down the steps to the arena floor. Crossing the crowded dance floor, she slipped into the ladies' room. The normally heavily trafficked facilities was unusually empty when Thandie entered. Going to the sink, she reached into her clutch and fished out her lipstick. When she looked back into the mirror, she realized she was not alone.

Standing behind her was Wife Number Five, Sophia Radcliffe.

Thandie whirled around. She had not come into contact with the woman since their awful introduction at Warren's home. Then, Sophia had been brandishing a knife. Thandie was relieved to see, aside from a tiny clutch purse, her hands were empty. However, this did not lessen her alarm at being near the woman. Thandie did not believe in coincidences. If Sophia was here, it was because she'd followed her.

In the luminous lighting, Thandie felt as if she were seeing Sophia for the first time. She truly was a stunning woman. Large brown eyes were enhanced in smoky shadows. Full pouty lips made her round face appear heart-shaped. Her curvy figure, was punctuated by large perky breasts. They were clearly fake, but the work was so nicely done, one could only admire. Thandie understood why Elliot and Warren had chosen her for a lover.

Thandie met her gaze directly. "Is there something you have on your mind?" she asked curtly.

Sophia's upper lip pulled back into an ugly snarl. "You may think he cares about you, but he doesn't. He doesn't care about anyone other than himself."

Thandie saw no reason to pretend. Clearly the *Look* article had made an impression on her. The woman was livid. Crossing her arms, Thandie casually asked, "And why should I listen to a warning from you?"

"Warning?" Sophia smirked. "A warning would imply I actually like you, and I don't."

"Fair enough," Thandie mused. "Now we know our feelings are mutual."

"Don't think for a minute your temporary status as Elliot's new bed partner will last long," Sophia jeered. "At first, he'll make you feel special, even honored, to be on his arm. You'll think you've changed him, that you're the only woman in his life. And then reality will set in. You'll notice the women who surround him, the long hours he works, and the sudden business trips he takes. By the time you get the stars out of your eyes, it'll be too late. He'll already be with someone else." She took a step toward Thandie. "I'm not warning you.

I'm telling you this to let you know when he does break your heart, I'll be watching and enjoying every agonizing moment." Sophia gave her one last pointed glare before storming out of the room.

Thandie stared after her. Sophia radiated hot anger and unveiled envy. She wondered what Elliot had done to hurt the woman to that degree. Did he even know? Had Warren known the depth of her feelings for Elliot when he'd married her? Or, she shivered, had Elliot begun the affair with Sophia after her marriage to Warren? The question sat in her stomach like a heavy rock.

Sinking her teeth into her bottom lip, she turned to look in the mirror. She was pale and visibly shaken. A burst of anger flared through her, but not at Sophia. Wife Number Five was inconsequential. Thandie was furious with Elliot. While she was receiving the snarling contempt of his ex-lover, he was probably still flirting with the Barbies.

The sudden desire to leave the club, hail a taxi and climb into her own bed overwhelmed her. Anything to escape her growing sense of unease. Sophia was the last person in the world she would trust, but the woman's words echoed her fears, and not for the first time.

She snapped her purse closed, and tucked it under her arm, and sailed out of the bathroom. With determined steps, she skirted the clusters of people, and exited the building. Tiny frowned when he saw her.

"Everything okay, Thandie?" he asked.

"Everything is fine," she said as she brushed past him and stepped onto the sidewalk. Thankfully, a taxi was parked alongside the curb on the opposite side of the street. Skipping across the busy road, she slid into the backseat of the car. "Star Island," she instructed brusquely.

She arrived at Elliot's home within fifteen minutes. After a quick shower, she climbed into bed and pulled the covers high over head. The house was so quiet, the sound of ocean waves crashed loudly in the distance. Staring blankly at the ceiling, Thandie realized she was not tired. Not even close. And so, for long minutes, she lay in bed letting her mind drift from one thought to another. Repeatedly, her mind circled back to one thought, or rather one question. What did she expect to come from an affair with Elliot Richards?

Thandie awoke to the wondrous feeling of a heavy male body stretching out on top of her. Soft lips trailed hot kisses against her cheek, making a blazing path to her lips. Her eyes opened to focus on Elliot's handsome face. If possible, shadows intensified his rugged good looks.

Feeling her gaze on him, he opened his eyes to look down at her. His silver eyes captured her breath. He searched her face before he kissed her again. She could feel him reach between them, grab hold of his shaft and guide his cock toward her wet center.

Thandie panicked. "Elliot, no!" She said in a heated whisper as she fought to close her legs. "Are you crazy? We can't do this here."

His head snapped up. "What the hell do you mean we can't do this here? We're in a bed, aren't we? Where else should we do it?"

"Not here." She groaned in frustration, unable to close her legs due to his lean form lying between her legs. "The girls are next door."

"Len and Raja are still at the club," he said confidently.

Thandie frowned. "What time is it?"

"Barely midnight," he said.

"Midnight?" The word confused her. "Shouldn't you be—"

"I left early," he said, cutting her off.

"Why?"

He gave her a hard look. "Why did you leave early?"

Thandie looked away, unwilling to tell him what was troubling her. Seeming not to care if he got a response from her or not, he lowered his head to kiss the curve of her neck. Annoyed, she pushed against his shoulders. "The girls will be here soon."

"So?" he snapped.

She took offense at his tone. "Don't talk to me like that."

"Trust me, pussycat, talking is the last thing I want to do right now."

"Why are you here? Shouldn't you be sweet-talking those twin Barbie dolls?"

He raised a brow at her comment and then his face relaxed into a knowing grin. "Are you jealous?"

"Get off me," she snapped.

Even in the darkness, she could see him look angrily down at her. But she didn't care. She was furious with him about Sophia, the twins, and a hundred other things she couldn't quite put together in a coherent argument.

She pushed against him again, this time more forcefully. This got an immediate response from him. Elliot suddenly leaned back. Thandie meant to slam her legs closed, but as if reading her mind, he grasped her thighs and held them apart.

"Let go," she hissed crossly.

He flashed her a tight smile. "Sweetheart, we're doing it tonight. Regardless of where you think it should happen. You can come willingly or not." His smile vanished as his voice deepened. "Either way, you're coming."

Seeing the determined look in his eyes, she understood that to fight him would be pointless. It would be a lost battle. She was already wet with desire. No doubt he could smell her, as well as see his effect on her form himself.

"Okay, Elliot," she said. "I surrender."

His chin lifted in obvious satisfaction.

"But not here," she insisted. "The girls will hear us."

"The girls would hear you," he said with a smirk. "If my memory serves me right, you are the noisy one between us." He saw her eyes lower in clear embarrassment. Had there been enough light, he was sure he would have witnessed her blush. Getting off the bed, he offered her his hand. "Come."

She accepted it. "Where are we going?"

"To my bed. As you know, my bedroom is on the other side of the house. If it is privacy you desire, then I am eager to provide it."

She looked down at his aroused nudity. "Do you want to get your clothes?"

He lifted his brow. "I didn't bring any." He swung open her bedroom door. "Hurry along, Thandie. I'm hungry for you."

His silken words cast a spell over her. Thandie felt a ball of heat growing in her belly and spreading throughout her limbs. And she hated him for it. The simplest word from him and she was putty in his capable hands.

Feeling her resistance, Elliot took action. He swiftly threw her over his shoulder, and went to his room. He kicked his door open and locked it behind him before lowering her to her feet. He turned his back on her and headed for the mini bar tucked in the corner of the room.

Thandie was thankful for the small privacy, for she was suddenly nervous. She was also aware that the T-shirt and panties she had fallen asleep in were missing.

Elliot returned to her holding a glass in his hand. He offered the clear liquor to her. She hesitantly took a small sip. The vodka burned her lips and throat. She muffled a cough.

"Slowly," he said. "Try another."

She did so, only to keep herself busy and to ignore that his hand was stroking her bottom. After the second swallow of the liquid fire, she pressed the glass back into his hand. He finished the remains in three steady swallows before placing the glass on the nightstand.

His eyes twinkled when he led her to his bed. Gently, he pushed her back across the bed. His body quickly followed. He lowered his head to kiss her. Light and teasing at first. She liked this. She began to relax and returned his kisses. But he made no further advances, just kissed her tenderly.

Soon, her arms were wrapped around his neck, and her legs were about his waist. The contact of her drenched center pressed against his naked manhood released his passion. The gentle lover vanished, replaced by the lusty rogue he truly was. He deepened his kiss. His hands scooped beneath her bottom and lifted her hips upward. He eased himself inside her, working every inch of his shaft deeper and deeper until he was fully submerged. He began to move inside her.

Elliot's weight pressed into Thandie, making it hard to breathe, but she liked the sensation. She could not escape him if she wanted to. She was his prisoner, both physically and mentally. Her legs tightened around his waist. Her back arched off the mattress. She pulled him closer. Her fingers raked his raven silk locks. He moved with liquid rhythm above her, every thrust flowing right into the next.

Her lusty moans furthered his craving for her. He groaned against her ear. He was on the brink of climax. Thandie let out a shout of elation and shivered beneath him. Her natural dew spilled forth, and she pulled him into her. Elliot was powerless to deny himself any longer. He came inside her. His hips jutted forward sharply, emptying his essence into hers.

When it was all over, a blanket of calm silence fell over them. Elliot lifted his head, balancing his weight on his forearms. Though she had not complained, he knew his weight was in part to blame for her choppy breathing. Looking down into her face, her classic beauty stirred him. He wanted her all over again.

Denying himself, he came off the bed. Pulling down the covers, he slapped her bottom lightly to indicate he wanted her to get beneath them. He watched as she slid under the sheets. She was clearly still upset with him. He could tell by the rigidness of her body.

Claiming his glass from the nightstand, he made his way over to the wet bar for a refill. Elliot drank the liquor slowly, as he made his way back to the bedside. Looking down at her with keen eyes, he marveled at the way the shadows played off the smooth contours of her body. Her skin was still flushed and dewy from their recent lovemaking.

"You're great, puss." His voice was warm and yet teasing. "I could screw you all night."

Although she knew he intended the words to be comforting, they had the opposite effect on her. Hearing the word *screw* so soon after sex made her feel cheap. The more she considered it, the angrier she became. It was the same feeling she had earlier tonight at the club when she'd seen him flirting with those women.

Abruptly, Thandie rolled onto her side, turning her back to him. She knew she was acting like a needy child, and she despised herself for it. But she despised him just as much for making her feel so insignificant.

She heard the delicate click of his resting his glass on the nightstand. Felt the mattress sag under his weight. His warm hand captured her shoulder, pushing it against the bed, urging her to lie on her back. He pushed her thighs apart and rested between them. Immediately, he was embedded inside her. She gasped at the invasion, but her body treated him like a returning emperor. Her womanhood cradled him by memory, clinging to him like a glove.

He groaned his approval. His gaze met hers. A slight smile played across his lips. "Why are you upset, pussycat?"

"Don't call me that," she snapped.

"Pussycat? But you are my pussycat."

She meant to roll away from him, but his hands were suddenly on her shoulders, pressing them into the mattress, diminishing any hope of escape.

He tsked. "You'll find any reason to hate me, won't you? Why?" He shrugged his shoulders dramatically. "I hold you on the highest level of adoration." He leaned forward to kiss her, but she turned her face away. "Thandie," he said, his voice losing its humor. "Your anger is misplaced, pussycat."

She bit back a retort, but her eyes threw daggers at him.

"Fine, Ms. Shaw." He lowered his head to take a taut nipple into his mouth. He sucked hard, forcing her to moan in response. "You want to play hardball. So be it. We'll play your game." Gritting his teeth together, he eased himself out of her sex. Still leaning over Thandie, he fixed her with a sharp and penetrating stare. "You have my undivided attention. What's on your mind?"

Thandie took her time meeting his gaze. When she finally did, there was a determined look in her eyes. "Tell me what happened between you and Sophia?"

The question caught him off guard. His expression went blank for a moment. It was possibly the first honest reaction she'd ever seen from him. She was slightly gratified to have invoked it from him.

"Well?" she urged. "Are you going to tell me?"

Elliot appeared to be considering the question. Finally, he bent forward, lowered his head and laved his tongue around her nipple before answering. "You already know what happened between Sophia and me. We fucked. End of story."

"She wasn't your girlfriend?"

"No." His answer was absolute.

"Do you want to elaborate?"

He shrugged his shoulders lightly. "We hooked up occasionally. When it stopped being fun, we parted ways."

"It sounds as if you were the one who parted ways."

"She wanted a relationship," he explained. "I don't do girlfriends. She had difficulty dealing with that. I moved on."

"You don't sound remorseful."

"Why should I? I was sleeping with other women before, during and after Sophia." He reached between her legs and slipped his fingers inside her. "You're wet. Do you enjoy hearing about me with other women?"

"No." She pushed his hand away and rolled over, giving him her back. "I don't like to hear you brag about your many conquests."

"I wasn't bragging. You asked me a question and I answered it."

"You...you..." She couldn't find the words to fully capture her displeasure with him. She was glad he couldn't see her face. She felt the lowest of the low. She was ashamed of her behavior around him. She'd seen the way women fell over themselves to get just the smallest piece of attention from him. She had seen the adoration in their eyes. They loved him on some base level and he regarded them as if they were merely dolls, silly playthings for his amusement. He spoke so uncaringly about his past lovers. It felt like a slap in the face because now her name could be added to that long list.

Elliot pulled himself up against her, wrapping his arm around her waist to fondle her breasts. "I know you turn your back on me when you're upset, but you're really doing me a favor. I love to look at your lovely bottom." He nuzzled her neck. "If you're still mad, tell me so I can begin to make it up to you." She moved to get out of bed, but his arm was unmovable. He held her closer. "Are you envious of my past... involvements? You shouldn't be."

"I want to sleep in my room."

"We can go there but I must warn you I have an extreme appetite tonight."

"I want to sleep alone."

He shook his head. "I can't give you that." He nibbled on her shoulder then laughed. "Damn. You're really pissed. I can feel the tension in your back."

"I won't share you, Elliot." Her words were spoken softly, but they might as well have been amplified through speakers. Each syllable fell between them like an avalanche of jagged rocks; weighing the bed down with meaning. "I won't tolerate you taking up with women at the club or anywhere else. If you want to keep me in your bed, it can only be us."

He did not need to search her face to know she meant every word. "You're not sharing me," he said quietly.

Thandie licked her lips, digesting what he'd just said. She clung to the words, desperate to believe them and too afraid to question their validity. And then she couldn't think, because he'd begun to brush his lips against her neck.

"Roll over," he whispered. When she did not immediately respond, he gently eased her onto her back. "I want to apologize properly."

His eyes glowed with intensity as he looked down into her face, but he said nothing, only stared at her until she was nervous. Parting her legs, he lowered himself until his head was cradled between her thighs. He used his fingers to push apart her pussy lips and stare at her. He looked up at her and smiled wickedly.

"I apologize, Thandie." He licked her slick nether lips. "Can you find it in your heart to forgive me for upsetting you?" He licked her again only this time he deepened the tease with an open-mouthed kiss. Her eyes rolled in the back of her head. She ran her fingers through his hair, pulling him closer to her. Her moans quickly turned to pants for breath. Elliot's hands reached up and cupped her breasts, squeezing them until they tingled from his touch. Just when she thought she couldn't take it any longer he pulled away and allowed her to come freely. Her body shook violently from the pleasure. When she was finally able to breathe regularly she opened her eyes to see him watching her. He was stroking his hard cock vigorously.

"Did you enjoy it, sweetheart?" he asked in a strained voice.

"How did you—how do you know how to make me…"

He hushed her words as her crawled between her legs. "I'm hungry for you, Thandie." He held the tip of his cock against her sex. "Tell me you forgive me."

"I forgive you."

Chapter Twenty-Three

A few hours later, Thandie woke. She'd slept fitfully, barely gaining more than snatches of slumber at a time. Her mind was crowded with unanswered questions and unspoken expectations.

Thandie eased out of bed, trying hard not to make a sound. She kept a careful eye on him as she slowly made her way around the bed. She did not want to wake him. With so much on her mind, she wasn't quite ready to deal with him first thing in the morning.

Her eyes stayed trained on him, measuring every breath he took. Then, a sharp pain shot up her leg. She looked down to see she had again stubbed her toe on the bench at the end of his bed. It was a cruel reminder that she had done this sneak routine before. She clamped her hand over her mouth, muffling a whimper of pain just in time, and limped out of the room.

The day passed slowly. Thandie and the girls busied themselves working on details for the next production at Babylon. When the time came to get ready to go to the club, Thandie did it with a sense of apprehension. She dreaded running into Wife Number Five again.

When they arrived at the club, the management meeting had just concluded. Adam, Markie and the rest of the team filed out of Elliot's office laughing and shoving one another like playful frat boys. Seeing Thandie and her assistants, they greeted them warmly before disbursing to their separate stations. Following Adam to the VIP area, the ladies got to work livening up the atmosphere.

When Elliot finally stepped out his office and entered the arena floor, Thandie's gaze latched onto him. She expected him to begin making his rounds among the guests. She was taken aback when he took to the stairs leading to the upper level and made a direct path toward her. He further shocked her by greeting her with a kiss to the neck. Len and Raja's eyes grew the size of saucers. If they hadn't know before that Thandie and Elliot were engaged in an affair, it was clear now. Slipping his arm around Thandie's waist, Elliot whispered into her ear, "Let's meet the guests together."

With Thandie at his side, Elliot began making his rounds. For many minutes, she was in a daze. It was the closest Elliot had come to publicly claiming her as his. Thandie felt like Cinderella hanging on Prince Charming's arm.

When Thandie came downstairs the following evening, she was startled by the sight of another large box resting on the dining room table. A single envelope rested on top, with her name spelled out in Elliot's crisp and precise handwriting. She stared at the box, still sleepy from a late night with Elliot.

Cautiously, Thandie picked up the envelope and read the short message. "4:00 p.m. this afternoon. Wear nothing underneath.... Or else.-E. P.S. You'll need your passport."

Thandie wrinkled her brows at the last words of his note. What did he have planned?

Putting the note aside, Thandie opened the large box. Inside was another dress. Pushing aside the tissue paper, she lifted the garment from the box. The dress was long, backless and had twin high slits on both sides. It was made of snowy white silk, which looked nearly transparent. Thandie peeked at the label and blushed. Elie Saab. Elliot certainly wasn't cheap when it came to fashion.

Gingerly, she put the dress back inside the box and carried it up to her room. There, she hung it in her closet and squandered several minutes simply gazing at the gown. By the time she finally stopped her daydreaming, she could hear Len and Raja moving sluggishly about in their rooms.

Thandie returned to the dining room and sat behind her laptop. When the girls eventually made it downstairs, Thandie was on her second cup of coffee, well into her emails, and grinning happily.

Len and Raja were discussing their approaching Key West trip. Apparently, they'd asked members of the Babylon staff if they wanted to join them. So far, the girls managed to sway the interest of three dancers, Adam, Michelle, Tiny and Warren.

When Lucinda arrived, Len and Raja followed her into the kitchen and felt compelled to regale her with trip details. Thandie, who'd been glued to her laptop the entire time, didn't have the heart to tell them Lucinda probably didn't understand a majority of what was being said.

The front door opened and Romero appeared around the corner. He nodded at Thandie before strolling into the kitchen. Neither Raja nor Len paused in their chatter to acknowledge him. Thandie imagined the girls were doing a good job of giving him the cold shoulder.

The atmosphere became noticeably frigid when Romero announced he was contemplating going to Key West with their party. There was a high-pitched screech, followed by something slamming.

Moments later, Len and Raja stormed into the dining room. Abruptly, they took their seats behind their laptops and began working, scowling the entire time. Catching movement from the corner of her eye, Thandie looked up to see Romero leaving the kitchen. She could have sworn he was grinning.

What remained of the day passed rather blandly. After Romero's visit, the girls refused to say anything else about Key West.

Meanwhile, Thandie struggled to stay focused. It was a futile attempt. Hourly, the dress seemed to beckon her back to the bedroom to marvel at it, or if nothing else, rub her cheek against the fabric.

Around two o'clock, Thandie gave up the fight and called it quits. Len and Raja leaped from their chairs, and changed into their swimsuits. By the time she powered down her laptop, the girls were lying poolside with earbuds in their ears.

Thandie retired to her room to get ready for her date with Elliot. After she'd showered, fussed over her hair and applied her makeup, she had little time to spare. As she was slipping on the heels she planned to wear tonight, it crossed her mind she should warn the girls she would be going out for a little while. She didn't want them to worry.

Slipping on her robe, she went downstairs. Without having to step onto the back patio she could tell it was no use. Both girls were lying comatose on their lounges. She could hear Raja snoring loudly from where she stood in the living room. Not wanting to disturb them, Thandie scribbled a note on a Post-it and adhered it to the patio door.

When she turned around, she saw Elliot standing in the foyer, watching her. She hadn't heard him. She hadn't even known he was in the house. As she came forward, she studied him. He wore a light gray suit and white dress shirt. The top two buttons were undone, hinting to the smooth skin at the base of his throat.

When she standing before him, he pulled her against him and his mouth was on hers. His hands slid over the curves of her bottom, caressing her possessively. Then he pulled his head back, stared down into her face and said, "You're not dressed."

"I just need to slip on clothes," she said thickly. "I should only be a minute."

Elliot released her and stepped aside. "By all means."

Slightly disorientated from his kiss and feeling unreasonably shy, Thandie slipped past him and hurried up the stairs to her room. She went to her closet and pulled out the gown. Again, she sighed at the sight of it. Taking it off its hanger, she stepped back and nearly jumped out of her skin when she heard a sound behind her. Thandie turned to find Elliot standing a few feet away.

His gaze was sweeping the room, examining the clothing piled on top an unmade bed. Thandie swore to herself, wishing she'd tidied up. Elliot sat down on the edge of her bed, and continued surveying her belongings. The room felt smaller with him in it. Carefully groomed and dressed in his tailored suit, he looked out of place in the cluttered room. However, he seemed unaware of this. He was much more intrigued by the items spilling out of her open suitcase.

Finally, his silver gaze settled on her. Lifting one dark brow, he asked, "Do you need help with your dress?"

She shook her head mutely. When he continued to stare at her, she realized he wasn't going to give her privacy. She supposed none was really needed. He'd seen and touched just about every inch of her body already.

Slipping off her robe, she tossed it onto the bed. Extremely conscious of her nudity, Thandie turned her back on him as she stepped into the gown. She could feel his eyes roving over her bare backside the entire time.

There was not much to the dress. There were no buttons or zipper to fuss over. Only two clasps at the nape of the neck held the whole thing together. Once fastened, the halter looped loosely over her torso, exposing glimpses of the gentle curve of her breasts on either side. The silk felt soft against her bare skin.

"You look lovely," he said in a low rumble.

Thandie glanced up at him from beneath her lashes. He looked enigmatic, as always. The only hint that she had any effect on him was the bulge at the seam of his slacks. For a moment she was transfixed on the swelling mass of flesh beneath the fabric of his trousers, well acquainted with what it was capable of.

Elliot coughed and suddenly stood to his feet. "If you keep staring at me like that, we aren't going anywhere." Taking her hand in his own, he said, "Come along, kitten. The world awaits." With just enough time to grab her purse, Elliot guided her down the hall. Locking the front door behind them, he guided her to the Range Rover.

When they were buckled into their seats, Thandie asked, "Where are you taking us?"

"You'll see," he said vaguely.

"And my passport?" she asked.

"Keep it close to you. It will come in handy."

When it became apparent he wouldn't say anything else, Thandie settled back in her seat and looked out the window. As they rode, Elliot reached out and placed his hand on her thigh. His hand easily slid between the dress's high slits. Thandie now understood why this particular dress might have appealed to him.

Some twenty minutes later, they passed a sign that read

Opa-Locka Executive Airport. Elliot turned onto a side road
that appeared to be for commercial use only. They soon pulled
into a small parking lot just outside a large but unpopulated
airplane hangar. When Thandie turned to Elliot expecting
an explanation, he only smirked in response.

Helping her out of the vehicle, Elliot led her inside the
building where a uniformed man welcomed them by name
and escorted them to a gleaming white private jet. Two more
men were waiting to greet them at the plane's entrance. Recognizing Elliot, both men shook his hand before turning to
introduce themselves to Thandie. She didn't catch their names,
but figured out she'd shaken hands with the captain and co-
pilot before being led on board. Thandie was vaguely aware
of being guided deeper into the cabin, and lured onto a long
leather couch that lined one wall.

The interior of the jet was a vista of buttercream leather
and polished woodgrain surfaces. It was grandeur on a level
she had never seen before. The plush seating was well spaced
out, able to easily accommodate fifteen people with room to
spare. Closed doors at the back of the plane hinted there was
more to be seen.

A handsome man with blond hair appeared from the rear
of the cabin. Introducing himself as James, their flight attendant, he turned to Elliot and asked if he were ready to depart.
Elliot nodded and the man consulted with the captain. Almost immediately the plane began easing out of the hangar.

After they were airborne, she turned to Elliot and asked,
"Is this your jet?"

"No," he said with a shake of his head. "This doesn't belong to me. I travel quite a bit, but not near enough to justify
purchasing something this ostentatious."

"So if it isn't yours…"

"I'm borrowing it from Nico. As well as his staff, of course."

"This is Nico's plane?" Thandie couldn't conceal the shock she felt. She looked around her luxurious surroundings. "What exactly does Nico do?"

Elliot made a waving motion with his hand. "I suppose he does everything, and yet nothing." He thought for a moment. "If you had to categorize him, he could best be described as an international investor."

Thandie nodded her head, intrigued. "And he just let you borrow his plane?"

A slow smile snaked across his lips. "We share quite a few things."

Thandie lifted her brow.

He patted his lap. "Come sit here."

"No, the steward will see us." She squealed when he scooped his hands around her hips, and lifted her onto his lap.

"There," he said. "Isn't that better?"

Thandie was too busy laughing to answer. When he slipped his hand beneath the folds of her dress and caressed her upper thigh, she sighed.

"This is the only way to fly," he said with a chuckle.

"I think it's time you tell me where you're taking me," she insisted.

"Someplace special."

"That's not an answer."

"I'll make a deal with you, Thandie. If I tell you, you can't ask any more questions until we land."

"Agreed. Tell me."

"Havana."

Thandie sat up straighter. "Havana? As in Cuba?"

Elliot tsked. "Remember our deal, pussycat." He kissed the tip of her nose. "No more questions."

"You can't take me away like this and not expect me to have questions."

Grazing his lips against her ear, he said, "We have some time to kill. Shall I give you the grand tour?" When she nodded, he smiled wickedly. "Good. I'd like to start with the bedroom at the back of the cabin."

Shortly thereafter, they landed at a small airport just beyond the city lights. Registering in the country was a bit too easy. Thandie and Elliot handed their passports to an official who glanced at their paperwork and handed it back with a smile and stamped visas.

A car was waiting for them on the tarmac. Sliding into the backseat, Elliot gave directions to the driver. Unable to understand the lengthy Spanish conversation that followed, Thandie turned her attention to the thriving city outside the car's windows. As the car whipped through the streets, Elliot explained they were now in the heart of Havana. He pointed out landmarks, marketplaces and local hangouts. His fondness for the city was obvious. The more he spoke, the more relaxed he seemed. Thandie found she enjoyed simply listening to the sound of his voice and watching his expressions as he leaned over her shoulder to peer out the window.

Elliot had the driver drop them off at a busy intersection that pushed up along the beach and a number of restaurants. He gave the driver a generous amount of Cuban pesos, then Elliot took Thandie's hand, and led her into the busy streets of Havana. Beautiful gothic cathedrals shared the same block as graffitied ruins. Nightclubs oozed jazzy Latin music and shouts of laughter.

Thandie got another shock when several of the shop owners called out Elliot's name and waved to him with wide smiles.

"Do they know you?" she asked when he returned their greetings.

"Yes, they know me rather well," he said with a laugh. "But mostly, they remember my father. He was from the neighborhood."

"How often do you come here?"

He thought for a moment. "At least once or twice a month, if I can manage it."

The streets were crowded with people coming and going, basking in the rhythm of Havana's nightlife. Elliot and Thandie walked the congested sidewalks, wandering in and out of the many clubs and bistros. Street musicians played their guitars and bongos, encouraging couples to dance for them. Included in the rustle of music and voices was the constant sound of cars bustling by and the crush of ocean waves crashing against the shore.

Eventually, Elliot steered them toward the beach. Walking hand-in-hand along the sidewalk, with the ocean on their left, they both felt light. Elliot filled the time by telling her about all the times his parents had brought him here when he was a child and pointing out storefronts he remembered.

He was mid sentence when he stopped and jerked his head back. Thandie turned to see what had caught his attention. A peddler had stationed his cart a few steps ahead of them. A variety of trinkets hung from the wagon: seashell necklaces, wooden toy cars, airplanes made out of recycled soda cans. Elliot stepped forward and peered down at a something small resting on a makeshift shelf. Thandie stepped closer to see it was a small circular object made of wood. Carved into the surface were the words *Industriales Havana*.

Elliot reached out to hold the object in his hand. He flipped it over in his palm and a diamond shaped emblem with a lion etched across it came into view, *Leones Azules*. An odd expression shadowed Elliot's face.

"What is it?" Thandie asked.

"It's a yo-yo," he said in a tight voice. Pulling a string Thandie hadn't noticed at first, he slipped his finger into the small loop, and dropped the wooden yo-yo. It rolled down the length of the string before snapping back into his palm, as if summoned by magic. He pointed to the carved emblem. "It's the *Industriales* symbol, a local baseball team." He palmed the toy in his hand thoughtfully. "I used to have one of these," he said. "It was a cheap little thing. Something your parents give you to keep you occupied." He squeezed the toy in his hand. "My father bought it for me when I was…six years old I believe."

"What happened to it?" she asked softly.

He shook his head. "I can't remember. I lost it."

"Do you want to get that one?"

Elliot abruptly shook his head and placed the yo-yo back on the chart's shelf with a loud smack. The old man working the cart, looked up in surprise. Elliot muttered an apology, fished out a crisp dollar bill from his wallet and pushed it into the man's hand. Without even looking back, he walked off. Thandie was left to stare after him. Giving the old man an apologetic smile, she chased after Elliot.

Yanking his arm, she turned him around. "What was that all about?"

He glowered back at the cart, as if it had done something to offend him. And then, without warning, he pulled Thandie to him and crushed her lips beneath his own. His mouth was hot and demanding, giving her no choice but to melt under the passion. With his hands stroking wide circles against her back, Thandie soon forgot the explanation she'd been demanding.

It was Elliot who eventually pulled away. His eyes were

cloudy with passion, but a smile tugged at his mouth. "I need you," he said roughly. Without another word, he guided her across the street, waving his hand to a man who lounged against his car.

It was the same driver who'd driven them from the airport. Elliot had somehow maneuvered their wanderings into a large circle, resulting in them ending up not far from where they started. He must have paid the man to wait for them.

It wasn't until Thandie was settled into the backseat did she begin to feel a dull ache in her feet. Leaning into Elliot's side, she listened to him and the driver chat. Again, she marveled at the sound of his voice. Low, distinct and controlled.

She must have dozed off, because the next thing she knew, Elliot was nudging her awake. She blinked sleepily at him and then looked around. The car was parked in front of a luxurious colonial-style villa in a rather desirable neighborhood.

Lights reflected off the white exterior, making the building appear taller than it actually was. It glowed in the darkness, emphasizing slender columns and numerous terraces.

"Where are we?" she asked.

"*Detrás de la Fachada,*" he said. "It literally means, 'behind the facade.'" Handing the driver a tip, Elliot slid out of the car before turning to help Thandie. "It is also my home."

"You live here?" she asked, inclining her head to the house.

In answer, he only smiled. Just as they were walking up to the gate that secured the perimeter of the grounds, the front door of the home opened. A native man came out. He smiled brightly at Elliot as he unlocked the gate for them. He and Elliot exchanged words before the man disappeared around a corner of the house. Ushering Thandie inside the house, Elliot locked the door behind him.

"Who was that?" Thandie asked, feeling like a broken record.

"Manuel," he said. "He and his wife are caretakers for the house."

"Do they live here?"

"Yes, in a small house at the rear of the property." Pulling his phone out of his pocket, he studied the screen, making a peculiar expression as he read whatever had caught his attention. "Make yourself at home," he said, still looking at the phone's display. "I need to return a call."

As Elliot drifted into another room, Thandie went on a tour. She floated from one room to another, marveling at the architecture and stylish decor. At the end of her careful exploration, she'd confirmed the villa boasted a small garden, terraces overlooking the sea, a living room, four bedrooms, three bathrooms and a large American-style kitchen.

"Does it pass inspection?"

Thandie jumped at the sound of Elliot's voice. He'd sneaked up behind her while she'd been looking out a window in what she assumed to be the master bedroom. Turning to look at him, she said, "I can't help but notice this villa looks brand new. How old is it?"

"It's just over five years old." He came to her, stopping when he was only a foot away. "What sat here before then was basically ruins."

"And you own this house?"

"Consider it my inheritance." He brushed the back of his hand against her cheek, and said in a low whisper, "No more questions."

Slowly, he reached for the clasps at the back of her neck. Thandie stood still while Elliot helped her out of her dress before stripping out of his own clothes. At his prompting, they showered together. And when they were done, Elliot dried them both off before leading her to the massive bed. She slid beneath him, opening her legs in a silent but desperate invitation. Elliot cradled himself between her thighs, and leaned forward to kiss her deeply, passionately. When he pulled back, they were both gasping for breath. Elliot's voice was husky when he said, "I intend to make you purr for me tonight, pussycat."

And then he did just that.

They slept well into the afternoon. The flight, a night of sightseeing, followed by satisfying sex had taken its toll on them. Elliot was the first to wake, and he made quick work of getting himself together. When he emerged from the bathroom he was dressed in white jeans and polo shirt. Thandie grimaced at how effortless it was for him to look picture perfect. He could have been posing for a Ralph Lauren photo shoot.

Leaving her to rest a little longer, Elliot went to a nearby shop to purchase her some clothes. When he returned, Thandie changed into the cotton dress he presented her with. When she asked about undergarments, he gave her a devilish grin and insisted Cuba did not sell panties.

By the time they finished eating breakfast, prepared by Manuel's wife, the car had arrived to take them back to the airport. The ride to the airstrip was brief. The jet's engines were running when their car pulled alongside it on the tarmac. Just as before, the crew welcomed them on board.

Taking his seat, Elliot immediately pulled Thandie into his lap. Five minutes later, they were airborne. As the plane climbed, Elliot held her close, and they watched Cuba disappear behind a veil of clouds. Then Elliot spent most of the flight talking on his cell phone. It had been ringing nonstop since they woke up.

Thandie tucked her face into the crook of his neck while she listened to him juggle one phone call after the next. Every so often, she smiled when she felt his palm stroke her breasts or upper thigh.

The flight back to Miami was over far too soon. Thandie regretted not having more time to see more of Havana, but she was thankful for their time away. She'd seen Elliot in a whole new light. He could be kind and responsive, sweet and caring. She felt something had changed between them during this trip. She was closer to seeing the real Elliot Richards than she had ever been before.

Chapter Twenty-Four

He was gone when she woke up.

Thandie knew he would be even before she opened her eyes. There was no bedside note waiting for her, filled with sugary words and passionate promises. He was simply gone.

Thandie felt vaguely hollow inside. However, it was probably for the best he'd left when he did; better for her, at least. She was suffering from charm-overload. She needed a break from the beautiful dresses, private jet and magnificent villa on a tropical island. One more week with that sort of treatment, and she would be completely smitten. Distance was a good thing.

For a long time she lay there, breathing in his scent. It was as heady and tantalizing as the man himself. Thandie tried to keep her emotions in check, but it was difficult. A million questions ran through her head all at once; questions she could not afford to ponder. Where was he? Was he alone? Was he with another woman?

No, she could not go *there*. Not even in the quiet recesses of her mind could she allow herself to fret over those questions. That type of thinking veered too much into the girlfriend category, and one thing Thandie definitely wasn't was Elliot Richards's girlfriend.

But did she want to be?

Their conversation from a few nights past came back to her. "I don't do girlfriends," he'd said. He'd meant every word. Not that she'd been surprised. Thandie had known Elliot was a ladies' man from the beginning. She'd entertained no fantasies that she was the only woman in his life, or bed. Their sexual encounters had been a combination of lust and convenience. Half of that scenario would no longer exist when she returned to New York in a few short weeks. So when had the situation changed for her? Was it the trip to Havana? No, it had been before that. But when?

Thandie squeezed her eyes shut, trying to block out the direction her thoughts were going. She could not let herself journey that dark path. She couldn't afford it. She would lose something valuable if she stumbled down that road. This was just sex. Plain and simple. It could only be about sex. Hard, satisfying, can-barely-walk-in-the-morning sex.

Thandie threw back the covers and stood up. She was just about to round the bed's edge when she came to an abrupt halt. She blinked. At the precise spot where she kept stubbing her toe, there was empty space. The bench was not there. Confused, she looked around. There, pushed along the wall, sat the offending piece of furniture. Had Elliot moved it? If so, why?

Refusing to place any importance on such an odd action, Thandie brushed past the spot and quietly tiptoed to the opposite side of the house. As soon as she was in her own room, she began to wash up.

By the time she'd pulled on clothes, there was a loud commotion from down the hall. Len and Raja's voices continued to rise by the minute. Thandie sighed tiredly. It was hard to imagine the girls could find something to argue about when they'd only been awake for half an hour. Stepping into the hall, Thandie quietly eased down the hall. The last thing she needed today was to be sucked into the fray.

Entering the kitchen, she began rummaging through the cabinets, searching for something appetizing. Grabbing a box of cereal from the pantry, she poured herself a bowl.

She heard the doorbell, and went to answer it. Warren stood on the doorstep, dressed in a suit and wearing his customary smile.

"Hey, kiddo!" he said brightly, giving her a hug as he stepped inside. "You look relaxed."

"Hi Warren. What are you doing here?" she asked.

"I promised Len and Raja I'd take them shopping weeks ago." He shrugged. "They finally called me with a date."

Thandie nodded her head. This would explain the arguing she's heard earlier. Waving him toward the kitchen, she said, "You never should have offered."

"I know," Warren said with a sigh. He looked around the living areas. "Is Lucinda here?"

"I'm afraid not. It's just me and the girls." She wrinkled her brows. "Aren't you a little overdressed to go on a shopping spree?"

"I had a meeting this morning."

Normally, Thandie wouldn't pry, but she could tell from the giddy expression on Warren's face, he was desperate to say something. "Did it go well?" she asked.

"Great." He slid onto a stool at the kitchen island. "Better than great... Stupendous."

Surprised, she asked, "Have things improved with your family?"

He grimaced. "Nothing new on that front I'm afraid."

"Oh," she said, a little disappointed for him. Taking another stab at it, she asked, "How are things going with the divorce?"

Warren's face split into a grin as bright as sunshine. "It's done," he said.

"Done?"

"Done," he said with a nod of his head. "We finally signed the papers. It's a miracle, Thandie. Wife Number Five has been playing hardball for the longest, and *voilà*." He snapped his fingers. "Just like that, she became agreeable. She accepted the original deal we offered her."

"That's fantastic, Warren."

"You're telling me! I guess she has a heart after all. Goodness knows, I never saw it during the time I was married to her." He grinned. "We signed the documents this morning. Now we wait for the judge to make it official."

"Wow," she breathed. "I'm happy for you. Congratulations."

"I'm a free man," he boasted. "The ladies of Miami had better look out."

Thandie sighed heavily. "Warren, have you thought about letting the ink dry on your dicorce papers before you get back out there?"

Warren furrowed his brows at her, as if trying to decode her words. "Why on earth would I want to do that? Life is too short to play it safe."

Thandie threw up her hands. "All right. Don't say I didn't try to be the voice of reason." Leaning her hip against the counter, she folded her arms across her chest. "So, now that you're single, what are you going to do next?"

Warren eyes crinkled at the beginnings of a smile. "You wouldn't happen to have a single and much younger sister, would you?"

Thandie laughed. "You never change, Warren." A thumping sound came from upstairs. Thandie was reminded the girls had been arguing. "Let me tell the girls you're here."

"Wait." Warren's hand shot out to stop her. "I wanted to talk to you for a moment." When Thandie turned to look at him, Warren went mute for a moment. Finally, he said a little too casually, "I see you and Elliot have gotten rather close."

Thandie wagged her finger at him. "That topic is off limits."

"I'm sure it is," he said. "And you know I wouldn't mention it unless it was important."

Thandie's brow shot in the air.

"Okay, okay. I admit I'm nosy," he confessed. "But this is serious." He gazed at her with pale watery eyes. "I like Elliot. He's a very sharp businessman, but he is not boyfriend material, Thandie."

"Warren—"

"Wait, just hear me out, and then I'll shut up." He took a deep breath before rushing on. "He always has an angle. He has a lot of moving pieces, if you know what I mean." When she was about to cut him off, Warren held up his hand. "Just let me finish. I care about you, Thandie. And as a friend, I'm telling you this because I know you're not ready for what will come of this affair." He paused before delicately continuing. "Elliot isn't a bad guy, Thandie. He's just not right for you."

"I know you mean well, Warren—"

"You don't know him," he cut in sharply. "You don't know him at all. I've seen a lot, Thandie. Believe me when I say you have no idea what Elliot is about."

The hard edge in his voice chilled her. Warren was rarely serious about anything. She'd only seen this solemn expression on his face once before—when she'd witnessed him drunk and depressed after meeting with his son. Just as it had been that night, Warren looked his age; weathered and broken. His sincerity was evident. He cared about her, and she loved him for that.

"I appreciate the warning." Standing up, she leaned forward and kissed the top of his white head. "But you don't need to worry about me. I can take care of myself."

Thankfully, Len and Raja chose that moment to come bounding down the stairs. Whatever disagreement they'd had earlier was apparently far behind them now, because they were all smiles when they saw Warren. With the ferocity of one of Florida's infamous hurricanes, they snatched up Warren and practically pulled him out the front door. He hadn't stood a chance.

After Warren and the girls had left, Thandie retreated to her room and threw herself across her bed. Warren's words reverberated in her head. He hadn't told her anything she hadn't already known. However, hearing a warning from Warren Radcliffe, the most irresponsible person she knew when it came to relationships, was ominous.

You have no idea what Elliot is about.

Thandie closed her eyes as the words echoed in her head. Warren was right, of course. Elliot was a mystery to her.

Again, she had to close her mind to the questions that assailed her, and try to think of ways to occupy her time. Without the girls around, she was a bit lost.

Thinking hard, she considered her options. She could go shopping or even squeeze a massage session in. However, the more she considered her choices, the more exhausted she became.

Spying her bikini, she changed into it. It was a beautiful day outside her window, and she could use a little sun. Collecting a towel, she thought she'd lie out by the pool, soak up the sun, and read a few fashion magazines.

Setting herself on one of the lounges, she pulled the latest issue of *Mode* magazine onto her lap. *Mode* was a national syndicate, quickly growing in popularity. Thandie had become addicted to it months earlier.

On its glossy cover was a picture of a beautiful woman wearing a dress that looked to have been painted on. Her tousled ash-brown hair, pouty lips and smoldering eyes gave her a sultry appearance. Beneath the photo, in large bold letters, read "31 Reasons Why We Love Tasha Tate." Next to the cover model was a subtitle reading "Sebastian Dunhill: Hollywood's New Heartthrob!"

Thandie flipped through the magazine, humming in agreement when a valid point had been made and folding down pages she wanted to reread. Her mind was racing. If she could get just one of these stars to make a guest appearance at Babylon, she would be immensely pleased. But it would mean little if there were no photos to publicize. She would have to talk to Elliot again, see if she could convince him to allow press into the club at the very least for the final show she was organizing.

Thandie continued to flip through the magazine, reading every article that struck her interest until she was exhausted by the possibilities. They had so much to do. She'd been in Miami for two months now and the amount of work required before her time here was done seemed overwhelming.

Tossing the magazine aside, she rolled onto her stomach and considered her options. She smiled quietly to herself. Yes, if she did this right, the results would be amazing. Visions flashed in her head of things to come. Yes, this could certainly work. She began running through her plans step by step. At some point, she drifted off to sleep.

Thandie awoke to the wondrous feeling of having all her stress washed away. She gave a satisfied purr of contentment and wiggled her bottom in delight. It was not until she felt a familiar warm caress cup her butt that she forced her eyes open.

Sitting on the edge of her lounge, his large hands massaging the backs of her thighs, was Elliot.

"The princess awakes," he drawled.

Thandie shielded her eyes against the sunlight. "What are you doing here?"

"How many times are you going to keep asking me that question? I live here. Where else would I be?"

"But why are you here?" The question came out much harsher than she'd meant it to.

"Enjoying the sights," he said with a wink.

Looking down at her cleavage, she placed a protective hand over her breasts.

He gave a wicked grin. "Haven't we done this before?"

"What do you want, Elliot?"

"What makes you so sure I want something? Maybe I just missed you, pussycat."

"Sweet words don't become you."

His dark brow lifted. "So you say." Looking out at the endless ocean, a gentle breeze ruffled his hair, making a thick lock fall over his brow. It made him look innocent and touchable. But the image was dashed when he raked his fingers through his hair, forcing the renegade tresses back into place. "I'm having guests over for dinner tonight," he said. "Afterward, they will be escorted to the club and treated as my personal guests. I would like you to join us."

"Who are they?"

"Does it really matter?"

"That depends," she countered.

Elliot stood and gave her one parting smile before coming to his feet and heading back to the house. Shouting over his shoulder, he said, "Dinner will be served at eight. Be ready."

And just like that, he was gone. Thandie watched him disappear into the shade of the patio. She couldn't help but marvel at his mysterious nature. How was it he could be both honest and elusive at the same time? She always felt he was being open with her, but there was a dark side to him, a secret he hid. A secret so well-hidden it no longer required effort on his part to conceal it, it just came naturally. She wondered if she would ever know the real Elliot Richards.

Thandie dressed carefully. She'd not yet had the opportunity to question Elliot again regarding his dinner guests. Were they business partners or friends? Elliot didn't seem to have many friends. She considered herself an example. They'd slept together often, and yet he was still an enigma.

She could feel the blood rush to her cheeks at the memory of their last time together. When they were alone, he was wonderfully real. She knew exactly what he wanted and when he wanted it. And during the few times she questioned him, he verbalized his desires, explaining how he wished her to move and how it made him feel.

He made her feel…beautiful. Yes, he made her feel sexy. Until now, she'd never really considered herself as such. Sure, she'd worked hard to maintain the body she had, but she'd always considered it a necessity to her job. The way most people considered a car, or a well-cut suit as part of their career attire.

She was always completely under his spell.

But outside of the bedroom, she was brutally aware of the fact she knew nothing about him. Nor he of her.

This train of thought concerned her, because it led to a series of questions she wasn't quite sure she wanted answers to and which confused her, affecting her judgment. She told herself it was too early to consider such things. This thing between her and Elliot was simply a fling. And who was to say they would ever sleep together again? He was a player. He would soon tire of her. With luck, she would be back in New York when that inevitable event occurred.

"I could fuck you right now."

She turned around to see Elliot standing in her room. She gave him a slow appraisal. He was wearing another one of his perfectly cut suits. This one was gleaming black, worn with an emerald green dress shirt. The colors complemented his dark looks superbly. Thandie didn't doubt he knew how breathtaking he was.

Elliot closed the bedroom door behind him, approaching her. "If I didn't know my guests would be here any moment, I'd rip that dress right off you."

"You've done it before."

"Yes, I have," he said slowly. "And the night is still young."

"Who's coming to dinner?"

"You'll see soon enough." Looking down at the necklace she held in her hands, he asked, "May I?"

Taking the necklace carefully into his hands, he stepped behind her and clasped the lock in place. He kissed the very spot the necklace joined at the nape of her neck. She could feel the goose bumps pucker all over her body.

"Thank you," she murmured.

"The pleasure was all mine."

She turned to face him. His nearness and the fact they were in the intimate surroundings of her bedroom made the simple task of breathing a challenge. Thinking up a sensible sentence was impossible.

"Where are the girls?" he asked.

"Warren took them out. I doubt I'll see them until morning."

"Convenient."

"For whom?"

"For us." His eyes went dark with want.

Thandie shook her head and took a step backward. "Elliot, I want to strike a compromise."

"What do you have in mind?"

"I want you to allow select journalists into the club."

"I believe I made it very clear where I stand on this issue." Turning, he left the room and sailed down the hall leading to the stairs.

"Yes, you have," she said quickly, chasing after him. "But I have an idea that might be of interest to you."

"No."

"Aren't you even curious about my suggestion?" She pulled on his sleeve, slowing his progress down the stairs. He turned, looking up at her with a somewhat annoyed expression.

"No, Thandie, I'm not." He continued down the stairs and crossed the living area. She caught up with him, stepping in front of him and forcing him to take note of her.

"Having press present will only help the club. The marketing behind it would be invaluable."

"It goes against everything I stand for, Thandie. People come to my clubs for the exclusivity. I make a lot of money to keep their party methods out of the papers. I'm not selling out so you can get your name in the press."

"This has nothing to do with me."

"You're a PR rep. You live to get your name in print."

"At least listen to what I have to say."

"My answer is no."

"Just one photographer. You can personally approve them if you like."

"No."

"They'll only have access to the arena floor."

"No."

Desperate, she pulled on his arm to stop him from walking away again. "Anything you want, Elliot. Just work with me on this. We need the press. I'll agree to any outrageous demands you might have."

"Anything?"

"Yes," she pleaded, "even if it's some obscure photographer no one has ever heard of."

"Anything." He said this quietly to himself.

"Yes, dammit. Now will you agree?"

"I'll agree to consider it."

She nearly jumped for joy.

"But," he said thoughtfully, "I'll need a lot of persuading."

She recognized his heated gaze, and she immediately re-leased her hold on his arm. "What kind of persuasion?"

"The kind only you can provide."

"But—we've already—"

He shook his head slowly. "Not even close."

"Am I interrupting?" Thandie gave a start at the sound of Nico's voice. He strolled into the living room wearing a smart gray suit and a big smile. "I can come back if you like."

Elliot gave him the same look of indifference he shone on everyone. "Prompt as ever."

"My mother raised me well." If possible, Nico grinned even broader. "Another car pulled in behind me. I believe Matrix has arrived with the Sinclairs."

Elliot nodded. And with that simple gesture, Nico left the room. Thandie was still frustrated by their earlier conversation and the sudden arrival and departure of Nico. She pressed her hands to her cheeks and hoped she didn't look as flustered as she felt. She glanced at Elliot and was surprised to see he was staring at her. A slow smile crept across his lips. Leaning toward her, he kissed her lightly on the lips. When their lips parted he whispered the words, "Not even close."

There was a burst of laughter coming from the foyer. After

a few seconds, Nico entered the room with three visitors trailing behind him.

"Look who I found," Nico announced.

Matrix appeared ahead of the group. Instead of shaking her hand, he surprised Thandie by kissing her on the cheek. He held her as long as possible before winking at Elliot, who only sighed tiredly before pushing Matrix aside.

Following Nico and Matrix into the room was a handsome couple. The man was blond-haired with clear blue eyes and a Colgate smile. He had a protective arm wrapped around the waist of a pretty African-American woman. She was physical opposites from Thandie. Where Thandie was tall and slender, this woman was petite and curvy. Her shapely figure was feminine and very sexy. Her long brown hair lay like silk over her brown shoulders, and her heart-shaped face glowed with life.

"Nick Sinclair," Elliot said as he approached them.

Nick's face split into a wide grin. "Elliot." The two men clapped each other warmly on the shoulder. "You remember Laney, don't you?"

"How could I forget?" Elliot said in a voice that was far too charming.

Nick didn't seem to like that, and he struggled to hide a frown. "Watch it, Elliot. Don't forget I'm quite jealous where my wife is concerned."

"More like a Neanderthal," Laney teased. Stepping away from her husband, she hugged Elliot. "It's great to see you again. Thank you for the wedding gift. You really shouldn't have."

"Nonsense. You two deserve to have a trip without business getting in the way." He winked at Nick. "Did you enjoy yourselves?"

"Absolutely," Laney said with a laugh. "Although I'm not sure if I'm as desirable with the weight I've put on." She smoothed her hand across what appeared to be a perfectly flat stomach.

Nick pulled her back into his side. "You're more beautiful now than you've ever been, babe."

Elliot rolled his eyes. "Newlyweds." He turned to Thandie and offered his hand. "Let me introduce you to my newest staff member. This is Thandie Shaw. Thandie, this is Nicolas Sinclair and his lovely wife, Laney."

After finishing the introductions, Elliot led them into the dining room, where the glass tabletop had been beautifully decorated. The smell of fresh-cut flowers made the air deliciously sweet. Small votive candles were placed around the table. The candlelight reflected off the glass surface of the table, making the setting look as if it were floating on a sliver of light. The feeling was intimate, romantic even, and Thandie could not help but be pleased she was seated at Elliot's side.

Thandie found dinner conversation to be delightful. Laney and Nick were a charming couple. They flirted with each other and even had the modesty to make fun of themselves. Elliot, Nico and Matrix entertained themselves by flirting with Laney, something that clearly annoyed Nick. Nick's obvious jealousy was endearing, and Laney was practically glowing with affection for her husband.

Laney was intrigued by Thandie's profession and literally radiated excitement when she asked questions. It fascinated her that Thandie actually knew famous people. Thandie was sure Elliot would certainly have more exciting celebrity stories, but he appeared quite content to sit back and listen to the women talk.

The questions kept coming—Laney wanting to know who looked better in person, who was a jerk, and where did they shop. The conversation grew, and the two became fast friends.

It did not take long before they were joining forces in quick word battles with the guys.

When they'd finished their entrées, Thandie stood to help the cooks Elliot had hired to prepare tonight's dinner clear the table. Laney, who clearly needed to stand and stretch, offered to assist. They made quick work of collecting the dinner utensils before disappearing into the kitchen to help prepare the dessert. This was an ideal situation. It gave Thandie a chance to speak to Laney privately.

When Thandie was sure they could not be overheard by the men in the next room, she asked, "How long have you and Nick been married?"

"Officially, two months. Unofficially, four months." When Thandie gave her a quizzical look, Laney lifted her shoulders in a slight shrug. "It's kinda complicated."

"I can't help but notice Nick's the first of his circle of friends to be married."

Laney looked toward the table of friends who were now speaking in low voices. Her expression looked momentarily troubled and just as quickly vanished. "Nick and I have grown a lot together. A year ago—heck, probably even a few months earlier—I don't think he would've been able to handle the concept of marriage. But—" she smiled to herself "—like I said, we've been through a lot."

"How long have you known Elliot?"

"Now we get to the heart of things?" Laney teased.

Thandie gave a shy smile. "I was hoping not to come across as obvious."

"You weren't. Don't worry." Laney gave the guys a quick look. "I haven't known him long. In truth, I've only met him a few times. But he's always been a complete gentleman. Very charming rascal. He makes quite an impression, wouldn't you agree?"

"I guess that goes without saying."

"Just keep your eyes open," Laney said.

"Are you going to expand on that tidbit of information?"

Laney shook her head. "Nope. You're a smart girl. I have no doubt you know what you're getting yourself into. Men like Nick and Elliot attract certain women, and they've become accustomed to the attention. I love Nick and I have no doubt he loves me, but every so often, I'm reminded of his past. So from one woman to another, the best advice I could ever offer is keep your eyes open."

"What are you two whispering about?" Nick strolled into the kitchen and wrapped his arms around Laney's small waist. "Are you trying to steal my bride away from me, Thandie?"

"I was thinking about it," she said mildly.

Nick kissed his wife of the cheek. "Well, take a number."

"Right behind me." Matrix entered the room, a wicked grin on his face.

"You'll have to wait your turn." Nico followed his friend. "Laney promised to run off with me first." He winked at Laney. She blushed. Nick frowned. Thandie laughed.

Elliot leaned in the doorway. "Are we going to have Laney—I mean, dessert—or what?" This made Matrix and Nico howl with laughter. Nick was practically growling.

They decided to eat around the massive kitchen island— miniature lava cakes with scoops of vanilla ice cream. They ate quickly; the playful banter continued, but the guys seemed to have agreed to a truce not to further annoy Nick.

When they were completely satisfied, they prepared to leave. They were going to Babylon, but tonight would be different. Neither she nor Elliot were working; they were VIP guests.

Elliot pulled her into the seat next to him, and he pressed his lips to hers for a quick skin-tingling kiss.

Upon arriving at their destination, Adam welcomed their group into the VIP area and led them to the elevator leading up to the Tower. Thandie yanked on Elliot's arm in warning. He only laughed.

When the lift doors slid open, the lush view of shiny satin cushions and candlelight filled her eyes. The room was completely empty, except for a bartender and waiter. She looked up to see Elliot grinning at her.

They made themselves comfortable on the cushions. They were each handed flutes of champagne; Laney received bottled water. They toasted to a night of friends. A second round of drinks was delivered, and the music soon became irresistible. They danced, and as the drinks kept coming, Thandie was grateful for the privacy of the Tower. Matrix and Nico disappeared. Nick, Laney, Elliot and Thandie settled into their own pockets of the room.

Nick began kissing Laney's shoulder, the base of her collarbone and then her neck, just behind the earlobe. As his lips made a slow progression, his hand, which had been on her knee at first, had now begun to slide up her leg, the fingers brushing her inner thighs. Laney released a bubbly laugh before pushing his hand away and closing her legs tightly. But Nick would not be denied the pleasures of his wife. In answer to her denial of his advances, he slipped his hand beneath her knee and, rather aggressively, pulled her leg up so that it hooked over his lap. Now, with her legs wide open, she was conveniently exposed to his eager hands.

Her dress fell over her thighs, which obstructed any view of Nick's seeking fingers, but there was no denying what was happening. Laney quit trying to detour her husband.

They kissed with hunger; one kiss melted into the next. Nick knew how to pleasure his wife, if her gasps and whimpers were any evidence. Laney's eyes sparkled with mischief, when she pulled his hand from between her thighs, held his fingers up to her lips and slowly began sucking them.

"So you like to watch," Elliot said from behind her. Stepping closer, he placed a hand on her hip, pulling her into him, pressing her against his growing erection. When he spoke, his lips brushed the lobe of her ear. "Is this how you like it, puss? Do they turn you on?"

Nuzzling her with his nose, she lifted her gaze to the couple. Thandie could not take her eyes off them. Laney's dress was tossed over her hips. Nick was on his knees, his face between her legs, his hands massaging her full breasts. So aroused, Laney's back arched deeply as she threw her head back and moaned.

"Do you like to watch them?" He nibbled on her shoulder. "That could be you. I could be deep inside you right now." He gave a soft chuckle when she moaned. "But you want to keep watching them, don't you? Oh, pussycat—" he cupped her breasts, grinding his pelvis into her backside "—you want me to take you while you watch." Elliot bit her shoulder, and she groaned in both pain and pleasure. "Wait until he gets her on her hands and knees," he whispered. "She does this thing with her back that should be illegal."

"You've seen them having sex before?"

He chuckled into her ear. "Wouldn't you love to know?"

Without warning, Elliot lifted Thandie and carried her to the nearest lounge. He dropped her onto the lounge. Pulling her legs into the air, he easily turned her onto her stomach. He forced her onto her knees by pulling her hips into the air. In one fluid motion, he yanked her dress up high over her hips. There was no time for foreplay. He was inside her within seconds. Thandie's groan came out as a scream. She was aching and slick with cream. A climax was rushing up her spine. She bit her lip hard as Elliot moved inside her. It was fast and hard, everything she so desperately needed right now. Her arms were shaking, and sweat gathered in the valley of her breasts and dripped off the tips of her nipples.

"Watch them, baby." He urged. "Watch."

The ability to concentrate on anything else but Elliot was absurd, if not impossible. She wanted only to climax. The need was so absolute it pained her.

"Watch them," he demanded in a hoarse voice.

Panting, she lifted her head to the couple. Nick had somehow managed to undo his pants, flip his wife onto her stomach and free his engorged cock. Laney was on her hands and knees, her ass swaying in the air as he eased himself inside her.

"I love when she does that," Elliot groaned.

With each inch, Laney's back arched deeply, and by the time Nick was fully embedded inside her, he was wild with desire. Gripping her hips, he rammed her backside with long strong thrusts. Laney's large breasts, now free of her dress, bounced and jiggled with every thrust. Their moans of ecstasy filled the room, and Thandie could feel herself coming.

A rush of cold white lightening rippled through her body. From her stomach to her neck, the spasms of pleasure rocked her body. She moaned as the feeling left her shaking uncontrollably. She was momentarily blinded by the sheer force of pleasure, and she fought to catch her breath.

She could feel Elliot's body tense before going into overdrive. His cock swelled as he jutted his pelvis determinedly. He cursed as he was overcome. He rode out the sensation, his breathing labored.

When they were both spent, he pulled the condom off and tossed it into a nearby receptacle. She turned onto her side, and he lay beside her. Easing inside her, he rocked against her while they watched Nick and Laney's lovemaking. Neither Thandie nor Elliot spoke. They kissed often and stroked each other passionately. In that moment, Thandie felt that something had changed between them. Something had happened, and they'd both felt it. She was suddenly overwhelmed with emotion. She felt like laughing and crying at the same time.

She turned her face away from him so he wouldn't witness the battle of feelings swimming inside her. Elliot ruined her plans by cupping her face and forcing her to look at him. He rolled on top of her and stared into her eyes, and for a second the world stopped. They were now playing on mutual ground. She saw understanding in his expression and yet he seemed distant at the same time. He lowered his head and kissed her. This was a kiss unlike any they'd shared before. It was both demanding and giving. It scared her. He scared her, and she had to close her eyes to stop from crying.

They came together this time. The moans and groans surrounding them became deafening, but they were in a world all their own. She became lost in their kisses, and with great panic, realized she had also become lost in him.

Chapter Twenty-Five

Thandie awoke in Elliot's bed the next morning and was unclear on exactly how she had gotten there. She remembered random scenes from the night before. Laney and Nick's naked bodies making endless love and Elliot and her taking each other over and over again, staring into each other's eyes, saying nothing. It felt as if it was a dream, something that happened long ago.

Thandie stared at the ceiling, the familiar scent of clean linens and light fragrance of lemons she'd come to recognize as Elliot's home filled her senses.

Elliot rested peacefully on his side. His dark hair hid his eyes and most of his nose. She figured she could gladly watch him sleep for hours. He was beautiful. As she stared at him, a strange feeling, identical to the one from last night, captured her. She felt happy and sad all at once. And again, just as it had the night before, it overwhelmed her. She turned away. There was something very wrong.

She managed to leave without disturbing Elliot. She had to put a little time and a lot of space between herself and him.

★ ★ ★

She loved him.

Thandie could hardly believe it, but there could be no denying what she felt. She was in love with Elliot.

She'd left his room, and returned to her own bed. She'd tried to get to sleep, but her mind was whirling. Then the revelation hit her.

Placing her hand over her heart, she tried to slow the erratic beating. It would do no good if she had a heart attack before she figured out what she was going to do about the mess she found herself in. She needed to get out of the house to clear her head. Throwing back the covers, she strode into the bathroom to clean up. After a quick shower and throwing on something clean, she headed downstairs.

Thandie was still in a state of shock when she drifted into the kitchen where Len and Raja were having breakfast. Over cold bowls of cereal and lightly buttered slices of toast, the girls were in the throes of another animated conversation. Some of their antics even made Thandie laugh.

"Sweet Jesus! All three of you together, and not arguing!" They all looked up to see Warren Radcliffe standing in the doorway, looking throughly pleased with the scene he'd just discovered.

Thandie, still laughing, rolled her eyes.

Len skipped across the room and wrapped her arms around Warren's neck, giving him a light peck on the cheek. Then she squealed. "Look at her!" And she pointed out the window at the pool where a woman lounged. Aside from the thin gold chain around her neck, her oversize sunglasses, and the tiniest of thongs, she was completely naked.

Thandie and Raja stood to gaze at the mysterious stranger. They had to practically shove Warren out of the way to get a better look. He shoved back to keep his vantage point. For five seconds, the three of them struggled with each other, completely unaware they were doing so in their efforts to gain the best view.

The woman had a rich golden glow all over her body. Every inch of her tanned skin was lathered with shiny suntan oil.

After getting over the shock of a semi-nude woman sunbathing scant yards away, the woman's other physical attributes became more defined. Her breasts were too perfectly shaped to be natural. Her chin was sharp, and her jawbones were uniquely high. Beneath her large sunglasses rested a long distinguished nose, which lay above full pouty lips. Tendrils of thick dark hair had escaped the knot of hair resting atop her head, causing them to fan the sides of her face. She was a very pretty woman…and very familiar.

Thandie gasped. She was the mysterious beauty Thandie had seen visiting Elliot at the club. And now she was here, in Elliot's home, sunning herself by his pool. How had she gotten in? Did she have a key to the house? And if so, Thandie wondered exactly how well she and Elliot knew each other.

"What's going on?"

Elliot's low voice broke the silence in the room.

Thandie turned to face him and was immediately sorry she had. His hair, obviously wet from a shower, was raked back from his temples. He wore fitted jeans which hung low on his hips. His shirt had been thrown carelessly over his shoulder, allowing him to adjust his wristwatch with his free hand. But it was his eyes that held her prisoner. His gaze said he had forgotten nothing that had passed between them the night before. The devilish grin tugging at the tip of his lips told her he'd relish reminding her.

His eyes never leaving Thandie, he asked, "What's the cause for all the pushing?"

"It looks like you have a visitor," Len said helpfully.

"She's making quite an impression on us," Raja added.

At these words, Elliot finally tore his eyes away from Thandie. Tall enough to see over all their shoulders, he looked past them toward the pool. His gaze was fixed. Other than his lips drawing into a thin line, he gave no outward reaction, making it impossible to read his expression. Elliot stared a moment longer before saying, "Excuse me."

They watched silently as he crossed the room and stepped onto the elongated patio. His long strides ate up the distance to the pool's edge, making a direct path to the woman. His back was facing them, but there was a stiffness in his broadset shoulders. They were too far to hear anything being discussed, but it was clear Elliot was not exactly thrilled to see her.

Apparently accustomed to his moods, the woman pulled her sunglasses above her head and gave him a slow smile. Elliot responded by saying something that unsettled her, because her grin faltered for an instant. Within seconds, it was quickly replaced. She slid her sunglasses back over her face and stretched her long limbs, doing so for his benefit rather than her own.

Elliot looked up and glanced over his shoulder toward the bank of windows that spread across the sunroom. When he turned back to the woman, he side-stepped a little to his right. His movement positioned his body so that her face and upper torso were impossible to see. With only her legs visible, Thandie, Raja, Len and Warren were no longer able to read their body language. Nor could they see her nudity. This only intensified their curiosity.

Warren swore under his breath. "The least he could have done was sat down and carried on the conversation like a gentleman."

Thandie continued to watch Elliot and the woman talk. Unable to read their lips, she was reduced to guessing at their exchange. Thandie's imagination ran wild.

Suddenly, Elliot handed the woman his shirt. The two of them traded words before she seductively pulled the dress shirt on, effectively covering her shapely form. Again, Warren swore under his breath.

Pasting a tight smile across her face, the dark-haired woman crossed the patio at an unhurried pace. The shift in position brought her closer to the windows and turned Elliot around so that he was now facing the group of onlookers. The woman picked up a set of keys resting on a patio table and slipped a vintage Hermes bag onto her small shoulder.

Elliot motioned to the shirt and said, "I'll be expecting that back."

The woman raked her fingers through her thick dark hair. "You know where to find me when you want it." She brushed her hand along Elliot's jawline, giving him another one of those suggestive smiles. "Feel free to stop by and...collect what's yours." Linking her arms around his neck, she pulled him forward for a slow kiss on the lips. The fact that he hadn't wrapped his arms around her seemed only to amuse her.

Thandie stared at the beautiful couple a few seconds longer before finally turning away. It was hard to pretend indifference after witnessing such scene. Having seen quite enough, Thandie called out to the girls, "Let's go."

The girls shot curious looks at each other, before doing as they were told. The three were climbing into the car in less than five minutes. With Thandie behind the wheel, they were sped off Star Island.

Elliot gripped the steering wheel of the Aston Martin tighter as he approached the winding stretch of land ahead of him. I-9 was famous for its oceanic views of the Atlantic, but Elliot barely noticed the million-dollar landscape. It was a blur of blue as he sped along the pavement.

Had not Warren insisted on riding with him to the investors' meeting this afternoon, Elliot would have made good use of this time, beginning with calling Laurent and reprimanding her for the performance she'd given his household this morning. No doubt her visit today had a double meaning. He'd known her too long not to figure out when she was up to something. Had it been strictly to get a good look at his houseguests or was there a more calculated motive involved? Knowing Laurent, he'd put his money on the latter.

They had an understanding that suited both of them. So why would Laurent step out of bounds? Whatever the reason, he intended to get to the bottom of it.

Visions of her naked body, slick with oil, flashed in his mind. He clearly remembered looking down at her, barely able to stop himself from shaking some reason into her. In a casually calm voice he'd asked, "What the hell are you doing here, Laurent?"

She'd given him an innocent smile as she spread her hands over her voluptuous body. "What does it look like I'm doing?"

"Very nice," he'd agreed. "You've made your scene. Now get out."

Her lips split into a wider smile. "Are you sure you want to go there with me?" she'd asked.

"Get your ass up, Laurent, or I'll do it for you."

"Now why would you want to do that?" she challenged.

"You know why." He nudged his head toward the house. "I have guests."

She shrugged her shoulders casually. "And?"

"Warren is here," he said.

That actually invoked a reaction from her. A silent understanding passed between them, before Laurent moved. She swung her legs over the edge of the chaise, her small feet touching the smooth surface of the patio. Pulling herself up slowly, and ever so provocatively, she stepped close to him. A devilish grin snaked across her lips. "We'll talk later," she said.

He said nothing in response.

Her smile turned predatory. "Don't be so cruel, my love. I would hate to respond in kind."

Pulling the dress shirt off his shoulder, he handed it to her. "Get out, Laurent."

Refusing to be ruffled by his rejection, she made a show of slipping on his shirt. She was toying with him, entering his home with an air of authority that annoyed him. It had always annoyed him. And she knew it.

What had gotten into Laurent? It was unlike her to goad him like this. And she'd never felt the need before to mark her territory over him. In truth, he should have seen this coming. She was curious about Thandie. She wanted to know who she was, and the depth of his involvement with her.

Sure, he could taunt her with the erotic details, but that had never been his style. Besides, it was the "not knowing" that would drive Laurent crazy. For a while, he'd enjoyed responding to her questions with vague noncommittals. But it would seem Laurent had taken matters into her own hands. By coming to the house, she'd upped the stakes.

And then there was Thandie. He wasn't sure exactly how much of Laurent's performance she'd witnessed. Apparently she'd seen enough, because when he'd gone looking for her, she was gone.

That had been the tipping point. He was frustrated with her for leaving before he'd had a chance to explain Laurent's visit. And that opened up a whole new can of worms. Why the hell did he feel obligated to explain anything to her? He enjoyed sleeping with Thandie, but that was it. What they had together was just sex. Elliot Richards was beholden to no one. So why did he have an undeniable impulse to set her straight?

Shaking Thandie from his thoughts, Elliot focused on the winding road before him. He had a busy day ahead of him. It would serve no purpose if he ran off the road before he had a chance to clean up Laurent's mess.

As if reading his mind, Warren found the courage to speak. "So, I see Laurent still takes good care of herself."

Elliot shot him a stony stare. "Do me a favor, Warren."

"Anything," he said eagerly.

"If this is going to work, stay out of my personal business," he said coldly.

Warren blinked a few times before nodding. "Of course," he mumbled. "If that's what you want."

"Yes, Warren," Elliot said sharply, "that is exactly what I want." Returning his full attention to the road, Elliot was pleased Warren hadn't made another attempt at conversation. Instead, they sat in stony silence while Elliot navigated the car.

Eventually, they arrived at the hotel. Handing the valet a twenty dollar bill, he and Warren entered the grand foyer, which had been painstakingly designed to impress any guest. Recognizing Elliot, the concierge greeted them energetically before personally escorting them to a room near the back of the building. The conference room had three wall screens. Nico's face loomed on the center screen. His hair was tousled, and he'd obviously not shaved.

Elliot glanced at Eddie, his accountant. "Are we live?"

Eddie nodded. "Nico's mic is online. We're waiting for the D.C. office."

Elliot turned toward Nico's screen. "Long night?"

Nico grimaced. "Hit me on my cell later. I'll tell you all about it." Nico's face split into a wide grin. "I've got pictures."

Elliot lifted his dark brow in question.

Nico nodded. "Quality."

Everyone laughed, but before Elliot could properly reply,

the far-right screen flashed to life. The image of a handsome black man appeared. Behind him, in large gold letters, read The Law Offices of Winthrop & Assoc. "Good morning everyone," he promptly greeted.

"Good morning, Adrian," Elliot said.

Adrian frowned. "Why is everyone laughing?"

Elliot waved his hand in the air. "Nico," he answered.

Adrian smiled. "I'd ask why, but my door is open and I'm afraid what my secretary might overhear." Checking his watch he said, "I'm on a tight timeline this morning, guys. I'm due in court by 2:00 p.m. and Dad has summoned me home for dinner."

"How is Senator Winthrop?" Warren asked, eager to make his presence known.

"Dad is good. Thanks for asking, Warren. Mom, on the other hand, remembers you from the Christmas party last year." Adrian shook his head. "Please don't be offended when I tell you she's banned you from all future parties."

Warren grimaced. "That wasn't entirely my fault. I sent a card expressing my apologies."

"Nevertheless," Adrian said, "you've been banned."

"How was I supposed to know that was your niece?" Warren asked helplessly.

"And with that said," Elliot cut in, "let's get down the business, gentlemen."

Thandie was furious. After having dragged the girls all over Miami on a wild goose chase, she returned to the house only to be reminded she had a meeting with Markie later. Not wanting to go to the club, she'd called him to see if they could meet somewhere else. Unfortunately, his schedule would not permit it. Markie was in between meetings and was squeezing time in with her as a favor. They had to iron out final details for the upcoming Drake performance, an event she was greatly looking forward to. The meeting had lasted just a little over an hour, before Markie had to join a conference call.

As she was leaving his office, she caught sight of a man's figure. And then he turned, and their eyes met.

Rex's handsome face split into a bright grin the instant he saw her. Before Thandie could anticipate his intentions, he pulled her into an embrace and kissed her on the mouth. Thandie tensed, and looked around them. The club was virtually empty. Only a smattering of staff members were around, but she felt a pause in the air. The few staffers there were watching her and Rex. She could practically feel the excitement bubbling inside them to repeat this newest development in their boss's overly publicized relationship.

For a moment, Thandie was too stunned to do anything. And embarrassed. She hadn't thought about Rex since the last time she laid eyes on him. And that was what...almost two weeks ago? Or was it shorter? She felt terribly shallow not knowing the answer. It hadn't even occurred to her to tell him things were different between them.

As politely as possible, Thandie eased out of Rex's embrace. Aware of the scrutiny they were receiving, Thandie took Rex's hand and led him to a table tucked in a corner. It wasn't exactly private, but it would have to do.

"How was your trip?" she asked, as she slipped into the booth.

"Busy," he said, settling in beside her. "Very busy. I hardly slept. But it's good to be back." He inched closer to her, and Thandie stiffened. Rex was still beaming, but he picked up on the tension on her body. "Is something wrong?"

"Um, yes and no," she began. "I have to tell you something."

"This doesn't sound good," he teased, his smile weakening.

"I'm afraid not," she confessed.

Rex straightened up in his seat. "Let's hear it. I'm all ears."

Not wanting to drag this out, Thandie got to the point. "I'm seeing someone."

Rex stared at her, genuine shock on his face. "You have a boyfriend?"

"It's complicated," she said lamely. "But I am seeing someone."

The juvenile question of her having boyfriend actually stung. Elliot was not her boyfriend. Hell, she didn't know what they were, but leading Rex on was not an option. She had to tell him she was involved. He'd been nice to her. He deserved to know the truth.

Rex seemed to weigh his response to the news. Finally, he asked, "Who is he?"

Thandie shook her head slowly. "It doesn't matter. I just thought…you should know."

"Do I know him?" he asked. "Someone from the club?"

Thandie held up her hand to stop him. "Rex, please don't ask me that."

"Is it Adam? I know you two are close. At first, I thought—"

"No, Rex, it's not Adam. "

He leaned back in his chair. "Why won't you tell me who it is?" he asked quietly.

"Because…it doesn't matter," she said lamely.

He studied her for a long while, battling within himself whether to be angry or congratulate her.

From somewhere above them, a door opened on the upper level. Seconds later, Elliot and Romero came down the steps. Both were on their cell phones, and looked to be in a hurry. Elliot's gaze flitted in their direction, and he paused. Rex turned to see what had distracted her. He was met with a cool gray stare.

Elliot inclined his head. "Rex. Thandie."

Rex waved in acknowledgement as Elliot continued walking, picking up his conversation with the person on the other end of the phone call.

When Rex turned back to Thandie, he searched her face, and then hesitated. Thandie looked away, but it was too late. She knew he saw the look in her eyes, the unbridled delight at seeing Elliot, and the longing to be near him.

"Oh no," he groaned. "Not him."

"It's not what you think," she said quickly.

"No, Thandie," he said in a tired voice. "It's not what *you* think. Elliot is bad news."

She folded her arms. "Please don't do that. I respect you, Rex. Please don't ruin it."

"I wish I could say the same." He got up quickly. "Elliot has women everywhere, you know. I thought you were smarter than that." He rolled his lips inwardly, fighting back the temptation to reveal something, to say something he knew would crush her. He decided against it. "I hope you know what you're doing, Thandie." He leaned forward, gave her a chaste kiss on the forehead, and left the club.

Thandie had mixed feelings about going to Babylon that night. Rex would surely be there. And Elliot...well, they hadn't talked since the beautiful woman was at his house, and then he'd stumbled upon her and Rex. Lord only knew what he'd made of that.

She'd considered calling him to talk about it, but somehow that felt like a bad idea. Mentioning it at all seemed to only put more importance on the incident. So, she'd resigned herself to pretend it had never happened. She and Elliot were not exactly dating, were they? Did she owe him an explanation? Did he even care enough to demand one?

Thandie took her time getting dressed. She'd let the girls leave for the club well before her, preferring they take the rental car while she took a taxi. As evenings with Elliot were often unpredictable, she'd rather see to her own form of transportation.

Dressed simply in a black mini skirt and blouse, Thandie arrived at the club a little past eleven o'clock. Tonight's theme seemed to be a kaleidoscope of color. The walls and ceiling glowed bright red, while pockets of purple and green lights splashed across the dance floor. Thandie searched the crowd, ever watchful for Elliot.

When she finally found him, she hissed. He was seated in one of the few reserved booths on the arena floor. He was talking to a man Thandie had never seen before. Judging by the number of champagne bottles clustered on the table and attractive women milling around, the man was obviously a high-spender. In spite of the circus unfolding around them, Thandie focused on one thing—the women seated on either side of Elliot. They did not appear to be part of his conversation, but rather pretty ornaments adorning his jacket sleeves. The blonde on his right leaned into his side suggestively. The brunette on his left, had her hand planted possessively on his knee.

Scowling, Thandie diverted her gaze and made her way to the staircase leading to the upper VIP level. She stared determinedly ahead of her, resisting the urge to look in Elliot's direction. As soon as she arrived, she caught a glimpse of Len and Raja at the bar, laughing with a pair of well-dressed men.

Thandie waved at them as she passed, looking for Adam. She found him leaning casually against the balcony railing. Next to him stood Rex. Thandie hesitated for a second and then forced herself to join them. When she was no more than ten feet away, Rex looked up. Seeing her approach, he said something to Adam, and deftly walked in the opposite direction.

His hasty retreat gave Thandie pause. Rex's reaction stung more than she'd thought it would. Seeing her expression, Adam came to her.

"He'll get over it," he assured her.

She pinched the bridge of her nose. "I feel like a total bitch."

"You aren't." Adam patted her back lightly. "Far from it. Rex will come around soon enough. It's just hard to lose the girl to the big fish in the pond."

The reference to Elliot made them both look down at the booth were he was seated. The blonde had managed to crawl into his lap. She did not look as if she was going anywhere soon. Shit. Something told her this was not a coincidence. Turning away from the scene she looked up at Adam. He actually looked embarrassed for her.

Fixing a tight smile on her face, she said, "I think I've had about all the fun I can stand."

Adam dragged his hand through his hair. "This is all a show, Thandie. He's just playing his part."

"Doing it rather well, isn't he?" she muttered. And then hated herself for revealing so much. "I'm sorry, Adam. Forget you heard that. I'm tired I suppose. If you don't need my help tonight, I'll head home."

He shook his head. "I have things under control here."

"Thanks." Kissing him on the cheek, she headed for the exit. She paused only once to tell her assistants she was leaving. She crossed the arena floor, cutting through dancing couples in her effort to take the most direct path to the entrance.

Just as she was reaching the grand entryway, someone took hold of her hand. Thandie whirled around to see Elliot. He was smiling at her, but the smile did not reach his eyes.

"Going somewhere?" he asked.

"Home," she said flatly.

"In a moment. I'd like to speak with you first."

Thandie crossed her arms and nodded.

"Alone," he said in a low voice. "In my office."

Her eyes narrowed with suspicion.

"This won't take long," he promised. Stepping aside, he said, "After you?"

Thandie was leery of his intentions, but tucking her purse under her arm, she stepped past him and headed for his office. Elliot followed so close behind, she could smell the faint scent of his aftershave. Heady as always, and so damned seductive.

As they climbed the steps to his office door, she wondered who might be watching them. She got the eerie feeling Rex's gaze was targeted on her back. It was as intimate a sensation as a hand caressing her. With a jerk, Thandie realized there was a hand on her body. Elliot's. His palm slipped down her spine until it was on her butt, and then he squeezed. Thandie stiffened. Elliot had never done anything like that before, not in full view of a crowd.

Had he done it for his own purposes, or for anyone who might be watching them?

Avoiding Michelle's gaze as she stepped past him, Thandie walked inside the office. As soon as the door closed, Thandie turned on him. With her chin jutted upward, and one hand cocked on her hip, she looked ready for war.

"Well?" she said. "What did you want to speak to me about?"

Elliot stared back at her, mischief dancing in his pale gaze. Then he began to tsk. "We haven't spoken to each other since that incident this morning, and that's how you greet me?"

Thandie said nothing in response.

"May I make you a drink?"

When Thandie shook her head, Elliot turned his back on

her and headed for the wet bar. While he poured himself a drink, Thandie looked about the room. She drifted over to the glass walls that overlooked the arena floor. The sight of swaying bodies and multi-colored lights was a little disorienting. Thandie was not sure when Elliot had moved behind her, but he was suddenly there, whispering into her ear.

"How is my little kitten doing?" His hands were suddenly on her hips, splaying themselves across her flat stomach and up to her breasts. When he reached her breasts, he squeezed them, the strength of his hold pressing her back up against his chest. "Have you been missing me?" he asked. In answer, her nipples became painfully taut against his palms. He chuckled. "I've missed you too, pussycat."

He kissed the curve of her neck and then nuzzled his nose against that very spot. Thandie closed her eyes, reveling in his touch.

His right hand released her breast, slid down her side, and behind the back of her thigh. In one deft move, he yanked her mini skirt up to her waist.

Thandie groaned at the brush of cool air against her skin and the press of his growing erection against her backside.

"Place your hands on the glass," he instructed.

Obediently, she did exactly as he said.

Placing his own hands on her hips, Elliot slowly lowered himself behind her, until he was on his haunches. Hooking his fingers into the band of the lacy panties she wore, he eased them down her legs, keeping them looped around her ankles. Sliding his palms over her calves, up the back of her quivering thighs and across her ass, he sucked in a long breath.

"I'm sure you know by now how much I adore your body," he mused aloud. In contrast to his softly spoken words, he squeezed her cheeks hard between his hands, pushing them up and spreading them apart. "But what I enjoy most about you, pussycat, is well…" He leaned forward and inhaled deeply. "When I see you across the room, the first thing I think about, aside from simply having sex with you, is how wonderful you taste on my tongue."

Thandie gave a strangled sigh when he skimmed the tip of his nose along her inner thigh. Digging his fingers into the soft flesh of her butt, he pushed her cheeks as far apart as he could without hurting her, exposing her creamy wet center to his gray stare.

"I'm going to make you come, sweetheart."

Pressing his face into her wetness, Elliot devoured her. His lips and tongue dipped, sucked and nibbled at her with such abandonment, Thandie was soon whimpering his name. When he reached one hand between the valley of her legs and stroked the tender bud of flesh, she quaked. Had she not been literally sitting on his face, her knees would have completely given out beneath her. Although she begged repeatedly for release, Elliot did not give it. He teased her until she teetered on the brink of climax and then pulled away to nip at the skin on her inner thigh or kiss the backs of her knees. The torture was soft and sweet.

When he knew she couldn't stand much more, he stood, freed himself and quickly sheathed himself as far as he could inside her. Gripping her hips, he plunged into her again and again. His thrusts were deep, slow and unyielding.

He took a decisive step back, pulling her with him. Her hands lost purchase of the glass and, just as he'd planned, she was forced to brace herself with hers hands pressed to the floor. With her ass in the air and her weight balanced on her toes and fingertips, she was completely at his mercy. Thandie had nowhere to go, no way the wiggle free or adjust herself to a new position. Thandie's moans turned into screams of rapture. He was knowingly hitting a spot within her that registered both intense pleasure and pain. He rocked against her with such strength, Thandie could think of little else but the mind numbing climax that was just a breath away. As his rhythm increased, his thrusts became sharper.

Something frail shattered within Thandie. She went stiff for several seconds before her body began to convulse around her. The orgasm that ripped through her shook her to the core, causing tears to spring to her eyes and ripping Elliot's name from her lips. She began to milk him, her wetness tightened around his cock and squeezed the very life out of him. Elliot gritted his teeth and swore under his breath.

Seconds before he was about to come, he withdrew. Hot strong spurts of liquid splashed onto her lower back. Using the flat of his hand, he smeared the moisture onto her ass and between her inner thighs. Turning her around, his lips were on her, kissing her hard and fervently.

It was at this point Thandie understood what this had all been about. He'd meant to make her pay for the incident with Rex earlier.

Hurt and wounded, Thandie shoved him away from her. Pulling down her skirt, she headed for his bathroom.

"I wouldn't do that if I were you," he said casually. "My next appointment will be here shortly."

"Appointment?"

He shrugged. "You're welcome to stay if you like."

Thandie did not know how to react. Elliot had never asked her to sit in on one if his meetings.

Elliot glanced at his watch, as if he had something better to do. The simple action made her feel cheap and insignificant. At that moment, Thandie hated him. Her eyes stung with tears and she turned away, but not before seeing a flicker of remorse in his eyes. It had only been there for a second, before vanishing.

There was a knock on the door. Elliot zipped up his pants, tucked his shirtfront in and raked a hand through his hair. He was perfect within a nanosecond.

Thandie on the other hand, having no time to react, looked as though she'd just had sex. Which was of course exactly how he wanted her to look.

"He's here," Michelle shouted from the door.

"Please let him in." Elliot said.

Rex stepped inside. He hesitated when he saw Thandie and Elliot. "I could come back," he offered.

"No," Elliot said. "I want to hear about your trip. Please, come in." Turning his dark head to Thandie, he asked quite coolly, "Will you be joining us?"

Thandie looked at Elliot, then to Rex, and back to Elliot. He'd set her up. The realization hit her like a bucket of cold water, drenching her in mortification. Her eyes blazed with anger. This was some malicious game of his. Too furious to speak, Thandie shook her head and headed for the door. She slipped out without a backward glance.

Chapter Twenty-Six

Thandie was furious with Elliot for what had occurred in his office. He'd used her to prove a point. And she had fallen into his trap.

When Thandie thought about how she must have looked to Rex, she cringed. With her hair mussed, her clothes disheveled and her lipstick smeared, she'd given the impression Elliot had hoped for. She looked as though she'd just had hot sex.

Thandie hadn't been able to meet Rex's gaze when she'd rushed from the room. With her head ducked, she'd left the club blushing with shame.

Asshole.

As soon as Thandie got home, she made a beeline for her bathroom. Locking the door behind her, she braced her hands on the sink. Hanging her head until her chin pressed against her chest, she promised herself she would not cry. She would not shed one tear over Elliot.

Lifting her head, she looked at her reflection in the mirror and was forced to look at the woman staring back at her. Gone was the independent, headstrong woman she'd always been so comfortable with.

The women who stared back at her was unsure and struggling to find balance and understanding.

She wasn't happy with what she had become. Under Elliot's charming persuasion, she had willingly become his sex slave, waiting and ready for his affections at a moment's notice. She was ashamed of her dependency on him, her anxiety to see him and even worse, her need to have him near her. When had this happened? When had she become his groupie?

Unable to bear the sight of herself, she turned away from her image and began to strip off her clothes. After a thorough shower, she lay in bed wondering how she'd allowed herself to plummet so deeply into this shadowy world of uncertainty? What was Elliot playing at? He'd embarrassed her by flaunting their physical relationship in Rex's face. But what had been the point of doing that? Just to prove he could?

Throwing her arm over her eyes, she tried to block out the waves of emotions that were crashing over her. She'd known the delicate strand holding her affair together would eventually snap, she just hadn't thought it would be this abrupt, or this vicious.

Rolling on to her side, Thandie forced further thoughts of Elliot out of her mind. If she was going to survive the final weeks of her stay in Miami, she would focus on what she'd come here for in the first place—her job. And the sooner she finished it, the sooner she could return to New York.

Thandie slept hard but short. Determined to get on top of things, she started working on promotion details early. Locked away in her room, she didn't dare leave to retrieve anything from the kitchen or dining room. If she saw Elliot's smug face she might just snap.

As much as she'd grown to dislike Mira Dietrich, Thandie was actually relieved she had a lunch meeting scheduled with her today. Not only would it get her out of the house for a while, Mira would also do a good job of distracting Thandie.

Leaving a note for the girls, Thandie slipped out of the house an hour and a half early. She took the scenic route, wasting time by exploring the Coconut Grove neighborhood.

When she finally arrived at Green Street, Mira was waiting for her. As usual, she was seated at one of the patio tables, a cigarette clutched between two wrinkled fingers.

Smiling pleasantly, Thandie took the seat opposite Mira's chair. "Hello, Mira."

"I haven't been able to get photos inside the club," she declared.

"I warned you security would be tighter," Thandie said.

"We all have wants, Thandie dear. If you want a nice fluff piece in *Look,* then I want photos. It's that simple."

"I'm working on it, Mira."

"Your time is almost up," the older woman pointed out. "You're on this project for what…three more weeks? Meanwhile, I have papers to sell."

"I'll handle it," Thandie assured her.

"I certainly home so. Otherwise—" her small ruby red lips split into a tight smile "—I'll have to report what I can get my hands on."

"Such as stories about Elliot and me?" Thandie asked.

Mira waved her cigarette in the air. "A necessary evil, as you well know. People want to know about Elliot and his fabulous lifestyle. He's intriguing. Thus, he will always be in the public eye. Anyone acquainted with him is bound to be caught in the limelight. So, if you don't like the heat, Thandie, I'd advise you to stay out of the kitchen." She tapped ash off the tip of her cigarette. "And you my dear are definitely in the kitchen."

"What does that mean?" Thandie asked wearily.

"You may not like my tactics, but pictures don't lie." Like

a grenade, Mira slid a newspaper across the table. "Don't say I didn't warn you."

Suspicious of anything Mira offered, Thandie spread the paper out slowly. It was another article printout with tomorrow's date posted at the top. She read the headline first: "Back Together Again!" Above the article was a picture of Elliot and the beautiful dark-haired woman arm in arm. They appeared to be leaving a restaurant together.

"Who is she?" Thandie heard herself ask.

"Who is she?" Mira repeated. "Surely you know who she is?" Realization came to her slowly, and when it did the smile that inked over her face was so evil she could been mistaken for the Grinch. "She's the reason why Elliot never hires women. Well, except for you, of course, but that was a rule of hers. Her name is Laurent." Mira paused for dramatic effect. "Laurent Richards. She's Elliot's wife."

For a moment Thandie just stared at Mira. She could feel the blood draining from her face. His wife? Elliot was married? The idea was so unbelievable, she had a hard time processing the words. But Thandie knew Mira was telling the truth.

This was the secret she'd always felt he was hiding. She could not explain it but somehow she just knew this was the closest she'd ever been to seeing Elliot for who he was. This was the true Elliot Richards.

Feeling Mira's eyes on her, Thandie abruptly folded the paper and slid it across the table. She swallowed hard before meeting Mira's hawklike gaze. "I guess I owe you thanks," she said in a voice barren of any life. "You spelled Elliot's name right."

Mira leaned back in her chair and studied Thandie. "You didn't read the story."

"I don't need to. Any news is good news, right?" Pulling her purse into her shoulder, Thandie smiled. "Forgive me, Mira. I have somewhere I need to be." Giving what she hoped was a convincing smile, she mouthed the words "I'll call you" before walking briskly to the patio exit.

Thandie couldn't wait to get into her car. She squeezed her hands into tight balls as she waited impatiently for the attendant to bring her vehicle around. When he finally did, she drove half a mile up the road, parked, and simply stared out the windshield.

He was married.

Somehow everything became clear. It was as if a veil had been ripped away from her eyes, allowing her to see for the first time in months. And then she plummeted headlong down a dark spiral.

Elliot was married.

She could not make herself say the words aloud. Even thinking them was painful. How had he hidden this from her? She gasped. Was she the only one who didn't know? Was this what Warren had tried to forewarn her of? A vision of Rex's angry face loomed before her. He'd been about to tell her something the day he'd figured out she was involved with Elliot. But he'd stopped himself. Had this been it? Had he stopped himself from telling her she was sleeping with a married man?

She felt betrayed. Why would anyone think she would be all right with sleeping with a married man? Did they assume Elliot had told her, so there was no need to make an issue of it? Were they really so jaded? For a span of five minutes, she berated them for not telling her. That eventually fizzled out, because it was had been Elliot's responsibility to tell her. He alone would bear the weight of her fury.

Thandie's mind went into overdrive, running through all the things she should have questioned. However, even in hindsight, there were few clues to go from. Elliot had been very good at concealing so much from her, it was hard to zero in on anything. But that did not stop her from trying. For a full hour, Thandie sat motionless in her car, searching her mind.

And after that, she began to plot.

Elliot slammed down the phone. He'd tried to call Thandie twice already, and both times she'd ignored him. It was bad enough he was feeling low about what he'd done the night before, arranging things so that Rex would see Thandie was his. He'd meant to belittle Rex by letting him know he wasn't in Elliot's league.

But he'd miscalculated badly. He hadn't anticipated the strength of his desire for Thandie. He'd meant to take her roughly, but not be unkind. As always, she melted into him, accepting his hunger with equal passion. He'd wanted to mark her, make it clear to her whom she belonged to.

It was not until they'd finished did he realize how poorly he'd treated her. And then Michelle had announced Rex's arrival. There was an instant when he'd considered not going through with it. For a breath of time, he'd thought he might be going too far. Her eyes were glassy with unshed tears, and he almost went after her. But he hadn't.

He'd made his point loud and clear. With the smell of sex still in the air, Elliot smiled tightly at Rex while he gave his stiff account of his time in Vegas. He could see the discomfort in the man's eyes, and was satisfied. He was a beaten man. But it occurred to Elliot, though he may have won this battle, he'd just lost the war in this chess match. He'd lost his queen to a petty affair, thus checkmating his own king piece.

After his meeting with Rex, he'd searched the building for Thandie, but learned she'd left the club. She was furious with him. He deserved that. He debated whether he should try to find her. He resisted the temptation. If she was as upset at him as he suspected, she needed time to cool off. Once she was calm, he would seek her out.

He decided not to go to her bedroom that night.

However, when she didn't come down for breakfast, he'd gone to her room. She wasn't there. Figuring Thandie was out running errands, he called her. No answer. He'd waited for her. Milling impatiently around the house, he'd frustrated his mother with his sulky mood until she'd given some excuse about visiting a cousin, before leaving the house.

Eventually, he'd had to go to his office for a meeting. He'd been cooped up in his office for hours, becoming more cross by the minute. Every time he checked his phone and saw there was no missed call from Thandie, his mood intensified. So far, Romero was getting the worst of it.

At the end of his third and final meeting, while people were still were filing out of his office, Elliot pulled his phone out and dialed Thandie's number. Again, he received her voice-mail. Refusing to leave a message, he'd hung up. For one sliver of a second he considered calling her assistants, but quickly rejected the idea. Thandie was protective of them. The last thing he needed was to create suspicion that he had any kind of involvement with either girl.

Deciding to wait until this evening seemed to be the best bet. If Thandie did not show herself tonight, he would have to go after her. Checking his watch, he furrowed his brows. Ten minutes until ten o'clock. The clock was ticking. He would give Thandie until midnight. If she wasn't in the building by then, there would be hell to pay.

The house was quiet and empty when Thandie finally returned to Star Island. Len and Raja must have taken a taxi to Babylon. Thandie had intentionally arrived late. She wanted to stay in her thoughts while she figured out how to settle things with Elliot once and for all. Of course, she'd considered packing up their things and getting on the first flight to New York. But that would be too clean, and far too easy for Elliot. He needed to be taught a lesson.

Thandie took her time going through her outfits. She wanted to pick something that suited the occasion. Selecting a bright red bandage dress and a pair of her best fuck-me pumps, she dressed quickly but with care. She wanted to look desirable and, most importantly, leave a lasting impression.

When her makeup, hair and clothes were just right, she climbed into the Expedition and headed for Babylon.

For a Thursday night, the crowd of people lined up outside the building was a good sign. She wanted an audience. Skipping the trail of cars waiting for valet service, Thandie pulled up parallel to the curb, blocking someone in. Cars honked at her for skipping the queue, but the staff who recognized her car went into action. All smiles and warm greetings, an attendant held the door open and helped her out of the SUV. Seeing a glammed-up woman receive such quick attention quieted the car horns. Security waved her forward, ahead of the line. They squinted menacingly at anyone who got in her way.

"You look killer in that dress," Tiny said as he held the door open for her.

"That's the plan," she said with a smile. Slipping inside the club, Thandie looked around the arena. The expanse was darkened with pops of green lighting along the walls. The hanging gardens had been lowered, giving the room a rain forest appeal.

Swiveling her head to the left, Thandie saw Elliot's door was closed. The management meeting was still taking place. *All the better,* she thought. Stepping toward the bar, she settled onto a stool. This was the best perch to watch Elliot's office door, and would give her ample opportunity to do what she'd come here to do.

Time being on her side, and knowing how particular Elliot was about keeping to a schedule, the office opened within minutes of when she'd expected it to. Eddie Bloom and Tom Comber were the first to exit the room, followed by Adam and Rex. Markie was the last to leave. The men filed out, taking the steps slowly as they chatted with each other. They looked noticeably less jubilant than the last time she'd seen them. Bad meeting?

A few minutes later, the office door opened again, and Elliot stepped onto the landing. Nicely dressed as always in a classic black suit and white dress shirt, he could have given James Bond a run for his money. Elliot bumped fists with Michelle, before looking out over the crowd. His expression was unreadable, but when his cool gray eyes landed on her, his expression was a mixture of surprise and then…relief?

Sliding off the barstool, Thandie glided up the steps, closing the distance between them. When she was no more than a foot away from where he stood, she whipped her hand back and slapped him hard across the face. The sound vibrated the air. "That's for not telling me about your wife!" she shouted at him. Thandie was gratified to hear a silence surround her. She had a crowd. Perfect.

Whipping her head around, she saw a stunned and scared looking Michelle back up, as if fearful her wrath would ricochet off Elliot and land on him. Thandie snarled at him for good measure, before turning around to storm off. She expected Elliot's shock to allow her enough time to exit the building. So what if he fired her? She no longer wanted nor needed his money. Hell, he could take a picture of the well-deserved slap she'd just given him and accept that as her resignation. Elliot Richards was the scum of the earth. If it were up to her, she hoped to never see his lying face again.

Thandie's determined ban on Elliot lasted a few more steps. She'd mistaken how quickly he'd recover. Within seconds, she felt his presence behind her just before an iron grip encircled her upper arm and all but dragged her into his office. He threw her up against the wall, ignoring the scandalized look from the guests seconds before Michelle closed his office door.

He spoke in a hard, even tone. "Next time you decide to make a scene, make sure you have the facts right. Laurent is my ex-wife."

"Why didn't you tell me—"

"And next time you think of slapping me, remember one thing." His eyes went cold. "I believe in self-defense."

In answer to his threat, Thandie lifted her hand to slap him again. Anticipating her action, he caught her hand and twisted her arm behind her back, causing her to whimper in pain.

"Get control of yourself, Thandie, or else I'll make this very embarrassing for you."

"Let go of me!"

Amazingly, he did. Thandie scowled at him as she clutched her wrist to her chest, rubbing the tenderness out.

With his jaw tight, he raked angry fingers through his hair. "Did I hurt you?" he asked in a low voice.

"Fuck off," she hissed.

Leaning one hand against the wall, he sighed heavily. "About Laurent—"

"You mean your wife," she snapped.

"She's is my ex-wife," he corrected. "Things between us are complicated."

"Yeah, I bet."

His faced darkened at her sarcasm. "We've been divorced for six years now."

"And you two are still sleeping with each other."

"It's not what you think."

"Why didn't you tell me about her earlier?"

"I didn't want you to—" He caught himself, pressed his lips into a thin line, and then tried again. "Laurent is inconsequential. She has nothing to do with us."

"She doesn't? You just sleep with her on occasion."

"Thandie—"

"How dare you react the way you did about Rex, when you're still involved with your ex!"

"We're not involved."

"No? So you think her showing up at your house to sunbath in the nude is normal? I saw her kiss you, Elliot!"

"She only did that to get a rise out of you," he snapped. "If you hadn't run off, I would have explained that to you."

"And the fact that she comes to the club all the time, is that normal too?" she retorted with a glare. "I don't know many divorced couples who behave like you two."

Elliot sighed. "My relationship with Laurent is complicated. I don't expect you to understand it."

"I told you I wouldn't share you."

"You aren't."

"Why don't I believe you? Why should I *ever* believe you?" Thandie pushed past him, and headed for the door.

"Where are you going?" he called after her.

"Why should you care?"

He moved ahead of her, blocking her exit. "I asked you a question."

She looked up at him with angry eyes. "Get out of my way."

"Tell me."

"I'm going to Warren's."

Elliot's handsome face twisted into an ugly smirk. "I'm sure he would be happy to help you."

"At least he's a gentleman," she threw back.

"Oh, he is? And you're basing that off what?"

Thandie gawked at him, confused as to why Elliot was always so quick to dislike a man who practically idolized him. "Warren is a complete gentleman in every sense of the word," she argued. "Unlike you, he would never allow a woman to be harmed. He's sweet and thoughtful, two qualities you have no concept of—"

"Thandie," he snapped, "you don't know what you're talking about."

"And you do?" she challenged. "You don't know Warren half as well as I do."

"Just how well do you know him?"

She jutted her chin up stubbornly. "I've known him for years. Believe me, I know a lot more about him than you. And you could stand to take a few lessons from him."

Elliot's face went stiff with anger. "The day I take lessons from Warren Radcliffe will be the day hell freezes over."

His words had been spoken with such menace that Thandie wondered what they were really talking about. How had the subject of Warren slipped into their argument? Surely discussing him couldn't be the reason for such disdain. What was Elliot getting at? What was really behind his scorn?

Once again, Elliot was confusing her with mysteries. Well, she was tired of it. Tired of him. Tired of Miami. Tired of this project. Having had enough, she stepped around him and threw back the door.

Pausing in the threshold, she said, "Just to be clear, we're done."

Chapter Twenty-Seven

The next day, when Thandie pried open her eyes, she was momentarily confused. Then she remembered the evening before and, most importantly, she recalled she was once again at Warren's home.

She blinked at the bedside clock and was surprised to see it was a quarter 'til noon. Amazingly, she'd been asleep for over twelve hours.

Rolling onto her back, she covered her eyes with her hand. More images from the previous day came hurling at her like blunt daggers. Mira and her Grinch-like smile. The picture of Elliot and Laurent. The sting of her hand after slapping Elliot. Anga standing in her robe when she'd arrived at Warren's after fleeing Babylon.

With a sigh, Thandie checked her phone. She'd turned it off last night after she'd received the umpteenth call from Len and Raja. Her call log was filled with more calls from her assistants and quite literally a roll call for the entire Babylon staff. The only person whose number did not appear was Elliot's. No big surprise there.

Easing out of bed, Thandie grabbed her store purchases and

went into the bathroom to wash up. Half an hour later, she wandered into the kitchen. Warren was seated at the breakfast bar, reading his newspaper. He flipped down an edge of paper when he heard her enter. A kind smile beamed from beneath his reading glasses.

"Anga cooked," he said. "She made plenty. Help yourself."

Although Thandie had no appetite, she piled a biscuit and a strip of bacon onto a small saucer and carried it to the table. For several minutes, she picked at the food while Warren pretended to be reading his paper. Watching him, Thandie was reminded of Elliot's animosity toward Warren. His reaction to her suggestion he take lessons from his business partner was unnecessarily chilling. She was certain the edge she'd heard in his voice was caused more from the heat of their argument than Warren, but still she worried about her friend. She wandered if Warren suspected Elliot thought so little of him?

"Are you ready to talk about it?"

Warren's quiet voice cut into Thandie's thoughts. She blinked, only to realize Warren had caught her staring at him. Looking down at the half-eaten biscuit, she shook her head. "No comment."

"I'm a good listener, you know? If you want this to stay between us, it will."

"Thanks, Warren, but I'm not up for sharing."

His eyes lifted with warmth. "Fair enough," he said. Reaching into his pocket, he fished out a key and slid it to her. "You'll need this."

"What is it?"

"A key to the house," he explained. "One of the copies I made for you and the girls when you first arrived in Miami." He cleared his throat uncomfortably, and said, "May I ask what you plan for today?"

"I have some work to do."

Warren nodded his head, as if this was the answer he expected. "You're welcome to do whatever you need to here."

"Thanks, Warren." She hesitated before adding. "For everything."

He patted her hand reassuringly, and then turned his attention to his paper. His pale eyes squinted as he focused through his glasses. She wondered if he needed a stronger prescription. When she was tired of pretending to eat, she cleared away her plate, kissed Warren on the top of his white head and went to her room to retrieve her items. When she returned to the kitchen, she announced she was going out.

It was a beautiful day in Miami. The sun shown bright and the sky was cloudless. The drive back to Elliot's home was a peaceful one, but tension grew inside her as she neared Star Island. She knew before she parked in the driveway Elliot was not there. His Range Rover was missing. A good sign. She relaxed a little.

Entering the house, she went directly to her room. It was just as she'd left it, cluttered with clothes and papers. Stripping off the dress she'd been wearing since last night, she took a long hot shower before going through her things and packing her essentials.

Pulling on a pair of jeans, a tank top and sandals, she went downstairs to collect her laptop from the dining room. This too was exactly as she remembered it. She wasn't sure, but she'd almost expected the house to be in some sort of disarray.

Just as she was packing her computer into its traveling case, her phone started vibrating. Her heart jumped into her throat. Was it him? Nervously, she checked the display. It was Adam. She gave a sigh of relief, before answering the phone.

"I've been trying to reach you for hours," he said.

"Sorry about that," she said. "I needed a little space. Is everything all right?"

"Everything is fine. I was worried. We all were."

"There's really no need," she said in a voice far more confident than she felt.

The silence that followed her words told Thandie she had yet to convince him. Finally, he asked, "What are you doing today?"

"Working on the last productions."

"Can you meet me for an early dinner?" When she hesitated, he said, "Come on, Thandie. We don't have to talk about anything you don't want to. I just want to make sure you're as fine as you say you are."

"But I have work to do," she said reluctantly.

"Great," he said a little too brightly. "We can talk about it. Bounce a few ideas around. It'll be a working meal."

Thandie pinched the bridge of her nose. "Okay, Adam. You've twisted my arm. But I'm warning you, I'm expensing the meal."

He laughed. "You won't hear me complaining. How about Peppers? It's a nice restaurant on—"

"I've been there," she cut in, remembering the first time she'd had dinner there with Elliot on her second night in town. "I can meet you there around four o'clock."

"Sounds good to me. See you then."

After hanging up, Thandie went to work gathering her items. She debated having the girls pack their things and move back to Warren's home. Or should she get a hotel room for the three of them? They had a little over two weeks left in Miami as it was. Would it be worth it to pay the expense of a hotel? Was it too much to ask Warren to take them in again? Was it safe to keep them at Elliot's home? In spite of her instinct to keep the girls close to her, she had to admit Elliot had been an exceptional host to them. This was partly due to the fact that he was rarely there. However, Thandie's protective nature kicked in, and after five minutes of thought, she decided the girls would move back to Warren's with her.

Remembering Peppers catered to a crowd, Thandie called ahead to ensure she and Adam got a table. She arrived ten minutes early. Walking inside the restaurant, Thandie got a strong sense of déjà vu. For it to be so early, the place had a nice-size crowd.

"Right this way, Miss Shaw." Lifting two leather-bound menus, the hostess guided Thandie across the dining hall, up a short flight of steps and toward the private booths. When she arrived at the very booth she and Elliot had shared, Thandie thought she couldn't sit there. Then she shook off the sensation.

Adam arrived a few minutes later and sat down with her.

Thandie flipped open her menu and began reviewing their choices.

Their orders were taken quickly and their food was to die for. Adam kept the mood high-spirited with light conversation. The closest they came to mentioning Elliot was touching on the upcoming events she and the girls would be hosting. Dinner wasn't the carefree affair she'd hoped for, but it was nice all the same.

Just as they were about to leave, a call came through on Thandie's phone. Recognizing it as Pitbull's agent, she waved Adam farewell, settled back into the booth and took the call. The conversation was brief but informative. By the time she hung up, she was desperate to get to her laptop to update her notes.

Sliding out of the booth, Thandie stood and headed for the restaurant's entrance. She paused when she felt a hand touch her arm.

"Thandie."

She turned to meet the dark eyes of Laurent Richards. Thandie stiffened and took a defensive step back. Laurent flushed at her overt recoil.

"Can we talk?" Laurent asked.

"I don't think so." Thandie slipped her arm out of Laurent's reach and was about to turn away.

"Please." Laurent said quietly. "We really should talk." When Thandie hesitated, she added, "I promise to be brief."

Thandie could see no malice in the woman's lovely dark eyes. It took a lot of the wind out of her sails. Grudgingly, Thandie followed Laurent to a secluded table along the back wall. Taking a seat, Thandie noticed from this position Laurent would have had a good view point of the table Thandie had just been seated at.

Noticing Thandie's observation, Laurent said, "Yes, I watching you."

"Why?"

"I needed to talk to you."

"Again, why?" Thandie pressed.

Laurent did not seem offended by her curt tone. She smiled pleasantly and said, "I figured you might have unanswered questions."

"And you were going to voluntarily give me these answers?" Thandie asked skeptically.

"I know this might sound strange coming from me, but I have no intention of deceiving you."

In spite of the sincerity Thandie heard in the woman's voice, she was unconvinced. There was a long list of reasons for Laurent to mislead her. Chiefly amongst them was Elliot.

"I'm sure you've seen the pictures of Elliot and me in *Look*." It was a statement, not a question. "I realize it may be hard to understand what those pictures convey." Laurent's fingers played with a thin gold chain looped around her neck. "Elliot met with me at my request. I made him an offer. He declined."

"No offense, Laurent, but I really don't care."

Laurent grinned knowingly. "I wish I could believe you."

"That's your problem. Not mine."

"I've seen the way you look at him, Thandie. Elliot means a hell of a lot more to you than you're willing to admit."

Thandie crossed her arms tightly around her. "As far as I'm concerned you can have Elliot. He's all yours."

She laughed softly to herself. "It's not exactly that simple. I wish it were, but it's not. As I'm sure you've discovered, nothing involving Elliot is ever simple."

Thandie shifted her weight in her chair, showing her discomfort with the direction of the conversation. "I have some things to attend to today. Can you please get to the point of why you wanted to speak with me?"

Laurent leaned back in her seat and studied Thandie, her gaze taking in every detail of Thandie's being. "I didn't think much of you when I first laid eyes on you," she said bluntly. "You're not exactly Elliot's type." She shrugged. "So you never got on my radar, until it was too late." Laurent gave a wistful smile at these words. "I'll admit, I was not happy about it. Elliot was vague as always, and that only infuriated me. You infuriated me."

"I didn't even know who you were until yesterday," Thandie said coolly. "I hardly see how I earned any of your animosity."

"Isn't it obvious?" she asked with a bemused smile. "I envy you."

Thandie's astonishment at these words could not be more evident. "Why would you envy me?"

Laurent leaned forward, looked her straight in the eyes, and said, "Because you have something I want."

Laurent was beautiful, perfect in every way. From what

Thandie could tell, she was well financed, and seemed to have an unlimited amount of class. "What could I possibly have that you want?"

"Elliot."

"Elliot?"

"I envy you because you have him."

"You're mistaken," she laughed. "I don't have Elliot. I never did." When Laurent did little more than stare at her, Thandie nodded her head. "It's true. Elliot does not belong to me, nor I to him."

"Thandie, I think you would be surprised how wrong you are."

"Did Elliot send you here?"

"No," Laurent said with a shake her head. "He would never send me to talk to you. In fact, he forbade me from talking to you. He would be furious to know I disobeyed him."

"Disobey?"

Laurent blushed. "Elliot is a very proud man, Thandie. I thought you would have known that by now." She tapped a manicured finger on the tabletop. "I'm sure you're wondering why Elliot and I divorced."

"Honestly, Laurent, I don't care what happened between you and Elliot. I don't want to have anything to do with your relationship."

"I cheated on him."

Her confession was so bluntly stated, Thandie stared at her. She couldn't help but wonder why any woman in her right mind would be unfaithful to Elliot. Physically, he was perfect. Thandie had never been as strongly attracted to any other man in her life. However, the emotional complexities had worn her down. Had he always been like that? Or was it a reaction to a bad marriage? And why was Laurent telling her this?

"I met him in college. We had a few classes together. Even

back then, he was quite popular with the girls. But he was very focused on his studies. He made excellent grades without really trying. I was on top of the moon when we started dating. I think I fell in love with him instantly. We were together for a year, and then I got pregnant. He asked me to marry him. I knew it wasn't what he wanted, but he was determined to do the right thing." Her fingers began to play with the necklace chain again. "I lost the baby six weeks later. And then I realized I was in a marriage Elliot never wanted to be in. I ignored it for a while. I was happy. I was Mrs. Richards. Even back then, that name carried some weight. I mean, you've seen him. He's absolutely gorgeous. He was good to me, but I knew he wasn't happy. Men like Elliot need to be free. They die a slow death when captured. He wouldn't say it, of course. He played his role perfectly. He provided for me, he was kind, and protective. But I could tell his heart wasn't in it. A woman knows when a man is in love with her. It's in the way he looks at her. The way the whole world goes still when she walks into the room." She leveled her gaze on Thandie. "I loved him very much. So much so, that I was willing to let him go."

"So you cheated on him?" Thandie heard herself asking in disbelief.

"I gave him a way out."

"Why didn't you just ask for a divorce? Why go through the dramatics of having an affair?"

Laurent shook her head. "Elliot would have never simply given me a divorce. He would have fought to make it work. He was determined not to make the same mistakes his father made. The only thing he could not forgive was infidelity. It was the only way to make him walk away from the marriage."

Thandie frowned. "Wait. Elliot's father divorced his mother?"

Laurent's dark eyes narrowed. "They were never married. That's why Elliot despises him so much. He will never forgive him for not marrying Lucinda."

Thandie shook her head. "Elliot doesn't despise his father. He adores him. He told me about how he taught him to sail, and the trips their family took to Cuba."

Laurent lowered her brows. "You're speaking of Luis Richards," she said.

"Yes, Luis," Thandie confirmed. "Elliot idolized him."

"I'm not talking about Luis. I'm talking about his father."

"What?" Thandie looked confused.

"His father left Elliot and his mother with nothing. If it weren't for Luis, I don't know how they would have survived those years."

Thandie shook her head. "I'm sorry. I'm confused."

"Luis was Elliot's stepfather," Laurent said slowly.

"Stepfather?"

Now Laurent looked confused. "Yes, he married Lucinda when Elliot was very young."

"But I thought he…" Thandie's words drifted off. She was trying to remember something Elliot had told her that night on the boat.

She sat up straighter and smiled warmly at Thandie. "The reason I wanted to speak with you was to help you understand my unique relationship with Elliot.

"I've made mistakes, Thandie. The biggest one was betraying Elliot. I loved him very much. I've been trying to correct things ever since. I told him I wanted us to give it another shot. I wanted us to reconcile. He said no. And I know why." She looped a finger around her necklace. "Do you know what I would give to have him look at me the way he looks at you?"

There was a vulnerability in her eyes that Thandie found impossible to look away from. She did not want to feel sorry

for Laurent. She didn't want to get pulled into her and Elliot's sick game of emotional cat and mouse. She didn't want
to feel anything for either one of them, but there was a tug of
sympathy there all the same.

Thandie abruptly came to her feet. "Good luck with that,
Laurent. Elliot and I are not on talking terms anymore. Feel
free to step in and sweep him off his feet."

"Believe me, I've already tried," Laurent confessed.

Slipping her purse onto her shoulder, Thandie quietly left
the restaurant. When she stepped onto the sidewalk, she took
a deep breath of warm air. Until this moment, she hadn't realized her hands were shaking.

"I leave town for a few days and all hell breaks loose."

Elliot blinked. He'd been staring aimlessly at his computer
screen for what…an hour? He looked up in time to see Nico
stroll into his office. As usual, his friend dominated the space
as if it were his own.

Falling into the chair opposite from him, Nico crossed his
legs and observed Elliot. "My sources tell me things have been
interesting around here."

"And who are these sources of yours?"

"If I told you, they wouldn't be my sources anymore, now
would they?" Nico scratched his jaw. "So are the rumors
true?"

"It's doubtful," Elliot said with a detached reserve.

"That's good to hear. I hate gossip."

Elliot frowned at his friend's good humor. "Where have
you been?" he asked.

"Traveling," he said vaguely. "Speaking of which, how was
your trip to Havana?"

"It went well."

"Oh, really?" Nico asked casually. "My flight crew tells me you had quite an enjoyable time."

"Stop fishing," Elliot warned.

"I wouldn't have to if you'd feed my curiosity." When Elliot said nothing, Nico gave him a wary expression. "How have you been?"

"I certainly hope that's not the reason you came down here."

Nico looked sheepish. "Not exactly, no."

Elliot made a circular motion with his hand, as if to say "get to the point."

"How is the lovely Thandie?"

"She's not talking to me."

Nico raised his brows. "That's surprising. The last time I laid eyes on you two, you were getting along exceptionally well."

Elliot recalled in vivid detail their night in The Tower with Nick and his wife, Laney. Thinking of it, and Thandie's absence made something in his gut tighten. A beastly creature wanted to tear its way out of his ribcage and attack Nico with savage desire.

"Elliot, are you all right?" Nico asked, eyeing him suspiciously.

"I'm fine," he growled.

Tapping his fingers on his knee, Nico waited for an explanation. When none appeared to be coming, he said, "Well?"

"Well what?" Elliot demanded brusquely.

"Are you going to tell me why Thandie isn't speaking to you?"

"Laurent," Elliot said irritably.

"Ah, yes," Nico said with a dramatic sigh. "A classic case of the jealous ex. Can't say I didn't see that coming."

"I didn't," Elliot muttered.

"Of course you didn't. You had your mind, and your hands, on other things, namely Thandie."

Elliot bristled at the words, but Nico was right. He should have known this would happen. If he hadn't been so caught up in seducing Thandie, he would have seen Laurent coming a mile away. It wasn't as if she'd been discreet about her interest in Thandie. Eventually, Thandie would have found out about her. But it irked him all the same.

"What are you going to do?" Nico asked.

"You know me," he said with a sigh. Elliot leaned back in his chair, his long legs stretched out. Linking his fingers together, he cradled the back of his head, and stared up at the ceiling. "I've always got a backup plan."

"Yes, I figured as much." Nico flicked an invisible speck of lint off his pant leg before continuing. "This is different."

"Excuse me?" Elliot asked, looking mildly interested.

"This is different," Nico said again. "I know you better than anyone, Elliot. So you aren't fooling me. I've seen you juggle women before, but this is different. Whatever is going on between you and Thandie—"

Elliot's face darkened. "Stop, Nico."

"But—"

"Stop."

"Fine." Nico tapped his hand on his knee. "Since you're not much for taking advice, maybe you can provide some to me." He waited for Elliot to argue, but when he was met with silence, he continued. "I'm considering investing in a fashion house."

Elliot fixed Nico with a curious stare. "Do you know anything about fashion?"

"No."

"Then, why?"

"Because I've developed a sudden interest in it," Nico said stubbornly.

Nico waited for a full minute before diving in and asking what had really brought him here. "Tell me what you know about Victoria."

This made Elliot sit up and look at his friend closely. "As in Victoria Day? That little girl with the mouth of a sailor?"

"She's far from being a girl," Nico said grimly.

Elliot laughed. "Please tell me you're joking."

"Tell me what you know."

"You aren't joking, are you?" he asked, losing his humor.

"Not even a little," Nico said quietly.

"I noticed you talking to her after the fashion show," Elliot said. "It didn't look to be going very well."

"She'll come around," Nico said with a shrug.

Elliot focused on Nico, furrowing his brows the closer he studied him and more specifically, the new piece of jewelry in his possession.

"Is that what I think it is?" Elliot asked nodded at the item that had captured his attention.

"Perhaps." Nico fingered the item nervously. "Now tell me what you know about Victoria—"

Elliot seemed to consider this, before answering. "Very little, I'm afraid." Elliot released a heavy sigh. "Most of her family works with her on her clothing line. She's a transplant here. Her family is from Florida, but she's been living in New York for several years. She just moved back to focus on her brand. She's got talent. That can't be denied. But from what I can tell, and from what little I've seen, she has no idea how to run a business." He ran a hand through his thick dark hair. "She's cute, Nico, but she's tiny as hell. Victoria could easily be mistaken for a child. And she talks more shit than any guy I know." Elliot suddenly looked up and stared at his friend, reading him well. "You're not interested in fashion are you? You want Victoria."

Nico shrugged. "Perhaps."

"Well then, good luck," Elliot said with a light smile. "I have a feeling you're going to need it."

Bad timing. It all came down to very bad timing. As Thandie looked herself over in the mirror, she wished she were anywhere in world but here. Of all the times she could have found out about Elliot's ex-wife, she would have to find out on the day before a performance.

Admittedly, her showdown with Elliot the previous night had not gone according to plan. Hindsight being twenty-twenty, she'd given little thought to what would happen after slapping him. The result was she'd shamed herself in front of his staff. And now she was trapped. The arrival of Pitbull obligated her to make an appearance at the club tonight. With her reputation on the line, Thandie felt compelled to handle the talent correctly. Not to mention, she and the girls had invested too much time organizing the final events. She'd like to see them through, if at all possible.

As was their routine, the girls left for the club early to ensure the stage setup and sound equipment were ready. When Thandie arrived, two hours before showtime, she could feel the tension in the air.

Out of habit, Thandie glanced toward Elliot's office door. It was closed. One sweep of the arena floor told her the managers were still in their staff meeting. A good sign. At least she didn't have to come face-to-face with Elliot at the beginning of the evening.

Thandie met Len and Raja backstage. After giving her an update of the preparations, they nursed their cell phones, waiting for arrival updates.

When Pitbull and his entourage finally arrived, Thandie and his manager, Guy, slipped away to finalize the financial obligations. When everything was squared away, they had less than thirty minutes to get everyone prepped. An impatient crowd could be heard chanting, "Pitbull! Pitbull! Pitbull!" When everything was finally in place, the stage manager ushered the entertainer on stage. The stage lights flickered and the audience went wild as Pitbull stepped forward and went into his first song.

From the safety of the backstage curtains, Thandie watched as swarms of people moved against one another, mouthing words to the song. This was the first real break she'd had this evening.

Thandie had no intention of staying. She would only be here long enough to ensure the performance went off without a hitch. Coincidentally, there was an unusually high number of celebrity guests in attendance. As PR events go, this was an immense triumph. However, Thandie took little joy in any of it.

What should have been one of the biggest nights of her professional career felt like an empty victory. She should have been rejoicing at the huge success of setting up such a star-studded event. Nothing could be further from the truth.

Every time she looked out over the crowd and caught sight of Elliot, her heart ached. And when she saw a woman wrap her arms around his waist and smile up at him in a wordless invitation, her eyes flared with anger. As much as she would like to believe she meant more to him than just sex, he'd wasted no time finding a replacement for her. It was a cruel reminder she wasn't the only woman in his life, and never would be. She scolded herself that her wounded pride was unnecessary and was exactly what she deserved. She had known long before getting involved with Elliot what he was about.

And even if she hadn't been warned several times before, he had made his intentions very clear.

I don't do girlfriends, he'd once said.

Cold as those words were, he had given her fair warning. She knew what she was getting herself into, so there was no one to blame for her predicament but herself. She'd been foolish enough to give her heart to Elliot Richards, fully knowing he would never feel the same. She was grateful her time in Miami would soon be coming to an end.

Leaving the backstage area, Thandie moved through the crowd, always aware of Elliot's exact location. It was easy to do. Elliot seemed to always be surrounded by a cluster of people.

Before her irritation got away from her, Guy, Pitbull's manager, approached her to discuss an issue. Thandie waved him toward Markie's office, where the two of them could talk in a more quiet setting.

Elliot was livid. The pretty brunette snuggled into his side to kiss his cheek. She had latched herself onto his arm and had done everything possible to let him know she wanted him to sleep with her. But despite the attractive company he kept and a successful turnout for tonight's production, Elliot was furious. And his anger was directed at Thandie.

He couldn't stop himself from watching her, watching who she was talking to and every time she disappeared, he went crazy until he located her again. Of course, he wouldn't approach her. He had absolutely nothing to say to her, however he had several sexual positions he wanted to put her in.

But that was out of the question. She had made it very clear she wanted nothing to do with him. He would like to think he could charm his way into any woman's bed, but after their last argument and those damned photos of him and Laurent, he had the sinking feeling even the best words would not soften Thandie. He'd been thoroughly rebuffed, and it drove him mad. It was not simply because he had been rejected. It was because Thandie had rejected him.

Elliot couldn't get enough of her. He'd found himself having sex with her tirelessly, hoping he would soon grow bored and move on. But things hadn't worked out that way. The more he took from her, the more he yearned to have. The feel of her beneath him, and the taste of her in his mouth obsessed him.

Even now, he wanted her. His cock hardened, just thinking about taking her.

He looked at Thandie again. Who the hell was that guy talking to her? Did she know him? If so, how well? Elliot saw her laugh brightly at the man. Apparently, she knew him well enough to hold a conversation with him.

And then she'd done the unthinkable. Placing her hand on his arm, she went with him toward the darkened hallway that led to some of the staff offices. Where the hell was she taking him? Elliot watched as the guy got familiar, touching her elbow as he followed after her. His hand skimmed down her arm to her back. Elliot was a heartbeat away from going over there and punching his teeth out.

Disgusted with himself, he wordlessly walked away from the clinging brunette. He had something to take care of. If Thandie was mad at him, that was one thing, but he would be damned if she offered herself to another guy. And in his own club, at that. It was disrespectful, and he would put her in her place.

Having concluded their discussion, Thandie accepted Guy's business card and promised to keep him in mind for any future opportunities.

They were about to leave when a dark shadow fell over them. Thandie looked up to see Elliot's tall figure standing in the corridor, filling the doorway to Markie office.

Guy gave Thandie a curious look. "Do you know him?" he asked.

"Unfortunately, yes," she said.

Guy glanced between the two of them and decided to take his leave. An uncomfortable moment passed when it became apparent Elliot was not going to step aside to allow the man easy passage. Guy paused, and was then forced to squeeze past Elliot's broad shoulders to exit the room, all the while being glared at.

When they were alone, Elliot stepped forward, kicking the door closed with his foot. He turned his intense gaze on Thandie. "Who the hell was that?" he demanded.

Thandie planted her hands on her hips and glared right back at him.

Elliot advanced on her. "I believe I asked you a question."

"You have some nerve even talking to me," she snapped. "Why don't you go find that brunette who had her hand in your lap all night?"

"Who was that?" he repeated slowly.

Fuming, Thandie marched forward, intending to brush past him and quickly lose herself in the crowd. However, Elliot had other plans. He gripped her upper arm and held her against him.

"Where do you think you're going?" he whispered.

"Get your damn hands off me," she hissed. "I told you, we're done."

"We're done when I say we're done."

"Let go of me or I'll scream my head off."

Elliot was furious, but wise enough to see she was serious. Releasing his hold on her, he eased her away from him.

Thandie quickly stepped past him, but before she was out of earshot, she heard Elliot's voice call out to her.

"Running back to Warren to cry on his shoulder?"

Angry, she whirled around on him. "What is it with you? Why all the animosity toward Warren? He's a great guy."

Elliot gave a dry laugh. "You don't know Warren like I do. All you see is the funny old man who hangs out in nightclubs, trying to relive his youth."

"He's never given me reason to doubt his motives."

"Because you're too caught up in his stupid jokes and money-flashing ways to care."

"Give me a break." She turned to walk away.

"Have you slept with him yet?"

That stopped her cold. Thandie spun on her heels to face him. "What did you just say to me?"

Elliot slid his hands into the pockets of his slacks and he met her glare with own of his one. "I asked if you'd slept with him." The words were spoken with icy malice.

Thandie stared at him, hating him for asking such a question. "No," she said coldly. "Have you?"

He stepped closer to her, measuring her. "He's tried to get you into bed before, right?"

"Why would that matter to you? My relationship with Warren is none of your business."

"Wrong again, pussycat." He drew his brows together. "Warren is my business."

"How in the world—" Thandie suddenly stared at him, seeing him for the first time. The furrow of his brows. That particular way that had always struck her as odd and yet…familiar. "Oh, my God," she whispered in a broken voice. Her eyes focused on him. How could she not have seen it before?

Elliot looked away, his jaw tight.

"It all makes sense now," Thandie said in a hushed voice.

She gave a humorless laugh. "You must really think I'm stupid. When were you going to tell me, Elliot?" She jabbed an accusing finger at his chest. "When were you going to tell me Warren is your father?"

Elliot's mouth drew into a thin line.

"He got your mother pregnant and left her for another woman." She said these words almost to herself, trying to recall Warren's drunken rant so many weeks ago. "You're the reason he moved to Miami. You and Lucinda."

"That's enough," he said in low voice.

"That's how he convinced you to hire me, isn't it? You did it as a favor to your father."

Elliot said nothing.

"But why?" she asked. "You don't care for him. You don't even like him. Why would you—" Thandie stopped herself when a chilling thought came to mind. "You slept with me, thinking that I'd had a relationship with him?" She sounded scandalized.

Elliot lowered his eyes, looking guilty as hell.

"Tell me the truth," she demanded, even though she was sure she already knew. "I want to hear it from you."

Elliot lifted his eyes to meet hers. They were as cold and hard. "When he first told me about you, I thought you were someone special to him. I didn't want to hire you, but I could see how much it meant to him. So I agreed, meaning to make your job as uncomfortable as possible. And then you walked into my office. You're certainly the type of woman he goes for: pretty, exotic and far too young for him. When he offered his home to you, I knew you were more than a passing fling for him." He broke their gaze. "I planned to seduce you."

"Why?"

"To hurt him."

"And me?" she choked out.

He fixed her with a defiant stare.

"Collateral damage," she finished for him. Thandie took a step away from Elliot. "That's what this has always been about, hasn't it? Hurting Warren." She took another backward step, catching her breath. "And I was just a pawn for your revenge." Her fists clenched together. "How could you be so cruel?"

"It wasn't all about revenge," he said. "At least, entirely."

"Havana," she whispered.

"Not Havana." He implored her with intense eyes. "That was all me."

She shook her head violently, and found she couldn't stop. Elliot took a cautious step forward. "Thandie, calm down." His voice was soft and even. "You need to breathe deeply and slowly. Can you hear me?" He moved closer, careful not to make any sudden movements. "Thandie," he said louder, "breathe slowly for God's sake, try to get control of yourself."

She wasn't listening. She continued to move away from him, shaking violently. When Elliot reached out for her, Thandie jerked back so abruptly she lost her balance and fell. She scrambled back, catching herself on her hands and feet. Elliot's arms were immediately around her, pulling her up and cradling her to him. With a strength Thandie hadn't known she possessed, she fought against him, struggling to shake off his touch.

Twisting free of him, she grasped the doorknob with frantic hands. Throwing the door open, she stopped short. Warren, Markie and Romero were standing there. They stared mutely at her tearful expression and then at Elliot.

Warren's eyes went wide with worry. "Kiddo?" he asked cautiously. "What's wrong?"

Thandie looked at Warren, seeing him clearly for the first time. She could not disguise the betrayal she felt. "Oh, Warren," she said in obvious disappointment. "How could you?"

Warren flinched at her words. Shame washed over his

weathered features. He glanced nervously at Elliot, swallowed hard and then said, "Let me explain."

"Get out of the way, Warren," Elliot barked. "Thandie, come here."

"Don't talk to her like that," Warren snapped.

She didn't want to hear another word from either father or son. If she did not get away, she was going to have a complete meltdown. Already, her breath was coming in quick gasps. Her legs were stiff beneath her, and colorful stars had begun to blind her.

Rushing from the office, she quickly put distance between herself and the sound of Elliot and Warren arguing. Barely able to see through the bright bursts of light exploding inside her head, she ran face first into Rex's chest. He steadied her by grabbing hold of her shoulders. When he looked at her, his eyes went wide. "My goodness, Thandie, what's wrong?"

She shook her head, unable to speak and gasping for breath.

"What has Elliot done?" he demanded.

Too breathless to give an excuse, she pushed away from him and moved toward the exit. Reaching the main hall, she flung open the entry door, causing it to bang loudly against the wall.

"What the hell?" Tiny said in surprise.

Sparing him no mind, Thandie shouldered her way through a mass of people waiting to get in. As soon as she was clear of the crowd, she gasped for breath, but the air never seemed to reach her lungs. Leaning heavily against the stone exterior of the building, Thandie forced herself to move as quickly as she could away from the club's entrance. She managed to hobble a few precious feet before she heard the club doors burst open again and Elliot's booming voice.

"Thandie!"

Chancing a glance over her shoulder, she saw Elliot's dark head swivel back and forth as his stern face swept the congested sidewalk. In one fluid motion, he reached into his pocket, pulled out his phone and held it to his ear. Thandie's phone began to vibrate inside her purse. Ignoring it, she stumbled a few more feet.

She just made it around the corner of the building when her legs collapsed beneath her. She slid ungracefully down the wall. Squeezing her eyes shut, she struggled for control. Determinedly, she focused only on her breathing and not the devastated remains of her broken heart.

Chapter Twenty-Eight

Elliot slept fitfully, and was happy when his alarm clock finally went off. The house was a lot different without Thandie and the girls there.

He'd returned home the previous night to an empty house, not that he'd expected a warm homecoming. But he was irritated all the same.

Thandie had removed all of her and the girls' belongings. They had been quite through. There wasn't a scape of fabric left behind. No doubt they were all at Warren's house. The thought alone pissed him off. He didn't want Warren anywhere near Thandie, but thanks to him, she was sleeping under his roof now.

Although he was tempted to go over there and demand Thandie return home with him, he was well aware he and Warren needed space. Another minute in each other's company, and things were liable to become violent.

Last night, he and Warren had had one of their worst arguments ever. Neither had been willing to back down nor allow the other to get a word in.

Finally, Elliot had been able to unleash all his anger at the man who'd fathered him. He'd ranted and raved about how little he needed him, and berated him for his cavalier lifestyle.

Warren hadn't taken it lying down. He'd ranted at Elliot for hurting Thandie and demanded he stay away from her. That hadn't gone over well. Not surprisingly, more angry words had been shouted and fierce glares delivered. It was like two bulls being unleashed in a small pen.

In the end, Elliot had to barrel past Warren to go after Thandie. If her panic attack was as bad as he feared, he had to get to her. Even if she hated him for it, he had to help her. But he'd been too late. Thandie was gone. She'd disappeared into the crowd.

He'd tried to revive the evening by greeting club guests, but it hadn't taken long to realize he did not have the stomach for it. Nor the patience. His fight with Thandie, followed by his showdown with Warren, had left him in a bad mood. Eventually, he'd retreated to his office and further aggravated himself by placing calls to Thandie's cell phone. Calls that were never answered.

He'd gone home.

Scowling, he'd gone to his bedroom and forced himself to go to sleep. It had taken some time before he was able to drift off. His thoughts had been filled with images of Thandie's shocked expression when she'd learned the truth about him. The look on her face was a cross between disbelief and resignation. Resignation. The word bothered him.

At the first sound from his alarm clock, Elliot flung his legs over the edge of the bed and stalked to the bathroom. After taking a quick shower, he listened to his messages while he dressed.

Message 1: "Elliot, it's Nico. I got your message. I'll do it, but I think we need to talk. Call me."

Message 2: "This is Matrix calling you back."

Message 3: "Hey, this is Eddie. There was a scheduling conflict today. The investor meeting had to be moved up an hour. I left a message with Romero, but I thought you ought to know."

Elliot gritted his teeth as he listened to the final message. Thandie had not returned his call, not that he necessarily blamed her. He'd been particularly cruel to her the previous night. He could have told her the truth a little more nicely. For that, he decided he'd give her time to cool off.

Seeing Romero waiting for him in the foyer was a reminder things had returned to their old cycle. But it did not feel right. Something was disjointed. His house had never felt emptier, or as quiet. He did not like it.

Elliot went through the motions of his normal routine. However, he did so in an unexplainable foul mood. By the time the investors arrived for their evening meeting, Elliot was practically growling. He glared at Warren the instant the man strolled into his office. As expected, his glare was greeted with equal hostility. It was the perfect beginning to a very tense meeting.

Elliot sat through the meeting, biding his time, waiting for the damned thing to be over so he could call Thandie and demand she come to the club so they could talk. He had to make her understand where he stood before things spiraled out of control.

His attention was snagged when Markie said, "I just found out the guest DJ dropped out. We need a replacement for tonight. I know a kid in Orlando who can probably stand in. I'll call his people to see if he's available."

"Nonsense," Elliot said. "You shouldn't be handling that." It was the first he'd spoken since the meeting got underway. "Have Thandie take care of the DJ replacement. That's her specialty." Having given the directive, Elliot turned his attention to his cell phone and began toggling through his messages, but the eerie silence that settled in the room drew his attention. He looked up to notice the stern faces of his staff. "What?"

No one said anything. They only stared at him. Elliot tossed his phone onto his desk and stood. Crossing his arms, he frowned at the group. "Is somebody going to tell me what's going on?"

Markie hesitated before saying, "Thandie's not here."

"Obviously, she's not here," Elliot said frostily. "Call her cell. Get her working on it."

Warren got up and, wearing a fierce frown, he confronted his son. "Thandie can't help with your DJ problem because she's gone."

Elliot frowned. "What do you mean 'she's gone'? Gone where?"

Warren lifted his brows. "Your guess is as good as mine. I would assume she returned to New York."

Elliot slowly turned on Warren. "You want to run that by me again?"

"She quit," Warren said bluntly. "We sent her off to the airport several hours ago."

"We?"

Warren fanned his hand around the room. "We," he clarified, "escorted Thandie and the girls to the airport this morning. She called us to notify us of her decision. She was eager to leave."

Elliot looked at his staff, recognizing for the first time the heated stares they were throwing in his direction. There was no mistake why Thandie had left, and they held him responsible. Damn it!

Elliot turned around to think for a minute. He could feel his anger building. She'd met with his team? How could she leave without talking to him first? He deserved that much. Had the woman completely lost her mind? Was this her way of ending things between them?

A multitude of questions ran through his head until he was burning with outrage. He rested his hands on the edge of his desk to gather himself. But it wasn't enough. In a burst of rage, he grabbed hold of the desk and flipped it over. The glass top shattered on impact, skittering across the floor in thick shards. By now, everyone was on their feet. Elliot knew he was out of character. Ever the cool and confident one, he knew his eruption set them all on edge.

Taking a deep breath, Elliot struggled to calm himself. He slid his hands into his pockets and turned back to his staff. "Everyone get out."

After learning the news of Thandie's departure, he'd stormed out of the club. The mess he'd made of his office would have to be addressed some other time. He simply could not remain at the club tonight. He was liable to do something stupid like get into a fight. Or worse, call Thandie and demand she explain herself. It was better that he leave and allow himself some time alone.

He was pissed off with Thandie for leaving, annoyed with his staff for obviously taking her side, and disgusted with himself for caring one way or the other. He was surprised more than anything. Through the haze of rage he was feeling, pure and unadulterated shock reigned supreme. It left him speechless. He might have called her, if he actually had something to say. He could not believe Thandie had left the way she had. She hadn't even given him a chance to explain himself.

Her sudden departure had blindsided him, and one thing Elliot hated above all things was to be caught unaware. He prided himself on being prepared, being two steps ahead of everyone. But Thandie had pulled a fast one on him. He hadn't seen this coming. He told himself this was the true reason he was in a funk. Thandie had outmaneuvered him. He hadn't thought it was possible for anyone to do that. Was he was losing his touch? On one hand, he had to give her credit. On the other, he was angry as hell that she'd slipped through his fingers.

Pushing the front door closed behind him, Elliot took in the silence of his home. It was the very silence he'd sought out. However, now that he'd found it, he discovered it was not as highly desired as he'd once thought.

Tossing his keys aside, he moved toward his bedroom. A shower was much needed—

"Elliot?" a female voice called out.

He froze in place. It was not Thandie's voice he'd heard, but the one person who had had complete and utter control over him. He closed his eyes, and prayed for patience.

"Elliot." It was not that she had said his name, it was how she said it.

"*Sí, mamá?*"

Lucinda glided into the room, drying her hands on her apron. "You're home early."

"Difficult day at the club."

She studied him in a way that only a mother could. He could never hide anything from her. She could read him like a book.

"I made your favorite," she said. "Come, have a bite."

Even if he wasn't in the mood to eat, Elliot had never turned down his mother's food. Especially if she'd prepared his favorite dish.

As expected, he followed her into the kitchen. The aroma of freshly baked dessert filled the air causing Elliot's mouth to water.

Lucinda patted a barstool, indicating she wanted him to have a seat. As he slid onto the stool, he watched his mother maneuver around his kitchen with far more grace than he ever could. She was poetry in motion, while she prepared a plate for him.

By the time she finally placed bowl in front of him containing a generous portion of warm peach cobbler and an equally large scoop of vanilla ice cream, Elliot's stomach was growling.

Without preamble, he dug into the dessert, eating nearly half before he realized it. Or even noticed that his mother was leaning against the countertop, studying him.

"Good?" she asked.

"Perfect," he confirmed.

Lucinda nodded her head, before casually asking, "Where's Thandie?"

Elliot stiffened and then said, "Gone."

She raised her brows. "Gone?"

"Gone."

"What do you mean by gone?"

"She went back home."

"To New York?" Lucinda said in surprise. "What happened?"

"She found out about Warren."

"I see."

"And Laurent," he added sheepishly.

"Hmm."

Elliot looked up from his near empty dish. "What does that mean?"

Lucinda gave a noncommittal shrug. "Well, what are you going to do?"

"Who says I'm going to do anything?"

"Because you're my son and I know you better than you know yourself."

Elliot rolled his shoulders back uncomfortably, committing to nothing.

Sweeping up his now empty dish and placing it in the sink, Lucinda began untying her apron.

"Where are you going?" he asked slightly alarmed.

She grinned. "I have a date."

"With whom?"

"That's none of your business." Tossing the apron on the counter, she held out her hand to him. "Walk me to my car."

Coming to his feet, Elliot took his mother's hand in his own. Pulling it to his lips, he kissed her palm. "You deserve to be happy."

She smiled softly. "So do you, Elliot."

Tucking her hand into his into the crook of his arm, the two walked side by side into the warm night air.

Just before tucking his mother into her car, Lucinda stayed his motion.

"Mi hijo?"

"Si madre." He turned to face her. He knew that she would not speak until she was confident she had his undivided attention.

"Don't be a complete idiot," she said simply. "If you miss Thandie, tell her so. Even a fool can see you care for her."

"It's not that simple," Elliot said with a sigh. "Besides, we're way beyond words."

Lucinda brushed dark curls away from his face and kissed his forehead. "You're never beyond words."

Chapter Twenty-Nine

Thandie checked the time. It hadn't improved much since she'd looked at it five minutes ago. Frustrated, she stared at her computer screen and tried to remember what she'd been working on. For the past few hours, she and the girls had been quietly working on assignments.

Since their return to the city a few days before, business had been booming. Their involvement with Club Babylon had had the desired effect, leaving Thandie with the daunting task of tackling her endless emails and responding to proposal requests. It was time consuming, but a necessary evil.

There were several small but high profile events happening throughout the city that appeared to be quite promising. There was even a job offer that would allow her to work abroad.

The assignment would take her to Ibiza, a small island off the coast of Valencia, renowned for its club scene. Thandie had spoken with the account rep twice already about the opportunity. The client, a Mr. Dominic Armenta, wanted her to host a birthday party for him. The assignment was projected to last no more than three weeks.

According to the rep, Mr. Armenta was some sort of real

estate tycoon. It was as vague an explanation as one could get. But Thandie didn't really care. She was intrigued by what the opportunity offered. Aside from generous billable hours, the project allowed her a chance to get away. The idea of escaping New York, and leaving her life behind was tempting. She could bury herself in her work and forget about Elliot. At least, she could try.

Thandie checked the time again. Same as before. Twirling a mechanical pencil between her fingers, she absentmindedly wrote the words *Dominic Armenta* on a bright pink Post-it and stared at it.

On a whim, Thandie typed the name into Google. A single picture of a well-dressed, silver-haired man, with a cavalier smile greeted her. A lovely, older woman stood at his side. Judging the wedding rings, and the gentle way the couple embraced one another, this must be his wife. Thandie was relieved to know Armenta was married. And old. No temptation there, she thought. No distractions.

She read his bio. It was a smattering of choppy, but direct facts; birthdate, marital status, one son and country of residence. It wasn't much, but more than enough to convince Thandie he wasn't another gorgeous, difficult club owner.

Goodness knows she'd had her fill of that variety.

Thandie clicked out of the search engine and returned to staring at her emails. She had a lot to do. There was plenty of new work to keep her busy, but not near enough to improve her attitude. Since her return to New York, she'd been cranky and quick to upset. As a result, the girls had been walking on eggshells around her, trying their best to stay out of her way and avoid eye contact.

Adding to the tension, Len and Raja were being rather cool toward each other. How long had that been going on,

Thandie wondered. She'd been so occupied wallowing in her own misery, she hadn't noticed the friction between the girls.

Finally, Amanda had had enough. She threw her hands up and shouted, "What is going on with you guys? Why is everyone in such a snit?"

Len and Raja traded dirty looks and Thandie pretended to be invisible. When it became obvious no one intended to answer her, Amanda planted her hands on her hips. "Well?" she demanded. "I'm waiting."

It was all the motivation Len needed. With a huff, she thrust an accusing finger at Raja and said, "Raja slept with Romero behind my back."

Thandie's head snapped and, against her better judgement, she echoed, "Romero?"

Raja jerked back as if Len had slapped her. "Ah! If I'd known ahead of time you'd already slept with him, I might not have done it."

"That's no excuse, Raja," Len fired back.

"Actually, it is," she retorted.

"Romero?" Thandie parroted again. "But—when?"

"On the drive back from Key West," Raja said at the same time.

"On the *drive* back?" Thandie said slowly.

Len made a coughing sound that sounded unmistakably like "slut."

"Key West?" Amanda said, looking dumbfounded. "But wait, I thought you were in Miami."

"We took a road trip to Key West," Raja supplied with a tired sigh.

"Keep up, Amanda," Len snapped.

Thandie found it hard to believe both her assistants had been involved with Romero. She'd been under the impression they loathed him.

"Who is Romero?" Amanda asked, clearly confused.

Len released a very loud sigh. "He's Elliot's assistant."

"Who is Elliot?"

"Elliot Richards," Raja said, releasing an equally dramatic exhale. "Seriously, Amanda, what planet have you been on?"

"Planet New York," Amanda snapped. "Now who is Elliot?"

"The owner of Club Babylon," Raja answered.

"And the most gorgeous man I've ever laid eyes on," Len breathed.

"And he was totally smitten with Thandie," Raja added.

Amanda's brows shot up so high, they disappeared into her bangs. "*Our* Thandie?"

Thandie could feel three pairs of eyes turn in her direction. In response, she became intensely interested in whatever was on her computer monitor. In unison, the girls leaned back in their seats, folded their arms across their chests and waited expectantly.

"It's your turn, boss," Raja announced.

"Excuse me?" Thandie asked, still avoiding eye contact.

Len smirked. "We fessed up about what was ailing us. Now it's your turn."

"Don't you girls have work to do?" Thandie asked.

"No," they chorused.

"That figures," Thandie grumbled.

"You've been in a pissy mood for days," Len declared, "and we've put up with it long enough."

"We deserve an explanation," Raja said in a matter-of-fact tone.

"They have a point," Amanda concurred.

Thandie shook her head. "I have no idea what you're talking about."

"We think you should talk to him."

"Talk to who?"

"Elliot Richards," Len and Raja said at the same time.

Thandie shook her head viciously. "I'm not talking to him."

"Why not?" Amanda asked.

"No one said you had to be nice," Raja suggested. "Call him up and scream at him, if you must. Just—" she sighed heavily "—get it off your chest."

"Has he called you?" Amanda asked.

"No," Thandie admitted quietly. *Not even once,* she thought.

That had been yet another crushing blow to her pride. She had purposely left Miami without speaking to him, but she'd secretly hoped he would try to contact her. At least to apologize. So far, no luck. Aside from her bonus check, Thandie hadn't heard a word from Elliot.

One person who had called her numerous times was Warren Radcliffe. He left a message on her answering machine at least once a day. Apologies poured from him like an unchecked faucet. He took responsibility for nearly everything, even things that had never been under his control, such as Elliot. Although he'd never mentioned Elliot by name, Warren expressed his remorse for not telling her the whole story of how he came to be in Miami and the "events" that had led to her hasty departure.

No matter how he pleaded, Thandie hadn't returned any of his calls. She simply wanted to forget Miami entirely.

Thandie sighed. "I appreciate what you girls are trying to do but—"

"We're not stupid, you know," Len said.

"And we're not blind either," Raja added.

"It's quite obvious whats going on," Len pressed.

"Girls," Thandie said in a warning voice.

Amanda looked around the room, in bewilderment. "Is somebody going to tell me what we're talking about?"

"Thandie's in love with Elliot," Raja said in answer.

"And she might as well stop trying to hide it," Len reasoned, "because everybody already knows."

Their words were quietly spoken, but they might as well have been shouted over a bullhorn. Thandie stiffened, preparing to deny their accusations, but what was the point? She was tired of being in denial, and even more tired of trying to hide it.

As if sensing her surrender, Len faced Thandie and asked, "Why do you think the female staff has backed off making advances toward him? Everybody at Babylon adores you, and they didn't want to see you get hurt. You obviously care about him, so do us all a favor, and call him up and tell him so."

Raja's almond eyes glowed with interest. "What's the harm, Thandie? Anyone can see he's crazy about you. The way he looks at you is sizzling hot."

"It's not that simple," Thandie said. "Nothing about Elliot is simple. Elliot and I are done."

"Thandie and Elliot were a couple?" Amanda asked, beginning to catch on.

Raja inclined her head and whispered quite loudly, "Thandie dumped him."

"We were never together," Thandie defended.

"It certainly didn't look that way," Len mused.

"Yeah, well looks can be deceiving," Thandie said with a snort.

"So you just ran away?" Amanda asked.

"I didn't run away," Thandie snapped. "I just…moved on."

"Before you got hurt," Raja finished.

Thandie wanted to scream at them, but emotion got the better of her. She took a deep breath. "We've already crossed that bridge." She turned away before they could see her eyes sheen with tears.

Apparently, she hadn't moved quickly enough. Len's mouth formed a small O, and Raja looked shamefaced. Thandie hated herself for being so pathetic, but she couldn't help it. The mention of Elliot had that effect on her. Clearing her throat, she awkwardly forced a tight smile on her face. "Don't worry about me. I'll be fine. I just need—"

The buzzer rang. The four women looked at each other with blank expressions. When enough confused shoulder-shrugging was shared, Thandie padded barefoot to the front door of her apartment and hit the intercom.

"Can I help you?"

There was a muffled sound before an unfamiliar voice said, "I'm here to deliver a package to…" he paused and shuffling commenced "…uh…Thandie Shaw?"

"You came to the right place," she said before buzzing him in. "Number 510."

When the messenger finally arrived at her door, Thandie signed a slip of paper, and was handed a single envelope in return.

She ripped it open, and inside was a certified check. No note had accompanied the check, and none was needed. She knew exactly what the check was for, and more importantly, where it had come from. She studied the information on the check. "E.R. Entertainments, LLC." It was her final paycheck for the Babylon project.

Thandie hadn't planned on receiving anything from Elliot. She'd mentally prepared herself to be shorted the amount owed to her, and because she was determined to sever all ties with him, she'd made no plans to insist he pay her for the hours she'd put in.

Looking down at the sizable check, she realized this was the final chapter of her time in Miami.

The check symbolized the end to a short but emotional

journey. Even the signature on the check spoke volumes. She recognized Elliot's precise signature. The familiar scrawl was heartbreaking. Thandie would have preferred a computer generated signature instead. Because knowing that at some point in time Elliot had held this very slip of paper, made the act of touching the check far more intimate than she would have preferred.

For an instant, Thandie wondered if this was yet another intricate twist in his mind games? Was this his way of showing her he had accepted her departure and had moved on with his life? Of course it was, she thought. Elliot was probably sitting in his office at this very moment, laughing at her, marveling at how easily he'd strung her along and how quickly he could replace her.

Instead of getting sentimental, Thandie got mad. How dare he write her off so easily? Did he think this check would make things square between them? Hell no. With jerky movements, she stuffed the check back into the envelope. If Elliot thought he was doing her a favor, he was delusional. And if he thought she would refuse the money, he had another think coming. She planned to cash the damned thing first thing in the morning.

But first, she had a phone call to make.

Crossing the room, she snatched up her cell phone and retreated up the steps to her private quarters. Her presence would not be missed, nor would her conversation be overheard. The girls were still arguing amongst themselves. Heedless of the time difference, she punched in a number and she waited for the call to connect. She was so upset, her hands were shaking. A curt voice answered on the second ring. Without preamble, Thandie got to the point.

"This is Thandie Shaw," she said into the phone. "Please tell Mr. Armenta I'm very interested in the position."

★ ★ ★

Elliot debated the wisdom of his decision. This was the last place in the world he wanted to be, but he was here nonetheless. He had to be here. It was as if his path had been destined to lead him here.

Before he changed his mind, he rang the doorbell. Silence followed. For a moment, he thought he'd gotten lucky. Perhaps no one was home, and he could leave telling himself at least he'd tried. And then he heard it. The soft shuffle of someone walking to the front of the house. He swore under his breath and braced himself as the door swung open.

Warren's face glowed with surprise at the sight of him. "Elliot?"

Elliot could not stop himself from glaring back at the man. Resisting the urge to say something cutting, he said, "We need to talk."

Warren nodded his head. "Yes, we do." He stood back, wordlessly inviting him inside. Elliot hesitated only for an instant before crossing the threshold. He stepped forward into the living room. His Thandie had been here. She'd run away from him to come here. It made him furious enough to lash out at someone. Namely Warren.

Refusing to take a seat, Elliot crossed the room to stare out the windows that overlooked a lush garden of tropical foliage. A backdrop of the ocean sparkled with sunlight, creating a liquid surface of golden glitter.

It was Warren who spoke up first. "I know you paid Sophia off to get her to agree to the divorce. I can't thank you enough." He waited to see if Elliot would turn to face him. When he did not, Warren continued. "I intend to repay you, Elliot. Tell me the amount and I'll make the arrangements."

Elliot did not immediately respond. In all honesty, he still didn't know why he had done it. His annoyance with So-

phia almost matched his contempt for Warren. He detested
the idea of calling his accountant to authorize a check being
made out to the gold-digging woman. So why had he gone
through with it? And why had he agreed to the ridiculous
amount she'd demanded? And why had he asked for so little
in return? The only stipulation he had insisted on was that
Sophia could no longer use her married name and she had to
leave Miami. It was an expensive deal to make, but she was
gone from all their lives. Good riddance.

"I didn't come hear to discuss Sophia," Elliot said abruptly.
He opened his mouth to speak, but was cut off when Warren spoke.

"Your mother is a good woman."

The comment caught Elliot completely by surprise. The
softly spoken words were so casually spoken, and so matter-
of-fact, for a moment Elliot thought he must have misunderstood. He turned to face the man. The two meet men stared
at each other with cautious expressions. The discussion of Elliot's mother had never been a topic between them. They'd
avoided any mention of Lucinda Richards at all costs. But now
it was as if the words had been said.

"Lucinda was good to me," Warren announced. "She loved
me, which was more than I deserved." His pale gray eyes flitted to the ground as he cleared his throat. "I, like most young
men in their prime, blew it. I didn't realize what I had, and
I was careless. She didn't deserve what happened. She didn't
deserve any of it."

Elliot's initial reaction to hearing Warren say his mother's
name was anger. Anger toward him for abandoning them, for
leaving him and his mother to struggle for pennies while he
lived in the lap of luxury, for breaking her heart.

But the wave of anger was quickly washed away, replaced
by pity. Warren might have had monetary wealth, but he had

little to show for it now. Elliot and his mother might have struggled to survive, but they had always been rich with love. It was the kind of love that made your heart swell in your chest at the mere thought. That was something Warren had never been able to buy. Despite his wealth, numerous divorces and twenty-something girlfriends, Elliot doubted Warren gained any real satisfaction from it.

"I've never asked you for anything," Elliot said.

"I know," Warren replied.

"And what I'm about to say changes nothing between us."

"I understand."

Elliot opened his mouth, and found the words refused to come out. He tried again, this time more successfully. "I need your help, Warren."

"All right."

"I need you tell me everything you know about Thandie."

A pleasant voice greeted her when she answered the phone. "Ms. Shaw," he said. "This is Joe, your driver. I'm downstairs. Do you need help with your luggage?"

"No, thank you," Thandie said. "I can handle it. I'll be down in a moment."

Thandie hung up the phone, marveling at how quickly everything had fallen into place.

Within hours of accepting the job offer, she'd received an aggressive itinerary. Apparently, Mr. Armenta was eager for her to begin working on his project. He wanted her in Ibiza by the end of the week.

Within a few short days, his rep had set everything up. A car would deliver her the airport, where Mr. Armenta's private jet would take her to Spain. It just didn't get any better than that.

Slipping her purse onto her shoulder, she gingerly lugged

her bags down the narrow steps of her loft. Amanda, Len and Raja were waiting for her in the living room.

Parking her luggage near the front door, Thandie turned to face her assistants.

"Well," she began, fanning her hands out to her sides, trying desperately to keep her emotions at bay. "Don't forget to lock up when you leave."

"We know," Raja said.

"Don't do anything foolish while I'm gone," Thandie warned.

"We know," Len said with a weak smile.

"In regards to the Tate party," Thandie went on, "your hours will be—"

"Ten to two," Amanda supplied.

"Right," Thandie nodded. "Same rules apply. No drinking, not even water, and always work the room."

"We know," they choroused.

"And remember to—"

"We know," they choroused again.

Thandie looked at the girls and smiled bashfully.

Raja hugged Thandie. "We're going to miss you."

"I'll only be gone for a few weeks," Thandie said in a low voice. "You won't even notice I'm gone." She blinked back tears. "But I'll miss you, too."

Len threw her arms around Thandie's waist. "Please call as soon as you get there."

Thandie patted her back. "I will."

Pulling away from the girls, Thandie brushed away tears from her wet cheeks. She was all business when she said, "I'll be depending on you while I'm gone. Don't let me down."

They bobbed their heads.

Suddenly desperate to leave town as soon as possible,

Thandie collected her bags, gave a hasty wave, and sailed out the door.

Her driver, Joe, was waiting patiently for her at the curb. He greeted her with a warm smile before opening the back-seat door to the town car. Thandie slid in, making herself comfortable while Joe quickly began stowing her bags into the trunk of the car. When he was done, he slid behind the wheel and drove away. Thandie was thankful Joe was not a talker. She relished the quiet drive, needing the time to calm her frazzled nerves.

They arrived at LaGuardia Airport and she exited the car. She quickly boarded the private jet. Unlike the grandeur of Nico's plane, this jet was somewhat smaller and much more modest in decor. Decorated in muted shades of gray and dark cherry finishes, the jet was practical, leaning toward functional, rather than pretentious.

She moved toward a pair of captain chairs, where a small workstation protruded from the cabin wall. She imagined this was where Mr. Armenta worked while he was traveling. Atop the table was a copy of the *New York Times* and a chilled bottle of Perrier awaited her.

Settling into her seat, Thandie looked out the window.

It was another dreary day in New York. Cloudy skies and drizzling rain. Leaning her head back against the headrest, Thandie closed her eyes, hoping the flight would be over as soon as possible. She was desperate to leave the city, desperate to escape the life she knew. The idea of Ibiza filled her with hope. A new start in a new city. Anything could happen.

Shadows moved behind her closed lids as the captain and his cocaptain prepared for take off. Thandie tried to block them out, choosing instead to close her eyes and rest. It was not easy. The sound of the cabin door closing and locking into place was the sweetest sound ever. Thandie felt as though she was finally safe—safe from her own emotions. Her eyes opened and flickered to the side, and for the first time she noticed a tiny black box on the edge of the desktop. It was tied with a black ribbon. A gift from Armenta?

Cautiously, she reached for the box. Like a child, she weighed it in her hand, trying to guess its contents. Nothing came to mind. Had it been meant for her? Nibbling on her bottom lip, she debated whether she should open it.

Her curiosity got the best of her. Thandie pulled at the ribbon, removed the lid and upended the box.

A single object slid into the palm of her hand. She blinked, and then she stiffened. She thought she would never lay eyes on it again, and here it was. A token of her foolish affection. Thandie was holding a small wooden yo-yo.

Thandie stared at the toy, a mixture of shock and confusion played across her face. A dark and imposing shadow fell over her shoulder.

Thandie looked up, just as a bolt of lightning shot up her spine.

In contrast, the man looked quite at ease. A slow smile appeared across his lips when he said, "Hello, pussycat."

Chapter Thirty

Thandie was unable to trust what she was seeing. Confused, she blinked several times. When the truth finally caught up with her brain, her eyes grew the size of saucers.

This can't be happening, she thought. Thandie watched the man walk casually to the seat across from her before settling into it. She could do little more than stare at him in utter disbelief. His cool gray eyes seemed to sparkle in the light, heightening his handsome features. He literally took her breath away.

Elliot. The man who'd stolen her heart and tossed it aside. The asshole who'd crushed her with his indifference. Elliot. A man who should be in Florida.

As if reading her mind, he said, "Judging from your expression, I gather you're surprised to see me. Although, I'm not sure why." He flicked a speck of lint off his jacket sleeve, before pinning her with his silver stare. "You didn't really think it would be that easy, did you?"

"What are you doing here?" she asked, surprised by the hoarseness of her own voice.

Elliot cocked his head to the side. "I thought the answer to that was obvious."

"What the hell are you doing here?" she snapped again. "Why did you come and why—wait a minute—" Thandie whipped her head around, an alarming thought gripping her. "How did you get on board?" she breathed. That's when she felt it. They were moving. Thandie peered out the window. Her heart dropped. The jet was indeed easing away from the terminal. The sound of raindrops pelted the windows as they picked up speed. Thandie glared at Elliot. When she opened her mouth to speak, words failed her.

"What's wrong, pussycat?" he cooed. "Cat got your tongue?"

"Y-you can't," she stammered.

A dark brow lifted in invitation. "I can't what?"

"You—you can't jump onto other people's planes."

"Why not?" he asked with mock surprise.

"It's illegal," she hissed.

"Not on a *private jet,*" he said.

Thandie stared at him in disbelief. Why did he have to be so damned arrogant? And why did he have to look so damned good while doing it?

As the plane climbed, the tension in the cabin thickened. Thandie stared at him, uncertain if she should start shouting at him or give him the silent treatment. It had been weeks since they had last spoken and suddenly, without warning, he was here.

Sparing him another heated glare, Thandie turned to look out the window turning the yo-yo in her hand. The aircraft was beginning to break through the clouds. From up here, the sky was clear and sunny. A perfect day. It was too bad she couldn't enjoy the view. Thandie's mind was working feverishly, trying to figure out how to handle Elliot's sudden appearance. If Mr. Armenta surprised them by greeting her at the airport, Thandie would have a lot to answer for. What would she say? How was she going to explain Elliot's presence to her new employer? The answer was, she couldn't. She'd be lucky if he didn't fire her on the spot.

"We need to talk," Elliot said, interrupting her thoughts.

"Talk?" Thandie repeated in surprise. "Talk about what? I haven't heard from you in weeks and suddenly you're demanding we talk?"

"Why did you leave before speaking with me first?"

Thandie crossed her arms over her chest. "You know why."

He tsked. "I believe I told you once before I wasn't finished with you."

"Stop treating me as if you own me," she hissed.

"I do, pussycat. The sooner you realize that, the better."

"I'm not interested in your games, Elliot."

"This isn't a game, Thandie," he said in a low voice. "Not this time." Elliot tore his gaze away from her, exhaling before continuing. "I admit my intentions may not have been virtuous in the beginning, but this is different. Forget all the other bullshit. That's not why I came here."

"Other bullshit?" she said quietly. "Would Rex fall into that category?"

A muscle ticked in Elliot's jaw. He was upset. She could feel his anger coming off him like a thick vapor. But Thandie didn't care. She was too hurt to consider taking his feelings into account. He was the reason they were at odds.

She'd always known Elliot wasn't the type to settle down, so she'd never dared to entertain fanciful notions. But if he'd only done things differently, Thandie could have left Miami with fond memories and few regrets. Unlike now. At this very moment she wished she had never gone to Florida, had never taken that call from Warren Radcliffe, had never heard the name Elliot Richards.

"I do not desire to talk about Rex," Elliot said in a voice so measured, it barely contained his wrath.

"No, you just want to have sex with me practically in front of him," she said. "Embarrassing me, humiliating me."

Elliot's eyes flashed a stormy gray and his handsome features hardened. "My methods may have been unorthodox," Elliot admitted, "but I believe I got my point across."

Thandie's eyes stung with tears. She couldn't believe he could be so callous about his actions. He couldn't even give her the satisfaction of pretending to look ashamed. "You didn't have to do it," she whispered.

Elliot tilted his head as he considered her. His icy stare grew ever more intense the longer he gazed at her. "In hindsight, perhaps not," he said.

"So why did you?" she insisted.

"Isn't it obvious?" he asked. "I was jealous."

"Jealous?" She found it hard to believe Elliot Richards, a man who had women falling over themselves to get near him, would be jealous of Rex. Elliot and Rex weren't in the same league, not by a long shot. "But why?"

"Because I loathed the way he looked at you," Elliot said in a near growl. "And I hated the way you seemed to revel in his company. You always seemed more at ease with him. It pissed me off and I retaliated. Granted, in the worst way." He paused. "My behavior was in poor taste," he admitted. "And for that, I apologize. I know I don't deserve your forgiveness, Thandie, but I need you to understand why I reacted the way I did."

"I accept your apology," she said in a voice devoid of any emotion. "But this doesn't excuse what you did."

Elliot nodded his head in agreement.

Needing a momentary distraction, Thandie turned to glance out the cabin window. The clouds were now far below them, revealing a beautiful bowl of cobalt blue sky. She could see no other planes in sight. It was as if she and Elliot were the only two people on the planet.

She turned to glance at Elliot. He was still watching her with those intense gray eyes of his. She could not count how many times she'd gotten lost in his eyes. He had a way of looking her that made her feel as if she were the only girl in the world. It was a spell only he could cast on her. And she fell for it every time. Even now, she could feel herself slipping under his influence, and it pissed her off.

When Elliot abruptly leaned forward, Thandie stiffened. Her eyes narrowed as she followed his movements. Even as she watched him, she was unprepared for what happened next. Elliot reached out, unbuckled her seatbelt and, without warning, scooped her into his arms and pulled her onto his lap. Settling her there, he buried his face into the curve of her neck. He inhaled deeply. His lips fluttered against her skin when he said, "You smell good." He nuzzled her with the tip of his nose. "And you feel even better." Elliot pulled away and studied her closely. "You're thinner," he observed.

She squirmed against him. "Elliot, don't."

He pulled her closer. "I can't help myself." He breathed in her scent once more. "I never could."

Thandie sucked in a calming breath, trying hard not to inhale the heady scent of him. "Why can't you ever play fair?" she asked.

"Fair?" he said with a frown. "I don't know the meaning of the word."

"I'm going to ask you a question, Elliot. And I want the truth."

"Ask me anything," he whispered against her ear.

"Why are you here?"

"I'm here for you."

This caught Thandie off guard. "Me? But why?"

"Because I want you."

"You want a lot of things," she countered.

"True," he conceded, "but you're different. You're special to me."

She shuddered at his words. "Why do you have to make things so difficult?"

The tips of Elliot's mouth curved into the smallest of smiles. "It's who I am. Nothing is ever easy with me. It's one of my more interesting traits." He brushed his knuckles along her upper arm. "It's why you're fascinated with me."

"And why are you so arrogant?" she moaned.

This time he gave a low chuckle. "If it makes you feel any better, you should know I'm completely mesmerized by you." His brow lowered into a frown. "Just when I think I have you figured out, you do something that utterly astounds me."

"Me?"

"You left me," he pointed out.

"You were being an asshole," she justified.

"You should have spoken with me first," he argued, his voice having lost all amusement.

"You shouldn't have lied to me," she fired back. Thandie released a heavy sigh. "Let's just call this what it was. We had sex. It was nice while it lasted, but it's over now."

"Is that what you think?" he growled. The twitch in his jaw was back.

"Isn't that what it was?" she countered.

"I wouldn't be here if that were the case," he said flatly. "You mean a hell of a lot more to me than that." He swore under his breath and looked away, seemingly counting to ten, until his temper simmered down. Finally, he turned back to her. "I can't blame you for having such a low opinion of me. I demanded a lot from you, and gave so little in return." He paused before continuing. "It scared me how I felt about you.

You snuck up on me, Thandie. I was surprised by how easily you got under my skin."

"I got under your skin?" she said, with a fair amount of surprise.

"More than you know," he said in a soft whisper.

Stealing herself against his words, Thandie squeezed her fists. She noticed for the first time, she was gripping something hard in her right hand. She opened her fingers to inspect the object. The wooden yo-yo rested in the center of her palm.

Elliot's gaze dropped down to the object of her attention. His expression softened at the sight. "I shouldn't have treated you the way I did. You were getting too close and it scared me. I reacted badly. You didn't deserve the way I behaved." Thandie opened her mouth to speak, but Elliot held up his hand. "Come back home with me."

For a moment, she was certain she hadn't heard him correctly. "What?"

"I'm quite certain you heard me, Thandie."

She shook her head in exasperation. "I can't go back to Miami."

Elliot's brow arched. "Exactly where do you think this plane is headed?" he asked.

Thandie blinked. When the weight of his words finally donned on her, anger welled up in her like hot lava preparing to explode. "You can't do that!" she flared up.

"I just did," he said smoothly.

In a burst of rage, Thandie pushed hard against Elliot's chest. Coming to her feet she, paced the length of the cabin, squeezing her palms tightly together, willing herself to calm down. After several minutes of fuming, she threw herself into her seat and glared at him. "You had no right," she hissed.

"You left me no choice," he said matter-of-factly. "Did you think I would simply let you walk away from me?" The question hung in the air between them, and for a moment, neither could speak, his pale gray eyes became cloudy with intensity. "Come back to Miami with me." The words were soft, and dangerously close to sounding like a plea.

"I can't."

"Why the hell not?" he asked, a hint of accusation in his tone.

"For starters," she began hotly, "My team is expecting me to return to New York in a few weeks. Not to mention, I have a new assignment I've committed to...and my mother is still there."

"The girls will be fine," he assured her. "And as for that assignment, I'm sure Mr. Armenta will understand."

Thandie sat up taller in her seat. "You know Mr. Armenta?"

"Of course I do," he said. "And so do you." When she didn't immediately respond, Elliot mouthed the word, "Nico."

Thandie stared at him in disbelief. "Nico is Dominic Armenta?" She shook her head and said, more to herself. "That can't be. I Googled him. Dominic Armenta is an older man."

"Dominic Armenta is an older man," Elliot agreed. "And quite formidable. His son, on the other hand, Dominic Armenta Jr., is the exact opposite. It's one of the many reasons he prefers to be called by his nickname."

Thandie's face fell. "You had this planned the entire time." Elliot nodded.

"But how did you know I would accept the job offer?"

"It was a calculated risk," he confessed, "but I know you. And I was willing to bet you would be eager to take a trip that would put considerable distance between yourself and me."

"Or in other words, you knew I would take the bait." Thandie sniffed.

"Your words, not mine," Elliot said carefully.

Thandie snickered. Her annoyance with him was growing by the minute. However, she couldn't help but admire his logic; and curse her own predictability.

She looked around the comfortable setting of the jet's cabin. Taking it all in with new eyes. She deduced what she should have noticed before. "I suppose this is another one of Nico's planes?" she asked.

Elliot shook his head. When she raised her brow in question, he said, "It's mine."

Thandie blink several times. "Yours?"

"Yes, mine," he said with a slow nod of his head.

"But I thought you didn't own a plane."

"I never said I didn't."

"But you—" she had to stop herself to collect her thoughts. "If this is yours," she began more slowly, "why didn't we travel to Havana on it?"

Elliot sighed before patiently explaining. "It's easier to pass through Cuban customs on Nico's plane because it's not registered in the United States. It's not a favor I ask often, but it has come in handy from time to time." He smirked at her incredulous expression. "Don't worry. I'm not taking advantage of Nico. He gets plenty of use out of my plane. If anything, I'm the one getting taken advantage of."

Thandie shook her head. There was so much she didn't know about him. She began to wonder, not for the first time, if she would ever know all the many pieces that made up Elliot Richards. Too wrapped up in her own thoughts, Thandie forgot to put up any fight when Elliot reached for her again. Like a limp doll, she allowed him to place her on his lap again.

Taking advantage of her lack of attention, Elliot pulled her closer to him, burying his face into the crook of her neck just as before. "Don't be upset with me," he said softly into her ear. "I had to find a way to see you again." Elliot inhaled deeply.

"I missed you. I didn't think I would, not to this extent. But damn I was wrong."

"I missed you too," she confessed, before she could stop herself. However, once spoken, Thandie felt an immense sense of relief because the words were true. She had missed him, and she loved him, more than she would have thought possible.

"Come back with me," he said.

"It doesn't sound like I have a choice," she said dejectedly. "I'm unemployed, stuck on a plane with you, and headed to a city I never intended to go to."

"I'm not such bad company, am I?"

"That depends."

Elliot actually laughed. "I don't think anyone has ever had that reaction to me before." He pulled her to him, encircling her in his arms. "You always have a choice, Thandie." Elliot paused, as if debating with himself. Finally, he said, "If you still want the job in Ibiza, it's yours. That was always a part of the deal."

"The deal?"

"Nico is an investor in the hotel holding your reservation. And he is hosting a surprise birthday party for his father. All of your accommodations are waiting for you, should you choose to take the job."

"And the compensation?"

"Per the original agreement."

"You did all of this for me?" she asked.

"There are a lot of things I would do for you."

Thandie wanted to shy away from his words, hold tightly to her skepticism, but it was impossible. When Elliot looked at her this way, she found she was powerless. Stealing herself against his softly spoken words, Thandie forced herself to focus on something of greater importance. Although she'd told herself many times before she did not care one way or the other, she knew that was a lie. She needed to know the truth.

"Warren," she began haltingly. "How are things between you two?"

For once, Elliot looked uncertain of himself. His handsome features lost some of their arrogant brilliance. "Things between Warren and me are…progressing," he said in a measured tone.

"What does that mean?"

Elliot exhaled before meeting her imploring stare. "We've been spending a lot more time together. I suppose I have you to thank for that."

"Me?"

"You're our safe topic." He used the tip of his finger to push a lock of her hair behind her ear. "To be quite honest, you're all we talk about. I insisted Warren tell me everything he knows about you. It took some persuasion on my part, but eventually he agreed." Elliot pulled back to look at her. "He's quite fond of you, Thandie. And he was none too pleased that I was the reason you left town."

"What will this mean for the two of you?" she asked.

"Who knows," he said with a shrug. "It's too new to tell."

"You two need each other," she heard herself say.

"Perhaps you're right," he agreed. "But I need you just as much."

"I'm not sure what you want me to say to that." She looked away from him. "The truth is, I don't trust you."

"I suppose I deserve that," he said. Catching her chin with his thumb and forefinger, he turned her face to look at him. "What can I do to convince you otherwise?"

"No more lies, Elliot."

He nodded his head. "No more lies," he agreed.

"And no other women."

Elliot actually looked surprised by this statement and, if possible, a little hurt. "Do you think I've been with other women?"

Thandie fixed him with a pointed stare. "Haven't you?"

"No, I haven't." The muscle in his jaw was beginning to twitch again. "I haven't been with anyone else since we became lovers."

Thandie wanted to believe him so badly it hurt, but she could not shake the feeling that trusting Elliot would only lead to disappointment. He would break her heart over and over again, if given the chance. And wasn't that the problem? She had few defenses where Elliot was involved. He might proclaim she had some power over him, but the truth was he had no idea how vulnerable she was with him.

Sensing her hesitation, Elliot slipped his hand through her hair, fingering the strands at the nape of her neck. "I want this to work," he said before pulling her to him to kiss her softly on the lips.

The tenderness of his kiss left her breathless, ending far sooner than she would have liked. "What now?" she asked weakly. "What happens next?"

"The way I see it, you have two choices." Elliot looped a lock of her hair behind her ear. "When we land in Miami, you and I will get off together. You will return to my home and we'll figure this out."

"What about my firm?"

"You made quite an impression during your time in Miami. I doubt you'll be hurting for business. And if you need help, I can make a few calls."

"Where would I live?"

"With me." He held up his hand. "And before you ask, the answer is yes, you'll sleep with me, too."

"And what would that make me?"

"We don't have to name it, Thandie. I just need you near me."

"Maybe we do need to name it," she said. "It's important to me."

Elliot nodded his head solemnly. "In that case, I suppose it would make you my girlfriend."

Thandie took a moment to take it all in. After a long pause, she said, "What's my other option?"

Elliot let his hand fall away. He studied her face, searching her eyes. "When we land, I'll get off. The plane will refuel, and you can go to Ibiza, just as you planned."

Thandie nodded her head slowly. "I need time to think about this," she said.

He lifted his wrist to squint at his watch, before nodding. "We have less than three hours," he announced. Raising her gently off his lap, Elliot came to his feet and removed his jacket. "That should be enough time."

"Enough time for what?" Thandie asked.

"For me to convince you." Slowly, he began to unbutton his shirt. "I must warn you, pussycat, I can be very persuasive."

Epilogue

Club Babylon
One Month later…

They'd made hot, sticky, draining love. Uncaring if the flight crew heard them or not. Clutching one another, they'd made love until they were exhausted. But in the end, it hadn't been enough. Thandie had left.

Even though he'd done everything he could, it hadn't been enough. He had failed to convince her to stay. He could see in her eyes, she was determined to go to Spain, determined to leave him.

Elliot was not accustomed to losing something he desired. He wanted Thandie, and she'd denied him. Nevertheless, he still wanted her. He missed her wide brown eyes, luscious curves and long endless legs. It would be a long time before he could forget the feel of her smooth skin against his. But it was wishful thinking to dwell on the memory of Thandie.

Many times, he considered traveling to Spain to appeal to her once more, but stopped short of going through with it.

Thandie had made her decision. He would have to respect her choice.

Elliot stared down into the lovely face of actress Chole Daniels. She was striking in that unusual way that all movie stars were. Her clear blue eyes were wide and expressive, sending him the clear message, she would like to know him infinitely better, and preferably without his clothes on. If her eyes didn't relay her point, the constant brushing of her breasts against his forearm made her intentions loud and clear.

"So it's your birthday?" She cooed. "Did you get everything you wanted?"

"Almost," he said casually.

Chloe placed a hand on his lapel. "Perhaps we can remedy that."

Fixing a smile onto his face, that he did not feel, Elliot grinned pleasantly at her. And then he stopped. From across the room, he thought he caught a glimpse of something, or someone. Leaning away from the bar, he stood to his full height. Looking over the crowd, he strained to see but it was too crowded, obscuring his view. And then it happened. The crowd parted, as if on queue, revealing her. She was a vision to behold. Tall, beautiful and absolutely perfect. Exactly his type. Her eyes met his and Elliot sucked in a breath.

Without another word to his Hollywood companion, Elliot weaved his way throughout the crowd, making a direct line toward her.

He stood in front of her and her gaze flicked over his shoulder, toward the bar. "I hope I'm not interrupting."

"You weren't." Elliot didn't bother turning to look. He knew all too well she was referring to Chloe Daniels. He could feel her burning a hole into his back. With a careless wave, he said, "She's a dime a dozen. She doesn't compare to you."

"Sweet words will get you everywhere," she said with a smile.

"I only need them to get me one place." Elliot let his hot gaze slowly roam over her body, lingering over every curve. Curves he was quite familiar with. Tired of the small space between them, he stepped even closer, then slid his hand around her waist and pulled her to his body. "I've missed you," he growled next to her ear.

I missed you too," she whispered.

"It's been too long, Thandie."

"I know," she confessed. "Was I worth the wait?"

"More than you know," he moaned. "Is this trip business or pleasure?"

"That depends."

"On what?"

"Are you still in the market for a girlfriend?"

"No." He squeezed her hip. "I already have one."

She smiled. "Then consider my stay indefinite."

Elliot leaned in to kiss her, but Thandie placed a hand on his chest. "On one condition."

Elliot answered her by lifting one dark brow.

"I can't leave my mother in New York. I would have to make arrangements to move her here."

He nodded his head. "Let me help you with this. I would like to meet her."

Thandie couldn't conceal the smile that began to spread across her face. "Can we *really* make this work?" she asked, a quiver in her voice giving away her uncertainty.

"It's already working," he assured her. Leaning forward, he kissed her long and slow. When he finally pulled away he looked her deep into eyes, before asking, "Would you mind stepping into my office?"

Thandie laughed. "I thought you'd never ask."

Elliot pressed his hand on her lower back, as he began to guide her through the crowd.

★ ★ ★ ★ ★